W9-AYD-568

RIVERSIDE PARK

Also by

LAURA VAN WORMER

RIVERSIDE DRIVE*
WEST END*
BENEDICT CANYON
ANY GIVEN MOMENT*
JURY DUTY
TALK*
JUST FOR THE SUMMER

The Sally Harrington Novels

EXPOSÉ*
THE LAST LOVER*
TROUBLE BECOMES HER*
THE BAD WITNESS*
THE KILL FEE*
MR. MURDER*

*In which characters from RIVERSIDE PARK previously appeared.

RIVERSIDE PARK
LAURA
VAN WORMER
MIRA®

ISBN-13: 978-0-7783-2652-6

RIVERSIDE PARK

www.MIRABooks.com

Printed in U.S.A.

For
Dianne Moggy
whose gifts as a publisher are many.

And with much love and appreciation to
Loretta Barrett, Nick Mullendore,
Gabriel Davis and Christine Robinson.

In thy face I see the map of honor, truth, and loyalty.

—William Shakespeare,

King Henry VI

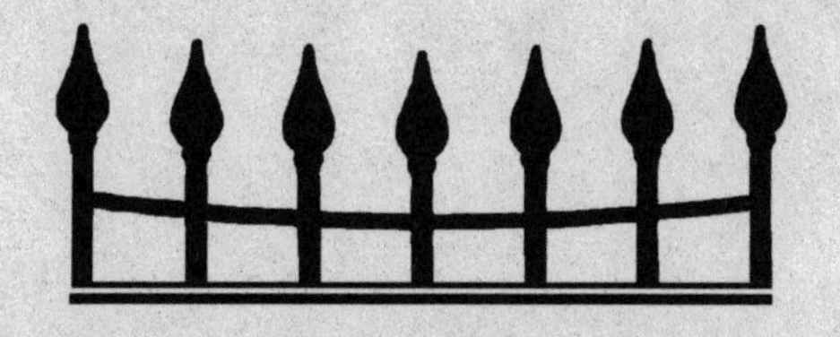

THANKSGIVING

WHILE CASSY COCHRAN wrapped her hair in a towel, she felt a kiss on the small of her back. She straightened up and smiled as arms slid around her waist to hold her from behind.

"So where do they think you are?"

"The office, to pick something up." Cassy turned around, allowing herself to be kissed. "As soon as they take off I'll come by to pick you up." She wanted to say something else but was prevented from doing so. For about twenty minutes.

And then she had to shower all over again.

Thanksgiving Dinner at the Darenbrooks'

BEFORE DINNER CASSY asked everyone to please hold hands during grace.

"Who's Grace?" someone said.

"Wait, wait!" pleaded a young second cousin of her husband's. "Look, look," she cried, jumping up to show everyone around the table the most recent issue of *City Style.* While Cassy exchanged looks with her husband, the fifteen guests politely admired the sight of the Darenbrooks splashed across the cover like movie stars. "Marriage of the Media," it said above their smiling faces. "Cassy Cochran and Jackson Darenbrook," it said below.

Their photograph might as well have been shot through linoleum for all the reality quotient it possessed. Instead of fifty-three and fifty-eight years old, the Darenbrooks looked on the far side of thirty. (There's nothing worse, in publishers' minds, than a life of grace, ease and luxury wasted on people readers could not imagine sleeping with.) The article was flattering, too. Cassy was billed as the stunningly good-looking woman of humble Iowa beginnings who dodged a career in front of the camera to become the founding president of the DBS Television network. Jackson was described as the brilliant Georgia heir who turned his father's newspapers into the massive empire Darenbrook Communications was today.

The Darenbrooks, according to *City Style,* had the world at their feet.

The article breezed over Cassy's divorce from producer Michael Cochran (and altogether skipped his alcoholism and how, the minute he got sober, he had dumped *her*), and mentioned the tragic accidental death of Jackson's first wife, Barbara (and graciously omitted how Jackson dumped his children on his sister so he could become an international playboy).

"Perhaps we can look at it after dinner," Cassy suggested.

The second cousin reluctantly took the hint (she did not get out much in East Binsley, Georgia), and leaned over to drop the magazine under her chair.

"Oh, Lord," Jackson began, his drawl pulling farther South than usual, "we thank you for this food we are about to receive and we thank you for allowing us to spend this special day of Thanksgiving together." Cassy's husband had wonderful cornflower-blue eyes and a ready smile. He was a tall, very well built man with an enviously thick head of hair that was real. "We ask that you bless and watch over our loved ones who cannot be with us today, both in heaven and on earth."

Jackson's voice trailed off and everybody waited.

"Merciful God," he continued, "please help the United States to be healed as a nation, and teach us to bring light and love to places of darkness and hate. Thank you, Lord, for your love and countless blessings for which we are so grateful. Amen."

"Amen," Cassy murmured, opening her eyes. "Very nice, Jack." She pressed the button under the carpet with her foot to signal the caterers in the kitchen. The twenty-six-pound turkey came out first and was set down in front of Jackson accompanied with several ooo's and ahhh's. He started to carve while a detail of three out-of-work actors began the rounds with serving dishes.

Henry Cochran, Cassy's only biological child, was seated to her immediate left. He had arrived two days earlier with his wife and young son. They were staying in the old Cochran apartment Henry had grown up in and which Cassy kept separate from the penthouse Jackson had created with the rest of the floor. Once there had been five other apartments on the top floor of 162 Riverside Drive, but one by one Jackson had acquired and added them to his new urban family manse.

At twenty-eight years old, Henry Cochran was still a good deal like his mother. He was tall, slender, blue-eyed and fair-haired (the latter, however, rapidly thinning, she noticed), but fortunately Henry had also inherited his father's deep voice and broad shoulders so that he had not (as he had feared while growing up) turned out to be a ninety-eight-pound weakling. He was ecstatic to be a family man and doing extremely well as an architect. The only problem was the younger Cochrans were moving from Chicago to San Francisco to be near Maria's parents, and Henry had been offered a new position that had made the move possible. Cassy felt she could not say anything because Maria was expecting another child and wanted more family around her, and living next door to the Darenbrooks in New York was not what Maria had in mind.

Cassy almost winced at the pain she felt in her heart at that moment. Having Henry living in Chicago had been hard enough; San Francisco seemed like the end of the earth.

"Good food, Mom," Henry said.

"I'm sorry, Henry," Cassy said, snapping out of her thoughts, "what did you say?"

"I said, 'Great food, Mom.' "

"I'm glad you're enjoying it," she said automatically with a smile, but looked down at her own plate with dismay. The food her in-laws had requested—including sweet-potato pie with marshmallow topping and mushy string beans cooked with fatback pork—was severely at odds with the regime Cassy's mother had pounded into her head as a child: six glasses of water a day and as much vegetables, fruit, fish and lean meat as she wanted. (Cassy's mother, in her glory days, had been a beauty queen representing the great state of Iowa. That is until, as Mrs. Littlefield was always careful to phrase it, "my horribly cruel and unfortunate marriage.")

Cassy had been blessed with beauty and a healthy body and, at fifty-three, was extremely grateful for both. She worked out with a trainer three days a week and thus far had only made some minor concessions to plastic surgery involving her face and eyes. It wasn't that she wanted to look younger, really; she just wanted to continue resembling herself. Her face always caught her by surprise when she had a moment to study it in the mirror. When had *that* happened, and *that* and *that?*

She had worn her long blond hair (now with occasional silver) up on the back of her head forever. Whenever she considered cutting it everyone around her freaked out, some declaring it was who she was while others maintained it best highlighted her features. Others said it was the promise of what that hair might hold—when and if it ever came down—that still kept eyes on Cassy when younger beauty was around.

Henry leaned over to say, "I love you, Mom," in the same way he used to as a child when he thought his mother might be upset. But Cassy wasn't upset, just tired. And sad, already missing her son.

She reached to give Henry's hand a squeeze. "I love you, too."

Suddenly mashed potatoes and peas splattered over the side of Henry's face and there was a screech of delight.

Ah, William. Cassy's grandson. If ever someone resembled her first husband, Michael, it was he. William had the blackest hair, was built like a tank and was shy about nothing. His current vocabulary consisted of *No, Mine* and *Rrraaarrrr* (Henry and Maria had two dogs), and his favorite pastime was throwing things at people. If they didn't sit on the child soon Cassy knew they would regret it. And as much as she loved Maria, she couldn't help but wish she had a little more steel in her mothering. Hopefully Maria's mother would help with that.

Cassy heard the deep laughter of her husband from the other end of the dining room table. Jackson had seen what William had done.

Sitting to Jackson's right was his alternately anorexic and bulimic daughter, Lydia, who, like Henry, was twenty-eight. Sitting on Jackson's left was his son, Kevin, who at twenty-six was six-foot-three and at least three hundred pounds.

After early go-rounds with Jack's children when they were first married, Cassy had pleaded with Jackson to go into therapy with them. He never had. On the other hand, Jackson had always taken Henry's word over that of his own children, never doubting that it was true, for example, that Kevin was stashing cocaine in Henry's room or that Lydia tried to have sex with Henry.

While Henry and Maria tried to cope with their screeching, food-throwing son, Henry's water glass was upended on the table. All of the out-of-work actors rushed into the kitchen and then rushed back out again with dish towels to blot up the water. William, at this point, was crying crocodile tears because his plate of ammo had been taken away.

"I would spank him," Cordelia Darenbrook Payne, Jackson's half sister, loudly advised from across the table.

"*Right,* Aunt Cordie Lou," Lydia cried, pushing her chair back to stand up. "We all know how much good your spankings did *me!* Excuse me," she added in exaggerated politeness to her father.

"Lydia," Jackson started to say, but she ignored him and walked out of the dining room.

Then Kevin excused himself and left the dining room, as well.

William was now screaming and Maria, blushing heavily, pulled William up out of his high chair. "I'll take him into the bedroom."

"Why don't you give him to me?" Cassy suggested, pushing her chair back slightly and holding out her arms. Maria seemed happy to hand him off. (At this stage of her pregnancy Cassy didn't blame her.)

"William," Cassy said sharply as she plopped him down in her lap. Her grandson stopped screaming to look up at her in a kind of awe. She handed him a dinner roll and picked up her fork, managing to take a few bites before she caught Maria's bewildered expression. "At this age they're better with anyone but their parents."

"He gets mad because he can't bounce on Maria's lap anymore," Henry explained.

If you think he's mad now, wait until the new baby comes, Cassy thought. She used her napkin to catch drool dripping from William's mouth as he gnawed on the roll, which killed her appetite.

Lydia reappeared and made her way to her seat smiling defiantly down the table at Cassy as Kevin came back in, as well. They were both high on something. Probably cocaine.

Jackson simply did not want to see it. Cassy supposed he was not unlike other fathers, figuring that by their late twenties it was none of his business what his kids did.

William fell asleep in Cassy's arms, the remains of the roll clutched in his fist. When she kissed the top of his head and stood up, everyone took it as a signal that Thanksgiving was officially over and they were excused. Lydia was out the door first. Henry, Maria and William were next to leave in a car for JFK, Cassy fighting back tears. Then she hurried to help her Southern relatives organize their bags. Everyone except Cassy would board a limousine bus to take them to the Darenbrook Communications plane in Newark. They would drop Jackson and her stepson off in Savannah and then conclude their flight in their home city of Atlanta.

"I don't know how you do it, darlin'," Jack said under his breath to Cassy as he gave her a hug and kiss, "but we almost resembled a family today."

Kevin kissed Cassy on the cheek. "Thanks, Cass, it was great."

She smiled, taking Kevin's arm and pulling him back a step. She leaned close to his ear. "If you ever bring drugs into this house again, I promise you, Kevin, you will never cross the threshold again. Have I made myself clear?"

Startled, Kevin stepped back.

"Oh, Cassy," Cordelia Darenbrook Payne said, swooping in, "it was *vun*derbar, *vun*derbar as always. And the black-eyed peas were so good we're taking them to eat on the airplane during the ride home."

"Okay, guys, we gotta move," Jack called to the group, tapping his watch.

"Mrs. Darenbrook?" The caterer appeared from the doorway. "We're almost finished in the kitchen. I want to make sure everything is the way you want it before we leave."

"Bye, darlin'!" Jack shouted over the crowd, waving to her.

"Safe journey, everyone!" Cassy called before closing the front door.

The kitchen looked better than it had when the caterer arrived and Cassy told him so. She gave everybody a small envelope (containing tips), and thanked them for such a lovely dinner.

"You made almost all of the food, Mrs. Darenbrook," the caterer pointed out.

"I hope you young people are taking the leftovers home," she said, addressing the group.

The workers held up bags of disposable food containers and thanked her.

Cassy saw the crew out the service entrance and walked down the long back hall toward the master suite, peering in at the state of the guest bedrooms, but not worrying about them since housekeeping would be back in full force in the morning. There was no trick to running any of the Darenbrook households, really. All it took was money.

The burden of Thanksgiving had been lifted and she felt her energy and spirits rising already. She vigorously brushed out her hair and then put it back up. She went into the bathroom to wash up a little and brush her teeth, then came back out to sit at the vanity to put on a little fresh makeup. She also exchanged the pearl earrings she had been wearing for two large diamond ones and took off her wedding rings. She threw a couple of things into a shoulder bag and hastily ran a lint brush over her dress. She went out to the front hall closet to retrieve a coat and suitcase and took the elevator down to the subterranean garage.

"I could have brought those down for you, Mrs. Darenbrook," the attendant said, rushing over to take the shoulder bag and suitcase.

"No worry," she said. She watched him put the suitcase in the trunk of her silver Jaguar. "I'm sorry you have to work today."

"I'm not. I get double time." He closed the trunk and hurried around to open the driver's-side door for her. "I'm through here at eight and then we'll have our big family dinner."

"Oh, I'm glad." She slipped down behind the wheel.

"So your house is finally quiet again, huh? That was a *lot* of people staying with you and Mr. Darenbrook."

"Indeed," she said, smiling.

"Mr. Darenbrook said he's racing his boat in the Caribbean this weekend."

"Yes, he is. With his son."

"Think he'll win? Oh, why do I even ask? Even when Mr. Darenbrook loses he still always seems to win somehow. Do you know what I mean?"

Cassy nodded, starting the engine. "Oh, yes, I know what you mean," she assured him.

2

What Happened to the Darenbrook Marriage

AFTER THE HUMILIATING defeat of her first marriage, falling in love with Jackson Darenbrook had seemed close to a miracle. Cassy remembered the day Jack realized he was in love with her very well. They'd been arguing (they had always been arguing in the early days of the fledgling network), and suddenly Jackson stopped talking and stared at Cassy with a sense of dawning revelation. Cassy knew then how he felt about her. And in that moment she knew that she had been falling for him, as well.

She was forty-four when they married and Jackson forty-nine. His family and friends were astounded by the changes in him by the time he stood at the altar. "He's a happy man, again," Cordelia told her. "Thank God he's a happy man again."

Cassy took her vows as sacred. She felt blessed and reborn to have such a commitment come to her at that point in her life, and she was determined to appreciate every nuance of it. With the exception of ongoing problems with Lydia, those first couple of years were blissful. When not traveling on business—which both did rather extensively—they were together at West End (the corporate headquarters of Darenbrook Communications on the Hudson River at Sixty-fifth Street), here at home on Riverside Drive, or at the house in Litchfield. They sailed and skied and traveled continents; they worked out together and often spent downtime just lazying around, reading newspapers, watching TV or movies, eating good food and making love.

Cassy felt loved, respected and redeemed.

She never tried to compete with the memory of Barbara, Jackson's first wife, because she knew she could never win in comparison to a saint who had died in her thirties.

Henry came home for brief periods while in college and he got on very well with Jackson. Kevin appeared erratically. They were married about two and a half years when Lydia tried to kill herself. Jack was away so Cassy hurried downtown to the emergency room of St. Vincent's where the police told her Lydia had slit her wrists and then had been walking around Sheridan Square. The doctor said Lydia was on a combination of alcohol, painkillers and cocaine.

Lydia was crying for her dead mother when Cassy saw her. Cassy tried to soothe her, explaining her father was rushing back to New York and would be here as soon as he could, that her father loved her so much—

Something akin to *The Exorcist* then occurred. Lydia's tears vanished and her eyes took on an eerie glitter while she told Cassy what a fool she was, what a stupid idiot she was. Didn't she know that Jackson was incapable of caring for anyone except himself? That he had conned her like he conned everyone? And the only reason he had married Cassy was that Aunt Cordie Lou had thrown in the towel?

"Don't you get it? He married you so you'd deal with me and Kev! *You are so fucking stupid!* You're a glorified housekeeper, taking care of things while he runs around getting his rocks off!"

Cassy gratefully agreed with the doctor that Lydia be held in psychiatric for observation for the three days they could legally keep her. Or at least until her father arrived.

Jackson ended up not flying straight home but continued on his trip because, he said, Cassy seemed to have matters so well in hand.

In retrospect those two and a half years of marital bliss had been a gift from the heavens above. If Cassy's world had exploded any sooner, she wasn't sure what would have happened to her.

"I came to say goodbye," the outgoing publisher of the Darenbrook newspaper in Charleston told Cassy, coming into her office at West End not long after Lydia's suicide attempt. "I handed in my resignation. I'm going to be the publisher of a new magazine in D.C."

"Well, I'm happy for you and miserable for us," Cassy said, coming around from behind her desk, holding out her hand. "Congratulations, Sheila."

"Thank you." Sheila glanced back over her shoulder at the door. She was an attractive woman, in her early forties, with dark hair and green eyes. "Do you think we can talk a minute?"

"Sure," Cassy said, going to close her office door, hoping Sheila was not going to try to pick her brain about how to effectively compete with the D.C. magazine Darenbrook Communications published.

They had scarcely sat down when Sheila burst into tears. Cassy didn't know her very well and felt a little embarrassed for her. She got up to get Sheila some Kleenex and thought,

I hope nothing's happened to her child. Sheila had brought her little girl to West End on bring-your-child-to-work day the year before.

"I'm sorry," Sheila said, trying to pull herself together. "It's just been so stressful."

"I understand. It was hard when I left my old job at WST."

"You are such a wonderful person, Cassy," Sheila said then, sounding miserable.

"I don't know about that," Cassy murmured. "Do you think you might have made the wrong decision, Sheila? That you'd like to stay on with us after all?"

Sheila looked at first stunned and then deeply pained. She brought the tissues up to press against her mouth.

"I might be able to help," Cassy said gently.

Sheila slammed her fist on her knee. "I can't stand it! I can't stand by and watch how he's deceiving you!"

It had hit her like a physical blow to the diaphragm. Cassy couldn't breathe and then an icy fear started down her spine. She gripped the arms of the chair and forced herself to resume breathing, to sit there and breathe, and to listen.

Sheila told her. That she and Jackson had been having an affair. For a while. Since before he had married Cassy, in fact, while Sheila had still been married. She told Cassy about traveling with Jack on business trips, about meeting him once for a quick tryst in the side yard outside Cordelia's mansion in Hilleanderville between dinner and dessert.

"For a long time I thought it was just me, and then you, too," she told Cassy. "I finally wised up when my secretary warned me that she would probably be leaving soon because, even though she had only slept with Jackson a few times, she was sure he was the man for her. Then she asked for my opinion of how long I thought it would take for him to divorce you."

Cassy excused herself, went in her private bathroom, quietly threw up, rinsed out her mouth and came back into her office.

"It's almost every day," Sheila said, starting to cry again. "He takes whatever attractive woman he can find. I don't know, maybe he buys them off, I don't know."

Jackson didn't deny a single thing Sheila had said. His eyes only took on deep, weary sadness. When Cassy had finished and was waiting for an answer, he took her hand, squeezed it and held on to it. "But it's you I love," he said simply. "That's why I married you."

She did not let herself cry. "Then why, Jack?" Oh, she had thought she knew why and it burned. He obviously found her sexually inadequate. ("How many times do you think a guy wants to screw Snow White?" Michael used to say.)

He had no explanation for his sexual exploits except to say that it had nothing to do with his love for her.

What alcohol is to the alcoholic, Cassy's therapist told her, sex is to the sexaholic. Then she went on about endorphins and about the brain chemistry of the drinker, the drug abuser, the gambler, the bulimic—and the sexaholic.

Cassy had held her face in her lap. "You're telling me I've done it *again?* I've married another addict?"

Like alcohol, the therapist told her, there was treatment for the disorder. Even rehabs specifically to treat it.

"No, I don't think so," Jackson said when Cassy asked him to see someone, a specialist that had been recommended. "I mean, not right now, Cass. I need to focus on this encyclopedia deal. I promise I won't—you know—until I go."

They continued to share the same bedroom in New York and Connecticut, and even started having sex again on the proviso he wore a condom until he was cleared of any possible sexual diseases. The encyclopedia deal had dragged on and he kept putting off going to the counselor but Cassy remained hopeful, particularly when after six months the tests came back negative. Lydia went off her rocker again in Mexico and they went there as a team this time, a united front. They resumed a more active sex life, no longer using a condom.

During this period she remembered why she had fallen in love with him. Jackson was infinitely kind and funny and endlessly interested in anything he sensed might interest her. He was also very affectionate, an element that had been sorely lacking in her first marriage, and they often held hands and almost always lay down together while reading or watching TV. He could also be extremely thoughtful about little things. He always tried to keep the newspaper fresh for her because he knew how much she liked a crisp paper. And if he had a cold and was coughing, he would quietly take himself off to a guest room in the night so as not to keep her awake.

He said he thought there was no need for them to go to counseling anymore. Didn't she agree? That things were good? They were happy? She had hesitated but then agreed, mostly because he had said this on a Friday and she didn't wish to ruin their weekend sailing.

When Jackson came back from a meeting in Atlanta the following week she knew. She knew because he had seemed distant and depressed and could scarcely look her in the eye. She said as much out loud while they were lying in bed, waiting to fall asleep. He said she was crazy, he hadn't done anything and snuggled closer. Instinct prevailed and she sat bolt upright in bed and told him she did not believe him. He protested he was too tired for this tonight. Then she got out of bed, wearing one of the red (ugh) nighties he liked her to wear, and said they might as well have it out, because if he was not going to counseling then he was moving into the guest room.

"Fine," he said in the darkness.

"Fine what?"

"Fine, believe what you want to believe, Cassy, but I don't need a therapist so I'm not going. If you want to sue me for divorce over it, then go ahead. I'm tired and need some sleep."

She hesitated, standing there in the dark, crossing her arms against the cold and feeling warm tears rolling down her face. (In the first years of their marriage she had only cried tears of gratitude. She had felt so good about the world, about herself, about their future. How had she not seen this side of him?)

"I mean it, Jack, if you won't go to counseling..." She wasn't sure how to finish the threat. She wasn't sure how she wanted to finish it. They had already built so many things together, their families, their homes, the network. And what would she say? How would she explain? To Henry, to everybody? Oh, and would Michael ever get a good laugh out of this!

"I'm sleeping in the guest room," Jackson announced, sighing heavily as he hauled himself out of bed.

She let him go and took a sleeping pill to knock herself out. The next morning when he came in to get dressed, she told him that if he valued their marriage at all he would at least go *with* her for counseling.

"I love you," he said, frowning at her. "But I'm not going."

"So you're saying that our marriage is over?"

"I think that's up to you," he told her, walking into his dressing room.

That was where they had left it six years ago. If she hadn't been so adverse to yet another public humiliation she would have left him then. The women, she had come to realize, had never stopped for more than three months in their entire marriage. A year later she sought the advice of a divorce attorney but then

Henry announced he wanted to get married and the thought of *that,* of having to participate in the celebrations by herself in front of Michael and his young wife, had been too much. To his credit, Jackson had acted the role of the perfect husband to a T.

Cassy was moving toward leaving him again when Maria had announced she was pregnant. Henry was so happy and scared and elated that Cassy didn't have the heart to do anything that would further worry him. And Henry would have worried about her. (If Henry had said one more time, "I'm so glad you have somebody, too, Mom," she thought she'd lose her mind.) So with Jackson acting the part of devoted and attentive husband (which reassured Henry and incensed Michael, whose second marriage had since broken up), and with Cassy acting the part of devoted and attentive wife (which elated her in-laws, who also happened to make up the Board of Directors of Darenbrook Communications), Cassy didn't know how she could ever get out of it. Or if she even really wanted to. So much, it seemed, relied on their pretense.

Perhaps the worst aspect of the situation was that their marriage was not *always* such a pretense. They still had their moments. Cassy wasn't particularly proud of the fact that, on occasion, usually around some family event, they would look at each other with great fondness and sometimes, sometimes, they would make love.

With a condom, of course.

This last part, that once in a while they still had sex, remained the Darenbrooks' special little secret, offering a little ghostly reminder of what Cassy had hoped their marriage would be.

Jack swore he still loved her more than anyone. Since there

still were so many women coming and going, Cassy could not see how this could be true. She did not say the same to him, though, that she loved him best. Because she didn't. She was very much in love with someone else, but that relationship was fraught with obstacles of its own. Still, it was wonderful to love and be loved.

Somehow Cassy was going to have to figure all of this out.

Amanda Miller Stewart's Family, a Pretty Girl, and an Attentive Young Man

THE PRETTY GIRL lived in their building and came and went at odd hours. Amanda knew this because their eight-month-old precious accident, Grace, was cutting her teeth and sometimes in the wee hours Amanda would take her down to the lobby so she could talk to the concierge and the night security man while walking the baby back and forth, patting her little back. (It was best, Amanda had found, to let the children's nanny, Madame Moliere, sleep through the night so she could get their two older children—Emily, age ten, and Teddy, age eight—organized in the morning.)

Grace had begun to fret at three-thirty in the morning on Thanksgiving, and since Amanda's parents and Howard's mother were staying with them, Amanda had quickly thrown on slacks and a sweater to scoop Grace up and pay a visit to the lobby. About fifteen minutes later a cab had pulled up to the entrance of the building and the pretty girl had come stumbling out of it. She had been rather astonishingly drunk. She was not as tall as Amanda, but taller than average, and had lovely dark brown hair. She also had a sleek body that only a girl in her twenties can possess. The girl had sworn under her breath as she banged her shoulder on the doorway, but did so in a manner that told Amanda the pretty girl was both well-spoken and probably well-educated.

Of course, if the girl lived in their building Amanda knew she must be a young woman of means.

The pretty girl had then almost collided with Amanda and Grace. She had reeled back, her large brown eyes trying to focus. She had looked at the baby and then back at Amanda. "You're always stuck with the kids," she'd said. "You should make Howard do more."

The night security guard, who was an off-duty NYPD police officer (who once showed Amanda's son the derringer he carried in his boot), had stepped forward to say he would see the girl upstairs to her apartment. Just as the elevator doors were closing, Amanda had heard the girl say, "Thank God I don't have any kids."

Amanda didn't speak of it—the fact that the pretty girl evidently knew her husband on a first-name basis—until they had returned from the Thanksgiving Day Parade and she and Howard were in the kitchen trying to pull things together for dinner.

"That must have been Celia," Howard said, squinting through the blast of oven heat, trying to see the meat thermometer.

"Celia who?" Amanda asked.

"Honey, I can't read this thing."

"Rosanne thinks we should sneak in a turkey with a whatchamacallit," she said, looking over his shoulder into the oven, careful to hold her hair back. She still wore hers long, basically because her husband liked it that way. (Sometimes when Amanda turned around on the street or in a store she could see the surprise in people's eyes that she was forty-four and not twenty-four. She had such beautiful hair still.)

"Fresh-killed turkeys from Ohio don't come with whatchamacallits."

"I know, darling," she said. "I think Rosanne meant that, when your mother isn't looking, we should just switch turkeys."

"But then it wouldn't taste awful and she'd know it wasn't the one she brought and then she'll start crying."

This was not the first time they had discussed the mysterious fresh-killed turkey Mrs. Stewart insisted on bringing with her from Ohio every year, or the meat thermometer she extracted from wads of tissue paper as though it were an irreplaceable heirloom. But Amanda felt bad for Mrs. Stewart, who was a widow and lonely, and wanted to make her mother-in-law's visits as pleasant as possible.

"Well, it is Thanksgiving," she murmured. "We can do it once a year."

Howard muttered something and used a dish towel to shove the turkey back into the oven and slam the door. "Okay, it's done."

"How can you be sure?"

"Amanda, we go through this—"

"Please just cut into it, Howard. We don't want to poison anybody."

They looked at each other and started to laugh. Howard slung the dish towel over his shoulder and moved over to Amanda, sliding his hands around her waist. "You must be exhausted."

"I am tired," she admitted, resting her head on his shoulder as he pulled her closer. She used to have such a narrow waist it was hard for Amanda to let Howard feel what she was carrying around now. She had been watching what she ate and exercised like a mad woman, but after Grace she could not seem to pull herself together like she had after Emily and Teddy. "How do you know this Celia?" she asked quietly from his shoulder.

"That girl? She's a bartender at Captain Cook's."

"A bartender?" Amanda raised her head to look at him.

"Once in a while I'll stop in and have a burger. And watch a game."

Amanda walked over to retrieve the kettle, fill it with water and put it on a burner. She needed to warm the silver serving dishes with hot water before filling them. (She had inherited the silver from her grandmother and it made Amanda's mother happy to see her using it.) "I didn't realize you frequented bars while we were away."

"Oh, that's me all right," Howard said, "in the bars, day and night. We're talking maybe once in a blue moon, Amanda. It does get a little lonely around here sometimes."

Amanda did not point out how, as a literary agent, and a very successful literary agent at that (president of Hillings & Stewart), Howard was inundated with people, phone calls and e-mail all day long. And when he did not have some professional soiree at night to attend, he always told her all he wanted to do was go home and collapse. He never said, "I'm lonely so I'm going to a bar."

Their living arrangement was becoming an increasingly unhappy situation for Amanda. After 9/11 Emily and Teddy were frightened of tall buildings, airplanes, staircases, fires and crowds. Like so many families, the Stewarts had gone into counseling with the children, but neither parent could bear the idea of not doing everything they could to make their children feel safer. So Howard found a gorgeous house and property in Woodbury, Connecticut, and after some discussion, Amanda and the children moved out there. Before this, it had never occurred to either one of the Stewarts that they would ever live anywhere but in their beloved adopted hometown of Manhattan.

The children were enrolled in school, and Howard hoped that when Emily and Teddy were older they would attend Taft as day students. There was a wonderful horse farm next to them, Daffodil Hill, where Amanda boarded a horse for herself and a pony for the children. Madame Moliere lived with them as well (the house was huge), so that Amanda could still get some work in on a book she was under contract to write, about the court of Catherine the Great. Howard tried to come out on Thursday nights and go back into the city on Monday mornings. Amanda would bring the children into New York at the slightest excuse; she did not want them to be afraid of the place their parents loved above all others, Manhattan, and more specifically, the neighborhood of Riverside Park.

Howard grew up in Ohio, where his father had a landscaping business, and Amanda grew up in Syracuse, where her parents were still both professors at Syracuse University. Howard had attended Duke and then book publishing lured him to Manhattan; Amanda attended Amherst and her (closet) gay husband had dragged her to Manhattan.

Howard's first wife had money, so he had not been pressed to make a lot of money while he worked his way up at Gardiner & Grayson to become an editor. He quit his job around the same time that his marriage broke up, started a literary agency, and had never looked back. It was with great pride that Howard had bought the Woodbury property on his own; Amanda knew her husband still considered this apartment as belonging to her, and that Howard wished as a family they did not still rely so heavily on the trust fund Amanda's grandmother had left her. The money Amanda had earned (and still earned) from her first book, a biography of Catherine the Great, was different, Howard said.

Amanda was extremely proud of Howard. Men liked his well-defined masculinity and sharp, well-educated mind, and women liked his curly hair, beautiful manners, deeply expressive eyes and easy smile. And while Howard appeared to be every inch the sophisticated New Yorker, he was, at heart, still a boy from the Midwest who loved life.

The Stewarts had come a long way in their marriage. Certainly Amanda had. When she had met her future husband she could scarcely leave the neighborhood. She had suffered a complete nervous breakdown in her first marriage and had retreated into her work and this apartment. Besides her parents, there had only been two people who she trusted enough to let in. One was her housekeeper, Rosanne DiSantos, and the second, her elderly friend Mrs. Emma Goldblum, who would come for high tea. They were still very near and dear to her, and were, in fact, present this day at the Stewarts' Thanksgiving dinner. If anyone had told Amanda that someday she would be running after three children, driving everyone all over hell and high water in a Lincoln Navigator and volunteering for The Parents and Teachers Organization in the Connecticut suburbs, she would have told them surely they were mad.

But that was exactly what she was doing.

Of course, had anyone told her she would ever agree to live apart from Howard for at least four days a week she would have said, "Never!" And lately it was more like six or seven days apart and getting worse.

"You can do whatever you like while we're away," Amanda said to Howard, trying to sound carefree. "I trust you completely."

Howard looked at her from across the kitchen. "Ditto, my dear."

Amanda only wished she knew why that pretty girl who called her husband by his first name kept parading around in her head.

Dinner finally reached the dining room table, and given the unusual collection of people they were entertaining went off rather well. Conversation with Amanda's parents, the professors Miller, could be difficult to follow when Mother got lost in life's metaphors and Papa wandered through lost civilizations, which is to say, to speak in their respective fields of English and history. Mother Stewart tended to talk about soap operas, so Amanda's older friend, Mrs. Goldblum, could help out a little there. There were Emily and Teddy, of course; Grace snoozing in her carrier; Madame Moliere, and Miklov, the assistant director of the children's soccer league in Connecticut. He was from the Czech Republic and the children called him Mickey-Luck. Also present were Rosanne DiSantos, no longer a housekeeper but a hospital LPN, Rosanne's beau, Randy, a detective in the Bronx, and Rosanne's seventeen-year-old son, Jason, who had to leave dinner early to go to work at Captain Cook's. Amanda walked Jason to the door.

"The tips are really, really good on Thanksgiving," he explained. Amanda had known this strapping young man since he was two years old. He was attending Bronx Poly Sci, hoping for early acceptance to the University of Pennsylvania to study engineering.

"Will Celia be bartending today?" Amanda casually asked.

Jason's head jerked in her direction. "You know Celia?"

"She lives in our building."

"Oh. Um, yeah, I guess she'll be working," Jason said, his face ringing with red.

Amanda returned to the dining room wondering if Jason was sweet on Celia or if he knew something about Celia he didn't want Amanda to know. Like the fact that Howard went there while she and the children were in Connecticut.

Amanda had never entertained uncomfortable thoughts like these until Grace was born. She didn't care what anybody said; carrying a third child at forty-three had almost finished her. Unlike her first two pregnancies, with Grace she'd been chronically tired and ill. She had also grown immensely heavy and the birth had been difficult, ending in an emergency cesarean. Mercifully Grace was fine, and after a few weeks, Amanda started feeling better. Physically anyway.

Most of the weight was off now, but Amanda's hormones—or *something*—were still out of whack. Her considerable sex drive seemed to have utterly vanished. And there was no way, not with how well her husband knew her, that she could pretend otherwise. And she knew this hurt Howard's feelings, that whatever sex life they could manage at this point was so one-sided.

Dinner flowed into dessert.

"Mickey-Luck's going to play us tomorrow," Teddy told Rosanne.

"He's going to play you for a fool?" Rosanne kidded.

"No, in soccer!" Teddy said, laughing.

"Is that your real name?" Mrs. Goldblum asked the soccer coach. "Mickey-Luck?"

"Miklov," he answered.

"Miklov," Mrs. Goldblum rehearsed.

"I've got a new recipe for it," Mother Stewart told Mrs. Goldblum. "Hot or cold, it makes no difference, it's wonderful meat loaf. Just ask Howard."

"With soccer and riding and music lessons," Amanda's mother was saying, "I'm beginning to wonder when these children have an opportunity to play."

"I told you I didn't like the play," Amanda's father said.

"Do you watch *All My Children?*" Mother Stewart asked Mrs. Goldblum.

"I watch all the children," Madame Moliere answered in her heavily accented English.

"The cheeldren are great," Miklov said, nodding. "They leesen, they practice and they do goot."

Amanda and Howard tried not to laugh but it was difficult. There were so many conversations going on there simply was no thread to follow. Everyone seemed happy, though, which was all that really mattered. Even Miklov, who usually featured a deep sort of Slovak scowl, was smiling.

He was a good-looking young man of twenty-six whose professional career in soccer had ended in his own country with an ankle injury. Amanda never really understood how Miklov had come to their soccer league but she hoped it would lead to better things. The job did not pay well at all, which was why Howard had engaged Miklov to conduct private sessions with the children, to give him some pocket money. (Well, and to make the children better players.)

Mrs. Goldblum, Rosanne and Randy departed shortly after dessert and the wife of the building superintendent arrived to clean up. Madame Moliere prepared the children to leave for Connecticut while Amanda endeavored to sort out her parents. Mother Stewart was flying out of JFK very early in the morning so Howard was staying in the city with her tonight. After he dropped her off at the airport he would join his family and in-laws in Woodbury in time for the children's holiday indoor soccer tournament.

Howard and Miklov took the bags down to the building's garage and secured them under a tarp on the Navigator's roof. Amanda's father sat in the front seat; Amanda's mother, Madame Moliere and Grace sat in the backseat; and poor Miklov was crammed into the rear jump seat with Teddy and Emily. Howard made sure everyone had their seat belts on and then walked to the driver's window. "Drive carefully," he murmured, giving Amanda a kiss on the lips.

"I shall," she promised.

One of the greatest surprises of their marriage had been Amanda's excellence as a driver. She loved it. Getting behind the wheel of a car gave her the same quiet thrill as when as a child, she had discovered someone had left the paddock gate open at her grandparents' farm. It was the thrill of freedom, of suddenly having the way and the means to go wherever she wanted.

The drive to Woodbury was pleasant and the traffic not too bad. They swung into a rest stop for Emily to use the bathroom and get some gas but then everybody except Madame Moliere and Grace got out for one reason or another and it took a while to load everyone back in.

When they reached the house, Ashette, their black Labrador retriever, was overjoyed to see them. Amanda dismissed the house sitter, got her parents settled in their room and made sure Madame Moliere had her eye on the children. Then Miklov climbed into the front seat and Amanda drove him home to the Waterbury housing complex where the league had put him up. They talked a little bit about the tournament that started tomorrow. A lot of the children were away for the holidays so Emily and Teddy would probably play their whole games, which was great since Amanda wanted her parents to watch them in action.

"How are you getting on, Miklov?" Amanda asked him. She had been surprised when Miklov had accepted Howard's offer of a bus ticket to join them for Thanksgiving dinner. Emily had not been, though. ("He's all alone, Mommy, oh, so very, very alone!")

"I miss my family," he admitted, brushing his hair out of his eyes.

"Of course you do," she said. "And I'm sure they must miss you."

"My mother."

She glanced over at him.

"My mother meeses me."

"Will you go and see her? For a visit, I mean."

"Not yet," he said, turning to look out his window.

He probably couldn't afford it yet. Maybe she and Howard could find some other parents who would engage him for private lessons.

While they drove through downtown Waterbury Miklov suddenly said, "This is a very happy day." When he smiled he was very handsome, although his teeth needed some work. She had no doubt that would come in time. Perfect-looking teeth was still a very American thing.

When she pulled up in front of the dreadful-looking building where he lived she said, "Here we are." She kept her foot on the brake, waiting for him to get out. She needed to pick up some milk on the way home. Her parents now only drank soy milk. What store would be open on Thanksgiving that would carry soy milk?

Mickey-Luck undid his seat belt and shifted to face Amanda, making the leather creak. "I will tell my mother about my American Thanksgeeving. I haf—" He looked down a moment and then raised his head to meet her eyes directly. "I say how kind you are."

"Our family is very fond of you, Miklov. You've made a big difference in our children's lives." *Because out here they miss their father terribly. So do I.*

Miklov's eyes traveled down to Amanda's mouth for just a second and then he turned away, searching for the door handle. When he found it he stopped again and turned around. "You understand how beautiful you are, yes?"

Amanda's eyes widened. And then she laughed a little. "Why, thank you."

He made a fist and pounded his heart twice. "I feel it there. For you. You are so beautiful."

Oh, save it, Mickey-Luck! she thought. *It is being American that you think is beautiful, our money is beautiful, this ridiculously expensive truck is beautiful, having a family is beautiful!*

"See you tomorrow," she told him.

He looked disappointed as he got out. Then he turned around, ducking his head back into the truck. "People think I am a peasant but I am not," he said in a rush. "My great-grandfather was a great general. My father went to school, he was a teacher. I am not a peasant, Mrs. Stewart!"

Somewhat startled, Amanda said, "Everyone knows you are a champion soccer player, Miklov, and an excellent teacher. And in America that is all that matters."

Miklov was searching her eyes and it made Amanda uncomfortable. But then his dark mood seemed to lift and he smiled, closed the door and walked away from the truck. He did not look back.

Amanda took a deep breath and regripped the steering wheel. Miklov was very attractive.

She set out to find soy milk.

Celia Cavanaugh

IT SUCKED BIG-TIME that she had to work. This was the first time in four years that Celia had the apartment to herself over a holiday weekend. But she did have to work, three until eleven tonight, three until two Friday and Saturday, and then three until ten on Sunday. Normally she cleaned up in tips over the weekend but on Thanksgiving? It might be okay today but she knew it would be dead over the weekend. To meet December's rent she was going to need an extra shift this week.

Celia and Rachel had been assigned as roommates in a freshman dorm at Columbia University. Celia did not have many Jewish friends in the Connecticut suburb she had grown up in, and Rachel did not have many white Anglo-Saxon Protestant friends in the New Jersey suburb she had grown up in, but they had hit it off in a big way and learned a lot from each other. For example, Rachel introduced Celia to lox and bagels, while Celia, Rachel joked, had introduced her to margarine and instant mashed potatoes. Both girls came from affluent families, had parents still married to each other, and had done well in their suburban training in piano, tennis, skiing and keeping secrets.

Celia's father was a partner at a Wall Street law firm, while Rachel's last name was synonymous with the largest independent truck leasing company in the world. Her father was really, *really* rich. So rich, in fact, that he had bought a two and a half bedroom apartment on Riverside Drive so his daughter could move out of the dorm her sophomore year. Celia was welcomed to move in with Rachel as along as she paid sixteen hundred dollars a month toward expenses. Celia's father asked why the heck should they pay sixteen hundred dollars a month to let her run wild when Celia could stay in the dorm for six hundred dollars a month and let her mother sleep at night. The girls put their heads together and figured out if they could just find someone who'd pay Celia's rent for the full-size bedroom, Celia could pay Rachel six hundred dollars a month and cram herself into the tiny maid's room off the kitchen, and then Rachel would have extra cash her father didn't need to know about.

They advertised in the *Spectator* and the son of a country-western star was happy to pay sixteen hundred dollars to live in such a nice apartment. After Celia's mother checked it out *and* the building *and* the neighborhood, she told Celia's father she had no objection to Celia moving in. If Celia wanted to live in a closet that was her business, but the Riverside Park neighborhood was now very in, Mrs. Cavanaugh told her husband.

They moved into the apartment in August and it was really great. Celia's father built her a loft bed so she could turn around in the maid's room. Then, on their third night in the apartment, Celia and the-son-of-a-country-western-star shared a couple of bottles of wine, one thing led to another and Celia never slept in the maid's room again. The next thing she knew, she was smoking cigarettes like the-son-of-a-country-western-star (Rachel put a huge standing fan in the hall to blow smoke back into their bedroom), and suddenly it was November and Rachel was calling Celia at the country-western star's palatial home outside of Nashville to say that if Celia didn't withdraw from their English class she was going to get an F because of her absences. Celia wasn't going to be able to make the time up, the teacher was an asshole. So Celia called the university from Nashville and withdrew from the class. Later when her parents saw the *I* on her report card she said she had actually gotten a B but the teacher had handed in the grades late.

The lies came easier and more often. Celia and the-son-of-a-country-western-star were drinking a lot and smoking a lot of pot. Rachel said after this school year that was it, Celia was out. Celia said that was fine, they were going to get their own place anyway. In February the-son-of-a-country-western-star wanted to take Celia to Aspen where his country-western-star parent had a place, but Celia explained she had a huge test coming up in history and couldn't go. But as she watched the-son-of-a-country-western-star packing his bags she changed her mind and went with him, deciding she'd just figure out what to do about her classes later. The solution she came up with was to call the school from Aspen and explain that she had broken her leg in three places skiing, was being forced to stay for medical treatment and could they please tell her what portion of her tuition could be applied to the following year since it looked like she would have to withdraw from school.

"Oh, Rachel's great, Mom," Celia would say, dragging on a

cigarette outside one of the Aspen ski lodges. "And she says hi. We'll probably go to the new place on Broadway for pizza tonight."

When Celia and the-son-of-a-country-western-star finally got back to New York in late March, Celia knew she had better get a full-time job so she'd have some money saved toward school; she had to somehow soften the blow to her parents that she had dropped out. She figured she would pay them back, start school again in the fall and be only fifteen credits behind.

That was five years ago and Celia hadn't been back to school since.

The week before Celia's twenty-first birthday, the son-of-a-country-western-star ran away with the newlywed wife who lived on the fourth floor of their building. Celia was at first stunned, then disbelieving, and finally devastated. (The newlywed husband wasn't so happy about it, either, although he did keep asking Celia if she wanted to come over to talk about it over drinks.)

Not long after that Rachel came into Celia's bedroom for a talk. Rachel made a great show of wafting through the smoke and sat down on the foot of Celia's bed. "You don't have to pay me for the maid's room anymore but someone has to pay the $1,703 for this room this month."

"I start bartending at Captain Cook's next week," Celia said, blowing smoke to the ceiling. (She had just smoked a joint with one of the doormen on his break and was still a little out of it.)

"Celia—" Rachel jumped up and kicked her way through the clothes and junk all over the floor to retrieve a handheld mirror from the dresser. She'd brought it back to shove in Celia's face. "Look at you!"

She hadn't wanted to particularly, but Celia did. Her

shoulder-length brown hair was unbrushed and her brown eyes had purple circles under them. Celia had also gained about fifteen pounds since she had replaced the-son-of-a-country-western-star with Oreo cookies, Cheez Doodles and Guinness in bed.

Celia sat up to stamp out her cigarette. "I'll move if you want."

"Oh, Celia, you never sleep anymore, you just keep doing drugs and drinking and locking yourself up in here." Rachel's eyes welled up with tears. "I want my friend back."

Since Rachel had threatened to throw her out the year before Celia didn't put too much on this threat. For whatever reason Rachel wanted to save their friendship, and did so with persistency which at that point had evoked from Celia mild contempt. Still, there was something about Rachel's near hysteria that got to her.

"My littlest angel, what is wrong?" her mother asked Celia the next night in Darien, as Celia lay sobbing on her old bed in her old room.

"Everything," she wailed. "I just feel like killing myself."

The next morning she found herself in a psychiatrist's office in Stamford. When she saw her mother's hopeful expression when she came out she felt enraged. She wouldn't tell her what she had told the man (which had been pretty much nothing). In the car, when her mother asked if they had discussed an antidepressant, Celia went ballistic, screaming, "I'm not going to be a high-tech zombie! So just forget it!"

"But, Celia—"

"The doctor said if I get all this sugar and nicotine and caffeine out of my system I'm going to feel better. And he said I had to exercise more and get more sunlight."

"And what about the drinking, Celia?"

"He didn't say anything about that," she lied. Actually what he had said was how much alcohol would increase her depression when it wore off.

"I'm going to cut way back anyway," she told her mother.

"Since you're only turning twenty-one next week and are already vowing to cut back on your drinking I'm not sure how to take that, Celia," her mother said, trying to remain focused on the road. This was how Celia remembered her childhood, her mother always driving Celia and her brothers somewhere. "But if you find changing these things doesn't help, you have to promise me you'll see the doctor again."

Although Celia said nothing about it, the doctor had lectured Celia on what a death sentence cocaine could be for someone like her. "You lose the ability to experience well-being because the cocaine burns up the chemicals that create it. That's why so many cocaine addicts kill themselves. They become physically incapable of feeling sensations of well-being. Think of a turtle whose shell has been ripped off."

Rachel was irritatingly elated when Celia said she was going to reform her evil ways. She quit smoking, started running in the park and Rachel went with her to a couple of Weight Watchers meetings so they could both get their food under control. (Rachel tended to be on the heavy side.) Celia started working at Captain Cook's and was amazed at how well the men tipped her; she was also perversely fascinated by people who drank too much. She swore off cocaine, stayed away from pot and began to sleep again.

All in all she started to feel whatever it was starting to lift. At least she could breathe without wanting to hang herself.

Her stint at Captain Cook's had worked out well. Mark Cook, the owner (who had sailed on nothing but the Staten Island Ferry), liked Celia from the start because she was really popular with the customers. She also didn't steal from the register like the other bartenders. Celia was made assistant manager of the bar. Not too long after that, when Celia lied to the other bartenders that the new guy was an undercover cop and the two worst offending thieves quit, Mark promoted her to manager of the bar.

In the meantime, Rachel got her B.A. and entered the master's program at Columbia in American studies. Although Celia looked and acted a thousand times better since her more wayward days, Rachel still worried about her.

"Oh, Rach, now what?" Celia said, making a strawberry-banana smoothie in the blender. "I've given up smoking, drugs and junk food. What else do you want me to do?"

"It's the stuff you're dragging home. All this junk all over everywhere."

It was true that Celia had found a renewed interest in well-made old things again. Finding and dragging home old things was something she had done even as a child. (Her parents said in her last life she must have been Queen Victoria.) "It's not junk," she protested, pouring some of the smoothie in a glass and sliding it to her roommate. She looked around and then snatched up a glass inkwell that had been drying next to the sink. "This is a mid-nineteenth century inkwell. It is not junk."

"It doesn't have a top, Celia, it's just more junk. But at least that's small. What are you going to do with that old window you dragged home the other day?"

"I'm taking it to storage," Celia said.

"It's *weird,* Ceil," Rachel continued. "I don't know anybody else who has a stone fireplace mantel lying on their bedroom floor. Do you?"

That made Celia laugh. And then Rachel laughed, too.

"We used to laugh all the time," Rachel said. "Remember?"

Celia nodded, feeling a little sad. When had everything gotten to be so hard?

"You spend too much time alone," Rachel continued. "If you didn't go to work I don't think you'd speak to anybody."

It was true, she had gone from being outgoing to wishing most of the time that people would leave her alone. She made all kinds of excuses to get out of family things. Her oldest brother was a lawyer like her dad and the other was a research scientist. This did not leave a whole lot of room for Celia to talk about her career in bartending. Even her mother was working on a master's degree at night at Fairfield University, in what Celia didn't even know. (She was almost afraid to ask what a Cotillion debutante who hadn't held a job in thirty years wanted a master's degree *in*.) The whole Cavanaugh family was so programmed for success Celia's throat tightened whenever she was around them.

At one time *she* had been a success in her family's eyes. She had made the National Honor Society in high school and made the varsity soccer and tennis teams. She had always been a class officer, and as a senior had been voted most popular, most likely to succeed and best legs. She remembered being happy, feeling full of energy.

Now, even in her reformed state of living, Celia felt as though everyone she had grown up with had run ahead and she couldn't catch up. It was as if she was stuck behind a wall of glass. She could see them but could not reach them. Rachel saw it because Rachel was the one who had to make up excuses for why Celia always ducked calls from old high school friends.

Celia pretty much ducked calls from everyone at this point.

After Celia encouraged Rachel to sign up for Match.com, the roommates' relationship improved because Rachel had something exciting going on in her life to focus on and all Celia had to do was listen to her talk about her experiences.

Celia's alarm went off at 2:15 p.m. She dragged herself out of bed, showered and put on her Captain Cook's uniform, which consisted of tight-fitting black jeans, a long-sleeved blouse (with billowed sleeves and plunging neckline; *aye,* like a pirate), and tucked a clean black-and-white bandana in her back pocket, which she would put on at the bar. She knew she should call home to wish everyone "Happy Thanksgiving," but if she did then she'd have to talk to all the relatives and deal with the questions her parents had not come up with satisfactory answers to: When was Celia going back to school? Was she seeing anyone special? Had she decided on her career?

She called her mother's cell phone. She knew it would be turned off but she also knew her mother would check it later when she hadn't heard from Celia. "Hi, everybody. I just wanted to say Happy Thanksgiving and tell you that I had a very nice day here but missed you guys and now I'm going to work. I hope dinner was good and Uncle Keith didn't break any chair legs in the dining room or anything again. Love you!"

A cold wind blew at her back as Celia walked to Columbus Avenue. Sometimes the wind off the Hudson was so strong between West End Avenue and Riverside Drive people had to walk backward to reach their buildings. And this was only November. Just wait.

The restaurant was busy but the bar was slow. "Three Diet Pepsis, a Shirley Temple and a zombie," one of the waiters said, putting in his order. "Identify the unhappy patron at *that* table."

It was a nice group that worked here. Most of them had come to New York to be actors.

Celia flicked the channels of the two TVs over the bar. She

turned the sound up on the NFL game and turned the sound off on the college game. The busboy brought in a couple racks of clean glasses and set them down on the bar. "Do you want me to put them away?"

"Not until you're twenty-one," she told him, smiling. Jason was terribly shy and young for his age, but he was a good worker.

Celia hefted the trays down into the bar and started putting the glasses away.

"Um," Jason said.

She looked up. "You'll be in the back?"

"Yeah," he said.

"Thanksgiving is the first day of Suicidal-Thoughts Season," a regular sighed to Celia. He was divorced, this one, and had moved into the city after his wife in the suburbs threw him out of the house. Why, he was not saying, but Celia suspected it had something to do with the way he drank. Celia almost never expressed an opinion about anything that mattered to her customers—like the way they drank—because the tips were much better if she didn't.

"I'm just thankful Thanksgiving's only once a year," another regular said from across the way, a heavily made-up woman with many miles on her. She'd been working at the Board of Ed for twenty-five years. She drank the house rosé over ice. She once told Celia she hung out at Captain Cook's because it was a nice place, the people were nice and if she *should* happen to find a man in here sometime then she would feel a lot safer about getting to know him.

Another regular, the unpublished writer, came in and sat down at the bar. He had on a tie and jacket, which was unusual for him.

"Happy Thanksgiving," Celia said. "What may I get you?"

"Arsenic or new in-laws," he said, loosening the tie. "Irish Mist on the rocks." He rested his elbows on the bar, watching her. "My agent's going to fire me," he said glumly, "I just know it. Asked me if I wanted to meet him for a beer. He lives around here."

"You're meeting him here?" Celia asked, pouring the whiskey. "On Thanksgiving?"

"I figure he wants to get it over with and tell me I'm going to be a fucking insurance salesman for the rest of my life."

"And with that kind of language not a very successful one," Celia observed, making everyone, including the writer, laugh. She wiped down the bar in front of him and slid a saucer of Chex Mix toward him. "He's not going to have anything bad to say," she said, "not on Thanksgiving Day. He wouldn't have called you."

"You think?" He was looking up at her with a kind of gratitude that translated into excellent tips. But that was not why Celia had said it; she meant it. She felt sorry for him. He'd been trying to sell something he'd written ever since she started working here.

"When's he coming?"

"I haven't called him back yet."

"Call him," Celia told him.

"You think?"

"It's Thanksgiving, I'm telling you, he must be calling with good news."

"I don't know what it is you should be doing for a living, Celia," the guy thrown out of the house in the suburbs said, "but it's sure not this."

Celia tossed the towel into the laundry bin and gave him a saucer of the peanuts she knew that he liked. "Why not this?"

"For starters, you sound like Martha Stewart and look like one of those women on *Friends.*"

"She does," agreed the lonely Board of Ed lady.

"Thank you," Celia said.

"Celia used to go to Columbia, you know," the writer said. Celia imagined he was building her credentials up in his mind so he would do what she had advised and call his agent back.

"Ceil," a waitress said breathlessly, careening into the bar. "I need two margaritas, a strawberry daiquiri and a mudslide as fast as you can make 'em."

"Got it."

A cold blast of air came in when the door opened. Celia glanced over and saw a man in overalls and a parka coming in. Keeping his coat on, the man slid onto a stool and briskly rubbed his hands. "Tenant blows uppa his stove and blamesa me. On a Thanksgivinaday, this I don't need."

Celia poured him a draft.

The second bartender for the night shift appeared. "Sorry I'm late, Celia."

"You haven't missed much," she said, putting ingredients for the daiquiri, margaritas and mudslide in three of the bar's six blenders and passing the order on to him because it was time for her break.

"Think it'll get busier?"

"Not until nine, when people get back into the city," she said, untying her apron and putting it under the bar. She went into the kitchen where, as usual, the crew was careening about swearing in different languages. (Their chef's dyslexia was pretty bad.) Celia walked over to the dishwashing area. "Jason," she called, and then she left the kitchen and headed for Mark's office. She unlocked the door and went in.

She was standing examining the shift calendar on the wall when he knocked. "Come in and close the door," she told him.

He did as he was told.

"And lock it," she added, walking over. While he was turning the dead bolt Celia placed her hand on the small of his back and felt him freeze. "Yes, I want to," she whispered into his ear. "Very much." She let her hand slide down and smiled to herself. Amazing.

She led Jason over to the low filing cabinet that also served as a makeshift table in the office. She sat down and pulled him to stand between her legs. And looked up at him. And smiled.

The teenager's eyes were half-closed and his breath ragged. It had been two weeks since the last time. While he just stood there Celia undid his belt, his pants, worked his zipper and then pulled his jeans down.

She took a sharp breath when she looked down. He tried to help her take his Jockey shorts down but his hands were trembling and Celia pretty much had to do it. As she sat back up it brushed the side of her face. She took hold of him and smiled, looking up. "You're really something," she whispered. Then she hastily stood up to take off her jeans and panties and moved back down onto the file cabinet. Jason grabbed at her thighs to pull her legs up and she scarcely had time to guide him into place before he shuddered and caved.

One of the hazards of an inexperienced teenage boy. The upside was Jason had been a virgin, free of disease, and now only knew the most acute desire to get into her. Which was fine with her.

"I'm sorry," he whispered.

"It's okay," she whispered back, pulling his head down to rest on her shoulder, "because you still feel so good inside of me." She was looking up at the clock. She had maybe ten minutes. She shifted, tightening her legs around Jason to keep him there, and started to whisper things to him. Nice things. About him, about his size and how he felt inside of her, about what she wanted him to do to her. It was not long before she felt him growing large again. The progress was slow but steady, and although he was not quite yet fully erect, she started moving against him because she had grown tremendously excited. He began thrusting back, making her moan a little, which got him more excited, and his increasingly harder thrusts made Celia's hips start to rise. She told him what was happening to her, what she was feeling, and then Jason became almost frantic, rhythmically banging the cabinet into the wall. She cried softly into his neck as she came and then shuddered violently; moments later he grunted loudly and collapsed on Celia, damp with perspiration.

Celia rolled out from under Jason and went into Mark's toilet to get some paper towels. She dampened some and used them to clean herself up and then wordlessly brought some out for Jason. She went back for the can of Glade and sprayed the air. It smelled of fake roses and when she looked at Jason they both laughed.

Rosanne DiSantos and Mrs. Emma Goldblum

"I HATE IT when you say things like that, Mrs. G," Rosanne told her eighty-nine-year-old former employer, longtime friend and roommate.

"I only said that it *appeared* the young foreign gentleman has a crush on our dear Amanda."

"And Amanda'll never notice because she never does," Rosanne said. "But now you're gonna make me worry about what's gonna happen when Mickey Muscles makes his move out there in wherever the heck she is." Having only lived in Detroit and New York City, Rosanne DiSantos was not a fan of the country.

"Connecticut," Mrs. Goldblum supplied, sipping her cocoa. "Amanda is quite capable of taking care of herself."

That shows how much you know about how she used to be, Rosanne thought. Amanda was like another person since she met Howie, and even like a third person after the kids started coming. As much as Rosanne wanted to believe the old Amanda was gone forever she still worried a bit now and then.

Rosanne had known Amanda and Howie for over fifteen years. When she earned her living as a housekeeper, they had been separate clients; Amanda was living by herself and Howie had been married to a first-class bitch that Rosanne hated.

Mrs. Goldblum's forehead furrowed slightly. "What is it, dear?"

"Oh, nothin'," Rosanne said quickly, forcing a smile. "I was just thinkin' how guys are always gaga over Amanda's boobs so she must be handling them, just like you said."

Mrs. Goldblum carefully replaced her cup into the saucer with a smile. "I might not have expressed it in quite that way, Rosanne dear, but I do understand what you mean." After a moment her smile faded. "And perhaps it's nothing."

Rosanne shot a look across the table. "Perhaps *what* is nothing?"

Mrs. Goldblum withdrew the lace hankie she kept tucked in her sleeve and patted her nose with it. "It's just that I've lived such a long time."

Oh, no, here we go again, Rosanne thought. Everyone got older, of course, but somehow she never thought it would happen to Mrs. G. She had always been a little frail, yes, like a little bird, but these "talks" she had started giving lately were giving Rosanne the creeps. Like she was trying to cram things into Rosanne's head at the last minute.

Rosanne couldn't think about life without Mrs. G. (How dumb was that? A licensed practical nurse who can't deal with people dying?) What had begun as a solution to the problem of an older widow with a rent-controlled apartment far too large for her and a single mother without a proper place to raise her young son had become over the years a very real family. Mrs. G had been one of her housekeeping clients, too, back in the days when Rosanne's husband, Frank, had been alive. (The Stewarts had been on Monday, Amanda Miller on Tuesday, the Wyatts on Wednesday, Mrs. Goldblum on Thursday and the Cochrans on Friday.) This apartment had been Rosanne and Jason's home for over a decade and Mrs. G was like a mother to her and a grandmother to Jason. Jason even called her Gran.

And what changes had unfolded! Jason went from six to seventeen years old and Rosanne went from housekeeping to night school to becoming an LPN at Hudson Hospital. The fact that Rosanne hated nursing was besides the point. She had risen from a blue-collar living to become a professional. People looked at Rosanne differently now. And no one seemed surprised that one of Bronx Poly Sci's academic stars was her son.

Living in an apartment overlooking Riverside Park and the Hudson River had been quite something, too. Particularly since Mrs. G had been living in this three-bedroom apartment for like sixty-five years and her rent was only $1,450 a month, half of which Rosanne paid. What would happen after Mrs. G died was not hard to imagine; they'd already seen it innumerable times. Rosanne and Jason would be evicted and the apartment would be renovated and sold as a condo unit for well over a million dollars.

What would she do then? Rosanne had no idea. Everyone expected her to marry Randy eventually but she preferred the relationship the way it was. Randy was a great guy and everything but while Rosanne worked steadily to improve herself and her lot in life, Randy wanted to keep everything the same. Change upset him. He wasn't stupid, but he wasn't motivated. He was a detective, but worked mostly behind a desk in an administrative capacity. Randy did his job, then left his shift on the dot to have a beer with the guys, maybe throw some darts and watch NASCAR. He had two kids by his ex-wife that he regularly saw and supported. The thing that really bothered Rosanne was how Randy never seemed to initiate any action on his own; if there wasn't someone always there to tell him what to do next he would basically do nothing.

Randy liked the way their relationship was. They went out on occasion, always saw each other on Saturday night (at which time they very pleasantly got on sexually), and Rosanne always cleaned his apartment so she could stand being there.

So they just went on and Rosanne found it reassuring to have him in her life.

"Okay, Mrs. G, you've lived a long time," Rosanne prompted.

Mrs. G moved her lips around a little before she spoke.

This had started recently, too.

"It's not good for a husband and wife to live apart," Mrs. G finally said.

"Amanda's not going to do anything." *At least I sure hope not,* Rosanne added to herself. "She's got the three screaming-mimis and Madame DeFarge to keep her busy."

"Hmm," Mrs. G said somewhat gravely.

Rosanne counted to five. "What do you mean, *hmm?*"

She adjusted her glasses to look at Rosanne and, eventually, stare Rosanne down. "When you live apart, you begin to think outside of the family circle. It's asking for trouble. A wife requires a certain amount of attention and Howard seems otherwise very occupied."

"Oh, Mrs. G!" Rosanne objected, wrapping her arms over the top of her head in frustration. She let her arms drop. "This is Howie and Amanda we're talking about. They both made mistakes the first time around and they knew *exactly* what they wanted when they got married. Which was each other. And the kids. They wouldn't hurt those kids for anything and I think it's rotten to even be talking about this!"

"I just worry," Mrs. Goldblum said vaguely, preparing to rise from her chair.

Rosanne had forgotten to steer Mrs. G into the kitchen chair with arms on it so now Rosanne needed to help her get up without Mrs. G realizing that she *was* helping her get up. Mrs. G had become extremely irritable whenever she tried to help her and had thrown an absolute fit last year when Rosanne installed bars in her bathroom and along the hallways (although, Rosanne noticed, she started relying on them at once).

"At what time may we expect Jason?" Mrs. G asked, now on her feet and reaching for her walking stick. (That's the way Mrs. G was—she didn't use a cane like normal people; she used a walking stick, a skinny little black ebony stick with a silver handle that her granny or somebody used ten million years ago.)

"A little after eleven," Rosanne said, glancing up at the clock. "They won't close the kitchen until ten."

"How we will miss him when he goes away to school," Mrs. G said, moving toward her favorite seat in the living room to pick up her book. As was her habit she would take her book with her into the bedroom to read before going to sleep, but lately she had been falling asleep before getting to the book—or even turning off the light.

The phone rang and Rosanne picked it up and held it under her chin as she cleared the cups and saucers from the table. She'd have to wash them by hand because they were Wedgwood bone china that had belonged to some other ancient relative of Mrs. G's. "Happy Thanksgiving," Rosanne greeted whoever was calling.

Very carefully she put the dishes in the sink and held the phone with both hands, taking a quick look back over her shoulder. "Yeah, sure. Don't worry about it. I'll be right down. I know it's hard, but you gotta do it. And I'll go with you." She swallowed. "Don't think about it, we'll just do it and get it over with. I'll be right down."

"Who was that?" Mrs. G asked, appearing in the doorway.

"Samantha Wyatt," Rosanne said, replacing the phone in the cradle.

"Is she home from school?"

"Yeah. And I'm just going to run over with her to see her parents. To say Happy Thanksgiving. Leave the dishes in the sink and I'll wash them when I get back." She kissed Mrs. G on the cheek and headed for the front hall closet.

Sam Wyatt

"WHERE DOES SHE find these guys, in a catalog of the weird and the strange?" Sam Wyatt asked his wife.

"I think she met him through work somehow," Harriet said quietly, putting the finishing touches on a second platter of hors d'oeuvres. They were on a second round because their youngest was two hours late and they were starving. They also had to entertain the latest boyfriend their older daughter had brought home to share their Thanksgiving meal.

Sam Wyatt's eldest daughter, Althea, was thirty-one, black, Methodist and worked on Wall Street. The guy in the living room had gray hair, was white, and with a name like Donnelly was probably Catholic and had some kook job on Seventh Avenue. Sam always knew they would regret having sent Althea to that Muffy-Buffy school on the East Side for rich girls. Althea had grown up with so few black friends it was no wonder she dated white guys.

Admittedly, Sam and Harriet revolved in a somewhat

rarified circle of New York. He may have started life as the youngest of six dirt-poor kids of an army sergeant who died young, but Sam had earned a college degree and today, at sixty-one, was a senior vice president of Electronika International, the second largest manufacturer of electronic office equipment in America. Harriet, whose skin was much lighter than Sam's, began in the training program at Gardiner & Grayson book publishers and today was Vice President of Publicity, Marketing & Advertising.

"Be polite, Sam, that's all I ask," Harriet murmured, picking up the tray of hors d'oeuvres.

"Yeah, yeah." He finished pouring the old white Catholic guy a second glass of wine. Sam hadn't had a drink in over twenty-one years, which was a good thing since it had been under only that one condition that Harriet had allowed him back into her and Althea's life. That was why there was an eleven year age difference between their daughters. Althea was from Round 1 of their marriage while Samantha was their AA baby, the child from Round 2 who benefitted most from her parents being in Alcoholics Anonymous and Al-Anon.

Where the heck was Samantha? he wondered, looking at his watch. Traffic, he supposed. Harriet said after the scolding they gave Samantha about her last cell phone bill she would probably claim it had been "uneconomical" to call them from the road.

"Cliff was just remarking on the boat," Harriet said when Sam came in, nodding in the direction of the framed picture of their sailboat.

Sam handed the old white guy his glass of wine.

"Thanks, Mr. Wyatt. Althea says you moor it in Manhattan for part of the year."

"At the Seventy-Ninth Street Boat Basin," he confirmed.

He sat down and took a sip of Crystal Lite. (It wasn't half-bad compared to the other low-calorie crap Harriet was always trying to get him to drink.) "This time of year we keep it at our place in South Carolina." One of the reasons they had been anxious to get the girls together was to tell them he had finally worked out early retirement with Electronika; he and Harriet could afford to stop working in the spring. They were planning to downsize from this apartment (thank God they had made the stretch to buy it) to a two bedroom and spend half the year in South Carolina and half up here in Manhattan.

Althea would be fine with not having them around half the year. After breezing through Columbia at their expense, Althea had gone off to Berkeley with her boyfriend at the time to get an MBA. With the degree (and without the boyfriend) Althea came back to New York and took a job on Wall Street, something she said she would do until she paid off her student loans from graduate school. She became an investment analyst, one of those brainy people who researched companies to see if the firm should underwrite a bond issue for them. If the analyst's recommendations were correct, the firm often made a ton of money; if the analyst was wrong, though, the firm might still make some money up front but its reputation could take a hit which ended in long-term loss. The analyst responsible tended to vanish.

When Althea had told Sam she wished to stake her career on specializing in alternative energy, Sam's heart had filled with dread. Leave it to whacked-out Berkeley to prepare his daughter to be the only person on Wall Street who would never make any money. But then, of course, the oil crunch came and a drawing of Althea's face appeared on the front page of *The Wall Street Journal* as the high scorer in a suddenly enticing field. Her recommendation to underwrite a bond issue for a small company holding a patent that promised to revolutionize the production of hybrid engines was a grand slam, while earlier bond issues—in wind turbos, micro-turbines, corn refineries and municipal thermal-dynamic energy plants—were sent flying around the bases. Her latest venture was underwriting an outfit reopening abandoned sugar factories.

Althea was going to make partner in January. Last year Sam and Harriet had been agog to learn Althea's salary was ninety thousand dollars—supplemented by a $650,000 bonus. To his daughter's credit Althea gave over seventy-five thousand dollars a year away, paid something like three hundred thousand dollars in taxes *(three hundred thousand dollars in taxes!)* and moved into a two million dollar loft in SoHo.

This kind of money seemed insane to Sam and Harriet. And yet their own apartment, overlooking Riverside Park, had been appraised at over a million five. (They had bought it for two hundred and fifty thousand!)

But that was the nature of the great have and have-not divide of the new America, wasn't it? The whole country seemed morally out of whack. You had everything or you had very little.

However lucrative Althea's career might be, she was paying for it in other ways. Her work was wildly intense and geographically complicated. When she was in New York she worked a minimum of twelve hours a day and otherwise was on the road for the better part of each month. It was not fun travel, either, or even sequential. It was "go to Sacramento to pitch a bond issue to the California state pension fund, then get back in time for the meeting with the partners and then get down to Knoxville to scout that company before anyone else gets there and don't forget next Monday is the public hearing on the Nova Scotia wind project, and Thursday is the

Westminster Bank summit in London, and the following week you must get in to see that nutcase in Venezuela" kind of travel.

The Wyatts were also particularly proud of Althea's personal agenda in her work, to generate jobs, products and energy options in places where there were few. Why not use the earth's earliest and most bountiful foods like corn and sugar to stretch our oil reserves? Why not harness desert winds to make electricity? Or turn the endless summer sunshine of Alaska into the electricity needed to run air conditioners in the continental United States?

Now as for Samantha, the Wyatts' nineteen-year-old, she was a very different matter. Frankly speaking she was a little spoiled and being that much farther away from them for six months of the year made both Harriet and Sam a little nervous.

"How much longer do we have to wait for Sammy?" Althea wanted to know, reaching for a piece of celery. She crunched down on it, showing the beautiful teeth from childhood orthodontics. Althea was a good-looking woman, tall, slim, with great cheekbones Sam recognized as his own. But it was Samantha who was the beauty of the family. Samantha looked like her mother.

"We'll give her another ten minutes," Harriet said.

Althea sighed, grabbed a piece of cheese and sank back into the cushions.

"So what exactly do you do on Seventh Avenue?" Sam asked the guy. (He wished Harriet would go into the kitchen to check on something so he could eat some cheese, too.)

"I'm a textile designer."

"Samantha will be so interested," Harriet said. "She's in a theater group at school and loves making costumes."

What the hell kind of job was it for a man to be a textile designer? Sam wondered. "I guess you have to be, uh," Sam said, "*inclined* toward that kind of work?"

Althea rolled her eyes.

"I'm afraid my husband gets slightly deranged when he's not fed," Harriet explained.

The white-haired guy was laughing. "It's okay. My dad had the same reaction."

"Your father's still alive?" Sam blurted.

Althea picked up a carrot from the tray and gently threw it at her father. It bounced off Sam's barrel chest to the carpet.

"It must be my hair," the guy said to Althea. He looked at Sam. "It's a family trait, Mr. Wyatt. A lot of us go silver before thirty-five." He smiled, looking hopeful. "I'm only thirty-four, sir."

"Don't bother explaining anything to him," Althea told her boyfriend, "because I won't be speaking to him again as long as I live." She glared at her father. "You got it now, Dad? Cliff is not gay, he is gainfully employed and he's thirty-four, okay?"

Sam mumbled an apology and then looked at his watch. "Where is that girl?"

"I vote we go ahead and eat," Althea said.

"Five more minutes," Harriet said, "and if she isn't here..."

"So, Cliff," Sam said, sitting back in his chair, "why don't you explain to me exactly what a textile designer does."

"Well, I'm a chemical engineer by training, Mr. Wyatt."

"Oh, a chemical engineer," Harriet repeated approvingly, raising her eyebrows.

"He went to MIT," Althea added.

"I work in a lab to create new fibers. For different manufacturers."

"He just created something for Ralph Lauren," Althea said.

"Good for you," Sam said, although it still sounded a little poofy to him. He turned at the sound of the tumblers in the front door.

"That will be Samantha," Harriet said, jumping up and going to the foyer.

"Hooray, food," Althea said, standing up.

"Oh, hi, Rosanne," Sam heard Harriet say in the hall.

"Rosanne?" Sam said, glancing at Althea. "What's Rosanne doing here?"

"I think Mom invited her to dinner." Althea balanced her empty glass on the hors d'oeuvres tray and picked it up. "But she was going with Jason and Mrs. Goldblum over to the Stewarts'." Cliff stood to pick up the other glasses and soiled cocktail napkins. "Rosanne was my babysitter way back when, Cliff, so be warned, if you don't mind your p's and q's at the dinner table she might pinch you."

Harriet reappeared in the living room and by her expression Sam knew something was wrong. "What's wrong? Where's Samantha?"

"She went to her room. She's not feeling very well." She turned to Cliff. "I hate to do this to you," she began.

"But it would be better if I left. Of course, I understand."

"Fix Cliff a plate to take with him," Harriet said.

"No way, I'm taking him to Captain Cook's," Althea said. "After making him sit here half the night the least I can do is give him dinner."

"No, Althea." The tone of Harriet's voice got everyone's attention. She added, in a quieter voice, "I wish you would stay. I think your sister would want you here."

A feeling of foreboding flooded through Sam and wordlessly he headed for Samantha's bedroom.

"Sam, wait—"

Rosanne was standing next to three suitcases outside Samantha's room.

"A lot of baggage for three days," Sam observed.

"Mr. W," Rosanne said, "we need to talk for a sec."

Sam went to the door and found it locked. He knocked. "Samantha? This is your father. Open this door."

"If I could just talk to you for one minute," Rosanne pleaded.

"Oh, Rosanne!" Sam heard his daughter wail from behind the door. "What's the use?" The handle turned and the door swung open.

"Samantha, what is it?" Sam asked, wincing as he looked at his daughter's tearstained face. And then he looked down, between the parted sides of her coat. When he brought his eyes back up his daughter's expression confirmed it. Samantha was pregnant.

Howard Stewart

HE KEPT PUTTING off telling Amanda about it and now he was running out of time. Christmas would just about finish him financially.

The deals he thought would set things right at the agency had never materialized. Instead, his number one associate announced she was moving to another agency and was taking two of Hillings & Stewart's biggest writers with her. To be fair, Howard had assigned these two midlist authors (writers who sold consistently well but never quite seemed to make a bestseller list) to her because they were taking up so much of his time. The associate placed them at new publishing houses where first one and then the other popped onto the bestseller lists. Now the income from huge new contracts for these two writers was gone with his former associate.

And then there was the death of Gertrude Bristol, the international bestselling romance-suspense writer Howard had edited at Gardiner & Grayson who had become his founding client. Year in and year out for eight years Howard had received a Bristol novel to sell to publishers in twenty-one countries, to Reader's Digest Condensed Book Club, to audio publishers and to movie and TV producers.

Gertrude had been ninety-three when she died so it wasn't as if her passing had come as a great shock, but what happened after did. It was not unusual for the longtime publisher of a bestselling writer to enlist a ghost writer to keep writing books under the name of the deceased writer. It was a marketing thing, where the author as a brand name promised to deliver a certain kind of book. Everyone from V. C. Andrews to L. Ron Hubbard had been writing from the grave for years, and Gertrude Bristol was the kind of traditional "cozy" novelist who had written so many books for so many years that more than one excellent writer could emulate her style. Howard found the right writer, the publishing house was ecstatic and ready to go, and then—

The niece, Gertrude's literary executor, said, "No."

Of course, since the niece had inherited some twenty-six million dollars and the rights to forty-seven novels, what did she care about money? What was important to her, she wrote Howard, was that her dear aunt's work remain her own.

Howard understood the niece's sentiments but he also knew this decision put his agency in bad straits. His accountant had been warning him since he bought out the distinguished Hillings & Hillings Literary Agency to form Hillings & Stewart that Howard was operating on a very slim margin for error. Howard did not let the people go from Hillings & Hillings that the accountant advised him to; Howard had gone ahead with what was considered the Cadillac of health insurance plans; and Howard also instituted a retirement plan the accountant warned could come back to haunt him if any of his young employees ever got serious about saving. Yes, the accountant admitted, Howard could comfortably meet these obligations now. But what if something happened and costs went up and income came down? What then?

And then 9/11. Besides the psychological fallout from the tragedy, property taxes skyrocketed and so did the rents on midtown office buildings. Insurance premiums of all kinds went through the roof. And then there was the fact that it took months for the book publishing industry to return to any sense of normalcy. And God help any author whose book had been published in the interim. A techno-thriller about terrorists Howard represented had had a first printing of four hundred thousand copies coming out in November. Because of its subject matter the publisher delayed publication by ten months, at which time it sold barely thirty-five thousand copies.

Howard's children had been badly frightened and so he had not even hesitated about buying the house in Woodbury. At the time he qualified for a good mortgage rate and he wanted his family safe. The house, in turn, started a slew of new expenses and it was not long before Howard was taking a lot more money out of the agency than the agency receipts could support.

By last year Howard knew he had to do something so he had put out a feeler with Henry Hillings about the possibility one of his grandchildren might be interested in learning the business. The old man instantly got fired up about the idea because he had one grandson, he said, "Who's just the ticket," and it was not long before a lawyer called Howard to express Henry's interest in buying his grandson into the agency as a partner. A partial cash-flow solution seemed to be near. But when it came time to show the agency books, Howard put it off because the agency at that moment was out over two hundred thousand dollars on a credit line with a bank that was failing. That's when he had hustled to get the Gertrude Bristol deal going and got shot down.

Subsequent meetings with his accountant did not go well. If Howard wanted the agency books to look good, he was told, he had to pay off the credit line, lay off at least three employees, sublet one of the offices and make his employees pay at least thirty percent of their health care premiums. Also, if he didn't want trouble with the IRS, he needed an extra hundred thousand to set things right. His finances, the accountant told him, were now officially a secret disaster.

Howard took out a second mortgage on the Woodbury property (bringing up the percentage he owed to one hundred and twenty-five percent), paid the IRS, paid off the agency credit lines and balanced the books. The accountant only shook his head, saying it was no good to put personal property at risk when the agency had been incorporated expressly to shield his family. Why did Howard do it?

Howard did it because Howard couldn't stand the idea that Henry Hillings would think he had sold his distinguished literary agency to a loser. In Howard's eyes it was a far better thing to be in a temporary personal financial bind than for even a hint of tarnish to appear on the Hillings & Stewart name.

He had told Amanda none of this because this was the one area—money—he had sworn to her she would never have to worry about on his end. He had learned his lesson with his first wife; Howard would make his own money. Amanda owned the Riverside Drive apartment free and clear and she also had a generous trust fund, the revenue from which they could rely on. Amanda didn't care how much money Howard made; she only cared that Howard did not drift into the financially carefree attitude he had developed in his first marriage. *That* was why he had been so excited about buying the Woodbury property. *He* was buying a beautiful home for his family; it was the money *he* had earned that would keep his family safe.

Amanda's reaction to the house had been everything Howard had hoped for. Her jaw dropped in disbelief and then she had burst into tears, telling him she couldn't believe it, how much he had achieved in such a short period of time, and how she and Emily and Teddy (for Grace had not yet even been imagined) were the luckiest people on the face of the earth.

"Howard," his mother said.

Howard blinked and then looked across the living room. His mother was driving him crazy tonight, talking about what a wonderful husband and provider Howard's father had been—even if he hadn't gone to college like Howard and hadn't had fancy friends. She was just declaring there was no shame in a man working with his hands when the phone rang.

"I'm proud of Dad, too, Mom," Howard said, jumping up to answer the phone.

"I'm over here at Captain Cook's if you still feel like having that beer," the insurance salesman aspiring to be a novelist told Howard.

"I'm glad you called," Howard said, trying to put on an act of grave concern for his mother's benefit. This would be his only chance to get out of here for a while. "I got an e-mail this morning from Australia I'd like to discuss with you. So don't move, I'll be there shortly. I'm sorry, Mom," Howard said, hanging up the phone, "but I'm afraid I have to go out."

When Howard saw Celia behind the bar at Captain Cook's he thought, *How weird is that?* Amanda had just asked him about Celia today and now here he was walking in like the regular he wasn't.

"How are you?" Howard greeted the insurance salesman who was sitting at the bar, shaking his hand and giving him a pat on the shoulder.

"Nervous as hell," the insurance salesman said, tossing back what smelled like whiskey.

Celia came over to their side of the bar. "He's worried he's going to have to sell insurance for the rest of his life," she told Howard.

"Hi, Celia."

"Hi."

"And he's scared you're going to give up on him," a strange woman with a lot of makeup said from the corner of the bar.

"He's been hitting it pretty hard," another customer explained.

"A Beck's, please, Celia, thank you," Howard said, sliding onto a stool. He looked at the writer. "I don't know about your career in insurance, but I did get an offer from an Australian publisher for UK rights on your novel. It's a modest offer, but you'll be published in Australia, England, Ireland—"

The writer threw himself at Howard to hug him. The customers at this end of the bar cheered. Howard laughed, slapping the writer's back, savoring the moment. This was the joy of his job. (Telling a writer that every publisher in America had rejected their manuscript was the worst.)

Celia placed a frosted mug and a bottle of Beck's in front of Howard. "Nicely done."

She was a pretty girl. It was funny, he didn't remember her as such. While the writer grilled him for details, Howard watched Celia and began to realize why she might have given Amanda pause for thought. She was one of those seriously

AWOL Fairfield County girls, a fascinating Waspy creature who could exude a kind of smoldering sexuality. Maybe it was the way her jeans fit her. She had a great ass.

When the writer left to use the bathroom Celia put a dish of pretzels down in front of Howard. "Thank God you had good news. He's been depressed for as long as I've been serving him."

Her eyes were nice. Very dark. Like her hair. "Which is how long?"

"Three years," she said, leaving to get another patron a drink.

When she came back Howard told her, "There is a school of thought that says it's good to keep writers depressed because then they stay home and write."

She laughed. It made her much more attractive. She had a great smile.

"I hear you ran into my wife early this morning."

Her eyebrows went up. "I did?"

"In the lobby. Around three this morning?"

Celia still looked uncertain and held up a finger, signaling that Howard was to hold that thought while she got another customer a drink.

Howard saw the writer standing just outside the bar area, holding a cell phone to one ear and covering his other with a hand. He guessed he was calling his wife with the good news.

"I got sort of hammered here after work last night," Celia admitted on her return. "I think I remember seeing her. With the baby. Your wife has really beautiful hair, right?"

"Yes, she does."

"And absolutely *huge* tits," Celia added.

Howard did a double take.

Celia covered her mouth, aghast. "I'm so sorry, I didn't mean it that way. My roommate and I watch this show on BBC

America, *What Not to Wear,* and this lady Trinny's always saying stuff like that so we've been saying it to each other. I didn't mean to be rude—"

"Miss?" a customer called.

"I meant it as a compliment," she said, moving away. "I mean, look." She gestured to her own breasts and then made a gesture of futility.

No, there wasn't much there, Howard had to agree. But Celia did have terrific legs and that great swing to her ass.

"My wife thinks I'm lying about the Australian publisher," the writer announced upon his return. "She thinks I'm saying it so I can stay out and drink and not have to deal with her parents. The busboy says he knows you, by the way. That one, over there. Joey or something."

Howard smiled. "Hey! Jason!"

The teenager untangled himself from a tray of dirty dishes and came over, smiling and wiping his hands on his apron before shaking Howard's hand. "Hey, Mr. Stewart."

"Long time no see," Howard joked. Jason was a great kid, but really shy. Of course, with a mother like Rosanne, Howard imagined it would be hard to get a word in edgewise. "Was that turkey gross or what?"

"It wasn't that bad," the boy said nicely. "At least it didn't have any buckshot in it this year."

They laughed.

"My novel's getting published," the writer told Jason.

"Congratulations. Is Mr. Stewart your agent?"

"Best agent in the world," the writer declared, but Jason's eyes had moved to something behind them. Howard turned to see what he was looking at. Celia. Jason was looking at Celia. When Howard turned back around he could see a rash of scarlet spreading across Jason's neck.

Jason had a crush on her.

"If you want, Jason," he heard Celia say, "you can have a second break."

Jason's eyes lit up. "Yeah. Yeah! That'd be great," he stammered.

"Then you better go and take it before she changes her mind," Howard said.

"Yeah. I guess." Jason stuck his hand out. "Thanks again for dinner, Mr. Stewart."

"You're welcome."

"Congratulations again on your book," Jason said politely as he backed away.

They turned back around on their stools to lean on the bar. "Seems like a good kid," the writer said.

"He is. I think he's going to do very well." For some reason this reminded him of the financial mess he was in and it made him feel sick inside. "I think I need a real drink," Howard announced. "What are you drinking?"

"Irish Mist."

"Sounds good to me." He looked around. "Where's Celia?"

The bartender servicing the other end of the bar came down to Howard. "Can I get you fellas something?"

"Where's Celia?"

"On break. What can I get you?"

Howard ordered two Irish Mists. The writer drank his pretty fast while Howard nursed his. Celia reappeared behind the bar about ten minutes later.

"You're a little young for hot flashes," the writer told her when Celia came over to see how they were doing. He had started slurring his words.

Celia blew the hair off her face. She did look hot. "Say that again?"

The writer repeated it.

"I think you've hit your limit," Celia said, smoothly swiping his empty glass from the bar. "So what can I get you? On me. Water, soda or coffee?" She put a dish of pretzels in front of him.

"Fuck that, I wanna real drink," he said, swatting the dish of pretzels off the bar. The pretzels went flying and the saucer clattered down on the floor behind the bar.

Celia looked at Howard. "Tell him I won't hold it against him tomorrow." And then she walked down to the other end of the bar.

"Fuck her," the writer growled, trying to get off the bar stool. Howard held his arm to steady him and the writer threw his hand off.

"Okay, okay," Howard said, backing off.

Without another word the writer staggered out of the bar.

"He left his coat," the woman with lots of makeup on said.

Celia came to wipe down the bar again and Howard apologized. He thought it had been that last drink that had done it. Celia agreed that had she been out here she probably would not have poured him that last drink. She said the writer got a certain look when he was on the verge of a blackout. "The cold will wake him up, though," she said with a smile. "How about a turkey sandwich? They're really good."

"Sounds good to me." Howard switched back to beer and ate his sandwich. It was good. The football game on television got pretty good, too, and he stayed on, having another beer, doing his best to stay in the moment and not think about his problems.

At eleven Celia said she was going off her shift so Howard closed out his bill and asked if she wanted to share a cab home. She said she would prefer to walk. He said that sounded like a good idea.

It was freezing out but Celia seemed unaffected by it. She

asked him a few questions about what a literary agent did, asked where he had gone to school (Duke) and who some of his writers were. (The only author of his she had heard of was Gertrude Bristol.) He asked her what kind of books she liked to read and she said Anthony Trollope.

"Which ones?"

She looked at him. "All of them. He makes me laugh and I like that time period. A lot of cool stuff was made back then. You know, books, paintings, furniture."

"Good evening, Miss Cavanaugh, Mr. Stewart," the night concierge of their building said. They said hello, and while Howard pressed the button for the elevator, Celia took her bandana off and shook out her hair. When they got in Howard pushed *11* and by the time Celia asked him to push *6* they were already past it.

"Sorry about that," he said, starting to get that sinking feeling again. He dreaded the ride out to the airport with his mother and dreaded going out to Woodbury to hang out with his in-laws in a house that might well get repossessed if he didn't think of something. He had to tell Amanda. And soon.

"It's okay," Celia said, leaning back against the wall and covering a yawn with her hand.

He sniffed the air, unable to identify the smell. "Is that your perfume?"

She laughed. "Perfume? It's rose-scented Glade. We use it in the restaurant office."

"Believe it or not," he heard himself saying, "it almost smells good on you."

A mysterious smile was playing on Celia's mouth and Howard felt a small shot of fear. He was afraid he was about to try to kiss Celia. She turned her head slightly toward him, as if she were reading his mind.

The elevator eased to a stop and he just stood there, looking at her.

"Your floor," Celia said, stepping forward to punch her floor into the directory as the doors opened.

Still, he stood there. They were only about ten inches apart. He knew she would let him kiss her. The doors started to close and Howard slammed them back, then took her in his arms to kiss her. When he tried to open her mouth the elevator doors tried to close again and knocked his mouth off hers. This time he let the doors close and Celia stepped back against the wall, putting her arms back to rest on the railing, as if to invite his eyes to run over her body while the elevator descended. He stepped forward to touch her but she twisted away. "I'm sorry, Howard, but I don't do married men. I don't think it's right."

It was as if she had slapped him across the face. At once he was ashamed and embarrassed. "I'm sorry, Celia, I'm sorry," he said quietly, turning away from her. "I guess I shouldn't have had that last drink, either."

The elevator arrived at her floor and she stepped out. "Howard," she said, waiting for him to look at her. "Forget about it. Because I already have." And then the elevator doors closed. He slapped *11* and took off his glasses to rub his eyes. *What the hell am I doing?*

Cassy's Monday Morning

"HOW GOOD OF you to telephone," Mrs. Emma Goldblum said to Cassy.

"I would have called before, Emma, but I only just got back in town and received your message." Cassy was speaking more or less in the direction of the speakerphone in her dressing room. She was slipping on a skirt, running late for the office. "How was your Thanksgiving?"

"It was very nice. We went to the Stewarts', as you know. Amanda cooked a very nice dinner. Her parents were visiting. And Howard's mother. Rosanne made a pumpkin pie and a mince pie. And you?"

Cassy had zipped up the skirt and was pulling down a pair of matching blue low heels from the organized shelves. "We had a full house."

"Yes, I know, you'll remember Henry brought over sweet William for me to see last week."

"Did you say *sweet,* Emma?" Cassy said, searching through

her vanity for earrings, necklace and a bracelet. She also hastily put on her wedding rings. "I love my grandson dearly, Emma, but *please.*" The sound of Mrs. Goldblum's chuckle made Cassy smile as she scanned the upper rack for her new fitted blazer. Why she had waited so many years to get a personal shopper was beyond her. All she had to do was say, "I'd like a blazer that goes with this skirt," and voilà, in a few days it appeared. (She knew why. Because they cost a fortune and she had not always had a fortune.)

"That is why animal crackers were invented, dear," Mrs. Goldblum said. "It makes all children sweet for at least five minutes."

Cassy laughed.

Scarf. She supposed she should wear a scarf. No, she hesitated, looking in the mirror, why start hiding her neck now with so many years to go? The sun did its work and that's all there was to it.

Cassy put on a scarf.

The outfit looked good, she thought, turning to view it in the three mirrors. She had always liked her clothes to be as perfectly in place as possible. It had annoyed her no end when a therapist once said that it was common for children of alcoholics to grow up that way, obsessed with external order in an attempt to contain the emotional chaos they felt inside.

"I know how terribly busy you are, Cassy," Emma Goldblum was saying, "but I'm calling to ask your help. Normally Sam Wyatt keeps an eye on my affairs but at present he is occupied with other matters so I am turning to you."

This got her attention. Cassy picked up the phone. "What may I do?" She walked into the master bedroom to look out the largest window. It was cloudy outside, making the Hudson look gray. It was windy, too, creating white caps on the water.

Directly below in Riverside Park the flag at the Soldiers' and Sailors' Monument was flailing wildly.

"I have some legal matters to attend to and I wondered if you would be so kind as to accompany me to my lawyer's office. It is downtown. I know it's a great deal to ask, but I need someone I can rely on and I prefer not to have Rosanne with me because I don't want to upset her. And she will be, that's just the way she is when it comes to—" she hesitated "—wills and such."

Emma meant death. Cassy imagined it was hard enough for Emma to face her mortality without Rosanne looking on.

"Did you have a specific day and time in mind?"

"I waited until I had spoken to you before making an appointment."

"I should be in town this week," Cassy said, "but let me get my calendar in front of me at the office and then I'll call you back. In, say, an hour?"

"I'm very grateful to you, dear." Pause. "I fear time is slipping away."

"Don't I know it," Cassy murmured. "Listen, Emma, is there something going on at the Wyatts'? You said 'concerned with other matters' in a rather ominous tone."

"I'm afraid nothing that I am at liberty to discuss."

After Cassy got off with Emma she went to the kitchen and flipped open the address book to check a number and make a call. "Good morning. Is Sam there, please? It's Cassy Cochran calling."

After a few moments Sam Wyatt came on the line. "Hey, girl."

"Girl, I *wish.*" She laughed, looking at her watch. She was late.

Sam had been a good friend to her. Their relationship had

been a baptism by fire in the final stages of her ex-husband's drinking. Cassy didn't know what would have happened had Sam not been there to help her through it. "I'm good, Sam, but I just got a call from Emma Goldblum. She asked me if I would take her to her lawyer's office, which I said I would."

"I would have taken her if she asked."

"She seems to think you have a lot on your plate right now and the way she said it—well, it made me wonder if everything was okay."

Silence.

"Sam?" She imagined he was reading something on his desk and was distracted.

"So Rosanne goes home and tells Emma," Sam said, "and then Emma calls you—is that how this works? I admire her restraint, it's been three whole days."

Cassy hesitated. She'd known Sam for years and was well acquainted with the fact that he could be—well, scratchy on occasion. Irritable. She wasn't offended particularly; that's just the way he was when stressed out. "Sam, no one has told me anything. And if everything's fine then that's great, I'll just hang up and get to the office."

"Now there's a plan," he told her.

Well, that was an exercise in futility, Cassy thought, hanging up and going back to the bedroom to retrieve her bag. She was using up so much energy living two lives to begin with she didn't need to nose into the affairs of her neighbors to expend any more.

"Mrs. Darenbrook?" she heard the housekeeper call.

"Good morning."

"Ah, there you are," the housekeeper said from the doorway. "You're usually gone by now."

Nothing like feeling unwelcome in your own home. Cassy

knew the housekeeper was anxious for her to leave so she could turn all the TVs in the house on to begin her daily regime. Oh, for the days of Rosanne! When someone arrived who was interested in the house and the family in it!

Cassy's plan to slip unobtrusively into the DBS News conference room had clearly failed; whatever discussion had been taking place stopped dead the moment she came through the door. She took the only seat left at the long conference table, which was at the other end from where their Senior Vice President and Executive Producer of DBS News, Will Rafferty, was presiding. She felt self-conscious with all of these eyes on her because they belonged to younger people, many of whom made their careers in front of the camera, which is to say they were trained to view their appearance critically and tended to do the same with everyone else.

Alexandra Waring was there, of course, the symbolic head of the news division and around whom it had largely been built. Alexandra recently celebrated her four-thousandth on-air hour for DBS News and, at forty-one, was, Cassy thought, even better looking than when they had launched the network. Maturity suited her. Alexandra had exquisite blue-gray eyes (which all five children of Congressman Waring, the longtime Kansas politician, had), high cheekbones, a full mouth and nearly black hair that had only recently begun to show an occasional gray hair. She also had a brilliant smile that was said to be able to generate ratings by itself.

Alexandra was fiercely bright and well-liked at the network, if not somewhat adored. She was demanding but fair and anyone who was trying their best usually found favor with her. A few people had come and gone very quickly at DBS News because it became quickly evident who fit in and who did not.

If someone understood what Alexandra and Will were trying to do he or she would do fine; if he or she disagreed with their direction and had no constructive alternative to offer, he or she soon *wanted* out. (The chill factor could be unbearable.)

Many of their key players in the news group had been with DBS since the beginning, when there had only been *DBS News America Tonight with Alexandra Waring,* Monday through Friday, for one hour at nine.

Sitting next to Alexandra was half of the anchor team for DBS's new 6:00–7:00 a.m. national news hour, Emmett Phelps. He was formerly a professor of law at USC and looked every inch the part, only younger. He was in his middle forties, had a nice head of hair, insisted on wearing horn-rimmed glasses and, regardless of the climate or season, a tweed jacket with patches on the elbows. Emmett was well-spoken and deliberate in his speech; he had the gift of being able to concisely summarize the complicated details of news stories that broadcast news could not stop to explain.

Across the table from Emmett was his more outgoing and outspoken coanchor, Sally Harrington, whose edge it was part of Emmett's job to smooth while Sally's was to make Emmett have one. She was almost thirty-five and possessed elocution no voice coach could ever teach. Sally was very pretty, with blue eyes and light brown hair streaked with blond. She had formerly served as a special producer for Alexandra, but also belonged to the Writers' Guild because she could write almost as well as (some said better than) her boss, the latter of whom notoriously believed a newscast was only as good as the writing behind it.

The jury was still largely out on Sally and Emmett and *DBS News America This Morning* but the November sweeps had been promising. Their biggest hurdle was making viewers want to forego their local news to tune in to DBS before the Big Three network morning shows began at 7:00 a.m., which meant *DBS Morning* going great lengths to cut back and forth to their affiliates to update local weather and traffic. Sally and Emmett had very high TVQs (the TV quotient of that ineffable "something" that made television viewers want to watch them), and while their ratings were slightly higher than anticipated it was still anyone's guess what would happen after the novelty of the news hour had worn off.

There were several other on-air talents and producers in this meeting. With the nightly news, the morning news, the half-hour daily newscast they produced for INS in the United Kingdom, the two magazine shows, the Internet newscast and the new podcast programming, the weekly meeting was an attempt to get the whole team on the same page of Alexandra and Will's playbook.

Cassy smiled at the expectant faces around the table who were evidently waiting for her to say something. "Good morning. I apologize for being late."

Instantly there were groans and people started throwing dollar bills down on the table, all except for Will Rafferty, who was picking out quarters from his change and shooting them down the table to Sally Harrington.

"You *always* win, Sally," Emmett grumbled, thumbing through his wallet. He took out a dollar bill and dropped it in front of her. He looked at Cassy. "I bet that your first words would be *'Sorry I'm late.'*"

"You'll never make it in curling," Sally told Will, lunging to catch a rolling quarter.

Alexandra was making change for a five from the pile of singles. "I bet you'd say, 'And what earthshaking events have I missed?'"

"I bet, 'Hi, everybody,'" the meteorologist said, pushing a small pile of bills down from his end of the table. "I could have sworn that's what you always say."

The producer for the morning news leaned over the table to look down at Cassy. "I guess you're really not a 'Hey' kind of person."

"You thought Cassy would come in and say, *'Hey'*?" Will said incredulously.

"Better than what he thought," the producer said, jerking his thumb in the direction of the twenty-two-year-old they'd hired straight out of Rochester Institute of Technology for the podcast. The producer laughed. "He said, *'Yo.'*"

"'Yo?'" Will repeated. He frowned at the young man. "You thought the president of DBS Television would come in here and say, *'Yo'*?" Everybody laughed.

The RIT rookie looked to Cassy. "Isn't that what your generation used to say?"

"Thank you for the compliment," Cassy said. "But I'm afraid my generation said, *'Peace'*—" she flashed the peace sign " *'Love'*—" she made an *L* with her right hand "—and *'Woodstock.'*" She put two peace signs together to make a *W.*

"This goes straight into the Feed the Starving Interns Fund," Sally announced, raking the pile of cash into her lap.

Sally was big on helping certain interns get by because she herself had once been a starving one. She shared something with Cassy on that score. Both of them had grown up, as Sally called it, "without money." (Sally was always quick to explain that "without money" denoted someone in a temporary phase with prospects for the future, as opposed to someone stuck in a permanent economic status that made them "poor.") Both Cassy and Sally had lost their fathers as children and both had put themselves through college. But where Cassy's fears about her future had led her to the altar with Michael, Sally, as younger women seemed to do these days, simply flung herself into the universe and made ends meet until she could support herself as a journalist.

Cassy had come to admire Sally Harrington a great deal. But Sally also kept Cassy in a perpetual state of anxiety since the younger woman was forever careening from one crisis to the next. Sally was one of those people who was addicted to the adrenaline rush, who felt most alive when the air was fraught with risk and urgency. While it had made her a star at DBS News—enhancing her ability to jump right into the fast track of breaking news—the same trait had also very nearly killed her. (Her last escapade had necessitated significant plastic surgery.) Sitting behind the anchor desk, however, seemed to be somewhat calming her down. That and being engaged to Alexandra Waring's older brother, a solid, reliable man who in nature was as different from Sally as earth is from wind.

The labyrinth of romance and nepotism in the Darenbrook media empire was vast and at times troubling. (She should talk!) Most dedicated people in mass communications tended to be workaholics and one of the challenges at Darenbrook Communications seemed to be how to prevent people from falling in love with one of the very few people they were regularly in contact with. Jackson's father began the trend when he married his personal secretary (his fourth wife, Jackson's mother) and she stayed on at the newspapers as an executive. Then Jack's best friend, the financial brains behind the company, Langley Peterson, married Jack's sister, Belinda. As the Darenbrook sons and daughters and nieces and nephews got older they needed careers (real or imagined) and they were placed throughout the corporation in the least damaging circumstances. Jack's brother Beau, who ran the magazine division out of L.A., was gay, and had set up housekeeping with the publisher of their most successful magazine. Jackson hired Cassy to launch DBS and ended up marrying her. Will Rafferty, sitting at the end of the table, fell in love with Jessica Wright, the DBS talk show host, and they were married. And so, in a way, Cassy reconsidered, maybe Sally Harrington falling in love with Alexandra's brother could scarcely be considered a conflict since David otherwise had nothing to do with Darenbrook Communications.

"Before I forget, Cassy," Will said, "Jackson will definitely be at the American Trust Foundation dinner in January, right?"

The Foundation's Awards dinner was a biannual event celebrating excellence in journalism. "He will be there," she confirmed. "But he thinks only DBS News is getting an award."

"What's Mr. Darenbrook's award for?" the young man from RIT asked.

"Lifetime achievement," Will answered. "And it's a surprise, so that information is not to leave this room."

"I should hope everyone at this table will be attending the dinner," Cassy said.

"Depends on how many tickets corporate picks up," Alexandra said while writing something. "The suits don't give us a whole lot of money for extracurricular activities." She looked up. "As you should well know, Cassy. And I do like your suit, by the way."

Everybody laughed.

"All right, guys, let's get back on point here," Will said, picking up his legal pad.

"Yo," Cassy concurred, making them laugh again. She slipped on a pair of half glasses and scanned the agenda that had been passed to her. When she looked up she saw that Alexandra was watching her. The anchorwoman smiled and looked away.

As she listened to Will, Cassy sat back in her chair slightly to cross her legs. Then she leaned forward, picked up her pen and made a note in the margin of the agenda. And then, somewhat idly, she wondered if she had ever not been in love with Alexandra Waring.

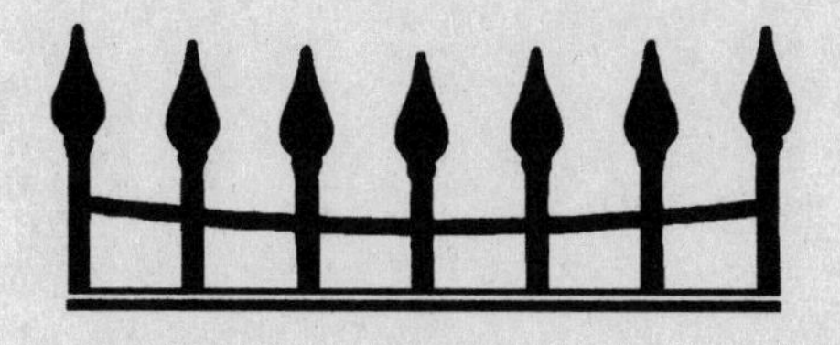

DECEMBER

Celia Has a Gift

A FRIEND OF a friend of Rachel's came to pick up their old refrigerator before the new one arrived. The guy was apparently some kind of fix-it whiz and he was somehow going to restore the Freon and put taps in the side to dispense beer and soda. Celia said if he could fix it why didn't they just hire him to fix it while the refrigerator was still theirs instead of getting a new one. "Daddy's getting it so don't worry," Rachel said. Celia was not worried in the least; she just hated what felt like arbitrarily replacing things for the sake of something new.

"Charlie," the man said when he arrived, holding out his hand to politely shake hers.

He was huge, this Charlie, filling the doorway. Behind him stood an upright steel dolly with big straps. He was much older than Celia had expected for Rachel's friend of a friend. He was like her dad's age, neatly dressed in a sweater (that Celia could wear for a dress), jeans, work boots and big blue parka.

"I feel kinda guilty," Charlie said later, sipping the cup of black coffee Celia made for him while looking in the back of the refrigerator. "I should just fix this for you."

"Thanks for the thought," Celia said, sitting at the breakfast bar, well wrapped in her terry-cloth robe, "but there're always appliances mysteriously falling off the back of one of my roommate's father's trucks. This time it was a stainless steel refrigerator." She was drinking coffee, as well. Nine-fifteen was early for her to be up; she didn't get home from work until almost three this morning.

"She'll never keep it looking clean," Charlie commented, coming back around from behind the old refrigerator, "not without a full-time maid."

"One of those hasn't fallen off the back of the truck yet," Celia told him.

Something on the counter caught Charlie's eye. It was an old door knocker, covered in years of crud, that was waiting for Celia to clean up. She bought it off a janitor last week who had been cleaning out a basement. The knocker was the head of a horse, made of what Celia believed to be solid brass.

"I might be interested in making you an offer for that," he said, moving closer.

"This?" Celia handed it to him. "Sorry, but I'm totally in love with it. Someday I'm going to buy a house with a front door that will do it justice. I think it's solid brass. Maybe a hundred years old."

"It is," he confirmed, hefting it in his hand. He took reading glasses out of his pocket and slipped them on to examine it further. "But my guess is around 1880. Where'd you get it?"

"On One Hundred and First Street. Guy was cleaning out the basement of the building. Ten bucks." Actually, she had paid the janitor ten bucks so that she could climb into the Dumpster to see what he was throwing out. Celia didn't know why she felt compelled to do things like this, but she felt no shame about it; she had always been fascinated by junk piles, looking for something that spoke to her. To a certain degree her mother shared her interest, but would never dream of the lengths Celia had been known to go.

Charlie carefully placed the knocker back on the counter. "He gave you two, two hundred fifty bucks for ten dollars."

"I guess it's going to have to be a very expensive house, then."

He looked at her. "You don't seem surprised."

"I don't know," she said, shrugging, "it's never really been about money."

"Spoken like a girl who grew up with a lot of it."

She looked up at him. "I beg your pardon?" She knew she sounded like her mother when she got on her high horse, but she didn't like the way he said it.

He held up his hand as a caution. "No offense. I just meant you obviously haven't had to try to make a living selling antiques. If you did, well, then, the money would mean a lot."

"I'm a bartender," she told him.

He frowned slightly. "You seem kinda classy for a bartender."

"I'm a classy bartender," she said, sliding off the stool to get more coffee. She was starting to feel depressed. "I just like old things."

"I work weekends at an auction house in the Bronx." When she turned around, holding the coffeepot out to him, Charlie nodded and she poured. "Thanks. That's why the money means something to me. I gotta kid trying to get through college. That's what I use the money for."

"Where is this auction house?"

He told her. It was way uptown, but it would have to be to

make any money. "So if you ever want to sell anything like that, the knocker, I can move it for you. That's the kind of thing people go nuts over."

Celia, standing there, sipped her coffee and lofted an eyebrow. "Maybe I should show you something, then." She led Charlie to the maid's room which she and Rachel shared as a kind of studio space. Rachel used her side for art stuff. Celia gestured to the wall and bookshelves on her side. There were various small oil and watercolor paintings and prints, some hanging in old frames, others in new, some prints vaguely speckled while others were almost clean. (She'd zap them in the microwave to kill the mold spores and then, if it was in good enough shape, use an artist's soft putty eraser on the spots. The paintings she left alone.)

Her best find in terms of a document had been rescued from a carton of ancient newspapers on the East Side that had been put out with the garbage. It was a single sheet, a 1787 playbill from the Drury Lane in London advertising Sarah Siddons and her brother, John Philip Kemble, starring in *Macbeth*. Celia had carefully matted it and used an old frame from another one of her finds, outfitted with new glass. She gave it to her mother, the intrepid theater goer, for her birthday last year and was amazed when her mother burst into tears, she was so moved. (Celia had been nervous her mother would think her cheap or something.)

On the shelves were other pretty or well-made things that had caught her eye: a variety of crystal doorknobs, an iron crucifix, a satin rope pull, a small circular silver serving tray, a crystal decanter (without its stopper), a silver calling-card holder. She also had a box holding Victorian calling cards she had been collecting forever.

Charlie was staring at the wall behind her. She laughed. "I

see you've spotted Madame X," she said, turning to look at the ink-and-watercolor sketch hanging next to the powder-room door. "It's *not* a Sargent sketch," she said, "but it sure looks like Madame X in the Met, doesn't it? My guess is someone made a sketch of the real thing. Or maybe they copied it from a print."

"Where did you get it?"

"I talked my father into buying it for me at an estate sale in White Plains when I was in junior high. I think I must have liked her attitude," she added, cracking a smile. *Yeah, Madame X in the old days. Just putting myself out there with all the confidence in the world.*

"You could get good money for that," Charlie told her, stepping closer to look at it. "It's well-executed, the subject is recognizable and it's got some age to it."

"What's good money?"

"Five or maybe even six hundred."

"You're kidding," she said, looking at it with new appreciation. "I think Dad bought it for twenty-five dollars." She grimaced. "But I love it, how could I ever sell it? Besides, my father got it for me."

"What I'm trying to say here, Celia," Charlie said, taking off his glasses and gesturing with his hands. He hesitated, looking for the words. "You've got," he said slowly, "an *eye.* And damn, little lady, I'd sure like to have whatever your father *didn't* buy you."

They laughed. She was starting to enjoy herself, starting to feel the same kind of connection with Charlie she felt with these things. It was hard to explain. "What about those doorknobs? I have no particular attachment to them."

"Well, you could go two ways. You sell them as a boxed lot or you could pitch each one on eBay, for example, to find those particular buyers who are looking to match or replace in a period house. That one's pretty common," he said, pointing, "but that—" he held one up to the light "—that looks European. Eighteen-fifty or so."

"I always look around on eBay but I've never registered or anything."

"Well, you should," he told her. "For someone like you it would be a lot of fun. You know, I mean, why not?"

"Charlie," she said, "I've got a ton of stuff in storage. Furniture, Victorian photo albums, tools, china, God, you name it. My roommate made me get it all out of here. Would you go through it with me? See if there's anything you could sell?"

"Sure! That's part of my job. Scouting. I get a bonus." He slapped his back pocket while explaining the sliding commission rates of the auction house, took out a well-worn wallet and pulled out a card.

"These are about to go into storage," she said, opening the closet door. They were simply boards, planking and slats standing on end.

Charlie put his glasses on again and went through them. "Oak, ash, cedar, burled walnut—that's gorgeous, that walnut."

"I know. It's that nutty color that makes me all zingy," she confessed.

"Kid, you gotta do something with this eye of yours," he said, closing the door and taking off his glasses. "You gotta make it a gift or I'm tellin' ya, it's gonna be a lifelong curse. People yelling at you to get rid of stuff and you can't."

"I know," Celia said, "because you just know it's important. But you don't quite know where in the scheme of things it's important. I keep thinking if I learn enough I'll know where all these pieces should go to make everything whole."

"It's an affliction all right," he said. "So what else do you have?"

She looked down at the Oriental rug. “Even Rachel loves this. I bought it from an estate sale in the building.”

He was turning one of the corners up. “She should love it. It’s all silk thread.”

She took him to her bedroom, apologizing in advance for the mess. It was even worse than she remembered, with clothes piled high, books and papers all over the place and then, of course, the stuff all over she always meant to do something with.

“Where did you get that?” he said, making a beeline for the steamer trunk she used as a table.

“It’s cool, isn’t it? It’s got like forty travel stickers from the thirties.”

“And that’s what people want, with the old stickers.”

“And what about this?” she asked him, gesturing to her bed. It was unmade, of course, and since she had a habit of pulling out all her sheets and blankets in the night, at the moment it looked sort of like a large animal nest.

He examined the headboard, which had boughs of leaves and flowers carved in it. “French,” he said. “Turn of the century. Nice.”

“It was my grandmother’s. What about the footboard?” she said, pulling the mound of covers up so he could see it.

He circled the end of the bed and then squatted, running his hand over the dark wood. Then he frowned and got down on his knees to examine the legs. Then he sat up. “This is friggin’ Regency, where did you get it?”

She burst out laughing. “It’s great, isn’t it? If you can believe, my brother and I found it on the side of the road in Massachusetts.”

“So what are you using as rails?” he wondered, lifting the comforter to look at the sides. “Not bad. Where did these come from?”

"I can't even remember," she said truthfully. "They were just up in my parents' attic and it was like, duh, I get it, Nana's headboard, these rails, the foot board."

"French headboard circa 1900," he said, getting to his feet, "English footboard circa 1820, American rails circa 1930." He smiled and threw his hands up. "It works. You couldn't pass this off as anything real—"

"I wouldn't want to," she told him. "It's my bed." Celia didn't tell him that no one except herself had ever slept in this bed. That it was the bed she had created after her boyfriend took off. That was the rule. No dirtying her nest. Never again. Not here, not where she was surrounded by the things she loved.

"Boy, I can sell that," he said, walking across the bedroom, pointing to the lamp on her dresser. It was a large, silver-colored metal sculpture of a nude woman holding up a globe of light in each hand. "The decorators from the Village will go nuts."

"I bought that off the street. But not with the globes. I had to pay more for those globes than I paid for the lamp."

"Which was how much?"

"Fifty, I think—which at the time I couldn't afford but I just had to have it. I didn't find the globes until last year. I think I had to pay around a hundred and twenty for those."

"I can get you a thousand. Net." He turned around. "After commission. A thousand bucks for that lamp."

She blinked.

"So when are we going to your storage unit?" he asked, eyes still roving the room. He walked over to her barrister bookcases.

"Anytime during the day, really," she said. "My parents gave me those bookcases."

Charlie straightened up and turned toward her, rubbing his

face for several moments, as if to judge whether or not he needed a shave (which he did). Then he dropped his hand. "You're in the wrong line of work, Cindy."

"Celia," she corrected him.

"People spend thousands and thousands of dollars trying to learn what comes naturally to you."

"I didn't know they had junk school."

"I'm serious," he said, sounding somewhat grave. "You shouldn't turn your back on this. You need to start doin' something with it. Make it the gift it was meant to be."

The intercom buzzed in the front hall and Celia went out to answer it. When she came back she told him someone else needed to use the loading dock downstairs. "So you better get your refrigerator before they tow your truck." She felt a spring in her step as she led him back to the kitchen. She wondered if maybe she really could do something with this. A general auction house sounded appealing. And eBay. She was going to have to sit down and do it. List something. Try the oldest doorknob. She needed to update her reference books, too, something she hadn't done since she had conned her parents into believing several volumes published by Antiques Collectors' Club were part of her required textbooks.

"Come to the warehouse Saturday," Charlie said, starting to maneuver his dolly into place. "The address is on the card. Be there about noon. There's an auction at two but I can show you around a little first."

"That'd be great," Celia said, crossing the kitchen to mark it on the wall calendar. Then, while Charlie wrestled with the refrigerator, she went back to her bedroom to throw on some clothes. Since they didn't have a fridge Celia would have to go out to get something to eat. She went down in the freight elevator to the basement with Charlie to make sure his truck was still there and then went back upstairs to exit through the lobby.

"Miss Cavanaugh," the concierge said. "I have some flowers for you." He disappeared into the holding room behind the desk and reemerged holding a gift bag and a cellophane sleeve of multiple flowers, the kind you got at the Korean markets.

"I guess I better put them in some water before I go out," she said, signing for them and walking to the elevator.

"A present?" the elevator operator asked.

"So it would seem," Celia said, waiting to get into the apartment before she looked in the bag. She cut the cellophane off the bouquet, snipped the ends off the flowers and stuck them in some water in a vase. She pulled open the gift bag, which was stapled, to find an iPod and an elaborate box of Godiva chocolates. There was also a square cardboard gift envelope which contained the new Norah Jones album. Utterly baffled, she tore open the card. There was a picture of a kitten and a puppy on the front. The inside of the card was blank, save for the inscription, "Love, Jason."

Uh-oh, Celia thought.

The Secret Life of Cassy Cochran

"THANK YOU FOR coming," Cassy said politely, shaking hands with the fourth set of producers shown into her office this morning. It was pitch day for DBS Sports, a time when freelance producers tried to convince corporate there was a sports program that broadcast television could not do without. It seemed to Cassy the program ideas this year had more to do with the entertainment division than sports. The head of the division complained the other networks had all the good sports coverage locked up.

At DBS the idea had never been to do what everyone else was doing, but to offer some kind of quality program the others didn't. They had made money, for example, by covering key overseas professional soccer matches and had also done well with occasional forays into collegiate hockey, baseball and even tennis. They also had some modest success covering Formula One qualifiers. But the division head, Cassy realized, was looking for a big score, the sports programming that would make waves in the industry and generate advertising dollars.

The last pitch had been for a TV reality show about a collegiate football camp with special emphasis on fistfights and catching players in the bushes with their pants down.

The pitch being thrown now was for a weekly how-to show on sports betting. Cassy didn't presume to know the legality of such a show (and DBS legal was here for that reason), and while she understood that millions of gamblers across America might like such a show she doubted the Darenbrook family would. They were particularly sensitive about gambling since their father had begun the media dynasty by winning a newspaper in a poker game, after which the previous owner had killed himself.

This was a team doing the presentation, a man and a young woman. She was reeling off the statistics about sports betting in America while he supplied dramatic enthusiasm and video snippets on his laptop computer of what the show would be like. They were persuasive; Cassy could see a brouhaha on this one. Some were going to say, "It will make us a lot of money," and others, "This is irresponsible," while Cassy, ever negotiating the line, would observe that betting on sports was not a sport, so if such a show was truly viable for DBS it should be produced out of the news department as an educational series. (That should kill it.)

She felt a nudge at her elbow and looked over at her brother-in-law by marriage, Langley W. Peterson. He tapped his pencil on his legal pad.

We can put it on after Stair Diving *and before* Make Your Own Moonshine.

Cassy covered her smile with her hand, cleared her throat, and then lowered her hand to look back at the presenters to reassure them they still had her attention (although they did not).

Few at Darenbrook Communications would believe that Langley Peterson, their Chief Operating Officer, ever made a joke, he was so straightlaced, but Cassy knew he had a fine sense of humor. It was just that Langley was so very, very shy. Jack considered Langley his best friend and Cassy counted him among her closest as well, which only underscored how bad she felt about deceiving him. Simply put, the reality of the Darenbrook marriage would shake all the faith Langley and his wife, Belinda, had in the world. They would be shocked and then outraged that Jack had not, as advertised, been reformed into a faithful husband. They would be shocked and disappointed the Darenbrooks had never made it to marriage counseling, and as far as Cassy carrying on with…

No. Langley would never understand.

Cassy first met Alexandra when Michael, Cassy's former husband, had hired her to anchor the New York news for WWKK. Alexandra had been intimidating to Cassy. She was twenty-eight, intellectually gifted, packaged in poise and beauty and possessed that ineffable aura of all-American class. Once Cassy knew for sure the young anchorwoman had not slept with her husband, Cassy relaxed a little, but then felt uncomfortable when Alexandra demonstrated some knowledge of the shambles Cassy's marriage was in. The situation became more uncomfortable when Alexandra confided in Cassy that she was bisexual. And then things became positively surreal when Cassy realized Alexandra was telling her about walking both sides of the street because she was hoping Cassy might cross over to see her.

After her initial surprise Cassy had been deeply flattered. She was forty-one at the time and at a very low ebb. Michael was bottoming out on his drinking and was almost a constant source of embarrassment and humiliation. Then Michael was fired from WWKK. And then he ran away. And it was not long before Cassy found herself starting to fall under Alexandra's spell. Perhaps, she had rationalized at the time, because Alexandra was a woman it would not really be cheating.

Well, whatever she had rationalized at the time, the point was Cassy did cross that street to see Alexandra. And how. For part of the spring and all of that summer.

When Henry returned from a summer spent hiking in Colorado and Michael returned from Lord only knew where to be hospitalized, Cassy had brought the affair to an end. She felt she had to. For one, however deeply she may have felt about Alexandra (which would take her years to sort out), Cassy was too emotionally beaten up to suddenly start swimming against the tide of social approval that had governed her entire life. Second, Alexandra's love had been so all-consuming, so endlessly deep that Cassy had begun to feel as though she was losing herself all over again, much in the same way she had when she'd married Michael. And third (which she tried to convince herself at the time was first), to encourage that side of Alexandra's sexuality would do her a severe disservice. If Alexandra were to have any chance of fulfilling her dream, to become the first woman to have her own national nightly broadcast newscast, then she would have to meet at least four of the five unspoken mandatory qualifications:

1) Must be male.
2) Must be white.
3) Must be Christian.
4) Must be from anywhere except the East and West Coast.
5) Must be married and heterosexual.

The fact that Alexandra had graduated *summa cum laude* from Stanford had no bearing whatsoever on anything. It was perfectly fine if the men got C's or had even dropped out of high school. No, what would count in Alexandra's favor was her race, her religion, where she was born and a husband.

When Alexandra left WWKK in New York to become a Congressional correspondent for one of the Big Three in Washington D.C., her old boyfriend moved in and Cassy was profoundly relieved. Michael by this time had gotten sober; the Cochrans stayed in touch with Alexandra and Cassy began to feel better about any wrong she may have imagined she had done her.

In his second year of sobriety Michael left Cassy for a much younger woman and asked for a divorce. That was right around when Alexandra and Jackson approached Cassy about coming on board the proposed DBS network as executive producer of the news division. When Alexandra and Gordon Strenn announced their engagement, Cassy accepted their offer and threw herself into building DBS News.

How had Cassy really felt about Alexandra at that point? She knew she loved her as a friend. Very much so. In fact, Cassy may have been somewhat wistful when she recalled certain things, but she had learned to simply shut that side of herself down in the same way she had shut down so many other feelings in her lifetime. Perhaps that was why Jackson's attentions made such an enormous impact on her. Falling in love with him—at least falling in love with the *idea* of falling in love with America's most dashing media tycoon—could and would solve so many problems.

Cassy was genuinely in love with Jackson by the time they got married and she considered herself heterosexual, with a mere blip on the screen otherwise, a time when she had been very down.

"Are you," one of her therapists asked, "heterosexual?"

"Yes," Cassy said.

"And you come to this conclusion how?"

"Because women have made passes at me before and I never responded. It was just that one time."

"You've said that all of your life men have been making passes at you."

Cassy nodded. That had also been part of why she had married Michael so young; she was sick of trying to deal with it on her own.

"Were you ever tempted by any one of those men?"

Cassy thought a moment. "Yes."

"And did you act out with any of those men?"

"No."

"Why not?"

"Because I was married and respected my wedding vows. That was the way I was brought up."

"But you had an affair with Alexandra."

"That was different. Michael had just run out on me."

"Okay. So what you're saying is, after Michael ran out on you, you felt you could break your marital vows."

"I think it was because she was there."

"There were no men you could have turned to?"

The question hung there for quite some time. "Yes," she finally said, "but Alexandra was a woman so it didn't really count."

"Yes, but you're heterosexual. You said."

And so on it went for years in therapy until Cassy was sick of talking about it. About talking about everything. She didn't understand why she couldn't just get a fresh start and get on with her life. And Jackson Darenbrook was the opportunity to do just that.

For more than a year after learning about Jack's infidelities

Cassy had felt frozen inside. She could see now that it had been a period of grieving, mourning the death of what she had believed to be her new life. One night she stayed late with Langley to sit in the control room of Studio A to watch the nightly newscast. By this time Alexandra had long since broken off her engagement to Gordon and had been treading water it seemed, dating no one in particular for any length of time. That night Cassy watched Alexandra on the monitors, wondering if she could ever allow herself to think about Alexandra in that other way again. Or rather, when had she begun remembering so much of what had happened between them? The thrill and the joy, the pleasure and the comfort. She tried her best to also recall the fear, the guilt and the hurt, but it didn't seem to be happening.

After the newscast she had gone home to 162 Riverside, opened a bottle of wine and went next door to sit in the living room of her old apartment. She had sat there looking out at the night lights glimmering on the Hudson, much as she had done so many nights over the course of her marriage to Michael, wondering what was the matter with her, why she was not more grateful, as if the answer was out there somewhere, maybe on a passing barge or in one of the apartments on the Jersey side of the river.

It was an incredibly romantic view from this window in particular, one that had always stirred a longing so deep inside her Cassy wondered why she had so long subjected herself to the torture of it. It never mattered how much Cassy longed for anything, because in the end she always did what she had been brought up to do as a wife, a mother and a professional: be true to her marital vows, care and protect her child and supplement the family's income in an honorable way—which translated into keeping up pretenses for the child's sake and making sure there was at least one paycheck that got to where it was supposed to go.

Only once had Cassy looked out this window with longings she had given in to. That had been six years ago, when she had given in to the longing to be loved by Alexandra.

Now she was back at that window, subtly horrified by the feelings that had been building. Circumstances were very different now, the consequences potentially even more disastrous on all fronts. Of all the people in the world was there no one else she could think about except Alexandra Waring?

The subject required more wine to contemplate.

The truth of the matter was, with the exception of Jackson, there had never been anyone else in her thoughts since Alexandra. The ferocity of those thoughts on that particular night were disturbing. The disturbance had finally given way to a quickening pulse in response to the impending danger of what she was about to do.

She called Alexandra. At half past one in the morning. And asked if she could come over. Alexandra had said yes, not asking a single question.

Cassy had taken a cab to The Roehampton on Central Park West. Alexandra's hair was wet when she arrived. She had wondered if Alexandra had simply come home from West End and taken a shower to wash off the studio makeup and hair spray, or if she had taken a shower after Cassy called. The first possibility made Cassy feel as though she had no right to be there, no right to interfere with Alexandra's life again, and the second made Cassy consider the possibility that Alexandra might be hoping she would interfere in her life again.

She asked Alexandra for a glass of wine, which Cassy was given, and when she was finally asked what was the matter, Cassy answered, "I'm here because I would like to make love with you."

The shock on Alexandra's face had made Cassy feel ashamed. Alexandra had no way of knowing that her marriage to Jackson was anything other than idyllic. And Cassy also knew she should be able to tell Alexandra up front about what, if Cassy got her wish and was taken to bed, Alexandra could expect to happen afterward. But Cassy did not have a clue. All she knew was that after trying to lock Alexandra out for so long she desperately wanted her back in. It wasn't very honorable. It wasn't even sane.

She waited for Alexandra to ask about Jackson but she didn't. She waited for Alexandra to ask her if this meant Cassy was in love with her, but she didn't. Alexandra simply stood up and offered Cassy her hand. Cassy waited for her to state some kind of condition, but she didn't do that, either, only led Cassy into her bedroom and, by the lights of the city, took her clothes off.

They made love for most of the night and when Cassy sat in a ten-o'clock management meeting the next morning she could still feel the imprint of Alexandra's mouth on her own. She managed to get through the day and felt both weak and elated when she saw Alexandra and Will come into the cafeteria in the late afternoon to join her for a cup of coffee. While they talked budget concerns the glint in Alexandra's eye and the slight puffiness of her mouth filled Cassy with a desire so intense it frightened her. She later sat in a finance meeting with Langley and the company controller and took inventory of the sensations in her body, knowing she had better go home and pull herself together. She did leave early and went home to lie down and think about what she had done. Six and a half hours later she was back at The Roehampton, twisted in the sheets, feeling herself rising again and again, crying out because she no longer cared about anything but this.

At five o'clock in the morning she had opened her eyes to find Alexandra watching her. She smiled that glorious smile and Cassy's heart ached. She got scared and told Alexandra that she was. And then she started to cry while Alexandra held her. She told Alexandra everything about Jackson, what had happened and what state their marriage was in. They agreed they needed to slow things down a bit until they could get their heads fully around what was happening. They agreed not to see each other until the following week, but Cassy canceled her plans and went out with Alexandra to her farm in New Jersey to spend the weekend, and caught up on a six-year absence. By late Sunday night the exhilaration and adrenaline finally wore off, the lovemaking lost its magic and the creeping sense of doom finally caught up with them.

Was Cassy going to divorce Jackson? Cassy needed time to think. Their marriage entailed a great many things that necessitated great care.

Was Cassy going to tell Jackson about them? Never. She was afraid of what he might do. To Alexandra.

Did Cassy love her? Yes, absolutely she did.

Did Cassy want to be with her? She didn't see how that could happen. For the time being this was all she could offer Alexandra.

So she was supposed to be Cassy's mistress? No (smile). Cassy would be hers.

Dazed, exhausted and progressively more nervous with each working day at the network, the tryst lasted another two weeks before Alexandra said it was intolerable that Cassy stay in that marriage. Cassy said she wasn't prepared to change things yet. Alexandra said then that was it, until Cassy at least separated from Jackson she couldn't—and wouldn't—go on like this. By that time Cassy had felt so many familial and professional pressures to keep the marriage going—at the very least she would have to figure out how to replace herself at DBS—and she told Alexandra she completely understood how she felt and did not blame her in the least.

So it ended as abruptly as it had started. However heartbroken Cassy felt, a couple of months later, when they briefly succumbed again over a long weekend, she felt a great deal better, thinking at least perhaps they could hold this pattern until Cassy felt she could make the break. They sated themselves three more times before Alexandra met the actress Georgiana Hamilton-Ayres. By that point it had become obvious that Cassy's affair with Alexandra had dramatically and inadvertantly improved Cassy's relationship with her husband.

"Jackson was regaling the newsroom this morning with tales of nonstop romance with his wife on the high seas," Alexandra had informed her.

The tales were true. After sailing in a race in the Caribbean, Cassy and Jackson had taken off by themselves for a couple of days, cruising in the islands, and, well, things just sort of happened.

"So what do you think, Cassy?" Langley Peterson said.

Cassy looked at him, drawing a blank.

"About *The Sports Gam.*"

She snapped back to the present. "*The Sports Gam?* Oh, the gambling show. I'd like to sleep on it, if I may."

"So you're not against it," the division head of sports said.

"I won't discount it until I've had some time to think it over," she told them.

When it really dawned on Cassy that Alexandra was serious, that if Cassy didn't leave Jackson she was going to pursue a full-time relationship with the beautiful Georgiana Hamilton-Ayres, Cassy had felt dangerously near becoming unglued.

"What do you expect me to do? Spend the rest of my life waiting for Jackson Darenbrook's leftovers? I won't do it, Cassy. It's not fair, and it's not right. Either you leave him or you let me go."

That night, in Alexandra's bed, Cassy thought maybe she could leave the marriage, but in the morning they both knew she wouldn't do it. So it was over. Really over.

"What has gotten into you?" Jack wanted to know when Cassy initiated sex not long after. "No, no, I don't want to know," he said, kissing her. "Just come here."

While Alexandra focused her time and attention on the actress, Cassy threw herself into developing new divisions of DBS and rededicating herself as a Darenbrook matriarch. Jackson was elated. Cassy's son, Henry, knew something was wrong, though. He kept asking her why she was driving herself so hard. Surely there were people she could delegate more to?

When Alexandra's relationship with Georgiana Hamilton-Ayres hit the tabloids Cassy was forced to sit in the meetings at Darenbrook Communications regarding the fallout with sponsors. Some had pulled their advertising from the nightly news and Cassy was instructed to have a heart-to-heart with Alexandra about what the hell she was doing. "Tell her I don't remember her being a dyke as part of the package when we agreed to build a news network for her," Jackson said angrily.

Langley, interestingly, was the calmest about it. It was his view the Hamilton-Ayres affair could serve as a lightning rod to define for sure who Alexandra's core audience was. There had long been criticism of the industry's primary ratings service because, the Big Three claimed, it was impossible that the *DBS News America Tonight* had a majority of viewers under the age of forty when their viewers were overwhelmingly *over* forty.

Langley was proven correct; the issue did clarify their audience, because with each new story about the celebrated "gal pals" there was a rise in the ratings of *DBS News America Tonight with Alexandra Waring,* a surge of viewers over forty, but then when that surge receded, DBS was left with the lucrative young demographics the ratings service had always claimed it owned. In the end, the relationship between the women actually attracted more sponsors to *DBS News America Tonight,* sponsors which wanted to reach that younger audience.

Though somewhat placated by this, Jackson still saw the relationship as a betrayal of his trust and demanded that Cassy and Langley set ground rules for Alexandra concerning her love life. That meeting, to settle the ground rules, would go down in the record books as one of the most bizarre.

"Of course there's nothing wrong with what you're doing," Cassy said, trying to ignore Alexandra's I-dare-you look. "The question is how everyone connected with DBS should handle it. We need to come to an agreement, some guidelines, so the sponsors know what to expect."

"I'm afraid Georgiana won't adhere to anyone's guidelines but her own."

Since Georgiana Hamilton-Ayres was one of the top ten box-office draws in the world, was wealthy beyond caring and the daughter of a tenth generation Scottish earl, there was little anyone could do to greatly impact her life at this point. Except, if they hurt Alexandra.

"Frankly," Langley said, "we're asking for your help with Ms. Hamilton-Ayres. Surely she would not want to see your career compromised."

"Understand, Alexandra, DBS is not in any way asking you to compromise your relationship," Cassy said, not quite able to meet Alexandra's eye. "We only wish you to observe a guideline that works in the best interests of DBS News as a whole."

"I can hardly wait to hear what this guideline is," the anchorwoman said.

"I believe you've been engaged to be married twice," Langley said.

Alexandra nodded. "Yes."

"That's good because it shows that you tried," he explained.

There was such a look of fury in Alexandra's eyes that Langley had been unnerved. "Well, I—" He faltered, at a loss, and looked at Cassy.

"We don't want you to say outright, Alexandra, that you're gay. Or that Georgiana is."

"And what do you suppose people think the nature of our relationship is?"

Cassy couldn't look at her and dropped her eyes down to her legal pad to doodle. "We don't care what anyone thinks," she said evenly. "We only care that you don't identify yourself with a specific lifestyle, just as we care that you don't identify yourself with a specific political party or movement."

"I see," Alexandra said. "So what am I supposed to say?"

Cassy glanced up briefly. "If someone asks you if you're gay, you are to say, 'No.' That's it."

"And if someone asks me if I'm straight?"

"Then you say," Langley said, "'Obviously not completely.'"

"'Obviously not completely?'" Alexandra threw her head back to laugh.

It was awful, but they had worked it out. Alexandra eventually admitted that what DBS was asking them to do was not very different from what Congressman Waring's chief of staff or Georgiana's agent had asked them to do.

"So we're straight on this?" Langley said.

"'Obviously not completely,'" Alexandra told him.

So DBS contrived its own "Don't Ask, Don't Tell" policy and it worked out—somewhat awkwardly—but it did work out. Cassy rewarded the sponsors who had remained steadfast throughout the controversy with bonus ad-runs in their new programming.

"Do you want to catch a bite to eat?" Langley said. "Cassy?" He leaned forward. "Are you okay?"

"Just a little tired," she said, pulling her papers together. "Sure. I'd love to have lunch with you. If Jack's around why don't we see if he wants to join us."

Amanda's Parents Come Back

THE PROFESSORS MILLER had no sooner left after Thanksgiving when they announced they wanted to come back to Woodbury for another weekend before Christmas. Since it was increasingly difficult to ever get her parents to leave Syracuse anymore Amanda was surprised. And worried. When she picked them up at the airport in Westchester she wondered if perhaps her mother was afraid her father might not be able to make the trip again. He was a lot older than she was.

When Amanda's mother, the former Miss Tinker Fowles of Baltimore, Maryland, called from school to tell her parents she was in love with one of her professors, she had unwittingly begun a scandal. The Fowleses (who had a tendency toward a lockjaw manner of speaking) fanned the flames of the aforementioned scandal by storming the chancellor's residence in the middle of the night with a battery of attorneys. The Fowleses were at once shocked and dismayed when their daughter arrived and issued her willful ultimatum: they could either accept Reuben Miller as their son-in-law or they could say goodbye to her now.

In the end the best the Fowleses could do was have Reuben sign a legal document that stated any children resulting from the marriage would be baptized and brought up Episcopalian. ("And since when is the child of a gentile mother ever a Jew?" Reuben had asked his beloved while signing.)

Amanda's parents had now been married for over fifty years.

When Amanda closeted her mother to find out the motivation behind this visit, her mother denied that anything was wrong. They just wanted to see a little more of her and the children and they so loved the house. Unfortunately Howard said if Amanda wanted him to do any of the Christmas shopping, which she did, there was no way he could come out for the weekend; she was on her own. Her parents were not difficult; the only problem lay in her father's preference for high cerebral exchange over activity, and her children's preference for activity over high cerebral exchange.

Amanda nonetheless tried once more to interest her parents in the children's indoor soccer games (which was no more successful than the last time, except this time they were really, *really* cold instead of just cold), and tried to interest her two eldest children in the advantages of learning Sanskrit so as to unlock ancient secrets. The only true success over the weekend was when Amanda's mother accompanied her to watch Emily and Teddy's riding lesson in the indoor ring at Daffodil Hill. The former Tinker Fowles had never lost the equestrian sensibility that had run through the Fowles ancestry for generations and she had only stopped riding herself five years before because of a torn roto-cuff that had since been repaired.

For their lesson with Jessica, Emily rode one of Daffodil Hill's small horses while Teddy rode their pony, Sweets.

Amanda, as she always did, saddled Maja and rode her around a bit before the children's lesson began and walked her around the ring during it. "All right, Amanda," her mother suddenly declared, waving at Amanda to dismount. She unsnapped the chin strap on Amanda's riding hat. "Let us see how *La Mère* may fair upon thy mare."

The children were agog when they saw their nana lead Maja over to the mounting block, ascend and swing her leg over the saddle. After Amanda adjusted the stirrups her mother took Maja in a posting trot. She was seventy years old but even time couldn't disguise the excellence of her seat and hands. When Amanda's mother pressed Maja into an easy cantor the children were beside themselves, and when Nana gracefully turned into the ring and soared over a jump, Amanda and the children started jumping up and down, clapping and cheering. "Just enough to start a family legend, dear," Amanda's mother said as she dismounted. The children would never look at Nana the same way again.

Howard had been brought up what Mr. Stewart used to call "a half-ass Methodist," which meant he was baptized, went to Sunday school for a while and then never went to church except for weddings and funerals. Before they were married Amanda and Howard attended a few churches around Manhattan because they agreed it would be a good thing as a couple to be grounded in some sort of spiritual community. They started with Episcopal and Methodist churches and then ran the gamut until they settled on joining a Congregational church. All three children had been baptized there and, if they were in town on the weekend, the children went to Sunday school there, too, but otherwise attended a Congregational church in Connecticut.

The children were at that age where matters of religion

were growing complicated ("What is an infidel, Mommy?") and for whatever reason Teddy suddenly expressed a fervent desire to attend Temple with his grandfather on Saturday. "By all means let him go," Howard said. "If anyone can convince Teddy there's a Power higher than himself I'm all for it."

Amanda's father reported that Teddy had behaved well and in general he was very pleased with his grandson's companionship. But then the next day Teddy fascinated his Sunday school class by announcing that his grandfather was a Jew like Jesus and explained that Jews didn't have crosses in their "Templar" because they knew Jesus before they killed Him so they didn't have to have one. ("You might want to spend a little time going over this with him," his Sunday school teacher advised Amanda.)

"What is this boy learning?" her father demanded of Amanda.

"To pledge his faith and obedience to a loving God," Amanda answered, hoping against hope her father would not turn around in time to see the children zinging his yarmulke around like a Frisbee in the living room.

"No cultural context, none," her father clucked. "Religion out of a cereal box, that's what you're spoon-feeding these children."

On Monday morning, while Amanda helped her pack, her mother suddenly took her hand, said, "My dearest darling child," and coaxed Amanda to sit down next to her on the bed. She held Amanda's hand in both of hers and squeezed. "I sense that things are not all they should be. Between you and Howard."

Amanda quickly reiterated the reasons why Howard couldn't come out this weekend and told her mother she shouldn't worry but her mother stopped her. "Howard is a hundred times the man Christopher was, but that does not make me want to see him hurt you."

"Mother—"

"I beg you to stop living apart like this."

"We don't like it, either, but—"

"Listen to me, Amanda, because I'm only going to say this once."

Amanda waited for her to say she thought Howard was having an affair.

"I know you. I'm your mother." She searched Amanda's eyes. "Amanda, I know what's going to happen out here if this goes on much longer."

"What are you talking about?" Amanda said, her voice rising.

"This young man—"

"*What* young man?"

"Miklov."

"Miklov?" Amanda said, bewildered.

"The children look at him the way they should be looking up to their father."

"He's their coach, Mother, of course they look up to him. They idolize him because he's a soccer star."

"They sense he's in love with you, that's what your mother's trying to say," Amanda's father said. She turned to see he was standing in the doorway. "We do not believe you're indifferent to him, either. Not love. But in the other way."

"God in heaven," Amanda cried, jumping up, "how can you say such a thing? You're saying that I—" She looked at her mother. "That it's *me,* that—"

"Howard won't forgive you," her father told her.

"No, he won't," her mother quietly agreed.

Amanda felt as though she had been thrust into a lunatic asylum. She tried to compose herself before speaking. "I really don't understand what you mean. I have never done anything to compromise my marriage."

Her father slowly made his way in to sit down next to her mother. He looked very old. The years of physical inactivity had caught up with him. Her mother held his arm as he stiffly sat down, as if she were afraid he might keel over. When he was seated they held hands. Her mother looked more like his nurse than his wife. "Why did you take him home by yourself?" her father said. "At Thanksgiving? Why did you not take one of us or one of the children with you?"

"Because it never occurred to me that my parents would think so ill of me. Now we need to get started to the airport, so if you'd like to continue this ridiculous conversation we can do so in the car." She walked over to close their suitcase, snapped the fastener and took the bag with her out of the room. She was floored. Mortified. And amazed at what had just transpired.

Then on the stairs she heard her father say, "It is always better to say something than to pretend not to see."

In Which Harriet Has a Meltdown and Sam Steps In

"WELL THAT'S JUST great," Sam muttered, pulling at the knot in his tie with one hand and throwing the mail down on the kitchen counter with the other.

"Now what?" Harriet said wearily. It had been a horrible couple of weeks. It was like an alien had dropped in from outer space to replace the daughter they loved. Sam kept rubbing his eyes and staring again at his nineteen-year-old daughter, trying to fathom what the hell was going on in that pretty head of hers, what the hell *had* been going on that had led to this. Sullen, angry, her abdomen looming large, Samantha spent most of her time sitting in the wingback chair with her feet up on the ottoman watching TV. She was being belligerent to *them,* as if this was all their fault.

"There's an eleven-hundred-dollar credit card bill for Samantha," he said, yanking his tie off with a flourish.

"I had to get some winter clothes," Samantha's voice said

from the back hall. "Or did you expect me to fashion a loose garment made of rags for protection against the cold?"

Harriet didn't bother trying to calm Sam down because now it was she who felt so distraught. She had been on a Planned Parenthood board for sixteen years and contraception had been such an important part of the girls' upbringing that she swore to Sam the only way Samantha could have gotten pregnant was if she had tried to get that way. But Samantha wasn't saying much. Just that the baby was due in February, the adoptive parents would pick up the baby from the hospital and then she would go back to school.

"Come in here, please," Sam said.

After a few moments, Samantha appeared. She looked radiantly healthy. She had her hair braided today and was wearing a flattering red dress. Sam held out the bill. "I'll pay this and then I'm cancelling the card."

"You can't, it's mine."

"I repeat, I will pay this and then cancel the card, and you will use your ATM card from now on, which means if you don't have the money in the bank to pay for something, then either you talk to us or you don't get whatever it is you think you can't live without."

She exaggerated her condition by plunking one hand on her hip and jutting out her hips. "It's my card. I'm over eighteen, I can keep it if I want."

"And who's going to pay it?"

"I will," she said, snatching the bill out of his hand.

"Yeah, right," he said, turning away.

When they heard her bedroom door slam Harriet came over to him. "Where would she get the money to pay it, Sam?"

"She doesn't have any money. She's just giving me b.s. to get a rise out of me."

"Sam—"

The tone of her voice made his heart skip. "What? *What?*" he said.

"She keeps saying the adoptive parents will come to the hospital. There can't be adoptive parents already, can there? Unless—" Tears welled up in her eyes and she reached out to the kitchen table for support as she sat down heavily in the chair and dropped her face in her hand.

"I don't get it. What do you mean?"

"I mean—" She looked up at him. "I think she may have already taken money for this baby."

"What? Are you out of your mind? What does she need money for? Why would she do that?"

"I feel sick," Harriet said, holding her face again.

"No, babe, no, hang on." Sam grabbed a paper towel, stuck it under the ice water tap on the refrigerator and then went over to put it on Harriet's forehead. She opened the towel up and covered her whole face with it. When he saw her shoulders start to quake—she was crying—he felt a kind of fury he had not felt for years.

"I just want to lie down," Harriet said, lowering the towel. "I'm fine, Sam, I'm just tired." He helped her up and walked her to their bedroom. She stretched out on the bed and he took off her high heels. He pulled up the quilt to cover her and sat down next to her. "I'm sure you're wrong. But I will find out."

"I'm so exhausted I don't know if I'm coming or going anymore," she said, covering her face with her arm.

"You haven't slept through the night since she came home."

"I'm just so scared, Sam. She feels like a stranger to me." She let her arm fall back on the bed. "Althea feels it, too."

"Althea's just upset because your heart's broken, honey, and she can't stand to watch. Not that I can."

She sighed. "I suppose." She closed her eyes, felt around for his hand and found it. "We'll get through this," she whispered. Then her eyes opened to look up at him. "We will, Sam, won't we?"

"Of course we will." He kissed her hand. "I'll make something for dinner." He got up.

"Could you make sure that Samantha eats something?"

"Obviously I can't make Samantha do anything, but I will try," he promised.

Fifteen minutes later he knocked on the door of his daughter's bedroom.

"Come in," she called.

Sam balanced the tray in one hand to open the door. "Since we're through yelling at you for the day," he began, "your mother thought you might want something to eat."

Samantha was sitting on her bed with a book and a highlighter. Any fantasies he had maintained that Samantha might be in here crying her eyes out with guilt were utterly dispelled. She looked extremely comfortable and happy in her flannel nightgown and slippers.

He put the tray down next to her on the bed. There were two slices of toasted seven-grain bread with peanut butter and sliced bananas on it. There was a tall glass of organic two-percent milk. There was also a quartered orange.

"Did Mom sneak wheat germ in this?" she asked, pulling the tray closer and peering at the suspect peanut butter.

"No," Sam said. "But I did." He walked around the bed and picked up her book. *"Abnormal Psychiatry and the American Social Model,"* he read. "Sounds like fun."

"It's pretty interesting, actually. How our system fails the most disturbed people, who then drag down the whole system so it can't function well for anyone else."

Sam was going to take a seat but the only chair was the old rocker and just now he couldn't face it. He had spent too many hours in that chair, holding Samantha in his lap, reading her stories.

She had been a beautiful child. She was still beautiful, with her square face, high cheekbones, aquiline nose and pouting mouth.

He walked over to the window facing 90th Street and rested his arms on the windowsill. He heard Samantha bite into the toast.

All he could think about was Samantha must have been pregnant last August when she had been working at a community health center. While she had been advising inner-city teenage girls of color about love, family and clean living. She also must have been pregnant when she was a bridesmaid in her cousin's wedding. For weeks and months Samantha must have known she was pregnant and yet had said nothing, only to show up at Thanksgiving and let her condition announce itself.

At first he had been furious with Rosanne for trying to run interference for Samantha. That quickly dissipated, though, because he had just been looking for somebody who was strong enough to endure his wrath. Rosanne had known Samantha her entire life. She had done the right thing. And she had run interference as much for the whole family's sake as for Samantha's.

Rosanne had always warned him that Samantha got away with murder simply because she was the daughter he carried no guilt about. ("No, that's not it," he would say.)

("Yeah, okay," Rosanne would say, "but you're not drunk anymore, so maybe you could just be a little nicer to Althea. Who's exactly like you. But we won't even go there, Mr. W, will we?")

"Your mother's afraid you might have already signed some sort of adoption agreement," he began, watching the dog walkers head toward the park.

"I haven't."

Thank God for that. "Samantha, you haven't taken any money from a couple or anything, have you?"

"No," she said.

"Your mother was wondering how you could afford to pay that credit card bill." He hazarded a peek over his shoulder. She was eating and didn't look in the least upset.

"I got a partial refund from school. I was going to tell you about it." She lowered the glass of milk. "But you made me mad. And I know I was wrong to charge all those clothes but I don't think I was completely sane when I did it, you know?" She was squinting at him. "My brain gets wicked weird sometimes."

"Hormones," he said, going over to sit down in the rocker. "You've got tremendous changes going on in your body. Your mother had that, too. With both pregnancies." He leaned forward, holding his hands in front of him. "We want to do what's right, Samantha. For you and for the baby. We get upset because we love you so much—" His voice started to break, but he cleared it and pressed on. "I know you said you got counseling in Utica, but we'd still like you to see someone here."

"Why?"

"Well, to start with, to make absolutely sure that you really do want to give this baby up—"

"I don't want it!" she said, voice rising. "I'll give birth to it, find it a good home and then I'm going on with my life, Dad. There's no way I'm keeping it."

He held his hands up slightly. "I understand. Don't get upset."

"You guys keep looking at me like I murdered somebody. I got pregnant, big deal, and I keep telling you, I'll take care of it."

"But it is a big deal," he said softly.

"I knew you'd want me to have an abortion, that's why I didn't tell you guys before."

"That's not true, Samantha."

"Oh, yes, it is. This isn't even really about the baby. It's about Mom's image in—" her head accompanied an imaginary dance step to the side "—*the community,* and what it will do when it gets out her teenage daughter is an unwed mother."

"With you walking in Riverside Park every day," Sam said, "you think anybody's *not* going to know you're pregnant?"

"Oh, so you want me to stay inside? You want me to pace in my room for the next two months?" She craned her neck forward. "Maybe you could send me to Africa, Dad. With any luck I'll get murdered in the Sudan and Mom's image problem will be solved. Then she can become a widely admired martyr and get even more awards."

She's jealous. Sam was thunderstruck. Samantha was jealous of how many people admired her mother.

"Enough nonsense," he said, getting to his feet. His back was killing him. "And for your information, yes, I probably would have advised you to have an abortion. But not your mother. Your mother only wants to understand why you wanted to get pregnant."

"Is that what she thinks?" she said, pushing the tray away from her. "That I did it deliberately?"

"She's worried about you, Samantha, get it through your head. You are her baby and she would do just about anything in this world to protect you. She's scared because she doesn't understand how you got to this place, why you couldn't come to her. Is that so hard to understand?"

After a moment Samantha relented, letting her head sag. After another moment, she said, "I thought about telling her."

"Were you raped?" Sam quietly asked.

She looked up at him in horror. "No."

"Because that's the first thing that crossed my mind."

Was it his imagination or did she smile slightly?

"Who's the father, Samantha?"

She shook her head.

"He has a right to know."

"He knows. I told you, I got counseling, all of that's been taken care of. So you can go tell Mom I didn't sell the baby down the river. It's a legit adoption agency."

"So you've talked to an agency?" He needed to get this straight.

"Yes," she said impatiently. "That's where I got the counseling."

"But you didn't sign anything."

"You can't sign off until after the baby's born. You're allowed to change your mind." She tossed her book to the floor and pulled herself toward the edge of the bed. "Anything else?"

"What's the father's race?"

She shook her head again. "It's not happening, Dad. And if you don't give it up I'm just going to leave." She pushed herself up from the bed.

"You will see the obstetrician, right? The one your mother made the appointment with?"

"Yes." She was looking around the room, he presumed for her robe, which was on the floor on the other side of the bed. Sam went over to pick it up. "Thanks," she said when he helped her on with it.

"And you won't sign anything for anybody without letting me see it first, right?" he said.

"Yes!" she said, exasperated. She turned around. "Are you through? *American Idol*'s on."

"Yeah. For now." He gestured. "Go on. Tell Simon he's an embarrassment to mankind."

He turned the bedside lamp off on his way out and went back to their bedroom. Harriet was sitting on the edge of the bed in the dark. "Well, she didn't sell the kid," he announced.

"So I heard."

He sat down next to her, making the headboard thump against the wall. "You heard it all?"

"I was right outside the door." She leaned against him and Sam put his arm around her. "I couldn't help myself."

He kissed the top of her head. "You're a good mother."

"You were wrong, Sam," she said after a moment. "I might well have told her to have an abortion. If it was early on." Pause. "I never thought it was ever going to be an issue. Not with all the contraception available to her."

"You could be right," Sam said glumly. "She might have done it on purpose. But why? What could she get out of it that she doesn't have already—or could have if she asked us."

"He's married," Harriet said. "I can feel it in my bones."

"What?"

Harriet sat up straight. "My guess is she wanted to tie herself to someone whether he liked it or not. Force him to make a choice." She sighed as she got up. "I guess we know what his choice was. Sam." She turned around. "You do know that we have to adopt this child ourselves, don't you?"

13

Cassy Takes Emma to the Lawyer's Office

WHEN EMMA SAW the limousine waiting outside her building she was upset Cassy had gone to so much trouble.

"Honestly, Emma, I didn't," Cassy said, walking slowly beside the older woman. Emma was holding Cassy's arm with one hand and using her walking stick with the other. "The car is something the company gives me so I can get everything done I have to get done." She gave Emma's hand a pat. "Like see an old friend once in a while."

As they emerged on the street a huge gust of wind blew up from the park and Emma's hand tightened on Cassy's arm as she stopped moving, closing her eyes against the cold. Cassy nodded to the driver who then hurried over.

There had been a great change in Emma Goldblum since Cassy had last seen her and she wondered how cognizant Rosanne was of what was happening.

"The last time I was in a limousine," Emma told the driver as he helped her in, "was for my husband's funeral." She allowed herself to fall the last few inches into the deeply padded seat. She smiled at Cassy. "The time before that was when I was married."

They rode along the West Side, chatting about the weather and whether it would snow in time for the holidays, when Emma suddenly said, "Rosanne has enough on her plate."

Cassy hesitated, wondering if this was the beginning or the end of a thought.

Emma, who had her stick planted on the floor of the car, kept looking ahead. "I worry, Cassy, because she dislikes nursing. Very much. And yet she is forcing herself to continue in advanced study at school."

Okay. Now Cassy knew where they were. "She may just need more time to get used to it, Emma. She ran her own business for so many years, it can't be easy to work for someone else."

The older woman was shaking her head, eyes still forward. "She doesn't want Jason to be ashamed of her."

"But Jason was never—"

"I know." She took a breath. "She doesn't want him to go to college and then be ashamed to bring his friends home."

"That's not about Jason, Emma," Cassy said. "That's about how Rosanne feels about herself. As if the job makes the woman. If you ask me, anybody who can make a decent living working for themselves as a housekeeper is worthy of anyone's admiration. It requires a heck of a lot more discipline than it does working for someone else who tells you every move you have to make, when and how, and never feels obligated to fully explain why."

Now Mrs. Goldblum was looking at her. Smiling. "Dear Cassy, I agree. That is why I wish you would talk to her. And perhaps assist her in finding another profession." She chuckled, covered her mouth with a gloved hand and, speaking around it, confided, "She says she hates being around sick people all the time. Can you imagine? A nurse who dislikes people who are ill? She says simply the most ghastly things about the doctors. And the head nurse. Oh, how she goes on and on about that nurse!"

The offices of Emma's lawyer, Attorney Thatcher (as Mrs. Goldblum respectfully referred to him) were located on Fifth Avenue in midtown and were particularly difficult to reach by car. The Christmas season was peaking and midtown was jammed with visitors wanting to see the window displays and decorations. Fortunately Cassy had allowed time for the traffic and she used the time to point out sights to Emma because Cassy knew she rarely came downtown anymore.

To a chaotic chorus of car horns the driver double-parked in front of the office building and helped Cassy get Mrs. Goldblum inside. It was positively freezing now, the urban canyon winds having grown strong.

"Mrs. Goldblum," Attorney Thatcher said at the door of his offices. Since no billing attorney Cassy ever knew spent time waiting for clients at the door she knew his affection was real. She supposed there was nothing like seeing a client whose whole life you had changed for the better, which had been the case some years before with Attorney Thatcher and Emma Goldblum. "We're all ready for you."

Cassy had assumed she'd be going in with Emma but Attorney Thatcher asked the receptionist to please see that Cassy was made comfortable while she waited. Emma took his arm and slowly off they went.

Well.

For some reason this errand was reminding Cassy of taking Henry to the dentist when he was little, wanting to go in with him but the doctor saying it would be better if she didn't.

She wished she had brought some work up from the car and thought about calling the driver. Then she remembered the traffic outside and figured he had enough to contend with. She hung up her coat, told the receptionist, yes, a glass of water would be lovely, and chose a comfortable seat and a copy of *Architectural Digest*.

Their penthouse had been in here. Cassy had frankly been appalled when she learned her new husband wanted to put their private home on public view, but it seemed to mean so much to Jackson she hadn't said anything. Her old apartment, she had made sure, was off-limits, but she was quite sure no one would be interested in it since she had decorated it herself, something between "early attic" and "soft and easy."

They were very different about the public-private thing. Jack loved the limelight and Cassy had never enjoyed it, feeling acutely self-conscious, but for professional reasons she had forced herself to get used to it. When she married Jack she realized too late how fully he intended to put their private life on view, at least those angles that flattered them most. Sometimes she wondered how much the secrecy of a relationship with Alexandra had inspired her to seek it again, to have at least one corner of her life be privately hers.

To see how little public criticism or fallout had resulted from Alexandra's relationship with Georgiana Hamilton-Ayres had been difficult for Cassy. No one seemed to blame either one of them for having fallen in love with the other; they were both such attractive young people. At that point it had only horrified and embarrassed Cassy to think of what she had expected Alexandra to endure in order to be with her. The envy and loneliness and sometimes downright misery Alexandra's new relationship caused her seemed to be appropriate punishment. Cassy wasn't young like Georgiana; Lord knows she came with caravans of emotional baggage; and yet she had expected Alexandra to sacrifice a full-fledged personal life in order to sleep with her on occasion.

Cassy was ashamed.

She remembered being at a dinner party at Jessica Wright and Will Rafferty's apartment one evening with Jack, Alexandra and Georgiana (the latter having been introduced to Alexandra by Jessica) and feeling absolutely horrible because Jackson, as was his habit in public, fawned over her as his beloved wife. It was horrible because Alexandra knew what their marriage was really like and because Alexandra was in love with the actress. Three women at that table were going to go to sleep that night in the arms of someone they valued above all others while Cassy would be alone. Jack had something else on for that weekend.

So Cassy threw herself into things that gave her a sense of accomplishment. She and Jackson took Henry and Maria and Kevin and Kevin's girlfriend on a safari in Africa; she got her mother resettled in an exclusive retirement community in Cedar Rapids; and she almost doubled the hours of DBS programming on the air.

Still, her depression deepened. Jackson came to believe he was the cause of it and made an effort to spend more time with her. If he stopped wondering out loud at how much more aggressive she was in bed she might have settled into permanent acceptance of her marital situation. But Jackson did not stop wondering out loud and kept asking her if she was seeing someone else. She would tell him, no, Jack, obviously absence must make the heart grow fonder.

How Cassy had gone from being a straight heterosexual woman to being heartsick over her ineptitude at loving a woman sometimes made her think she had lost her mind. But then she would remember her marriages and think, *Aha! That's right! I'm inept at falling in love, period!*

One Sunday afternoon Alexandra and Will stopped by the Darenbrooks' penthouse for Cassy to sign off on special expenditures before she left for England the next day. Jack and Langley had already flown over. They went over the paperwork and Cassy signed off on it (*almost* all of it; "Damn, we were hoping you might not notice that part," Will said, seeing what item she had drawn a line through and initialed) and then Will left and Alexandra stayed behind.

They were in the den and Cassy walked around the bar to get Alexandra the glass of water she'd requested. Then Cassy just stood there, frozen, and let her head slump down. She felt so utterly beaten suddenly. Alexandra asked her if she was all right and Cassy didn't answer her. She couldn't. In a moment Alexandra came over to stand next to her, lightly touching her back. "What is it? What's wrong?"

"I miss you," Cassy whispered, head still cast down. "I know I shouldn't say it, but I miss you so much I don't know what to do anymore."

Alexandra had done the right thing, of course, which had been to take her hand away and take a step back.

"I wish you would go now, before I completely humiliate myself."

She thought Alexandra would say something like, "You couldn't humiliate yourself with me, Cassy." Or something. But she didn't. Alexandra simply left, as all people in committed relationships should do, and later acted as though nothing had happened.

Cassy was startled from her thoughts when a large man came barreling through the doors of Thatcher, Wyndam & Lamont.

He gave a nod and a grunt to Cassy and said something to the receptionist which prompted her to hurriedly pick up the phone. "Mr. Tarnucci has arrived." The receptionist hung up the phone and stood up. "I'm to take you right in."

Cassy wondered if this could be Tarnucci the real estate developer. If it was, he was an extremely wealthy man. He had swooped into Manhattan after the stock market decline to start buying buildings.

"Are you sure I can't get you something other than water?" the receptionist said when she came back out. "Attorney Thatcher said it may be another half hour."

"No, I'm fine," Cassy assured her. She did call her driver, though, and gave him the new time estimate.

"She knows," Alexandra said to Cassy a few years ago, closing Cassy's office door behind her. "Somehow Sally Harrington knows."

Cassy rose from behind her desk. Sally Harrington had been writing a major profile on her for *Expectations* magazine. "Knows what?"

Alexandra met her eyes. "About the first time I lived in New York. What happened."

Cassy felt a chill run through her. "But how could that possibly be?"

"I don't know," Alexandra said, starting to pace, "but believe me, she knows."

It was an important moment because it was the first time Cassy found herself being caught in the pretense of her image. She and Jackson had just paraded *the* perfect marriage for Sally's benefit the weekend before in Litchfield. Having an affair with a young woman who was now her employee did not at all fit the profile Cassy had just presented to Sally.

At the very least, such a bombshell in *Expectations,* that Alexandra Waring had once had an affair with the female married president of DBS Television, would force one of them to leave DBS. More than likely it would be Alexandra. Cassy knew how the Darenbrook family operated: they would rally around Jack, and then around Cassy to forgive her, and then they would cast Alexandra out as the villainess who had taken advantage of Cassy while her first marriage had been collapsing.

Thank God, Sally Harrington turned out to be not only scrupulous, but clever. The publisher of *Expectations* had counted on Sally to hatchet Cassy's image in exchange for a career in the big leagues. Instead, Sally handed over the evidence of the affair to Cassy and then somehow got something on the *Expectations* publisher that made her altogether kill the story.

"It was a journal my therapist made me keep at the time," Cassy later explained to Alexandra, after Sally had returned it to her. She pointed to the fireplace in the den. "I burned it after she left. Can I get you something?"

"A vodka tonic," Alexandra said, throwing herself down in a low, overstuffed chair.

Cassy stared at her. In all the years she had known her she had never seen Alexandra drink hard liquor.

"Please," Alexandra said.

"Yes, of course." Cassy walked over to the bar and made the drink for Alexandra and also made one for herself. Without asking she used diet tonic water, Grey Goose and a lime from the bar refrigerator. "It must have been taken in our robbery in Litchfield last winter," Cassy said, handing Alexandra her drink and sitting down on the couch. "It was in the *attic,* for heaven's sake." She took a large sip of her drink. "I had no idea it was gone. At the time we didn't even think they had gone up in the attic."

Alexandra took a long pull at her drink. "This is very good, thank you. So, did you have anything else like that?"

Cassy shook her head. "No. I'm not even sure why I kept it. Because I hated keeping it." She looked at Alexandra. "And I wrote a lot of things that weren't even true. So it was stupid for me to hold on to it."

Alexandra rested her drink on the chair arm. "I wish I could have read it. Because then maybe I'd finally know what had really been going on in your head."

"You know what was in my head at the time."

"No, Cassy, I don't." She took another sip of her drink. "I thought you were head over heels in love with me. And then one day—" she snapped her fingers "—it vanished. Gone. It was like nothing had ever happened between us."

"It wasn't like that."

"Oh, yes, it was," she insisted, nodding.

"That's not how I felt."

"Oh, no? So tell me what you wrote in the journal."

"I told you, I wrote some things that weren't true."

"Then what did you write that *was* true?" She brought her drink up to her mouth again. "Hmm?" And then she drank the rest of her drink down, the ice falling against her mouth.

Cassy took her time answering. "I wrote about how wonderful you were as a friend, and then later I wrote about how wonderful you were as a lover." She swallowed. "That was true."

A little color appeared in Alexandra's face. Then she launched herself out of the chair, heading for the bar. "And what did you write that wasn't true?"

Cassy didn't answer. She watched Alexandra pour herself another drink. A hefty one. To see her doing this astounded Cassy. And unnerved her. Alexandra was the kind of all or nothing person for whom adding alcohol might not be such a good idea. Particularly when for years Alexandra had always said she didn't drink. Cassy wondered what other habits Alexandra might have acquired while being with Georgiana Hamilton-Ayres.

"I think I have a right to know what Sally Harrington read about me." Alexandra sat down again, this time holding her glass in her lap. "Well?"

"I wrote that I cared about you, but I knew I was not in love with you. I wrote I was heterosexual and I was very sorry I was going to have to hurt you. Because I had to. Not only for my family's sake, but for your sake."

"Yes, well, I knew all that," she said, sipping her new drink.

"I should hope you know what parts of that weren't true, but were lies to myself to prepare me for ending it," Cassy said. "I was in love with you, Alexandra. And clearly I was not heterosexual."

"That much I did notice," Alexandra said under her breath, putting her glass down in a crystal coaster on the coffee table with a distinct clink. "So what did you tell Sally?"

"I didn't tell her anything. I just thanked her."

Alexandra had rubbed her eyes for a moment and then dropped her hand. "So Sally Harrington thinks we had an affair, but you turned out to be heterosexual and I turned out to be gay. So now you're happily married to Jackson and I'm happily attached to Georgiana."

Cassy nodded. "That's about it."

Alexandra thought for a long while. "So we lucked out," she summarized.

"We lucked out," Cassy echoed.

Alexandra let her head fall back against the chair to look up at the ceiling. "So the story is, once upon a time, somewhere in the universe, two planets collided before continuing to the orbits God had intended."

Cassy couldn't help but smile. "Only to collide again a couple of times."

"Yes. Yes, they did," Alexandra said. She put her elbow down on the chair arm and dropped her face into her hand. "I can't stand how things are between us." She lowered her hand. "I don't know how things got so messed up."

"It got messed up because you deserved a full-fledged partner, Alexandra."

"The problem has always been," Alexandra said with sudden animation, shifting in the chair to more directly face Cassy, "that the part of you that has always cared for me is the part of yourself you've never liked."

"That's not true."

"Or the part you've never respected." She pointed at Cassy. "You've always viewed your feelings for me as a defect in your otherwise perfect character."

Cassy cringed. Then she shook her head. "No. Maybe way back in the beginning, Alexandra, but I haven't felt that way for a very long time. I know, I've always had that good-girl syndrome. But it's that wanting to be a perfectionist, it's *that* which comes from my self-loathing. My feelings for you, my love for you, Alexandra, has always come from that part of me that *loves* me, if that makes any sense. It's the healthiest part of me. Unfortunately, I've always hated myself a lot more than I've loved myself. And that's why I have always messed it up."

Alexandra got up out of her chair, turned away from Cassy and looked up at the ceiling again, her hair falling back over her shoulders. "I can't believe you tell me this now. When I'm with Georgiana."

"I love you, Alexandra. I always will," Cassy heard herself say. "But I also know that at my age I'll never be able to change enough to make you happy. Georgiana was the right decision. She loves you for you, she's your age, she can even give you children—"

"Stop it," Alexandra said, wheeling around. "Just stop—*stop it!*"

"But it's true," Cassy told her.

"What is the *matter* with you, Cassy?" Alexandra said, coming toward her. "You know I love you! Georgiana wasn't a *decision.* She was a *reaction.* She was a reaction to you wanting to stay in that hideous marriage instead of trying to figure out a way to make a life with *me.*"

"I think we're saying the same thing but in different ways," Cassy told her.

"No, we're not," Alexandra said, straightening up and throwing her shoulders back. "You're telling me that I'm better off with Georgiana. And I'm telling you, take me away from Georgiana before it's too late."

At first Cassy thought she hadn't heard Alexandra correctly. But she had. She looked down. "I can't."

Alexandra walked over, sat down next to her and took Cassy's hands in her hands. "Look at me."

Cassy raised her head. Alexandra's eyes were searching hers. Over all this time, regardless of the situation, Alexandra's eyes had always held the same question. *How much do you care?* "This really will be goodbye," she murmured. "You know that."

Cassy nodded.

Alexandra kissed her. *There is no use to this,* Cassy thought as familiar sensations began to register, of Alexandra's mouth, of Alexandra's hands moving over her arms, her back, her waist, her breasts. Alexandra fell back across the couch, pulling Cassy on top of her.

"All set, Mr. Tarnucci?" the receptionist asked. The big man had come out but there was still no sign of Mrs. Goldblum.

Cassy took a breath, crossed her legs in the other direction, and offered the man a polite smile on his way out.

Woodbury

THE ELEVEN-HUNDRED page outline of *The Royal Court of Catherine the Great* was finished and Amanda was trying to figure out how she might clear a period of time to transform it into the first draft of the book. Only through an intensely focused period of days and weeks would she be able to achieve the brief omniscient view of the masses of material to flesh out the book into a whole. After that it would be back to mere mortal paperwork, checking and rechecking and cross-referencing the working manuscript, page by page, line by line, stitching everything into place. Then she would take another intensely focused period to revise the book straight through, taking care to remove those stitches in an effort to make it appear seamless.

Amanda's biography of Catherine the Great, which had been published over a decade before, had taken ten years to write. This book, about her court, made use of research from that first book but it was still taking another ten years to write.

Why was it taking her so long? The answer was simple: Emily and Teddy. And the minute Amanda had thought she was really free to write full-time again—hello, Grace!

Now, with Madame Moliere here, Amanda had a chance to work again, but she balked at the idea of emotionally withdrawing from her children at a time when their father seemed so distant. And, too, because Madame Moliere had not warmed to her older children the way she had hoped.

Amanda glanced up at the kitchen clock, called to Madame Moliere that she was going out, put on her coat and went outside to meet the school bus. There had been a time in her life when Amanda had feared she could never be a good wife or mother; now she only worried about the wife part, which was the part that for years had felt like her most successful venture.

Howard wasn't happy. The children complained he wasn't fun anymore, that Daddy was always tired and always cranky. Over Thanksgiving weekend Howard had only looked at Amanda oddly when she made a romantic overture. She could have been a hooker trailing after him down the street for all the welcome she had received. Then he apologized, saying he was wiped out. That was not what had bothered her, though, that their sex life seemed to have utterly disappeared. What bothered Amanda was that instead of holding her as they fell asleep, as he had done for years and years, he had turned the other way and balled himself up around a pillow, mumbling something about being used to sleeping alone now.

And yet Amanda's parents were shaking a warning finger at her! She understood why they had said what they did; they knew the only person whose behavior they might possibly affect could be Amanda's, so they had fired a warning shot over her bow to provoke her into changing course. Amanda had also come to realize over the years that her mother had been far more aware of Amanda's sexual lifestyle after Christopher, and before Howard, than Amanda had known at the time.

Her mother was also what was once demurely referred to as a "warm-blooded creature." As a child Amanda had been dimly aware that her parents were hopeless romantics but when she herself had become more sensually inclined she refused to consider her parents in that light at all. Amanda still could not endure thinking about her parents in that way but evidently her parents *did* view *her* in that way.

But she was not going to have an affair with anyone! The question was, when had Howard started one, or when was he going to? The guilt she sensed in him was unlike anything she had experienced before.

The other day Madame Moliere had been watching a talk show in the kitchen and when the show started talking about the signs to look for, to tell if your spouse was having an affair, Amanda stopped to listen: sudden new interest in improving his looks: a diet, working out, new clothes or a special new effort made with hair; a sudden change in routine or schedule; blocks of time unaccounted for; a sudden increase in sexual appetite at home. Howard didn't seem to have any of those signs (except hanging out in bars when Amanda was in Connecticut! She was still getting over that revelation), but all kinds of things were setting him off when he was not by nature an irritable man.

"What makes you think anything has to be going on?" he snapped. "Did it ever occur to you I'm just tired?"

Amanda walked down the hill to the bottom of the driveway. Ashette followed her to the barrier of the electric fence, barked a couple of times in protest, gave up and then sat down to wait for her return. Amanda checked the mailbox. A lot of bills, none of which appeared terribly inviting. It was not even Christmas yet and look at all these bills: oil, electricity, telephone, Internet, satellite TV, satellite radio and credit card bills. Amanda had never owned a credit card before she met Howard. Now they seemed to have several. Or at least Howard did.

She heard honking and looked up to see a red pickup truck coming down the road. She smiled, holding her hand over her eyes, unsure who it was. As the truck bounced closer, squeaking on its springs, she saw it was Miklov. She had never seen him drive anything other than the league's van on occasion because he didn't own a car. He had come to the States with essentially the clothes on his back and Amanda knew he sent money home to his mother in the Czech Republic. The brakes of the truck gave an earsplitting screech as he pulled over and the engine shuddered a few times before shutting down. Miklov jumped down from the cab. "How do you like? It is mine!"

"You have your own truck?" Amanda said, clapping her hands together, wanting to appear excited because he so clearly was. The truck must represent a great deal to him, she knew. It represented Miklov's first opportunity to go when and where he pleased. There must be the feeling of accomplishment from having purchased it. (Did she dare make sure Miklov understood all the ins and outs of registration, insurance and emissions testing?) "Congratulations!"

"It is not new," he noted with a hint of apology.

Amanda was not particularly aware of changing styles in trucks but she did know the rounded roof of this one reminded her of a pickup on her grandmother's farm thirty years ago. She also knew the paint should be shiny, not dusky, although she rather liked this textured brick color better than what might otherwise be an obtrusive red.

The school bus was coming. The driver slowed and stopped at the edge of their driveway and Teddy pushed past Emily to get down the stairs first. “Cool!” he declared with wide eyes, promptly running around to the back of the truck to climb up and look into the flatbed.

Shifting her backpack, Emily got up on her tiptoes to peek inside the driver’s side window.

“Isn’t it wonderful?” Amanda said. “Miklov has his own wheels now.”

Miklov grinned. “Do you like it, Emilee?”

“The seat’s all torn up,” Emily observed.

“Em,” Amanda said under her breath.

“I put in new seats,” Miklov explained. “I only own for one hour.”

Emily caught her mother’s expression while turning back to her coach. “I think your truck is very nice just the way it is, Mickey-Luck.”

He beamed.

“Trucks are supposed to be beat-up,” Teddy announced, elbowing his sister to try to see in through the window. “It’s a guy thing. Can we go for a ride, Mickey-Luck?”

“I’m afraid you’re going to have to go another time, Teddy,” Amanda said, looking at her watch. She wanted Howard to take a look at this truck before she allowed the children in it. “You’ve got homework and then dinner and then your father’s calling to talk over your social studies project.”

“Blech,” Teddy said, “who needs social studies?” He looked up shyly at his coach. “I bet I could be a mechanic if Mickey-Luck would let me work on his truck with him.”

“At least seet in the seat, Teddee,” Miklov said.

Teddy dropped his backpack on the ground. He had to use two hands to press in the button on the door handle. With a squeal and a bang the door opened. Miklov helped him up. The steering wheel was big and thin, and while Teddy couldn't turn it much, he pretended to with great dramatic flair and sound effects.

A piece was missing out of the truck's dashboard, Amanda noticed, or perhaps a piece of the dashboard remained and it was the rest of it that was missing. Amanda supposed it depended on one's perspective.

Emily by now had lost interest and was running up the hill to see Ashette.

"Come on, Teddy, we need to get moving," Amanda said. "Thank you for stopping by to show us your new truck, Miklov."

Miklov bent over from the waist to pick up Teddy's backpack and when he came back up Amanda found his face significantly closer to hers. He was smiling, his eyes happy; she could smell mouthwash and some kind of aftershave. She thought of what her parents had said and, indeed, she could see genuine affection in Miklov's eyes, but not the love her parents had spoken of. She and Miklov were comrades in this distant outpost; theirs was a friendship that had developed after spending so many hours thrown together with the children. He was very lonely, but now with his truck Amanda imagined he would shortly have a girlfriend because now he could finally leave the herd of soccer moms to go where the eligible young women were.

"Pro-gress, you know," he said.

"Yes, I do and you're doing very well," she acknowledged, dropping her eyes to her son. "We are happy for you, aren't we, Teddy?"

"Mickey-Luck rocks," he acknowledged. "I'm hungry."

They said goodbye and started up the hill, Teddy running

ahead. Physically he took after Amanda and at eight looked somewhat like a colt. The doctor said he would be quite tall, perhaps as much as six-foot-three. Emily was sturdier, like her father, and unfortunately about as graceful. Ballet had helped with the latter, however, and it was her endurance that made her a valuable player on the soccer field.

Miklov honked as he drove away and they all turned to wave.

In the kitchen the children helped themselves to graham crackers and milk and settled down with their books at the kitchen table. Amanda went into the study to put Howard's mail unopened in his desk drawer. Then she picked up the phone to call him. Maybe he was in a better mood today.

Howard didn't pick up on his cell phone so she called the agency. "I don't know what to tell you, Amanda," Gretchen, her husband's assistant, said to her, "because he's not here and I'm not sure where he is."

"If he doesn't have anything on his schedule he could be touring bookstores." Her husband was well-known to do this, to pause at the window of one bookstore and then spend hours touring bookstores all over midtown to check out what was selling, what was placed where in the store and, most importantly, to get a sense of how his authors' books were being sold and in what quantities. Amanda crossed her left arm to support the arm holding the telephone. "Is something wrong? You don't sound like yourself."

"It's just been really crazy around here today."

"It is always very crazy there," Amanda reminded her, looking out the bay window. There were birds in the dogwood tree near the window. She hoped the cat didn't get them. "Is there anything I can possibly assist you with?"

Gretchen dropped her voice. "He'd kill me for talking to you. Kill me first and *then* fire me."

Amanda's stomach tensed. "What is it?"

"I think there's some kind of trouble at the bank. They called and he got pretty upset. I think that's where he might be. At the bank."

Howard was a fanatic about the agency books. He must be at the bank screaming from the rafters about some kind of error the bank made.

"I'm sure he'll sort out whatever it is," Amanda said, thinking how upset Howard would be that Gretchen had spoken of it. She tried to turn the conversation into a neutral one again, half joking that Gretchen might want to get some Dove chocolate in anticipation of Howard's return because it tended to have a sedative effect on her husband. She compared notes on Christmas shopping and they speculated on the chances of snow.

"Are you talking to Daddy?" Emily asked from the doorway.

"No, darling," she said, hanging up, "he's going to call us a little later."

"I want to tell him about my math test."

"You'll get a chance a little later," Amanda said, steering her back into the kitchen.

"Why can't Dad live with us all the time?" Teddy asked. The remains of graham crackers floating around in the glass of milk in his hand was disgusting and Amanda couldn't look at it.

"I'm working on it," she told her son.

"It's Mickey-Luck!" Teddy suddenly cried, slamming his glass down and bolting from the table.

The young Czech was standing at their back door, smiling through the glass, with Ashette barking and dancing around him in glee. When Teddy opened the door Miklov held out a large package wrapped in white paper and tape. "I forgot your gift!" he called to Amanda. He laughed, moving the package high over his head so Ashette couldn't get it. "She knows it is steck!"

"I love steck!" Teddy declared.

The next thing Amanda knew Miklov was staying for dinner and she found herself smiling as she prepared it, pleased to have such a grateful and enthusiastic guest joining them.

Celia Talks to Jason

WHEN JASON CLOSED the office door behind him Celia said, "You don't have to lock it." His expression, when he turned around, was not a happy one.

"Here's the iPod," she said quietly, putting the box down on the desk. He made no move to get it. "It was very generous of you, Jason, but I thought I explained before—"

"I told you, I didn't *buy* it. Somebody gave it to me and I already have one." And then more forcefully, "I *wanted* to give it to you. What's wrong with that? It didn't cost me anything. It's not like a Christmas present or anything."

"Jason," she said, crossing her arms and sitting down on the low filing cabinet. In the next moment she remembered their history with this cabinet and moved behind Mark's desk to sit. When she looked up she could plainly see Jason was thinking the same thing. "I was wrong to do what I did with you."

He gave her a look of disbelief. "Why? I can handle it."

"You more than handled it," she told him and Jason's face

instantly brightened. "It's time for you to have a real relationship. You know, have a girlfriend." He was starting to scowl. "Look, Jason, I don't want to be emotionally involved with anyone right now. And I think you do. So you should get a girlfriend."

"I'm not emotionally involved with you," he said.

"But we've become friends, and that *is* an emotional attachment," she said. "And I don't do, you know, the other—" she gestured weakly "—with a friend. I just want us to be friends."

He hesitated. "You acted like you liked it."

She felt her face burn. "Yeah. But—" What was she supposed to say now? Why didn't he just leave? Go away? And why was his erection getting bigger? "Anyway, take the iPod. You can give it to someone for Christmas."

"I'm not going to give you anything anymore," he said. "So why can't we just—" He shrugged. "You know."

"I can't do that anymore, Jason. It was wrong."

"Why is it wrong?" he asked, stepping forward. "You don't have a boyfriend and I don't have a girlfriend."

She heard a belt buckle and looked up in alarm. Jason had undone his belt and was pulling down his zipper.

"What the hell are you doing?" she nearly yelled.

"I know you still want to do it," he said, moving around the desk.

"Stop it," she said, looking away.

"I know you do," he said, pulling himself out of his pants.

"What if someone comes in and sees you like that?" she demanded.

"I locked the door." He reached for her hand. "Come on."

She yanked her hand away from him and violently pushed her chair back. "I'm not kidding, Jason, stop it. Zip up your pants and stop being an asshole."

After a moment he turned his back to her, zipped up his pants and did up his belt.

"I know it's confusing," she said miserably, looking down at the floor. "That I was doing it and now I don't want to do it. And I know you don't get it but I get it now. I'm too old for you and I shouldn't have done it."

He turned around and she saw that he was crying. Crying!

"I love you," he said. "I'm sorry but I do."

"Oh, Jason—"

"I know what I said before but I do care. I'm in love with you, Celia."

She didn't say anything because she didn't know what to say. She didn't want to make it any worse for him.

He wiped his eyes with his sleeve, sniffed and then looked at her again. "You don't—?"

She shook her head. "I'm sorry. No."

He stumbled over to the door.

"Jason, your iPod—"

He turned around to swipe it off the desk. Then he unlocked the door, hesitated and turned to look at her. "I'm never coming back here. Ever." He threw the door open with a crash and left.

Howard Scrambles to Form a Plan

"I'LL CALL HER as soon as I get off with you," Howard lied to Gretchen while he walked through the cars stalled on Fifth Avenue. He had no intention of talking to Amanda until he had some idea of how he was going to meet the next hurdle of this financial mess. Then he would be calmer and would call her. And after he successfully made it over this hurdle he would, he swore, sit down with Amanda and tell her everything.

His visit to the bank had badly shaken him. The personal banker who had been so nice while extending him large credit lines was no longer very nice. He told Howard he had to pay a big hunk of money by December twentieth or there was going to be tremendous trouble. When Howard explained there was a cash-flow problem that would soon work itself out, the personal banker said that's good, so Howard could pay something today out of the agency account at the bank, which currently had over three hundred thousand dollars in it.

Howard explained this was not his money, but money that belonged to his clients, and the personal banker sat back in his chair and said the account had the name of Hillings & Stewart on it, did it not? That it was his company, was it not? Howard quietly explained that if the personal banker touched a penny in that account he would see his personal ass in prison on charges of extortion and racketeering.

No, the meeting hadn't gone so well. Still, Howard had gotten an extension until the middle of January. Now he needed to get the Hillingses to examine the agency books before then.

He'd been walking the streets for hours now, trying to clear his head and get some sort of plan of action together. With the extension he should be able to scrape together the agency Christmas bonuses. His employees also expected to be paid for the week between Christmas and New Year's when the office would be closed. He had his family gifts to buy and the endless envelopes for their households' workers to fill with cash.

He entered the front door of The Pierre Hotel and headed for the bar. It took a minute for his eyes to adjust to the lighting but he spotted Kate Weston sitting around one of the low tables in an overstuffed chair. There was a glass of white wine and a glass of water in front of her. Kate had just been promoted from editor in chief to publisher of Bennett, Fitzallen & Coe. He kissed her hello, congratulated her again, and then apologized for being late. She told him he was not late, but in fact early, and Howard ordered the same as she was drinking, a glass of Chardonnay and a glass of ice water.

"Aren't the lights something?" Kate asked him once he was settled.

"What lights?" he complained, pushing his glasses higher and looking around. "I never can see a damn thing in here."

She laughed. "I meant the Christmas lights, Howard. On Fifth Avenue." She leaned forward. "Hello, Howard, are you there?"

He gave her a sheepish smile. She was an old friend. "Yeah, I'm here."

She leaned a little closer. "I'm sorry I didn't like the novel you sent me. I hope you're not upset with me about it."

"Of course not," he said, picking some nuts out of the dish and popping them into his mouth. "Why would I be upset when I was counting on you to offer me three hundred and save me the time and trouble of having to go out to everybody with it?"

"It's not that it was badly written," she said.

"So you said." He washed the nuts down with the water.

"I'm sorry, Howard, but I just *hated* it. I didn't like the narrator and I hated reading it."

Howard looked at her and then burst out laughing. He had to. What else could he do? "Thank you for such a highly detailed editorial review."

She was laughing, too. "I just don't know what it was about her writing, but I had Mark read a few pages, too—"

She was married to Mark Fiducia, a prominent editor at another house.

"And I'm afraid it didn't go over very well with him, either."

"There is a school of thought, you know," Howard said, "that says your feelings of revulsion might indicate the presence of brilliant artistic talent."

"Well, as long as she works her artistic talent somewhere else—"

They both cracked up again. He assumed Kate was as tired as he was. Everybody in publishing was tired all the time because nobody ever had a chance to read anything until night, which only kept the anxiety of everything everybody had left to do pricking the edge of any sleep they managed to get.

When Howard had quit his job as an editor he had imagined that running his own agency would mean more control over his time and workload. In a sense that had been true—so long as he wasn't very successful. As soon as his first book hit the bestseller list (which had been right away since it had been one of Gertrude Bristol's), the insanity had begun. And the thing was, if worked sucked now, he only had himself to blame, whereas in the old days at Gardiner & Grayson he had always had a slew of scapegoats to blame for wreaking havoc in his life.

Today was one of those days Howard hated his boss and wanted to quit.

"So let me tell you why I really wanted to see you," Kate told him. "I'm desperate for a big book to sell at the London Book Fair. You represent Georgiana Hamilton-Ayres, don't you?"

Georgiana Hamilton-Ayres was one of the most popular actresses in the world. Her mother had been a huge Hollywood sex symbol and her father was some kind of Scottish peer. Georgiana's childhood had been well-documented in the press since she was the object of a custody battle that lasted for years and involved all the best elements a drama could offer: beauty, wealth, power and sex, acts of implied depravity and acts of Parliament, glamorous Beverly Hills mansions and romantic Highland castles.

Georgiana grew up to be somewhat of a blond blue-eyed bombshell like her mother, except with a degree of class and acting ability her mother had never possessed. She was very successful as a movie actress early on and when she got married the general opinion was that Georgiana Hamilton-Ayres was showing amazing resiliency from her deeply troubled upbringing. Her mother was institutionalized because of the ravages of drug and alcohol abuse, and her father was a famous eccentric whose estate now depended upon the kindness of his daughter to exist.

There had been some sort of scandal about Georgiana having an affair with a woman while shooting a movie and then her marriage blew up. It was unclear for a while what she was doing or who she was sleeping with. Then, out of the blue, she was linked with Alexandra Waring, the DBS News anchorwoman, and while the women readily acknowledged they were "best friends," it seemed pretty clear they were lovers. That relationship seemed to be over now and Georgiana Hamilton-Ayres was supposed to be running around with a cameraman or something.

"Vaguely," Howard said. "She wrote a storybook when she was seven years old that we still handle—"

"Which is still in print."

He nodded. "Yes. So if you wanted to count that, then, yes—" He shrugged. "I suppose you can say I represent Georgiana Hamilton-Ayres."

"But you know her. Right?"

He nodded. "Oh, yeah."

"Because I want her to write her autobiography," Kate said. "And I want you to convince her to do it and then sell it to me. There'd be a few stipulations in the contract about what she has to talk about in it—"

"Like what?"

"Her relationship with Alexandra Waring—"

"Oh, is that all," he said sarcastically, reaching for his glass of wine.

"What it was like being shuttled between her father's castle in Scotland and her mother's home in Hollywood, her mother's movie sets and then, you know, just about her life since she's been on her own. The movies, the costars, what she's learned about herself and life—"

"And she would want to write this *why?*" he asked skeptically.

"She told Spencer Hawes she was interested in doing it."

Howard considered this. If anyone would know something like this it would be Spencer, who was married to a powerful tastemaker in the form of a glossy magazine publisher. "But I thought Spencer was leaving you guys."

"He is. He and Verity have this deal to start up a new magazine in L.A. *New Yorker* gone Hollywood, or something. That's why he was talking to Georgiana about it and then brought the idea to me. Spencer gets exclusive first serial rights to the book and uses her as the cover for their premiere issue."

"And how did I get to be so lucky as to be brought in on this?"

"Georgiana's changing agents, to Johnny Kohrbach's new group, which doesn't have a literary division. And Spencer and I both think you'd work very well with her."

"I'm flattered, thank you. And tell him thank you."

"Just get us what we want, Howard," she laughed.

Howard sipped his wine, thinking. His eyes moved back to Kate. "So she really is interested in doing this? Airing her dirty laundry?"

"It doesn't have to be *dirty* laundry," Kate said, "we just want her to address the fact that the laundry exists."

Howard could feel the excitement building in him. "I can't imagine her family's going to be pleased about such a project."

"Her mother's wet-brained and the earl's off his rocker and you know it will all be in done good taste. I mean look at the woman. She does whatever she wants and her fans only love her more."

They raced on in their discussion and both made notes (although the lighting had been designed to discourage overt signs of business being conducted in this genteel atmosphere). Kate was talking a million on signing which would mean a one-hundred-fifty-thousand-dollar commission right off the bat. It would be enough to break the logjam if he could just hold on that long. Of course he had to talk Georgiana into wanting him to represent her but it sounded as though Kate and Spencer Hawes had already done a lot of that work for him.

They left The Pierre and walked up to 72nd Street. "You're so lucky you got out when you did," Kate said. "I'm already beginning to feel like the Moses of book publishing and I'm telling you, these tablets are getting heavy."

He laughed.

"I'm serious. After Spencer leaves I'm wondering who I'm going to have left to talk to. For whatever faults he might have, Spencer's pretty good on the inherent challenges of making enough money to satisfy the owners and still publish books that you're proud of."

"So where does Georgiana Hamilton-Ayres' autobiography fall?" he asked her.

"Hopefully somewhere in the middle."

They walked on awhile, each in their own thoughts. "Do you ever think about coming back on this side, Howard?"

He stopped walking. "Are you kidding? You come to me about a three-and-a-half-million-dollar deal and then in the next breath ask me if I'd like to slash my income and be bullied and kicked around by a bunch of foreign owners?"

She sighed. "What's wrong with me, do you suppose, Howard, that I can't seem to leave it? Do something like you're doing?"

They started walking again. "Who's to say you won't be doing what I'm doing some day? In fact," he added, looking at her, "maybe that is something you and I should talk about down the road. You coming in with me."

"Oh, don't tempt me!" she cried.

He pressed his shoulder slightly into hers. "I'm serious, Kate. Just keep it in mind. Between you and me, I'm looking to expand. To bring in one or two agents as partners. You know you'd be fabulous." By the time he put Kate in a cab Howard was in better spirits. Even if Kate Weston never left Bennett, Fitzallen & Coe, it was nice to know she thought highly of him.

Though the night was cold Howard walked across Central Park toward home to think about things. If Georgiana were to write the book Kate wanted, it occurred to me him that DBS might not be too happy about it. He wondered if it might prove to be a little awkward with the Darenbrooks when he saw them. When he was on Central Park West he cut over to 89th Street to stop in for a quick cheeseburger at Captain Cook's. As he approached the door to the bar, Jason DiSantos came barreling out, nearly crashing into him. "Sorry," Jason muttered, swerving away.

"Jason?"

The teenager turned around. He was obviously upset, but didn't say a word; he only stood there, breathing heavily.

"You need a coat, Jason," Howard finally said.

"I'm okay," Jason said and hurried off into the night.

Howard stuffed his gloves in his coat and hung it up. He slid onto a stool at the bar, plucked the small menu out of the holder and looked up to see that ESPN was on.

"Hey," Celia said, coming over.

"Hi. I owe you an apology," he said as he looked over the menu.

"For what?"

He looked up. "For my behavior on Thanksgiving. I was in a very strange frame of mind and shouldn't have done what I did."

She batted the apology out of the air with a flick of her hand. "Apology accepted. It never happened." She smiled. "I recommend the salmon, if you like salmon."

He did like salmon and sipped on an icy Beck's while he waited for it, thanking God he hadn't done anything with Celia—particularly now, when there was a chance of sorting this financial mess out.

Maybe it would be a happy Christmas after all.

Cassy Takes Emma to the Lawyer's Office (continued)

CASSY LOOKED AT her watch. She'd been waiting for Emma Goldblum at Thatcher, Wyndam & Lamont for one hour and fifty-five minutes. She turned the page of the magazine she was not reading.

The whole country had seemed fascinated by Georgiana Hamilton-Ayres' gal pal relationship with Alexandra, particularly since the tabloids continued to link Georgiana romantically with whatever male costar she was working with. Cassy tried to shut it all out except in the narrow line of view as network president.

Work went on as usual for several months and then Alexandra dropped a bombshell. "The first thing is, I'm absolutely fine. I received a complete clean bill of health this morning."

Cassy had covered her stomach, the lurch in it had been so strong.

"I had a small cancerous tumor in my right breast. I had a lumpectomy and I just finished six weeks of radiation. I've come to tell you this because I would like to go public about it now, promoting awareness that, yes, indeed, women under forty do get breast cancer. And the trick is still early detection."

They had worked together so closely and for so long Langley did not think it was unusual that Cassy had started to cry, wiping her eyes, saying how happy she was that they had caught it in time. Langley simply gave Cassy his handkerchief and went over to give Alexandra a tremendous hug, which for him was tantamount to crying.

Once Alexandra accompanied Cassy down the hall to Cassy's office, however, Cassy had closed the door and lost it, railing at Alexandra how dare she suffer a life-challenging illness and not tell her.

"It was easier for me to cope if I didn't," Alexandra said. "Georgiana doesn't even know."

Cassy had stared at her. "What do you mean?"

"It seemed like a good time for us to have a little time apart anyway. Sally was keeping an eye on me. If something had gone wrong, she would have told you."

"Sally?" Cassy very nearly shouted. "You told Sally Harrington and you didn't tell me?"

Alexandra nodded. "I'm very grateful to her."

"And I'm going to wring her neck," Cassy said, walking around her desk to sit down. She slipped on a pair of reading glasses, pulled a legal pad closer and picked up a pen. "All right. So we'll talk to Eric about a press conference. When do you—" She stopped and took off her glasses, trying to think. "Are you well enough to go to the West Coast for any of the Mafia Boss Murder Trial?"

"Oh, yes," Alexandra assured her.

Cassy was on the verge of asking about her separation from Georgiana but didn't. It was just as well since within two weeks Cassy learned from Sally Harrington that Alexandra was back with Georgiana. Probably for keeps.

The receptionist at Thatcher, Wyndam & Lamont had taken her coat out of the closet and was putting it on. "Do you want me to check again before I leave to see how they're coming along?"

"I'd appreciate it, thank you," Cassy said. "I need to let our driver know."

All Cassy had required to know something was up was to see Alexandra, Georgiana and Alexandra's brother, David, leaving West End together. And when David said later he just felt like coming East for a visit with his sister (never in David's life, Cassy knew, had he taken such a whimsical detour from his work) somehow Cassy had guessed what might be going on, and she had been proven correct.

"When are you planning to tell DBS about the baby?" Cassy said to Alexandra when the men, Langley and Will, dropped behind them as they walked down Park Avenue. They were attending a memorial service at St. Bart's for a reporter who had worked at their local affiliate here in New York.

"When there is one, I should think," Alexandra smoothly answered.

"I assume one is coming that will look a lot like a Waring."

"That's the plan," Alexandra said, glancing over as they started up the stairs. "As of a week ago, at any rate."

The world had started to spin for Cassy in that moment but

she had continued on, as she always continued on, numbly taking her place in the pew reserved for them. She saw Alexandra get up to speak about the reporter but Cassy did not comprehend much of what she was saying because it was sinking in, really sinking in, that there would be no going back, that she had lost Alexandra once and for all.

Alexandra had only given her a decade to get her act together.

The thought of merely working around her was dismal and Cassy had examined her options.

"We both know you won't leave DBS in the next five years," the chairman of a group of cable networks told Cassy. "It's still learning how to walk, it needs its mother. So I don't even know why I'm bothering to talk to you about this job."

"You don't want to leave DBS for us," the CEO of one of the Big Three said to her. "You've got freedom, profits and fun at DBS, where we're experiencing something akin to the fall of the Roman Empire. It's no fun, Cassy."

"For crying out loud, Cassy," her old boss at WST said, "you *are* DBS. You've got the same problem Dr. Frankenstein had. The creature only seems to respond to you and the whole village is trying to kill it. There's no way DBS can survive without you right now. You'll never be able to live with yourself."

"Geez, Louise, Cass," Jackson said one evening, coming out of his dressing room while using his electric razor before they left for the theater, "where are all of these rumors about you leaving DBS coming from?"

"Attorney Thatcher says Mrs. Goldblum will be out in five minutes," the receptionist reported, bringing her back to the present.

"Thank you." Cassy called the driver to relay this information and leaned over to pick up an issue of *Kiplinger's.*

Not long ago her accountant had announced she was officially rich and didn't have to work another day of her life if she didn't want to. When Cassy asked him what she would do with her time he suggested gardening and perhaps golf.

Cassy and Jackson were awakened at almost one o'clock in the morning by the telephone. Cassy's heart skipped a beat as it always did when they got a call at that hour. Had something happened to Henry? Her mother? Was Lydia on the loose? Kevin? She had moved over in the bed closer to him as Jackson rolled over to pick up the phone. "Darenbrook."

She held her breath, resting a hand on Jack's shoulder. "She is?" He turned to Cassy. "Alexandra's downstairs."

She froze a second. "It must be something important."

"Yeah, send her up." He hung up the phone, turned on the light and swung his feet out of bed.

Cassy was already standing and putting on her robe. "Go back to sleep, Jack."

"How can I go back to sleep when I know the whole world's probably blown up," he grumbled, thumbing the waist of his boxer shorts as he walked to the bathroom. "That's the only reason why she'd turn up at this hour."

Cassy was standing in the doorway when the elevator arrived and Alexandra emerged looking pale and utterly wrung out. She was still in her studio clothes and her makeup was a mess. "Is Jackson here?"

Cassy nodded, stepping back to hold the door open for her to come in.

"Oh, God, forget it," Alexandra said, turning back to the elevator.

Cassy moved quickly. "Please. Don't go."

"What's goin' on, girl?" Jackson said, his looming figure filling the doorway. He was tying the belt of his robe.

"The world at large I believe is safe, Jack," Cassy said, shielding Alexandra a bit from view. "Alexandra thought I'd still be up."

Jackson peered around Cassy. "You okay, kid? No, you're not okay. Are you?" The last was said gently. He stepped up next to Cassy. "Is it like a woman thing or— You know, I—" He looked at his wife.

"Why don't you go back to bed, Jack," she suggested softly.

He nodded, looking over at Alexandra. Then he impulsively went over to touch her arm and kiss her on the forehead. "Anything we can do," he murmured. "You know. We're here for ya."

"Thank you," Alexandra said quietly.

Cassy waited until he left. "Let me get the keys. We'll go next door." When she came back she unlocked the door of her old apartment and Alexandra went in ahead of her. Cassy turned on the foyer light and followed Alexandra into the kitchen where, a moment later, she found Alexandra leaning over the sink with her eyes closed and her forehead resting on the faucet.

"Can I get you some water?"

"I just told Georgiana I can't do it," Alexandra said. "I told her I could not be responsible for bringing a child into this world when I knew in my heart we wouldn't last."

Cassy pulled a stool out from the breakfast bar and slowly sat down.

Alexandra straightened up, turned on the water and washed her face with her hands. Cassy got up to get her some paper towels. Alexandra finished splashing water over her face, drank a few handfuls and then dropped her head down in the sink. "God, I wish I was in Kansas," she said. "I could take my pillow and blanket and go outside in the moonlight and hide in the cornfield, because then I could sleep knowing nobody could find me. Except maybe a fox." She took a deep breath and stood up, reaching for the paper towels. "Thank you."

Cassy retrieved two glasses from the cabinet and filled them with water while Alexandra sat down at the breakfast bar. "Everyone gets scared about becoming a parent," Cassy said, handing her a glass.

"It's not about being a parent." She drank down half of the water and put the glass down. "It's about trying to force myself into a commitment I don't want to make."

Cassy nodded slightly, sipping her water. "You've got a lot going on, and are under a lot of pressure—"

"Cassy," Alexandra said sharply. "Please." She blinked. "Look at me. Do I look like someone who's in love, wants to get married and have a child? Or do I look like the rat I am who never should have gotten involved with Georgiana in the first place, much less lead her on all this time, when I damn well knew it wasn't going to work."

"Maybe you need some time."

"Maybe you should just listen to me for a minute," she said, dropping her eyes.

After a moment, Cassy said, "I'm listening."

"I don't care if you stay married to Jackson," she said, her eyes still cast down. "I won't ask you to make changes, to change anything, if you don't want to." Finally she brought her eyes up. "I'm only asking you to love me, Cassy, and be with me when you can." Her eyes filled. "I can't— I don't want to go on without you. Do you understand? Whatever I have to do—you tell me, and I will do it. But I've got to have you in my life."

"This is, um—" She looked at Alexandra, overwhelmed. "This is really—"

"I know," Alexandra said.

"A part of me has been praying for this moment," Cassy admitted.

Alexandra didn't move.

"But it's not fair to you."

"It's not fair for me to pretend I want anyone else," Alexandra said. "I did it, Cassy. I found the ideal person. I gave it my best— I got everything I wanted." She swallowed. "But I love you, Cassy. I always will. So I don't care anymore, do you hear me? I'll be with you under whatever conditions you say." She smiled a little. "You might say that you lost the battle but you won the war." She swallowed again. "If you still want me."

"Of course I do," Cassy said. "And I'll try, as I can, to sort it out—"

In the next moment Alexandra was holding Cassy in her arms. After about an hour, she went home.

They had been, as best they could, together ever since.

"Here I am at last, poor girl!" Emma Goldblum said as she came into the waiting room on Attorney Thatcher's arm. She was already bundled up to go outside. "This has been far above and beyond the call of duty."

"It was rather nice, actually, to have a little time to myself," Cassy said, standing up. "Did you get your business settled?"

"Most satisfactorily, thank you, dear."

"Are you getting Botox or something?" Jack asked Cassy not long after she and Alexandra had taken up again. Cassy had been finishing her makeup before they attended a clubhouse dinner and Rangers game at Madison Square Garden. "No. Why?"

"'Cause you're looking so gorgeous all of a sudden," he declared. "I mean you're always gorgeous," he said, leaning over to kiss her cheek, "but you're just bloomin', girl." Then he looked at her in the mirror. "Is there something maybe you want to tell me?"

"No."

She should have known Jack would check up on her. When they arrived home late one night after an opening at the Metropolitan Museum the doorman handed Jack a large manilla envelope that had been dropped off for him. Jack looked at the return address, raised his eyebrows at it and ushered Cassy to the elevator. He smiled at her on the way up, tapping the envelope behind him on the wall. They went into the penthouse and he followed her into the bedroom. "So," he said, lounging in the doorway of her dressing room, "are you going to tell me who it is or do I have to read this?"

"Who is what?" she called.

"Who it is that's puttin' that smile on your face."

Cassy's blood ran cold. "What are you talking about?" she said, slipping out of her dress and heading to the bathroom.

"I gotta report here in my hand that is gonna tell me what my wife's been up to."

Cassy tried to mask her fear by taking the offensive. "Now why would you do something like that, Jack?" she said, putting on her robe and sticking her head out the door to look at him. "It's not fair. There aren't enough private investigators in all of the United States to keep track of you."

"I'm going to open it."

"Fine," she said, closing the bathroom door. She had used the john, washed her hands and face and brushed her teeth. Then she flossed, hands on the verge of a tremor.

"What is this, a joke?" He pounded on the door.

"It's not locked," she called.

The door flew open behind her. "This clown says you're meeting Alexandra at an apartment on East End Avenue."

She was. Alexandra had turned out the tenant in her old co-op to give them somewhere to meet. "I meet Alexandra all the time in all kinds of places," Cassy said, checking the skin around her eyes in the mirror.

"But she lives on Central Park West." He was looking through the sheets of paper, trying to figure it out.

"Excuse me," she said, sliding past him. She went into the bedroom and turned down the bed.

"Cassy!" he yelled, stomping in a moment later. "Is *Alexandra* fucking you?"

"You do have a way with words," she said, taking her robe off and getting into bed.

Then he read something else that made him drop the papers to his side and stare at her. "Alexandra went from Georgiana Hamilton-Ayres to *you?* I don't believe it."

She looked at him. "Thanks, Jack."

"I don't believe it," he said, dropping down on the edge of the bed. "I just don't fuckin' believe it. I build her a whole goddam news network and she fucks my wife."

Cassy propped herself up on her elbows. "I do have some say in it, you know."

"Why she would do this to me, I do not understand."

"How *dare* you," Cassy said, sitting up.

"What?" he said, turning. "What did I say?"

"Is that snow?" Emma Goldblum asked with a note of concern in her voice.

"No, I don't think so," Cassy said, leaning closer to the window. "I think that's soot from somebody's furnace."

"Oh," Mrs. Goldblum said. "I'm afraid my eyes are not what they once were."

"I know how you feel," she said. "Mine aren't, either."

Mrs. Goldblum put a hand on her arm. "You won't mention our little jaunt to Rosanne just yet, will you?"

"Emma," Cassy said, "I don't even know what this little jaunt was about. But if Rosanne asks me where we went, what do you want me to say?"

"That it is a surprise," she said. She patted Cassy's arm. "I am very grateful to you, Cassy dear. You've always been so lovely."

"You're very welcome."

"You must promise me you'll continue to watch over Rosanne. She respects you so."

Cassy frowned slightly. "Emma, you really should tell me if there is something going on."

Emma thumped her stick on the floor. "Samantha Wyatt is expecting a child in the beginning of February—"

"What?"

Emma took a little intake of breath as she nodded, saying, "Yes. It's no longer a secret. She intends to give the baby up for adoption and return to school. Needless to say, her parents are beside themselves and Rosanne has been trying to help."

Cassy's mind was reeling. With Harriet's views on birth control, how did this happen? Harriet had to be devastated she wanted to give up the baby. And Sam.

"So my timing is not the best, I find," Emma said. "Everyone has enough on their plate without having to deal with me."

"I was just pleased I could take you," Cassy told her.

"Yes, and so was I, but what I mean, dear, is that I'm dying, and I'm afraid it might be sooner rather than later."

The Wyatts

"DIS COFFEE TASTES like piss!" the loudmouth said, following with a string of expletives that made the newcomer to AA cringe.

Some are more sober than others, Sam tried to remind himself before he lost his temper and dumped this nasty piece of work headfirst into the garbage. "If you don't like it," he said, putting a reassuring hand on the shoulder of the newcomer, "then *you* come early and make it." He steered the newcomer back into the safety of the church basement kitchen.

"It tastes like piss, I tell you!" the loudmouth yelled through the serving window.

"I'm sure you would know," Sam mumbled under his breath and he was pleased to see the newcomer crack a smile. He was all of sixteen days sober and terrified.

The loudmouth started coughing then, that horrible early emphysema sound Sam had heard so many times in so many people who had passed through this particular meeting over the years. The Upper West Side may have given way to big money—almost all the old single-room-occupancy hotels were gone now—but there was still an underside to Broadway and Amsterdam Avenue this meeting catered to. The meeting was considered hard-core, where wet-brains and advanced illness were not uncommon. Harriet had given up trying to convince Sam to drop this meeting (she worried he might catch tuberculosis); Sam had found it an excellent contrast to his Friday midtown luncheon meeting that looked like a roll call for the Fortune 500. The only concession he made was to take greater care to make sure he washed his hands at this meeting.

"I'm still having trouble reading," the newcomer told Sam. "I couldn't really see the directions on the coffee can. I hope I don't have cancer or something."

"We'll try getting you some glasses," Sam said, reaching for a jar of instant coffee. "When was the last time you had your eyes checked?" When the newcomer didn't answer, but only jammed his hands into the pockets of his jeans, Sam knew it was probably never. He noticed the newcomer was wearing the same pair of blue jeans and green shirt again, but they were clean and his hair was still wet from a shower. He had come a long way since Sam picked him up from the drunk tank thirteen days ago.

"We'll get you some cheaters at the drugstore after the meeting," Sam said. "Reading glasses, magnifiers," he added when he saw the newcomer's puzzlement. "So listen, here's a trick about the coffee." He held out the jar of instant coffee and poured some into a foam cup. "Now," he prompted, leading him back out into the meeting room. He took the lid off the massive coffeemaker, grabbed a bunch of paper napkins to lift the steaming basket out, took a furtive look over his shoulder and dumped the instant coffee in. Then he used the basket stem as a stirrer, replaced the coffeemaker lid and, holding more napkins under the basket and stem, winked at the newcomer and carried them back into the kitchen.

"Would you be my sponsor?" the newcomer stammered while watching Sam dump the grinds in the garbage.

"I already am," Sam said with a grin. "But it's always nice to be asked."

Even after all this time an AA meeting still put Sam on an even keel. If he was very happy a meeting brought him down a notch, reminding him of his precarious vertical position when he had first arrived in AA, and if he was very down, as he had been since Samantha had come home, watching the initial despair of newcomers slowly turn to wonderment always brought him up a notch.

"Hey, babe," he called when he arrived home.

"In the kitchen, honey."

"Hi, Dad," Althea greeted him. She was sitting on the other side of the table from Harriet. Mother and daughter were evidently having a chat while they were eating what Sam hoped was a Cobb salad. (At least there would be some meat in it.)

"There's a salad for you in the fridge," Harriet reported.

"Great, thanks." He was already there and was surprised to see quite a lot of bacon in it, which meant Althea must have made it. "I thought you were in Budapest, kiddo."

"I was. I got home this afternoon. Thought I'd come over."

He glanced back over his shoulder. "Where's Samantha?"

"She went to the movies with Rosanne."

"How do you suppose she thinks we're going to explain the situation to people?" he asked himself. "They see Samantha all over town, pregnant out to here, and then later when they ask how the baby is, we're supposed to say, 'Oh, we all gave it up for adoption because Samantha said she would never come home again if we didn't'?"

When Sam and Harriet had broached Samantha with the idea of raising the child themselves, they were stunned and then heartsick over Samantha's rage. She'd screamed at them that everything was arranged, to just leave her alone, "Or I swear to God I will never come near you again!" Then she'd made some crack about old people and wheelchair races and locked herself in her room.

It wasn't as if Sam and Harriet were thrilled with the prospect of parenting all over again. If they did raise the child it would mean selling their place down south, because no one under fifty-five could live in that community full-time. Even as they had discussed it Sam swore he could feel his arthritis getting worse by the second. Committing every day of their lives for the next eighteen years? Yeah, high school graduation at eighty-two and eighty years old, that would be interesting.

He'd have to hire somebody to teach the kid how to throw a ball.

"Daddy," Althea said, Sam noticing at once she had addressed him in a way she had not for decades. "I want to adopt Sammy's baby."

Sam lowered the salad dressing cruet to the counter and looked straight ahead, examining the grain in the cabinet. Then he picked up the cruet again and poured dressing over his salad. "Are you proposing the child should bring itself up while you're traveling around the world?"

"I'll hire a live-in nanny," Althea said. "And I can alter my schedule, group my meetings together. Like other mothers do."

Like other mothers do. Althea was about as much like other mothers as gales at sea were like windy days at a swimming pool.

He knew she meant well. Althea couldn't stand the idea of letting the child go, either. "It would be a huge commitment," he said, joining them at the table. He pretended not to see Althea exchanging looks with her mother. "It would mean a life of self-sacrifice on behalf of an innocent being, whose fault none of this is."

"Yes, I know."

Sam imagined this was the same tone of voice Althea must use in business meetings, when people trusted what she had to say. He wished he had not brought up Althea so he could trust everything she said, too. Althea had been running so hard and so fast for so long she scarcely knew who or what she was anymore—so how could he trust what she said were her true feelings?

"If you did this," he said, "interfered with Samantha's plans, you realize your sister might never speak to you again."

"Oh, I think she'd come around—if she knew the child thought she was his aunt."

Now there was a healthy start, Sam thought, let's just lie to the baby right from the beginning. *Here's your aunt Samantha. Oh, don't mind her, she's just moody.*

"And with Samantha parading around the neighborhood in her condition how are we to keep the secret that she is more than the child's aunt?" He speared some salad but then had to put his fork down. He couldn't eat when his stomach was tied up in knots like this.

"We'll figure it out, Dad," Althea said. "We'll take it as it comes."

We'll, she said. Althea was counting on their support. Well, she should. The child would need grandparents, a father figure.

He tried to quell the sudden streak of joy he felt in his heart—a father figure! *But it's not about what we want,* he reminded himself, *it's about what is best for the baby.*

"What's important," Althea continued, "is that the baby would have a loving parent and loving grandparents and would always know he or she was loved and wanted."

"And the baby could also have a loving mother *and* a father and *two* sets of grandparents if it were adopted," Sam said.

Althea cocked her head to the side. "You gotta problem with a single mother?"

"I don't have a problem with one, I just wouldn't choose that situation for a child."

"Where the hell do you think I would be if I *hadn't* had a single mother, Dad? A single working mother? While you were out doing whatever it was you were doing?"

Althea was referring to those years Harriet raised her by herself, before Sam got sober.

He pushed back from the table slightly, running his hands on the edge of it, trying to control his temper. "I know your heart's in the right place, Althea."

"I want the baby, Dad. I want it more than I've ever wanted anything."

"A child is not a pet," he said, looking up. "And you've wanted a pet for years and you still don't have one, do you? Why? Because you've always said with the kind of life you lead it wouldn't be fair to the animal. So why do you think it would be fair to a child?"

"Because I will make changes in my life to make it fair," she argued. "I would be the child's *mother*—"

She stopped speaking when they heard the front door of the apartment slam.

Slammy Sammy they had called her when she was little.

"Hi," Samantha said, coming into the kitchen and dropping her keys in the bowl. She disappeared down the hall.

"Hi," Rosanne said, her jacket still buttoned and her hands in her pockets, trying to sound cheerful but not quite succeeding.

"Can I get you something?" Harriet asked her. "Coffee? Tea? Hot chocolate?"

"Dad's salad?" Althea added, pushing his plate over an inch.

"No, thanks, I can't stay." She rested her back against the counter, looking first at Sam and then back to Althea. "I guess I'm interrupting something."

"No, no," Sam said.

Althea frowned, looking at him.

"We were talking about the future," Harriet said quietly, staring down into her mug. Then she looked up, lowering her voice. "How did you find her?"

Rosanne glanced at the doorway before answering. "She's pretty much the same. Angry, angry, *angry* and I dunno who at."

"Maybe us for so badly mistreating her," Sam said sarcastically. He looked at Harriet. "We should have doubled her allowance, bought her the car she wanted, given her a mink coat. We should have catered to her every whim day *and* night and then everything would be okay."

"We know, Dad," Althea sighed. "None of us knows what's going on with her. Not even me."

"What about the father?" Sam said. "Rosanne, what do you know about him?"

She shook her head. "Nothing."

"Like does he *know* he's going to be a father and the baby's going to be sent down the river?" Sam continued. "And is he white, is he black, is he purple, does anyone know?"

"Shh," Harriet said. "She's coming."

Samantha walked in and went straight to the refrigerator. She stood there, unconsciously using her hands to help shift her bulk as she shifted her weight from one leg to the other. "Don't we have anything to eat?" she complained. "There's no cookie dough."

"In a month you can eat all the junk food you want," Rosanne said, saving Harriet the trouble.

Harriet pushed her chair back and carried her dishes to the sink. "I'll make you some toast with peanut butter and banana."

"Yeah, all right, thanks," Samantha said. "What?" she said to her father. "What are you looking at?" Frowning, she shuffled over to the table and sat down in her mother's chair, a hand over the baby.

"I just wondered if you wanted my salad," he lied. He was thinking how huge she was and wondered if she might not be a little further along than she'd said.

"Salad, yuck," she said. "It'll make me barf again."

Sam stood up and took his salad over to the counter.

"So I gotta get going," Rosanne said. When no one said anything, she added, "Yeah, okay, don't everybody fight to see me to the door."

"Bye, Rosanne," Samantha said. "Thanks for going to the movies even though it sucked."

Sam walked Rosanne to the front door. "The atmosphere is so pleasant here," he whispered, "I can't understand why you don't want to stay and enjoy the festivities."

"Just hang in there, Mr. W," she said, patting his arm. "I gotta get home and check on Mrs. G. She's not so hot these days."

"She is getting up there, Rosanne."

"Mrs. C took her to her lawyer's today. I'm not supposed to know but I do."

"She's probably getting her will in order." He met her eyes. "The last will she had was from 1972."

Rosanne covered her face with her hand for a moment and Sam put a hand on her shoulder. "I know. It's difficult," he said. And then he gave her a big hug. As if Rosanne was in AA, too.

Amanda Goes for a Ride

"I'M SORRY, I can't, Amanda," Howard said. "If you want me to take time between Christmas and New Year's I have to stay in this weekend and work."

"It's not a matter of *my* wanting you to take time," she began.

"Yeah, I know, I know. And I want to. Look, I just can't get out of here, Amanda, and that's all there is to it."

"God forbid you should ask me to bring the children in." He didn't answer. "God forbid you should ask *me* to come in."

He sighed heavily. "It's better if you didn't."

"Yes, I'm sure it would be. Goodbye," she said, hanging up on him. He didn't come out last weekend and now he was not coming out for this one. It would be three weeks since they had seen him and the man was not even seventy-five miles away!

Their marriage was taking on a surreal quality and Amanda could feel herself getting so angry she had to make a conscious effort to calm herself before driving the children anywhere. And drive she did. School, piano lessons, choir practice, play-dates, grocery shopping, Christmas shopping. Having to get a Christmas tree with the children and Madame Moliere and decorate it without Howard felt close to being the last straw. How had she gotten from winning the Greistenberg Prize in history to being a *hausfrau* schlepping around making excuses for why her husband was failing his family? What could possibly be more important at this time of year?

The telephone rang again and it was Howard. "Amanda, listen, I swear, after the holidays you and I need to sit down and I will explain everything that's been going on."

"At least you're finally admitting something *is* going on. That could be construed as progress, I suppose."

He paused. "I can't talk about it yet."

"It better be sooner than later, Howard," she warned.

"Look, I've got to go," he said.

"Fine, go," she said, but he had already hung up. She put the kitchen phone back in the cradle a bit harder than she meant to and it bounced out of the cradle and crashed to the floor. They tended to go through mobile phones in this house rather quickly, but this would be the first one she had broken.

She picked it up, turned it on and listened. A dial tone. She almost wished she had broken it.

Amanda looked up at the clock and walked to the front hall, aiming an ear toward upstairs. She could hear the music box in the nursery; Madame Moliere had already put Grace down for her nap.

Amanda sat down on the stairs and rested her chin on her fist, looking at the sky through the fan-shaped window spanning the front door. It was bleak outside; the forecast of snow had elated the children this morning but only filled her with a greater sense of loneliness. She would not build a fire in their bedroom tonight, as she and Howard had always done to celebrate the first snow of the season. When everyone was safely asleep, there would be no need to keep quiet because there would be no one to make love with.

It gave her a hollow feeling inside to think those days were gone. Even if Howard was the slightest bit attentive to her she would probably still feel numb. It was frightening actually, how Amanda was starting to feel so little about anything connected to her marriage. She knew how much she loved Howard; she couldn't remember, though, how it felt to be in love with him.

She simply *must* pull herself together. It wasn't as though the children didn't miss their father, too. No, she would pull herself together and build a big fire in the family room and after dinner they would toast marshmallows and she would take Howard's place and tell Teddy and Emily a ghost story.

"Mrs. Stewart?" Madame Moliere said quietly from behind her at the top of the stairs. "Grace is asleep. Is there anything you wish me to do?"

"Thank you, no, Madame Moliere," Amanda said, turning around. "I will be going out for a little bit, though, so please do mind Grace."

"Of course," she said, with a slight bow.

The warmth Amanda thought would have materialized with Madame Moliere was still not in evidence. And had Amanda known she would still be calling her Madame Moliere, instead of Isabel—or even Madame M, which they had tried and to which Madame Moliere had looked at them askance—she never would have engaged her. On the other hand, Madame Moliere was meticulous in her care of Grace and was many times undaunted by Emily and Teddy's high-flying spirits.

Amanda went to the mudroom to put on her barn boots, a heavy leather coat, knit hat and gloves and took the car keys off the rack. She'd stop at Daffodil Hill to see Maja and Sweets before going to the grocery store.

She started the Navigator and wondered again about the hybrid truck they had agreed to purchase. There was nothing like living through a Connecticut winter to become aware of their desperate dependency on oil. With six of them and the winter roads out here a full-sized four-wheel truck was a necessity. And when the temperature dropped below freezing and then stayed there for weeks one would do almost anything to keep fueling the furnace. They had further winterized the house last summer, which was a help, but they wanted to demonstrate to the children they had some kind of plan to cut back on gas, oil and emissions. The hybrid had yet to materialize, however; Amanda supposed it was yet another thing on hold while Howard was off doing whatever it was he was doing.

Miklov's truck turned in just as Amanda was coming down the driveway. It was looking and running much better now. When he started the engine a large cloud of pollution no longer ballooned from the exhaust, and when the ignition was switched off, the engine cleanly shut off, too. After Miklov had passed the test (driver's license, insurance card, registration, emissions test), she had allowed Teddy to ride home yesterday in the truck after practice. Teddy had been on cloud nine. First he was able to stay and close up the soccer center with his idol and then he got to ride "in a real truck, like men drive."

It seemed that Miklov was standing in for Howard in Emily's life, too. In a match with a team of notorious ruffians from a nearby town, Emily, who had been playing halfback, had been deliberately smashed into the boards. Amanda had jumped out of her seat when she saw her daughter go down clutching her elbow. The ref had not seen what happened and no whistle was blown. Amanda had almost leapt over the wall onto the playing field but then Emily scrambled to her feet and hustled to rejoin play. When the next whistle blew to stop the play, Emily went over to the player who had shoved her and—what did they call it?—*got in her face.* When play resumed the bully shoved Emily again, but this time Emily shoved back, sending the girl flying to the ground. Play was stopped. Both coaches came trotting out onto the field. The bully refused Emily's offer of a hand up while the bully's father started screaming obscenities at Emily. Emily looked up at the man, squinted, and then put her hands on her hips and turned her back to him, looking to the ground as her teammates gathered protectively around her.

Howard should have been there. After she knew Emily was all right, that was almost all Amanda could think about, how Howard should have been there. Emily and the other player were both pulled out of the game and it wasn't until the game was over that Amanda realized that Miklov had put Emily's elbow on ice. "It was important to Emilee she stay for whole game," he explained. "But now we go for X-ray, I believe."

Miklov rode with them to Waterbury Hospital. By the time Emily was in X-Ray Amanda still had not been able to reach Howard. Fortunately there was no serious injury so Amanda took them to the Barnes & Noble café down the road for a sandwich and then encouraged everyone, Miklov included, to pick out a book. Emily chose a mystery taking place on a horse farm and Teddy a book explaining how the pyramids were built. For Miklov they found a manual for old Ford trucks and Amanda chose for herself Flora Fraser's biography of the princess-daughters of George III.

Howard should have been there.

Miklov had also talked at some length with the children about the difference between holding one's own against a dirty player and becoming a dirty player yourself. While he felt Emily had acted honorably, he warned her that it could have cost them the game had she been ejected any earlier. ("How *do* you keep them from pushing back?" Amanda asked him on the side. "You don't," he told her.) They dropped Miklov off at the soccer center to pick up his truck and when they got home, after ten o'clock, Emily was delighted to find several phone messages from her teammates who were ecstatic Emily had given the bully a taste of her own medicine.

Finally reaching Howard had been anticlimactic and by the time Emily tried to recreate the game scenario over the telephone for her father even she had lost interest.

"Hello!" Miklov greeted Amanda, extending his hand out the truck window.

She smiled, rolling her window down. "Hi."

"That girl, who pooshed Emilee?"

"With the charming father, how can I forget?"

"She is out three games. She pooshed Stratford gerl into boards last night."

"Really?"

"She is ten. I bet she in preezon by twenty."

Amanda laughed.

"I also want to tell I am away for Chreesmas." He nodded. "Yes, I go. Thank you for invitation here."

"I'm very happy for you. Where are you going?"

"I go to cousin in Queens. Three days." He grinned. "Vacation, huh?"

"That's wonderful. The children will be devastated, though."

He waved his hand. "Ehh. I run them and run them, they will not mees me."

They both laughed. "And how many practices before Christmas?" Amanda asked him.

"One." He held up his index finger. "Then on vacation, I am now beeg shot." He smiled again, turning his head slightly. Amanda noticed he had gotten a haircut. "What are you about now?"

"I am off to the grocery store," she said. "You run the children and I feed them, you see."

"Get in my truck, I take you," he said, reaching down to pat his door from the outside.

"Thank you, but no," she said. "I need to see the horses, too."

How could it be that talking to Miklov for two minutes could make her feel so much better? Because he liked her so much. Because he thought she was worthwhile. And she did think he found her attractive. She thought he was very attractive, too. But it was innocent. They were both so lonely out here, how could they not wish to cheer each other up?

"Come on. I drive you," he said. "You see how nice the truck now."

The truck meant a lot to him, but Amanda knew she shouldn't go with him. Her parents had been right about that, it wasn't completely proper for her to be alone with Miklov.

On the other hand she felt a surge of excitement about doing something different from what Howard obviously imagined she was always doing out here. She wouldn't be changing a diaper or windshield washers; she'd be running around town with Miklov in his truck while the children were in school!

"All right," she said, rolling up the window and backing up the driveway. She parked the Navigator and by the time she had emerged from it, Miklov had driven his truck up and was standing next to it, proudly holding the passenger door open for her.

"Golly, you have done a lot of work, Miklov," Amanda declared. The big old ratty seat was gone, replaced with two nice bucket seats from Amanda didn't know what kind of car. But they were bolted firmly in the floor and had shoulder and lap belts of the same color. The dashboard looked ten times better, too, and there were new mats on the floor and a leather cover over the steering wheel. The whole interior was as clean as it could possibly be.

"Heat works," Miklov announced, pulling off his glove and holding his hand over the vent. She did the same and agreed it was working.

"This is wonderful, Miklov. This is a fine truck."

"And the radio," he added, snapping it on. He had it on News 880. "Helps me with my English. Okay. Here we go." He put the truck in Reverse and carefully backed up.

Amanda, out of habit, glanced back over her shoulder, too, and casually wondered what Madame Moliere would think of this scene if she were to see it from her bedroom window. She noticed out the small back window the cargo in the truck bed. "Are those bags of sand?"

"Yes. To traction." He ducked his head to look up through the windshield at the sky. "It is snow today."

"Yes," she said, as he drove slowly down the driveway.

"Horses?"

"Right next door," she told him. "Over there."

"A coffee first? To take?"

"No, thank you, Miklov, I'm fine," she said.

"Okay." He stopped at the end of the driveway, put the truck in Park, yanked up the emergency brake and turned to face her, resting his hand on the back of her seat.

She should get out right now. Tell him she forgot something and get out and go back into the house. He'd understand. He always did.

Instead she felt a small thrill run through her when she thought, looking at the earnestness in his eyes, that she could divorce Howard and marry Miklov if she wanted. Trade Howard and the Riverside Drive apartment for this house and give the children a young father who adored them. Miklov could coach. He could get his college degree and teach. That's what he should do. She almost laughed out loud; imagine, her with a twenty-six-year-old former Czech soccer star in Woodbury!

Oh, my, she shouldn't even joke about it. Poor Miklov was so lonely he'd go for it in a second, although she was pretty sure he'd get over her in a hurry when she told him she wouldn't be having any more children.

Or maybe she would have just one more.

"What you thinking?" he asked her, smiling.

"I am thinking about what a lovely wife, family and home you shall have, Miklov."

"Thank you." He gestured toward the windshield. "Have you seen up there?" He pointed across the road to her neighbor's vast property.

"I don't think anyone is allowed up there," she said, looking up.

"There ess chain, yes," he said, "but I log for him, the owner."

She looked at him in amazement. "You do?"

He nodded. "I cut wood." He smiled, eyes twinkling. "I haf wood for you. For Chreesmas. Can I show you?" Excited now, he released the parking brake and put the truck into gear. "I stack tomorrow. At your house." He drove down their road and pulled into the dirt road that led up to what the children called The Mountain. The road was blocked off with a steel gate and chain. There were a lot of problems around here with people on all-terrain vehicles.

"I have key," Miklov said, yanking the emergency brake again and hopping down out of the truck. The lock came off and the chain dropped to the ground and he turned around to point out to Amanda the sudden break in the clouds. "The sun!"

Amanda was grateful. Even with the heater working, she was getting cold.

Miklov walked back to the truck in the easy gait that identified him at every game. "Wait till you see." He drove the truck through and then hopped out again to close the gate. "Mr. Fenn nice guy," he said, climbing back in.

"Is that who owns the land?"

"Yes." Miklov put the truck into gear and the springs started squeaking as they moved over small pits and rocks. "Cutting wood in this place makes me feel…" He pounded his chest once with his fist and Amanda thought about the night he told her she was beautiful. "Wait till you see."

"It's a very narrow road, isn't it?" she said as the fur trees seemed to close in on them.

"You must care for deetches." He nodded his head toward her side of the road. "For rain."

Amanda looked down. Indeed there were ditches on the side of the road. "Promise me, Miklov, that you won't bring Teddy up here. Because if you do he will try to sneak over here and then we'll never find him."

"He leesten. You do not have to worry."

"*Some*times he listens," Amanda said.

"We see when older," Miklov said, downshifting into *2,* the gears working hard as the road dramatically steepened. "Maybe one day he work with me. Make him strong."

"Is that snow?" Amanda asked, leaning into her window. The trees blocked out so much of the light it was difficult to see.

Miklov pulled the headlights on. "Snow," he confirmed.

In a short while they reached a landing of sorts and Miklov carefully parked.

"Oh!" Amanda said, when a view suddenly opened before her. It appeared they were on the top of a cliff, a granite ledge, and were looking out over the Woodbury hills. Perhaps on a day clear of snow or rain one could see houses but right now all Amanda could see were the rolling hills of Connecticut. It was absolutely beautiful.

"A reserve," Miklov said, pointing to a lake in the distance.

"Reservoir," she said gently.

"Resevwar," he said.

Amanda reached for the door handle to get out. He quickly turned off the engine and jumped out to open the door for her. She climbed out and walked nearer to the edge of the cliff. Once the truck door was closed it was completely silent. Beautiful. The snow was coming down.

Miklov came up to stand next to her. "No build at resevwar," he said, gesturing. "But here—" He stamped in place. "Here can build." He looked at her. "I dream build here."

She smiled.

"Mr. Fenn know I save for thees."

Amanda grimaced slightly. "I'm afraid it will be very expensive."

"Here? No. Must have generator, well, septic. Mr. Fenn keep rest of land."

Her head kicked back a little. "You wouldn't have electricity up here? Or water?"

"No. Zooning?"

"Zoning."

"But," he said, accentuating with his hands, "he say, and town say self-suffishent fine. Pass inspectzion, and okay. I am fine." He held his hands up as much as to say, Voilà! "Oh. My geeft," he said, leading her around to the other side of the truck.

"Good grief, Miklov," Amanda said, slightly agog at the tremendous pile of firewood in a clearing in the woods.

"Not all!" he laughed. "One cord, that is Merry Chreesmas. I bring and stack tomorrow."

"You're very, very generous," she said, looking around. "Did you clear all of this? By yourself?"

"I rent equipment, bring it up and then breeng it down. Yes, I do this all." He was smiling, clearly very pleased with what he had accomplished. "Mr. Fenn say put llama here maybe."

"Llama?" She looked around and shrugged. "I suppose."

Miklov walked her around, explaining Mr. Fenn's plan. (Amanda vowed to find out more about this amazing Mr. Fenn. Either he was Miklov's guardian angel or was planning to take terrible advantage of him.) They walked back to the cliff while Miklov built his imaginary house in front of Amanda's eyes. It was stone. A roof of hand-planed cedar shingles. Forest-green shutters that really closed over the windows. Two fireplaces. A large wood-burning stove in the basement. Duct work to rooms. Solar panels behind screen of firs. Stone house with generators. Red barn with wood-burning stove.

They stood in silence for a while, then, each admiring his house and view.

"I luff you, Amanda," Miklov said.

She turned to look at him. She didn't smile. She didn't frown. She just stood there. "Yes, I think I've known that," she finally said. "I'm sorry, it's not fair, is it?"

Judging from his expression he understood what she meant.

"You make me feel good, Miklov. My children love you so much. And you are my friend." She swallowed, wiping some snow off her face, and tried to smile. "We laugh a lot, don't we? All of us?"

Miklov nodded. "Because it's happy."

"Yes." She looked back out over the cliff, wondering where to go from here. She had asked for this, had she not? Coming up here with him? She wished she could even remember what Howard looked like right now, remember when he had cared, or looked at her even remotely the way Miklov was looking at her now.

She might kiss Miklov, she realized. If for no other reason than to remember what it felt like to feel something again. Because she did feel something right now. She felt like an attractive woman alone with a good-looking young man who thought he was in love with her. He didn't know yet, which one day he would, that what he was in love with was America. That what he saw in her and her children was a sense of belonging to this great country.

She represented his future to him. And so he didn't see anything but that.

Miklov held his hand out to her.

All Miklov needed was someone to steep him in manners and etiquette. He needed to learn a few ballroom dancing steps, to read a newspaper each day and be outfitted with khakis and Oxford shirts and loafers and a blazer. He needed a hand-tailored suit, navy-blue, some dress shirts and black shoes with tassles. (He had found the right haircut, she saw; and he was personally well-kept to a fault.) If Miklov was given this life-kit Amanda was certain she could find him an educated American wife with a little background. He was nice-looking, hardworking, had a good heart and possessed that male prowess that Amanda's son instinctively knew he wanted. No doubt when he became an American through marriage Miklov would become a Republican, a thought that almost made her laugh out loud, but nonetheless she knew would be true.

She had waited too long to respond to Miklov's gesture because he came over to take her hand and bring it up to hold against his chest. "No, I'm sorry," she quickly murmured, taking her hand away and stepping back. She wasn't the least bit afraid of Miklov. It was what she felt inside, her insidious imagination taking flight and building that house up here, a place where she could escape with Miklov during the day and sometimes at night until he tired of her or she had brought him far enough along to marry him off. That would be her gift to him, in return for making her feel alive again and feel like a sexual being again, like a woman with a life of her own and choices of her own, including how to fill the hours her husband had abandoned her with.

Miklov stepped forward and took Amanda in his arms to kiss her. It startled her, how well he kissed, and she thought he was as graceful in all things as he was in things athletic. His arms tightened around her, pulling her more firmly against him, and he brought his lower body against her, sliding his tongue into her mouth.

It was astonishing, really, how strong the urge came back, how much she longed to give herself to him, and he knew what he was about, yes, he certainly did, because he effortlessly moved them over to the truck without breaking off the kiss or the pressure of his lower body. He reached behind him to open the passenger side door and then pulled her around it to back her against the seat. Still kissing her he slid down the zipper of her coat and plunged his hands inside to touch her breasts through her sweater. He groaned then, sliding his hands under her as he pressed into her again. Then he did the most extraordinary thing. He grabbed her hands and pulled them down to feel the bulging mass in his pants, and he held her hands in place and began thrusting against them. Very quickly afterward he broke off their kiss to utter a small cry next to her ear. Then he gave one last heave against her and shuddered.

He collapsed against her, a dead weight, panting. Then he pushed her hands away, the job finished. When he slid his hand between her legs she said, "No." He pulled his hand away and then, a moment later, pushed himself up. He did not look at her, but stood there, his hands now in his coat pockets. He was looking at her breasts.

"I want so long," he said. His eyes came up. "I want—"

"No," she told him and she pushed herself up from the truck and walked away a few steps, rocks crunching under her barn boots, and zipped up her coat. Then she looked up at the sky, the snow falling wet on her face.

In Which Sam Overhears a Conversation

THE DOORMAN SAID Harriet had arrived fifteen minutes earlier and since Sam was home early, too, and Harriet had not said anything about coming home early he knew something was up. No doubt whatever it was had to do with Samantha. That's why he had come home early without telling Harriet, to have another go-round with Samantha before Harriet came home and was upset by it.

He let himself in the front door quietly, put his briefcase down, stuffed his gloves in his pockets and slipped off his overcoat to hang it in the front hall closet. He thought he heard talking as he crossed the living room and tried to pretend he was walking with his usual heavy tread but knew he wasn't. When Sam reached the back hall he stopped because he heard Harriet say, "No, it's *not* good enough, Samantha."

Samantha said something he couldn't make out.

"It *is* important, young lady," Harriet said. "With *all* the advantages you've enjoyed in your life, with *all* the education you've received, with *all* the emotional and financial support at your disposal, how could you have allowed yourself to get pregnant when you have absolutely no intention of keeping the child?"

"I coulda gotten an abortion," Samantha said.

"That's not the issue, Samantha," Harriet said. "The issue is *how* you got pregnant. *How* you could have unprotected sex. Or *why* you would deliberately have unprotected sex so that you would get pregnant."

"It's a little late to be worrying about that now, don't you think?"

"Darlin' child, you're not even twenty years old. I can only pray I'm being early for the next crisis you're bound to have since you seem to have learned nothing from this experience."

"You're not even curious about how long I've been having sex? *Mommy?*" The way she said the last made Sam clench his fists.

"Samantha."

After a long moment. "What?"

"You can fool your father but you can't fool me. I know you got pregnant on purpose."

"I didn't do it on purpose," Samantha said.

"Oh, I think you most certainly did."

There was a long silence in Samantha's room.

"He's married, isn't he?"

Sam frowned, his stomach churning.

"I'm going to take that as a yes." Harriet sounded very tired suddenly. "So my next question—how old is this man?"

"Why? What difference does it make?" Samantha said, her voice rising.

His daughter's nerve was finally starting to give. A crack was widening in the wall of stubborn willfulness. At last.

"Because you adore your father and it would not surprise me if you were attracted to someone somewhat like him."

"You think I want to—"

"No," Harriet said angrily. "You know perfectly well what I mean. We all grow up with the adults around us being role models. We associate love with certain traits of those people we grew up loving. So what I'm saying, Samantha, is, it would not surprise me if you felt drawn to an older man because your father was older when you were born, and if he *is* anything at all like your father, then it would mean he has a family."

He couldn't hear if Samantha was saying anything or not.

"Let me guess. He's tall, right? And a big man, right?"

"Stop it," Samantha said. She was crying.

"How long has this been going on?"

Silence.

"Samantha—"

"No! I'm not telling you! You'll wreck everything!"

Sam, feeling dry-mouthed and weak, leaned into the wall and held the bridge of his nose in his hand. He imagined Harriet would be near apoplexy at this point. She was on the right track, though.

"What kind of man would leave you down here all by yourself while you're about to give birth to his child?" Harriet said. "Forget the fact he's married, Samantha. A real man, a man who cares about you, would have shown up here by now to talk to me and your father. Not sneak around and call you while we're not here. Samantha, he's not even sneaking here to *see* you. Don't you see? You cannot throw this baby away simply because it would be inconvenient for *him.*"

"He doesn't want it," Samantha said, starting to sob. "I can't even see him until it's *gone.*"

The crying went on for some time. "Sugar, don't you know

how much your father and I love you?" No answer. "Don't you think we would go to the ends of the earth for you if we thought this relationship was something that would make you happy?" No answer. "But to punish us, and to punish your sister, because this man—"

"You don't understand, I love him!" Samantha wailed.

Sam gritted his teeth, pushing his forehead against the wall.

There was no talking for a while, only the sound of crying. He imagined Harriet might be trying to calm her. "Is he one of your professors?" she asked quietly after a while.

"No." He heard Samantha blow her nose and then clear her throat. "He works at a pharmaceutical company. He's a sales director."

"How did you meet him?"

"In Starbucks."

"When?"

"About the second month I was in school."

Pause. "When you were a *freshman?*" Silence. "Does he live in Utica?"

"Binghamton." She cleared her throat.

"So how did you see him?"

"He comes to Utica on business sometimes." Pause. "Sometimes I travel with him. He picks me up and we go on trips."

Sam felt the rage starting.

"Trips to where?"

He couldn't hear what Samantha said, but it was a long rambling narrative.

"We wouldn't care, Samantha," Harriet said, "if he was a good man, a good man for you, your father would get over it. His color would make no difference to us as long as you were happy."

He's white.

Samantha was talking again.

A string of expletives were running through Sam's mind. Of course the son of a bitch was in sales, no doubt he was good-looking, quick on his feet, smooth, always with an angle… He'd heard enough.

Sam walked back to the front door and opened it. Then he slammed it so hard the front hall mirror shifted against the wall. *"Hello, I'm home!"* he called, opening and slamming the front hall closet. "Where is everybody?"

He had to keep his cool. Somehow.

He took a deep breath and let it out slowly.

Harriet had gotten Samantha started and now he needed to subtly confer with her before she went any further. She had to get a name on this guy, even just a first name and the company, and then Sam knew he could find him.

Amanda is a Mess

THERE WERE NO words that could fully express the loathing Amanda felt for herself.

Silently she got into the truck. Miklov walked over to pick up her hat from the ground and brought it into the truck with him.

She stared straight ahead. The snow was really coming down now.

Miklov started the truck, turned on the lights and the wipers, carefully backed around and started slowly down the mountain. When he stopped to open the gate she climbed down out of the truck and told him she wished to walk home. He hurried over, saying something about it being too dark.

"What I have done is unforgivable," she said to him.

"But you did not—"

"If I did not have my children, Miklov, I swear I would go home and slit my wrists." Then she looked down, shaking her head, thinking, *That is why I want to slit my wrists, because I don't deserve to be their mother.*

"Leesten—" Miklov had firmly taken hold of her arm and given it a shake. "I luff you."

"I do not love you, Miklov," she said. "I did a bad thing. I hope someday you will forgive me." She pried his fingers loose. "Please don't hurt my children because of me." And then she started down the road.

Emily's mother. Teddy's mother. Grace's mother. Madame Moliere's employer. Howard Stewart's wife, for better or for worse, Mrs. Stewart.

If what transpired on the mountain did not so sharply remind Amanda of what she had once been like she might have found some small space left on which she could stand to forgive herself.

The sickness she felt inside reminded her of how much she did love Howard. She remembered now what it felt like to fall in love with him. Miklov had even reminded her of what their passion had been like. So her body wasn't dead, it was just their relationship.

She climbed the driveway and stripped off her gear in the mudroom. She went upstairs to tell Madame Moliere she was back and then went into their bathroom to take a long hot shower, crying while she did so. She was slightly better afterward; at least she could carry on a conversation with Madame Moliere. The children came home and while Amanda listened to how their day went she knew she had to do something because her marriage was falling apart, she was falling apart. And if she fell apart, the way Howard was lately, the whole family would fall apart.

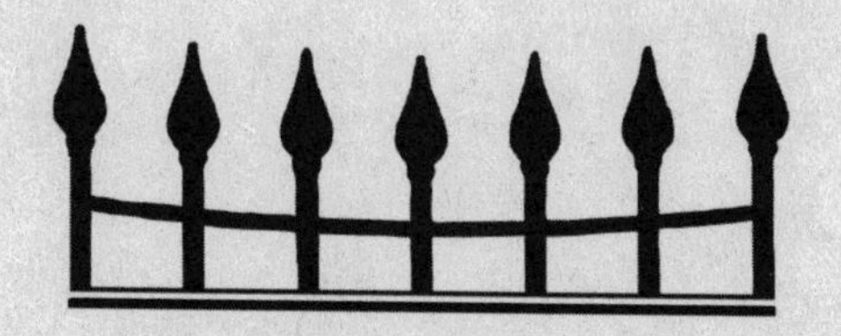

JANUARY

Cassy

IT WAS A heavy burden that Emma had given Cassy to carry over the holidays, particularly when, between Christmas and New Year's, Emma's health failed so quickly Cassy needed to stay in Manhattan, scrambling to find hospice care.

"They said I could try chemotherapy," Emma explained, "but I told my doctor that was nonsense at my age, I would do no such thing."

"But why, Emma?" Cassy said, feeling so deeply saddened. Why was it that wonderfully loving and giving people like Emma had to go when people like her own mother, who was going to be bitter and angry and venomous to the very end of her life, seemed to stay on forever? She didn't wish her mother dead, certainly, but there was no sign whatsoever of the mellowness Cassy had been told to expect her mother to achieve at a certain age. Soon even Cassy's hefty "donations" to the resident's board wouldn't keep her mother where she was. ("If your mother would just stay away from the clubhouse," they would tell Cassy, "it might be all right, but she plants herself in the middle of everything and says the most unkind things to people.")

"Because my turn on this earth is coming to an end," the old woman said with a smile. "And I am ready to go. Daniel is in a better place," she explained, referring to her son, "so I don't worry about him as I once did. My affairs are now in order and Mr. Thatcher gave me his word my final wishes shall be carried out to the letter."

Cassy smiled encouragingly, feeling her throat tighten.

"It is Rosanne I worry about." Mrs. Goldblum sighed. Her eyes got a little teary and she withdrew a hankie from her sleeve, removed her glasses and patted her eyes, blew her nose, and then replaced everything where it had been. "I had hoped by now she and Randy would be married but that does not seem to be in the cards. Young Jason will be going off to college and I—I fear for her happiness," she continued. "After all that schooling and expense, golly oh, my, Cassy, to find that she loathes it! She has a degree and experience—"

"She can get a job anywhere."

"The poor dear is miserable and I— Well, I've simply run out of time."

Cassy blinked back tears. "You know I will help her, Emma. You don't have to ask."

"But I must ask. Because she is so proud— Oh, dear Cassy, there is no need to cry."

She had been trying so hard not to.

"No, no," Mrs. Goldblum murmured, reaching for her hand. "I long to be with my husband." She looked out her living room window at the river. "I dream about him almost every night." After a long moment, she turned back to Cassy. "I am so tired, dear, so very, very tired." She smiled then. "So many people I love are waiting for me."

Cassy's daughter-in-law, Maria, had been due to give birth at any moment and so the young Cochrans had remained in California for the holidays. Jackson had gone to Georgia for Christmas and then on to Idaho to ski. Cassy had spent Christmas Eve night with Alexandra and had ended up driving her out to Connecticut the next day, where she'd sat down to dinner with Sally Harrington's family and Alexandra's brother, David. After dinner Alexandra, David and Sally had flown out of Hartford to make the trek to Waring Farm in Kansas.

The day after Christmas the task could be put off no longer. Cassy had been forced to sit down with Rosanne and Jason. Rosanne, she knew, was aware that Emma was failing but her first reaction was one of anger, how could Mrs. G not take the treatment that was being offered, but even while Rosanne had been saying this, the anger had left her voice and then she stopped speaking altogether and looked at Jason. "To be honest, Jason, I bet it was optional treatment. I don't think your gran could have taken very much of it before— You know how fragile she's gotten."

"So she's going to die?" Jason asked.

Rosanne nodded. "Yes. And I think Mrs. C is here because your gran wanted her to help us arrange things." She looked at Cassy. "She wants to stay here, doesn't she? Her husband died in the bedroom by the window."

"Here?" Jason said, panicking. "Gran wants to die *here?*"

"That's her wish," Cassy said quietly.

"But she's got to go to the hospital!" Jason said to his mother. "Everybody goes to the hospital to die."

"The thing is, Jason," Cassy said as gently as she could, "she does not want to go to the hospital anymore. She wants to be here, in the place she loves most."

"It's not going to happen today, sweetie," Rosanne sighed, pulling her son's head down to her shoulder to hold him, as though he were still a little boy.

When it comes to death, we all feel little, Cassy thought.

"I'll petition for family leave next week," Rosanne said.

"Rosanne." This was the tricky part. "Emma does not want you nursing her."

"Well, that's her all over, isn't it?" Rosanne said, kissing the side of Jason's head as he pulled out of her embrace. "For Pete's sake, Mrs. C, who could be a better nurse than me?"

"A stranger." Cassy let her answer hang there a moment. "She wants hospice to come in. She doesn't want you to remember her, well, less than presentable. She wants you to remember her being—" Cassy smiled against her tears "—neat and tidy, as always. So you can enjoy your time together."

"What are you talking about?" Jason said, looking at his mother. The panic was still in his voice.

"We'll have nurses' aides come in. One for each twelve hours. If we're lucky, though, and we find the right agency, maybe we could have one aide and have her stay around the clock. So your gran won't get confused." Rosanne looked at Cassy. "We'd make my room the nurse's station, I guess."

Despite all the estate planning Attorney Thatcher had done, trying to organize hospice care, or even to find the right agency, wasn't easy. "If the president of the fifth largest TV network in the country can't make head or tail out of these medicare and insurance forms, just who the hell can expect the elderly to deal with them?" Cassy demanded of the poor medicare worker she had on the phone.

"You can't just get a wheelchair," Rosanne explained to Cassy. "You gotta have the doctor write out a prescription for one or it's not covered."

"That agency has only been around for a year," Rosanne explained, "I wouldn't use them."

"No guy. She'll flip out," Rosanne explained to Cassy. "It's gotta be a woman. Ask if they have anyone from Jamaica. Those gals are always great readers and it would be great if they could read to her."

It took Cassy, Rosanne, Attorney Thatcher and Cassy's accountant to sort everything out.

"Darlin', just get whoever you want in there and write a check!" Jackson told her.

"That's exactly what Emma fears and I promised her I wouldn't. It means a great deal to her to be able to see her way on her own resources."

"Yeah, well, this is costing like eight hundred dollars an hour of your time."

"It's no different than what you did for your aunt Biscuit, Jack."

"At least I was related to her."

"Well, at this point, I *am* related to Emma."

"What about Amanda Stewart? Why isn't she wrestling with all this paperwork?"

"Because Amanda doesn't know yet. Rosanne and Emma said we should wait until after the holidays. The Stewarts are staying in the country this year."

By the time Cassy returned to work in January she was exhausted. The hospice care was in place, however, and Rosanne and Emma both liked the RN in charge of Emma's case, the nurses' aides that were brought in, and also the social worker who served as a family therapist overseeing the process.

★ ★ ★

"So who is your designated health care proxy?" Alexandra asked, emerging from the bedroom of the East End apartment, tying the sash of her silk robe. She had come in from the studio not ten minutes before and gone straight into the shower.

Cassy had prepared one of Alexandra's favorites, a platter of Mediterranean roasted chicken and vegetables and was just taking it out of the oven using pot holders.

"Oh, wow, that looks great," the anchorwoman said appreciatively, sniffing over Cassy's shoulder and then giving her a quick kiss on the neck. "So who is your proxy?"

"I'm beginning to think," Cassy said, carrying the platter in to the dining room table, "the rule against talking about work here should extend to issues of health care." She had taken all the leaves out of the table to make it a small round one, spread a white linen tablecloth over it, and set it with silver, cloth napkins and candles, the real deal because they had not seen one another privately since Christmas and she wanted to make an effort.

"So it's Jackson," Alexandra surmised, turning the chandelier lights off as she came in to sit down. "Cassy, this is just beautiful. Thank you."

"You're very welcome."

Alexandra started to put her napkin in her lap but then got up again and came around the table to kiss her. "I mean it, thank you." Her eyes were large and luminous in the candlelight.

"You're welcome, darling," Cassy murmured, reaching for the carving utensils.

"I find that I'm missing you more rather than less as time goes on," she said, returning to her side of the table with a swish of silk.

Cassy started carving the chicken. "You were expecting to care for me less?"

"You're the one who always says, 'Familiarity breeds contempt.'"

"That must have been another lover," Cassy said, laughing, putting white meat on Alexandra's plate. "What I've always said is, 'Surely there will come a time you won't find me sexually attractive anymore.'"

"How many times in the past have I wished that to be true," Alexandra sighed, watching her.

Cassy added roasted Bermuda onion, new potatoes, tomatoes and olives to the plate and handed it to Alexandra. Cassy smiled to herself when she recognized Alexandra's expression. She was thinking about sex. As tired as she was, the mere thought of Alexandra thinking about it did something to Cassy. Was this normal? To be aroused so often at her age?

Certainly it was a credit to Alexandra's proficiency in matters so intimately physical. She smiled to herself as she served herself.

"Would you be my health care proxy?" Alexandra asked.

Cassy raised an eyebrow, putting the serving utensils down on the side of the platter. "If you would like me to be."

"I assume you're Jackson's," Alexandra said, sipping water from her crystal glass, "because those kids would kill him the first chance they got."

"Yes, I am Jackson's," Cassy said, picking up her fork, "but he is not mine."

"No? Who is?"

"Henry." She ate some of the food. It was, if she did say so herself, excellent.

"Was Jackson ever it?"

She swallowed, nodding. "When we were first married."

"And then you changed it?"

Cassy sighed and put her fork down. "Yes. I changed it."

"Do you think I will ever be it?" Alexandra asked her.

"Must we talk about this now?"

"No, we don't," Alexandra said.

They continued eating in silence for a while. Then Alexandra started telling her stories about how Sally Harrington got on with her future in-laws in Kansas. Evidently they had all had an interesting time of it. "Do you suppose you'll ever come with me? To Kansas?"

"As what?" Cassy asked, sipping her water.

"Well, how about the love of my life?"

Cassy looked at her. "I think your parents would drop dead of shock." She cocked her head slightly. "What's going on with you?"

Alexandra shrugged, finishing the last piece of chicken and onion on her plate and put her fork down. "I was just wondering—" she patted her mouth with her napkin "—if I were dying, Cassy, would you leave Jackson then? If I asked you to?"

Cassy's heart jumped into her throat.

"No!" Alexandra said quickly, "I'm fine. I'm healthy as a horse."

"Thank God," Cassy said, slumping back against her chair. She threw her napkin on the table. "For a second—"

"Actually," Alexandra said, putting her elbows down on the table and resting her head in her hands, "if I were dying, I wouldn't ask you to live with me. Because it would be too sad. To finally have you where I've always wanted you, since the night I first met you, but knowing I had to die to get you there."

It was Emma's situation that was stirring this up. Cassy wasn't immune, either. She had been thinking a lot about the things she might want to do before the end of her life and at this point she couldn't pretend Alexandra didn't figure heavily into it.

Cassy pushed her chair back to stand up and left her napkin on the chair. She circled the table and knelt by Alexandra's chair. She took her right hand, pressed it to her mouth and then lowered it. "I do want to get there," she said quietly. Then she dropped her forehead to rest on Alexandra's thigh. It amazed her to think Alexandra did not seem to know all that she meant to her. Which had, very quickly, it seemed, come close to everything. She raised her head. "Darling, if I move in with you, it will be because I intend to spend the rest of my life with you. And nothing less."

Alexandra slid out of her chair to her knees. She touched Cassy's hair, her eyes thoughtful. "Could it be that we're really getting somewhere?" She smiled, meeting Cassy's eyes. "Do you think?"

"I'm not really sure," Cassy said truthfully, "but it feels like it."

Over the course of the night it became clearer to Cassy that, yes, they seemed to really be getting somewhere.

Jason Tells His Mother

"HELLO?" ROSANNE SAID into the phone as she pulled sheets out of the washer and put them in the dryer.

"Mrs. DiSantos?"

"Yes."

"This is Celia Cavanaugh calling from Captain Cook's."

"Jason's not here, Celia." She considered explaining that he was staying in the Cochrans' old apartment because Mrs. G's illness and the nurse's aide were upsetting him to the point he couldn't sleep, but decided it was none of her business. "I can take a message, though."

"I wanted to let him know a good job's opened up at Park West Café. I've already talked to them about him. And I think if he'd just go over tonight and see a guy named Rich he'll get the job. It's bussing, but I think it'll turn into waiting tables in June."

Rosanne made a face, straightening up. "He's got to work tonight."

There was decided hesitation on the other end.

"Don't you work tonight, too, Celia? I thought you worked Tuesday nights," Rosanne said, tearing off a sheet of fabric softener and tossing it into the dryer. She closed the door, set the timer and turned it on.

"I just wanted to make sure he heard about this job, Mrs. DiSantos."

"Uh-huh," Rosanne said, stepping out of the laundry area and closing the louver doors. The nurse's aide was in the kitchen getting more ice water. She was trying to get Mrs. G to drink more water. Why she thought Mrs. G would drink more water now when she disliked drinking it even when she was in the pink of health Rosanne had no idea, but then, everyone kept telling her that Virginia was in charge of Mrs. G, not her.

"I'll see he gets the message, Celia," she promised before hanging up. "Virginia, I'm going out for a little while. Can I pick up anything? I thought we'd have sole tonight. Mrs. G said she thought it sounded good to her."

"I love filet of sole," the aide said. "That would be very nice."

She had given Virginia her bedroom to use as a sitting room so she could hear if Mrs. G needed her. Rosanne in the meantime was bunking in Jason's room and Jason was over in Mrs. C's old place. He came to visit Mrs. G every day. He just couldn't sleep here, he was so nervous about her dying. The social worker said it had to do with how his father had died when he was young.

The reality hadn't fully dawned on her yet, Rosanne knew.

"Why aren't you getting ready for work?" Rosanne asked Jason, closing the apartment door of Mrs. C's old apartment and following him into the kitchen.

His school books were all over the breakfast bar. His shirttail was hanging out over his jeans and he was walking around in his socks, which is what Rosanne had asked him to do so he wouldn't mess up Mrs. C's floors. He took his place at his books, picked up a pencil and twiddled it next to his ear.

"Jason?"

"I had this paper to do," he began.

"You just took two weeks off and now you're taking tonight off?"

He sighed heavily, eyes on the book in front of him. "It's sorta complicated, Mom."

"Well uncomplicate it," she told him, taking off her coat. "September's going to be here before you know it and you'll be grateful for every single penny you save. Or at least *I* will." She tossed the coat on one of the stools. "So what's this paper?"

"It's like a calculus thing."

"Not my favorite thing," she said, looking over his shoulder. "Before I forget, Celia called. She sounded a little vague on the subject of you working tonight, too."

Her son's reaction was almost visceral. Now he looked at her as though she had plunged a knife in his back. "Celia Cavanaugh?"

"She said there was a job bussing tables at Park West Café that would probably turn into waiting tables in June. She said if you're interested you should go there tonight and ask for Rich. She said she already talked to him about you and says if you go over tonight you'll probably get the job."

He had turned away from her and the back of his ears had turned very red.

"Jason, did you get fired?"

He shook his head, his back to her still.

Rosanne shifted her weight onto her left foot, plunking her right hand on her hip. "What's going on, Jason?"

He hung his head a little. "I quit."

"I thought you loved working there."

"Not anymore," he mumbled.

She took a step closer and softened her tone of voice. "Jason. Turn around and look at me, please." Reluctantly he did. "When did you quit?"

"Just before Christmas."

"Why didn't you tell me?"

"I was gonna." He shrugged. "Then Gran got sick and everything." He looked up at the clock and started to slide off the stool. "I guess I should go over to Park West Café."

Rosanne pushed him back down on the stool. "What happened at Captain Cook's?"

He tried to meet her eyes but failed. "I was tired of it."

She put her hands on his shoulders. "Tell me the truth."

"I just didn't want to be there anymore." His ears were still burning red.

"Jason," she said warningly.

He twisted away from her and got up off the stool. "It's not something you talk to your mother about."

The only things boys did not talk to their mothers about were sex and drugs. And maybe violence. Since she knew two were not presently at issue she assumed it was the first. "There's a girl there?"

Bingo. The flush spreading across his face told her she was right.

"She's not a girl," he mumbled, jamming his hand into his pocket and tracing the kitchen door jam with the toe of his sock.

What did *that* mean? "How old is she?"

"Twenty-four."

Twenty-four! It had to be a crush, then, right? He was in high school. "Celia Cavanaugh?" she guessed.

After a moment he nodded, eyes still on the doorjamb. "She doesn't like me the way I like her."

"She's a lot older than you are, Jason."

His head kicked up and she could see anger in his face. "That's not it, Mom. I wasn't too young for her. She just doesn't want a boyfriend, she doesn't want a relationship."

Rosanne felt the tiniest sliver of fear. "Just how far did this relationship between you go?"

"It was just—you know," he said, sliding his hands into his back pockets. There was the slightest touch of pride in his voice and Rosanne started to feel light-headed. She swallowed, trying to see her son in the same way strangers might: tall, nice-looking, the new need to shave regularly, his sweet nature.

"No, I don't know," she said trying to keep her voice even.

"I have to go to that restaurant," he said, turning away.

"Don't you dare take another step. Not until you explain to me what has been going on between you and that bartender."

When he turned back around she saw a mixture of fear and defiance in Jason's eyes. This was one of those defining moments Mrs. C used to warn her about. "Okay, Mom. Have it your way."

She waited.

"Go on, ask me, if you want to know so bad."

This was not how she had imagined Jason's first love would be. He still played video games and watched cartoons on TV.

"I screwed her, Mom, all right?" he suddenly said. "Isn't that what you want to know?"

Rosanne caught her breath and then straightened to her full height, throwing her shoulders back. "Jason Frank DiSantos, you will *never* use that kind of language again, do you hear me? And you will *never* use that kind of language about what is—what *should* be—a sacred act between two people." *Yeah, right,* she thought, *that's me and Randy, sacred every Saturday night.*

"That's what you care about, Mom?" he said, angry, coming toward her. "My language? Aren't you even worried she might be knocked up like your sweet little Sammy Wyatt who you spend all your time with?"

She slapped him. Hard. Rosanne had never done that before and the red mark it left on Jason's face made her feel sick. "You have no right to judge other people," she told him. They glared at one another until she finally stared him down and he backed away a step, turning his back to her. "So Celia the bartender is *not* pregnant, is that right?"

"Right," he said, resting his hands on the breakfast bar.

"You're going in for a complete physical." She took a breath. "You're going to get tested for AIDS, for herpes, for—"

"She's not like that, Mom."

"And how could you possibly know that?" she said, grabbing his arm and turning him around. "How can you know where she's been, where the men she's slept with have been—"

"She's not like that, Mom, so just shut up about her."

"This is what tells me you are still a child, Jason. That's why I am scared. Because whether you like it or not, a twenty-four-year-old woman has no business messing with a boy in high school!"

He suddenly whirled around to pound the breakfast bar with his fist. "Shut up, Mom!" He turned back around, tears threatening. "She's not like that. She's a wonderful person. And I love her, Mom. Okay? And I wouldn't love her unless she was something special."

Oh, she's something special all right, Rosanne thought.

Sam Has a Visitor at the Office

THE EXECUTIVE COMMITTEE meeting dragged on. On the table was whether or not Electronika International would altogether close down its plant in central Connecticut and, if and when they did, would they build a new plant in a right-to-work state or move that entire end of production to China. No one at the company wanted to shut down the plant but they couldn't afford the northeast union wages and benefits anymore and they were getting hammered with taxes on their property and equipment.

"What do you think, Sam?" the president asked from one end of the long boardroom table.

Since Sam's thirty-year career at the company had largely been spent in marketing, he knew the question was being asked in terms of public relations. Just how bad would the fallout be for pulling the manufacture of high-end office equipment out of the States? And should Electronika even care about fallout since their key competitor had already moved production to China and was killing them with lower prices?

Sam leaned forward, folding his hands somewhat gravely in front of him, his wedding band catching the sunlight. They were on the twenty-third floor and had a view of the East River. He was one of two people of color in the room. The human resources director, a woman, was half Puerto Rican and half something very white. Skin did not get much darker than Sam's, and he liked how the crisp white cotton sleeves of his Brooks Brothers shirt looked against it.

"I think we should consider going public with our problem," Sam said.

"If we delay shutting down that plant it won't just be a problem anymore," the controller said, "it will be our disaster."

"Go on, Sam," the president encouraged. He had been in the office for four years now. At forty-five he was the youngest president they had ever had.

"From here on in let's make the whole process public."

"Would that be including the pending brain-cancer lawsuits?" someone said sarcastically.

"I think we call the *Times* and say, this is where we are, these are the choices we currently have and we want the public to understand what's going on. Then we tell the governor of Connecticut we can't afford to do business there anymore, which is the absolute truth. Then we set up a summit with the governor and Connecticut union guys to see what, if anything, can be done to keep us there. And then we set up a summit with, say, the governor of Arizona, about what would be possible in a right-to-work state. We give the numbers out to the public all the way, what it costs to do business in Connecticut, what it costs in Arizona, and then what it costs in China to produce what we need."

"To a certain extent we're already doing that," the president said.

"What about the brain-cancer suits?" someone said again.

While legal started talking about that, Sam made some notes regarding an overall corporate image rehab. He was somewhat startled when his secretary came in to drop a note in front of him.

Althea is here to see you. She says not to hurry, she brought work to do.

"I am telling you," the controller said, "unless union workers increase their contribution to their health care we can't use union workers anymore, period."

The meeting went on for another half hour, during which nothing was resolved except the president was going to make a highly publicized trip to Connecticut and Arizona.

When Sam returned to his office he couldn't help but smile when he saw Althea sitting on the couch, typing away on her laptop. When she was very little she sometimes came in with him on Saturday mornings and sat on the floor and colored on the coffee table. By the time she was six she was scribbling nonsense on sheets of paper—alternating between being president of the United States and a movie star—doing somersaults down the thickly carpeted hallways and looking for other workers who had come in to catch up because they might give her some candy.

Now Althea made twice the money he and Harriet did combined.

"Hi," he said coming in, "this is a nice surprise."

"Hi, Dad, hang on a sec—" She finished typing something. He made his way to his desk, tossing his legal pad on it and took his seat. Althea walked over to the door. "Do you mind if I close this for a minute?"

"No, not at all," he said. He watched her as she closed the door and came back to sit down in front of his desk. It was hard sometimes to equate the little girl looking for candy with this poised and confident woman. Althea was like him in that she loved well-fitted and finely made clothes, but she had a grace in her movements he had never possessed.

"Would the great and powerful Oz also mind coming out from behind that curtain?"

The desk. She didn't like to talk to him while he was behind it. Sam smiled, shaking his head, and got up out of his very comfortable leather chair and walked around to sit down in the chair next to Althea. "So what's this?" he said, reaching for the folder.

"Wait a second," she said, pulling it away. "You can't open it yet until I explain."

"Okay." She gave it to him and Sam sat back in his chair, crossing his leg to rest his left ankle on his right knee, and tapped the folder against his leg. "Explain."

"I wanted to talk to you without Sammy or Mom around, Dad. Because I know if you back me on this then it'll happen."

"And if I don't back you?"

"I'm going to do it anyway," she told him evenly.

He nodded, biting the side of his lower lip. "I take it we're back to the baby."

She nodded. "I've served notice to the adoption agency in Utica that I'll be suing to stop the process."

"Althea," he began, shaking his head, "your mother and I—"

"Are going around in circles," she finished for him. "And it's not your fault, but you're damned if you do anything and you're damned if you don't." She brought her hand to her chest. "I don't care what Sammy thinks right now. This child should not leave our family and I'm not going to let it. And no offense, Dad, but you guys are way too old to be anything but grandparents."

Sam rubbed his face. "And what about your sister?"

"I want you and Mom to tell Sammy that unless she allows me to adopt this child then you will cut her off financially."

"You want us to commit extortion on your own sister," he said dully, opening the folder and looking through it. There were a number of legal documents.

"Whatever it takes," Althea said. She touched his arm. "She wants to get rid of the baby, Dad, so she can chase that man. You're not going to be able to stop that. She thinks she's in love with him. But you can't just let her out of this without her having to face up to the consequences for her behavior. She has to do the right thing. She has to let us keep this baby."

"So you think she did it on purpose," he said.

"I know she did," Althea said without hesitation.

Sam closed his eyes, feeling nauseous.

"It was the only way she could think of to call his bluff. To get him to leave his wife."

"Jesus," Sam said, swiping the folder and standing up. "Jesus Christ, help us all," he said, going to the window.

"It happens, Dad."

"Not with one of my daughters it doesn't," he said, pivoting around. "She was not raised this way, Althea!"

"I know," Althea said, standing up. "And Mom's dying of a broken heart. But if you just stop and think about how spoiled Sammy is, everything she does makes sense."

She stopped when she saw Sam glaring at her. If one more person said how he and Harriet had spoiled Samantha he was going to start breaking up the furniture. He had *not* raised his daughter to carry on with a married man, he had *not* raised a daughter who would try to trap a married man—

He threw himself in his chair behind his desk, tossed the folder on his desk and bent over, pretending he needed to retie his black Oxford shoe. When he sat back up he felt more in control. "Tell me again why it's fair to take away this child's chance to have a mother *and* a father?"

"You're fixated on that. Just because your childhood was miserable, Dad, doesn't mean every other child's has to be. We're not talking six kids here, Dad. We're talking about one. And imagine if Grandma had made the kind of money I do. You don't think your life would have been a lot different after your father died? Of course it would have been. Grandma would have given you the world if she could." She was leaning over his desk now. "You of all people should understand why I, as a successful black woman, cannot allow to see my own flesh and blood be given away when the child can have a warm and loving and thriving home with me." She had tears in her eyes. "You of all people, Dad, should understand that it was *you* who raised *me* to be this way, to succeed and to be independent and to have the courage to stand up and be who I am. And who I am, Dad—and I know this with all my heart—is the mother of this child."

Sam heard her. He really heard her this time. He pulled his chair closer to the desk and opened the folder again, thumbing through the papers.

"I want you to be with me when I talk to Sammy, Dad. I want you to back me up on this. If you do, I know she'll agree."

"And if she doesn't?'

"I'll sue to stop the adoption."

He nodded, turning a page. There was a document in here for Samantha to sign away all of her legal rights as a mother. It would be something she signed after the birth of the baby. There was also one for the father. The name of the father was blank.

"What if Samantha changes her mind and wants to keep the baby?"

"She won't. She's too narcissistic."

"But what if she does?" he asked, looking up at her.

"I'd want her to live with me in New York," Althea said. "Transfer to NYU. So the baby has some stability."

"And if she refuses to come back to New York with the baby? What would you do then?"

"I'm not sure. But I do know I would keep tabs on the child and make sure it wanted for nothing. Time, attention and love included."

Sam took in a long, deep breath, looking down at the papers again. Althea's commitment was there. She meant what she said. Come hell or high water she would be the guardian of this baby.

"Okay, babe," he murmured. He closed the folder and looked up at his daughter. "I'm in. Let's do it."

25

Celia Receives a Visitor at Home

CELIA WAS NOT even up yet when Rachel came into her bedroom and woke her up.

"Ceil, Ceil," she said, shaking her shoulder.

Celia raised herself up to look at the clock and then collapsed facedown in the sheets again, pulling a pillow protectively over her head.

"Damn it, Celia," Rachel said, yanking down the covers, "wake up. There's a cop at the door."

"A cop?" Celia mumbled.

"With some pissed-off lady. The cop wants to see you."

Now Celia rolled over and sat up. She tried to think. Yes, she'd had a few drinks after hours at Captain Cook's last night and then she and Jimmy the waiter had shared a joint on the walk home. But she didn't have any blackouts or anything; she hadn't done anything except come home, strip her clothes off and go to bed.

Rachel had her wardrobe open. "Where's your robe?"

"Somewhere," Celia said, surveying the piles of clothes around the room.

"Celia, come *on*. It's a cop!"

She got up and slipped on the closest pair of jeans lying on the floor, pulled a T-shirt over her head and headed for the door.

"You can't go out there like that!" Rachel whispered, frantic.

"Watch me," Celia said, walking out into the hallway. She yawned and covered her mouth. "Excuse me," she said to the uniformed officer and a short lady who were standing just outside the open door. "I work nights so I'm not really awake. What may I do for you, officer?"

"Are you Celia Cavanaugh?"

"Yes." The short lady was looking her up and down as if she was some kind of nasty garbage. "And you are?"

"Never mind who I am. You'll find out soon enough," the woman snapped.

"Officer Kellaher, New York Police Department," the officer said. "This lady has made a complaint against you concerning the sexual assault of a minor."

"I'm calling your father," Celia heard Rachel say from behind her.

"No, Rach," she said quickly, turning around. She turned back. "Officer, I have not the slightest idea what you're talking about."

"Having sex with a minor is against the law. Arrest her!" the woman instructed the cop.

Celia's elderly neighbor had opened her door just in time to hear that.

Celia was awake now. "I'm sorry, there has to be some kind of mistake."

"I'm Jason DiSantos' mother," fumed the short woman.

"Do you *still* think there's a mistake? Since you forced my son to have sex with you in order to keep his job?"

Celia tried to push down the fear. "Forced?" She shook her head and looked at the cop. "Officer, I'm a bartender at Captain Cook's, over on Columbus."

The space cadet neighbor on the other side of them had now come out of his apartment to ask if Celia needed any help.

"She's being arrested for the sexual assault of a minor," the old lady neighbor from the other side explained to the space cadet.

"I am not," Celia told her neighbor.

"You are, too!" Jason's mother said, stamping her foot. "And you'll rot in jail if I have my way. What kind of freak are you?"

"What I was trying to say, Officer," Celia sputtered, "is that her son works at Captain Cook's, too, as a busboy."

"He *used* to work there. That's where she raped him!"

Celia tried to ignore her. "You have to be at least eighteen to work in a restaurant that serves liquor. That's the law. You know it and I know it. Otherwise Jason couldn't work there. So I don't know what this is all about. He's an adult. He's a legal adult!" she shouted at her old lady neighbor.

The police officer looked at Jason's mother, who seemed to have lost some steam. Jason was probably only seventeen. Still, a seventeen-year-old boy was not considered a sexual minor.

"What the hell's the matter with you that you have to go after high school boys?" Jason's mother said to her. "Why did you have to sink your claws into Jason? He's a sweet kid and you raped him and then you dumped him and you hurt him. I've got half a mind to deck you, you smug little bitch—"

Celia stepped back, using the door as a shield, but the police officer got a hold of the woman. "Dammit, Rosanne," he said, grabbing her arms, "cut it out."

That was a weird thing for him to say.

"I'll just get her out of here now, Miss Cavanaugh," the cop said, dragging Jason's mother toward the elevator.

"You're a sick woman!" Mrs. DiSantos yelled as Celia slammed the door.

"What the hell was *that* about?" Celia cried to the ceiling on her way to the kitchen.

Rachel was just hanging up the phone. "Your dad's on his way," she said breathlessly.

"My what? Rach, I told you not to—" Celia dove for the address book and quickly dialed her father's cell phone. She got flipped over to voice mail. "Dad, forget whatever Rachel told you, it was a gag from someone at the restaurant. Call me." She hung up. Moments later the phone rang.

"A gag?" her father said. "Molesting a child's a gag?"

"That was the joke. There's this eighteen-year-old that has a crush on me."

"That's a pretty sick joke, Ceil." Pause. "So you're all right?"

"I'm fine," she said, going over to make coffee. She looked over her shoulder to see Rachel's new boyfriend standing in the doorway, looking at her as if she was a freak.

"I could run up anyway, Ceil. Take you to lunch."

Her father's love and concern only depressed her for some reason. "Thanks for offering, Dad, but I'm fine."

"Celia," her father said, "honey, listen, your mother and I are serious about you coming out for a couple of days. Just to talk about things."

"What things?"

"How you're doing."

"I'm doing fine," she said, spooning the coffee in, flipping the filter into place and turning the machine on.

"For your mother's sake, then. And mine." Pause. "Does it

ever occur to you that we'd just like to see you and spend some time with you sometimes?"

"To talk about how I'm doing," she repeated, getting three mugs down from the cabinet on the assumption Rachel and the boyfriend would want some coffee, too.

"To spend time with you," he said. "Check at work, will you?"

"I don't know, it's really busy."

"It's important, honey."

She promised she'd try (and wondered if she would) and got off the telephone.

"They were going to arrest you for the molestation of a minor?" the new boyfriend said. He was working on a doctorate in the English department. Something about Richard Brinsley Sheridan and *Masterpiece Theatre.*

"He's eighteen," Celia said, looking over at him. "Didn't you have sex when you were eighteen?"

"No," he said.

Celia poured coffee and held the mug out to him. "Do you think you would have wanted to have sex with me when you were eighteen?"

He reached for the carton of milk on the counter a little wide-eyed. "I'll say."

"I rest my case," Celia said, picking up a mug for Rachel.

"And if you look at her like that again," Rachel told her boyfriend, "my father will break your legs."

Randy and Roseanne

ROSANNE STORMED PAST the concierge and the doorman out to the street.

"It was a misunderstanding," Randy explained to the concierge. "I apologized for barging in."

"I'm glad it was mistake," the concierge told him. "Miss Cavanaugh's a nice tenant."

"What did you say to them?" Rosanne demanded of Randy when he emerged from the building.

"I apologized for making any disturbance."

"What disturbance? You didn't do anything! You should have at least cuffed her or something—throw a scare into her."

"I think you're enough to scare anyone, Rosanne," he said, steering her by the elbow toward his patrol car, double-parked in front of the building. "If that girl reports my badge number, Rosanne, I'm toast. I'm supposed to be at 156th Street and that's where I'm goin' now."

"Well, thanks for nothing!" she said. Then she relented,

watching him open the patrol car door. "Randy. I'm sorry. I'm just angry, that's all. Thanks for doing what you could."

"Hi, Rosanne, hi, Randy," Howard Stewart called, coming down the sidewalk. He was in one of his natty suits and the black dress coat Rosanne thought made him look like he owned New York. Or ought to.

"Hey, Howard," Randy said. "I gotta get back to work." He kissed Rosanne on the forehead and got into the patrol car.

Howard waited for Rosanne to come over to the sidewalk. "Everything all right?"

After a moment she shook her head. Then she walked between the parked cars to reach him.

"What's wrong?" he said quietly, leaning slightly to see her face.

"Everything."

"Like what?"

She looked up at him. "Like that whore bartender in your building seduced my son and broke his heart and made him lose his job and taught him love is something painful and horrible."

Howard, behind his glasses, blanched.

"Yeah," she told him.

"You can't mean Celia."

"Oh, yes, I do. Celia the whack-job bartender whore-slut." The last she said through gritted teeth, her eyes moving past Howard.

"Rosanne, there's got to be some sort of misunderstanding here."

"No misunderstanding, Howie." Her eyes, when she brought them back to him, had a deep sadness in them. "There's something else. Something I gotta tell Amanda." She looked up at him. "It's bad news and it can't wait anymore."

"What kind of bad news?"

"Mrs. G's dyin', Howie. She's got cancer. It's happening fast. She wants to stay at home until—" Tears sprang into her eyes and Howard put his briefcase down on the sidewalk to put his arms around her.

Lifetime Achievement

JACKSON STOPPED IN to pick Cassy up. She was so pressed for time she had to change in her office for the American Trust Foundation dinner. She was high as a kite, though, just back from San Francisco where she had held her brand-new little granddaughter and namesake, Catherine, in her arms.

Cassy was almost ready, but still pulling herself together in her office bathroom, the door slightly ajar.

"So what's the little gal like?"

"She's pretty, Jack, very pretty. And has dark hair and dark eyes. She's beautifully formed. She looks a lot like Maria's mother."

"How much did she weigh?"

"Six pounds nine ounces."

"That's a good size. And how's Maria?"

"Maria's amazing. Of course she's younger than springtime, which always helps." Cassy inspected herself in the mirror on the back of the door. She was wearing a pale gray silk gown Alexandra had had made for her, which made the most of what

Cassy had (and downplayed that which was leaving or was never there to begin with). The strapless bodysuit she wore under it simultaneously smoothed her body, pumped up her bosom and made sure everything that should be softly rounded out was. Her tan was sprayed on but was nonetheless effective, making her eyes look bluer than blue and her smile very bright.

She was wearing Jack's mother's diamond necklace and earrings, which would eventually go to Lydia. Cassy turned her head to examine the positioning of the diamond piece in her hair that Jack had given to her for her fiftieth birthday.

Diamonds were a crucial prop in the Darenbrook family image.

"So what are they going to call this kid?"

"Catherine," she answered, coming out. "The whole nine yards. Not Cassy, not Cathy, but Catherine."

Jackson let out a low whistle when he saw her. "Creepin' crickets, lady, they're all just gonna roll over and die—" this came out sounding like *dah* "—when they see you."

"You look very handsome, Jack," she told him, straightening the bow tie of his tux. "And you got a good haircut. Chi Chi?" she called.

Her administrative assistant appeared and appropriately complimented them on their appearance. "Doesn't she look amazin'?" Jack said, taking Cassy into his arms to kiss her. This was one of the games he liked to play, to see how far he could go with Cassy in public before she pulled away.

"Now you have lipstick on." Cassy moved to her desk for a tissue to wipe his mouth. "Chi Chi, could you give Cleo a call and tell her we're on our way down? I need a last-minute check and—" she squinted at Jack's face "—my husband needs something to cover the dissipations of the town."

"Madame, your dissipated husband is ready to escort you," he said, offering his arm. She retrieved her evening bag and walked out with him.

"Either you're going to get skin cancer," Cleo told Jackson as she applied some makeup under his eyes, "or someone's gonna mistake you for an old piece of luggage and put wheels on you."

"I'm probably gonna need wheels," he laughed, flashing his brilliant smile at the DBS hair and makeup person in the mirror.

"I'm serious," Cleo said. "Mr. Darenbrook, you have to wear sunblock, a hat and zinc on your nose in that boat."

Once Cleo had all but perfected them Jackson and Cassy headed out to the driveway where several limos were waiting. They walked to the lead car and as they passed the others, windows came down and employees shouted greetings. Everybody was in particularly high spirits since everyone except Jackson knew about the award he would be receiving tonight.

Langley and Belinda Peterson were already waiting in the lead car for them so the procession set off immediately. The dinner was being held at the Mandarin Hotel, scarcely a few blocks away, but the traffic was tricky in the evening around Columbus Circle and there was some waiting before being dropped off at the entrance.

Jackson hopped out first and helped Cassy out while a few photographers took pictures. The Darenbrooks waited for Belinda and Langley and then went inside, crossing the hotel lobby to ride up to the thirty-sixth floor.

The ballroom was lovely, with soft lighting and wonderful flower arrangements on the tables. The podium was set up on the dais in the front and behind it tremendous glass windows looked out over Central Park South. There would not be a cocktail hour at this function tonight, essentially in an attempt to make more money on it as a fund-raiser, and to keep the journalists more sober than they usually tended to be at dinners like this. The American Trust Foundation dinner was to be a straightforward gathering of one's two hundred and sixty closest industry friends.

Cassy had created the seating chart for their table of ten. She made a point of seating Will Rafferty on her left and Jackson on her right so that Jackson and Alexandra (the latter sitting on the other side of Will) could not see each other unless they leaned forward over the table.

When Will and Alexandra came to the table, Jack stood up until Alexandra had taken her seat. "I like your new haircut," Alexandra told him.

"Thank you," he said with a slight bow. "I intend to win favor with my gorgeous wife so I may ravish her at the conclusion of these lofty proceedings." Alexandra politely half smiled, as did the others around the table.

The DBS table was rounded out with the morning news anchors, Sally Harrington and Emmett Phelps, and the British anchors of the DBS-INS international news hour, Ronald Law and Leona Thistle. They talked about nothing over dinner, as they always did at dinners like this, and occasionally someone from another TV or radio network or newspaper or magazine came over to say hello. Every time someone did, the men put down their napkins and stood up, so it took longer for them to eat.

When coffee and dessert were being served Cassy excused herself to use the powder room. (One never knew how long the night might drag on.) Alexandra and Belinda went with her. There was a line of spacious lavatories with slatted doors and Cassy headed for the far one. She carefully minded her dress and heard Alexandra call, "Anyone else having wardrobe issues?"

There was laughter. In dresses like these there always were. Alexandra looked as though she had been poured into her gown.

"Hang on," Cassy called. She came out to wash her hands and then went over to where Alexandra was standing.

"In here, quick please," the anchorwoman said. "I can't fall out of my dress on the stage." Cassy slipped into the stall and Alexandra closed the door behind them. "If you could just fasten that part, that would be great," she said, which was utter nonsense since what she did was kiss her. "That's it," she said after a moment. "Thank you. That's much, much better, thank you." She smiled, cleared her throat. "I can take it from here," she said, stepping back to open the door for Cassy.

"Wardrobe malfunction," Cassy explained to a waiting woman.

This was insane, she thought, returning to the table. And yet this was her life. This is where she was, with a husband and a lover both determined to stake territory on her.

Jackson stood up and held out her chair for her. "Where did you get that?" she asked him, nodding to the brandy snifter at his place setting.

"I've got connections, lady," he whispered. "Why, do you want one?"

She shook her head. Jackson stood up again because Alexandra and Belinda had returned. Not long after the lights of the ballroom dimmed and the program began.

The master of ceremonies was terrible. As he droned on and on Cassy was sure everyone must be fighting sleep as much as she was. And then it suddenly got very, very cold in the ballroom.

"To keep us awake, no doubt," Jackson whispered. He offered her his coat. She wanted it but said no because she knew he was soon going to be called to the stage. Mercifully the awards segment finally began, which Cassy enjoyed if for no other reason than to see what the winners were wearing. The heat came back on, too. Jack was bored, though, and started practicing his disappearing coin trick.

When they announced DBS News had won for best broadcast television coverage of domestic news, Alexandra and Will went up to the stage to accept the award. There was a very good round of applause but Cassy knew how few outside of DBS were happy about them receiving this award. Somehow it didn't seem fair that while the old dinosaurs staggered around (buckling under the onslaught of cable and online news) DBS News was almost embarrassingly unencumbered with overhead.

Cassy stood up as Alexandra and Will climbed onto the dais.

Alexandra moved across the stage with an elegance and grace that made Cassy smile. Alexandra was only forty-one. (*Better keep stretching, Old Girl,* she told herself.)

"By DBS winning this award," Alexandra said into the microphone, "the news divisions of CBS, NBC, ABC and PBS also win this award because it was their decades of dedication and commitment to a standard of higher journalism that lay the groundwork for DBS News to be created on. So we thank the American Trust Foundation for this honor, we pledge to try even harder in our quest for fair and balanced news coverage, and we salute our industry colleagues for making it possible."

The crowd liked that and this time everyone stood up to applaud.

"Can we get out of here now?" Jack whispered when Alexandra and Will were led away.

"Just a little while longer," she whispered.

Jack straightened up in his chair and then leaned toward her again. "Can't I just go? I'll take a cab and leave the car for you."

"No," she told him. She frowned because he was loosening his bow tie. She reached over to retie it with Jackson squirming like a child.

"Can I at least go to the men's room?"

"No."

"Geez Louise," he said through clenched teeth. "This is torture."

"Ten more minutes, that's all I ask," she whispered.

When the emcee was announcing the next category, the lifetime achievement award, Cassy saw that Jackson was practicing his coin trick again and she took the coin away from him.

"What is your *problem?*" he whispered.

A huge screen had descended from the ceiling, the lights were turned down very low, and the retrospective on the life and career of Jackson Darenbrook began. It was only when Jackson saw his own face ten feet high in the front of the room that he snapped to attention. The DBS documentary group had put this together, with Alexandra narrating the story of "one person who has contributed so much to so many in the field of journalism."

There were pictures from his childhood, working at the paper with his mother and father, pictures of him growing up with his siblings and older half siblings, his college days, his marriage to Barbara, the birth of his children, his working partnership with a gawky young Langley Peterson. It showed the long list of newspaper acquisitions Jackson had made, the printing plants he built, the launching of the Darenbrook satellite, the expansion into magazines and then textbook publishing and then into electronic information systems and then, most recently, on the Web.

When the lights came up Jackson was coming out of shock, blinking back tears, and then he saw that standing across the dais were all of his siblings, applauding him; Elrod, Cordelia, Norbert, Noreen, Beau and Belinda. Cordelia stepped up to the microphone to read the inscription on the award.

"The American Trust Foundation names Jackson Darenbrook recipient of its Lifetime Achievement Award for advocating journalistic excellence in the fields of newspaper, magazine and book publishing, broadcast television and Webcasting." She looked up. "Well, come on up here, Jackie, and get *yor awahd!*" Everyone laughed and Jackson, hastily wiping his eyes with a handkerchief, kissed Cassy and made his way up to the stage. He kissed his siblings and then took the microphone.

"I was sittin' there tellin' mah wife I wanted to get outta here. She's tellin' me to sit still and I'm tellin her, 'What is your problem, lady?'" He grinned. "I guess now I know." People laughed.

His acceptance speech was wonderful and Jackson demonstrated why his employees loved him when he reeled off names of key employees from the past thirty years he thought deserved to share this award with him. He then looked up to thank his mother and father in heaven, which made his sisters start to cry, and the crowd was utterly charmed.

They stayed on for a while after the ceremony, going to the press area with Jackson's family for a few pictures. It was nearly eleven when Jackson's siblings allowed him to leave and only then on the promise they would all have dinner tomorrow.

They left Langley and Belinda behind with the rest of the family and went out to the car.

"We need to get this polished," Cassy said about the plaque. "It's got everybody's fingerprints on it. I think you should put it up in the lobby so people can see it when they come into work in the morning."

"I want to polish *you,*" he said, pulling her to him. He kissed her, his hands starting to roam. He must have felt her stiffen. "Come on, Cass," he murmured, sinking his mouth into her neck. "Come on, darlin'." His hand slid down her thigh.

She just sat there. After touching her for a while he abruptly sat up. "This is a very big night for me," he said, pulling her hand in his lap. He smiled. He whispered in her ear, "I'm like a city block long here, we really need to do something about this."

"I'm sorry, Jack," she said, taking her hand away.

He brought his head back to squint at her. "Why not?"

"I don't want to."

"Well, we know how to make that go away," he said matter-of-factly, touching her breast.

"Please. No," she said.

"Oh, criminy cripes, what's wrong?" He said this as if they had been in marital bliss for the last ten years.

"It's Thursday, Jack, aren't you supposed to be going somewhere?"

"I'm spending tonight with you."

"Oh, I see. Now all of a sudden *I'm* your Thursday night date."

"Fine," he said, flicking his hands as if to rid himself of any trace of her.

"You don't get it, do you? A wife is not something you substitute your girlfriends with once in a while."

"You've never been a substitute for anything or anybody, Cass, that's why I married you. Because I love you."

They'd only been through this about a hundred times over the last seven years, but now in the last year a new part had been added, which Cassy was now waiting for him to start.

"And you're no dyke, Cass, that much we both know. How long you're going to go on with this charade to get back at me, I don't know—"

"You are a sex addict, Jack, we also both know that. A very happy sex addict."

"So what if I took the cure?" he said suddenly, shifting in his seat. "I mean it! What if I go to one of those places, Cassy, and get my balls electrocuted or whatever it is they do? If I went, and I got cured—" he held his hands out "—then what happens?"

"We'll talk about it after you go."

"No, no, no, wait a minute," he laughed. "I want to know now, before I go. Do we get to start over? Be newlyweds? Only be true to each other? Hmm?"

She didn't say anything, but only looked at him.

He rapped on the glass divider. "Pull over when you can," he told the driver. "Sorry it didn't work out for us tonight," he told Cassy. "You're still mah wife, ya know. Lord knows how much I'd like to show you." The car pulled over and Jackson flung the door open and got out. "Have fun, 'cause I intend to, darlin'," he said before slamming the door.

After a moment, the driver asked, "To Riverside Drive, Mrs. Darenbrook?"

"Actually, no. Central Park West at Eightieth, The Roehampton. Then please drop this plaque off at West End. I'll call ahead and tell the guard to expect it."

Amanda Receives Unwelcomed News

WHEN TEDDY STARTED whining about why they couldn't have an Xbox, Emily soon joined in, claiming everyone in their school had an Xbox except for them. When they had advanced as far as everyone in the whole universe had an Xbox, and that some people even played their Xboxes in the car, Amanda went downstairs to get a large box from the basement that immediately elicited groans from the children.

"Oh, Mom," Emily said, covering her eyes. "Nobody else's mother does this! It's weird!"

"I want an Xbox, not that stupid box," Teddy grumbled.

"Every time you complain about not having enough computers in our lives," Amanda said, "it's time for this box."

"Dinner will be postponed for thirty minutes," Amanda announced to Madame Moliere. Amanda had already covered the kitchen table with newspapers and was placing a large sheet of paper in front of Emily and one in front of Teddy. She gave each one of them an inkwell and then held out an array of feathers for them to choose from. Emily took a swan feather and Teddy took a gull feather. Amanda unscrewed the tops of their inkwells. "You are to write a list, please. I want you to write down five ways Abraham Lincoln amused himself at home, in the evening, with his family, when he was your age."

Emily plunked her chin in her hand and sighed. "Who wants to do math on the back of a shovel?"

"They didn't do anything in the olden days, Mom," Teddy announced. "They were all very sad."

Suppressing a smile, Amanda sat down and folded her arms to rest on the table. "Why were they sad?"

"Because there was nothing to do!" he expained, throwing his hands out.

"Think, Teddy. There was no electricity, no TV, no computers, no radios, no DVD players, but I promise you, oh, darling child of mine, people did amuse themselves." Somehow Teddy had already gotten ink under his fingernails.

"Abraham Lincoln could carve things," Emily said, carefully dipping the end of her feather into the inkwell.

Howard often wondered out loud when Amanda would graduate the children to at least metal pens but she said never. Looking for feathers gave the children something to do on their walks.

"Carve stuff?" Teddy read, craning his neck to see his sister's paper. "Cool, a knife," he said, looking back down at his blank sheet. Suddenly his hand shot up in the air. "Knife fights!" When he saw his mother's expression he slowly brought his arm down and, discouraged, slumped in his chair.

"He could read books," Emily said next, dipping her feather into the ink. She would have to do it several times, but she had the knack of it.

The whole process took almost an hour but Amanda finally received her lists. Emily had carefully penned:

carve things
read
tell stories
sing songs
shadow puppets

Teddy wrote:

catch spiders
arm wrestle [ressal]
play with dog
clean gun
scare sister

Howard called at seven and the children shared their lists with him on the speakerphone in the kitchen. Howard asked them what they had done to provoke their mother into bringing the dreaded box out. They told him about the Xbox.

"Darling, I need to speak to you a minute," Howard said. His voice was gentle; it reminded Amanda of how he used to sound most of the time. Attentive, loving. The holidays had been so awful. Howard, when he was here, had been moody and distant. And Amanda was still sick with self-loathing. Thank God for the children because they gave them something to focus on besides each other.

"I love you so much, Howard," Amanda found herself saying into the phone as she took it into the family room.

Clearly he was surprised by this sudden declaration. But that was how it felt, a sudden, overwhelming love and need that rushed up at the sound of his voice. His old voice.

"I love you and the children more than anything or anybody in the world and I think I would die without you," she rushed on.

Pause. "Amanda— What's going on out there?"

"I can't stand the way things have been," she said, tears starting to rise. "I miss *us.* I'm starting to hate it out here. Without you. I think we just could spend some more time together, Howard, somehow we can get past this—this *abyss* between us. That's what it feels like."

He was silent a moment. "If you feel comfortable leaving the children with Madame Moliere, then maybe you should come in, Amanda."

"I'll come in tomorrow."

"The thing is, Amanda," he began. "Mrs. Goldblum isn't very well. I ran into Rosanne this afternoon and she asked me to call and tell you."

Her heart sank. "It's very bad, isn't it, Howard?"

"I'm afraid so. But nothing's going to happen right now. Rosanne thought you should know and Mrs. Goldblum would like to tell you about it herself." Pause. "But she wanted you to be prepared. There's been a big change, apparently."

"Oh, Howard," she said, sinking down on the arm of the couch, holding her face in her hand. She couldn't ignore the timing of this news. It was as if to remind her that whatever pain she could cause herself was nothing compared to what the world could offer.

"It's supposed to snow tomorrow," Howard continued. "Maybe you should take the train."

"We already have three inches out here," she said, looking

out to the driveway. "If it's too bad I'll take the train." She sniffed, wiping her eyes with the back of her hand. She felt a hand on her arm. It was Emily. She sensed Amanda's sadness and slid her arms around her mother's waist to comfort her.

Celia's Parents Sit Her Down

"I DON'T THINK your mother's going to be wild about me bringing you out in the bar car," Celia's father said, carefully balancing his beer cup against the rocking motion of the train.

"Call it the club car and she won't mind so much," Celia said, reaching for her beer in the holder. They were on their second and both were starting to unwind—as much as her father could unwind. While the other men in the bar car had loosened their ties, some altogether taking theirs off and stashing them in their suit pockets, her father's remained firmly knotted and in place.

Since Celia had met her father at the gate in Grand Central she'd seen at least ten people she knew from Darien. There was a neighbor, friends of her parents and then, weirdly, like four kids she had gone to high school with who were now commuting to New York. Talking briefly to Chip, the art director at the ad agency, was okay; Suzy at *Glamour* magazine was okay, too, and even old Charles, their class buffoon, who was working at the Rockefeller Foundation, hadn't bothered her, either. It was only when they ran into Bethie that Celia began to feel uncomfortable. Bethie had that whole Darien-to-Vassar-to-the-Upper-East-Side thing going, wearing a chic dress, jewelry and high heels and flashing a rock of an engagement ring. (So *what* if Celia wore jeans and a pirate's bandana on her head every night to sling booze? She'd scored higher on the SATs than Bethie.) But it was Bethie's announcement that she was working at Sotheby's that killed Celia. The jealousy that swelled inside her was so violent she could barely speak. And then when Bethie, with a sigh and a casual wave of her diamond, said it was "just something to do until the wedding," Celia practically choked on her anger.

So what? she told herself, her face ringing red as she followed her father through the Metro North cars. *So what?*

Even her father noticed Celia's funk after they had crossed paths with Bethie. "You never liked her, did you?" he asked her when he had come back to their seats with their first cups of beer.

"Oh, she was all right," Celia shrugged, refusing to get into it.

After a while her father leaned over. "Maybe you could see about her job when she leaves."

The comment simultaneously surprised and enraged Celia. She was surprised her father thought she still had it in her, the ability, as her mother called it, "To clean up well." And then she was enraged all over again because she could never do it. Her life was too much of a mess.

"You probably have to have your degree, though." He sipped his beer, unfolding a fresh copy of the *New York Post*. (That was the drill: the *New York Times* on the way in and the *Post* on the way out.)

Celia spent the rest of the train ride trying not to let her unhappiness show. The train arrived on time and they walked down the long staircase and then under the railroad bridge on Leroy Avenue to reach the parking lot where her father left their old Toyota every morning at seven. (He kept his Lexus in the garage.) Celia's mother drove a Mercedes SL now, instead of a Volvo wagon, because she didn't have any kids at home anymore to carpool around. And after the Cavanaugh's golden retriever finally died of old age, Celia's parents had even downsized to a miniature Dachshund.

"Your brother wanted to come down from Providence," her mother said, standing in the garage doorway to greet them, "but he got stuck at—" She stopped after her husband's kiss hello. "Have you been drinking and *driving,* Hal?"

Her father mumbled something about "a beer" and continued into the kitchen.

"Hi, lovey," Celia's mother said, hugging her. She released her and stepped back. "Where's your bag?"

"I can't stay, Mom. I've got the lunch shift tomorrow."

"Oh, Ceil," her mother said, following her in.

Celia nearly tripped over the little dog. He still took a little getting used to. She put her purse on the kitchen table and squatted down. "Hi, there, little one," she said, picking him up in her arms. He frantically licked her face, making her laugh.

"He's been a little devil today," her mother announced, waltzing over to the stove to lift the top off a pot and stir whatever was in it with a wooden spoon. "He dragged one of the pillows down off the living room couch and into the front hall closet."

"Did you go to sleep-away camp?" Celia asked his little face. He gave her nose a happy lick.

"Do you want some wine?" Celia's father asked, coming back into the kitchen. He had changed into corduroys, but still had his work shirt on and was rolling up the sleeves.

"Are you asking me or Celia?"

"Both of you."

"White for me, please," her mother said. "Celia, I made the seafood casserole you like."

"That's great, thanks," she said, putting the dog back on the floor. "White for me, too, Dad."

"White it is," he said, going out to the bar area between the living room and dining room.

"So how are you, Mom?" Celia asked, leaning on the kitchen counter.

Her mother gave an answer that lasted nearly twenty minutes and included news about everyone, it seemed, Celia had ever known in Darien. They sat down in the dining room to what really was a great dinner—a casserole of crab and lobster in a cream sauce, over rice, and a salad with mandarin oranges and strawberries—but by the end of the meal Celia wished she was anywhere else. None of her answers to her mother's questions were satisfactory. Her mother hated that she had dropped out of college, hated that she was a bartender, worried about Celia being a single woman alone in New York and couldn't believe that Celia still didn't have a boyfriend. (She had hated the-son-of-a-country-western-star.)

"So that's it?" her mother finally said. "No parties? Rachel's not up to anything?"

"She bought a new refrigerator," Celia said, being sarcastic.

"Really, what kind?"

It was something in the way her mother said it, an innocent attempt to be interested in whatever Celia was willing to talk about, that made Celia start to cry. She bolted from the table and went to her old room, closing the door and throwing herself across the bed. Her mother gave her five minutes before knocking on the door and coming in.

Celia sat up and wiped her eyes with her sleeve.

Her mother let go of the doorknob and came over to sit beside her on the bed. "What is it, angel? What is so wrong?"

"I just wish I were dead sometimes, Mom. It's just everything *sucks.*"

Celia heard the clicking of her father's knee—a college football injury—coming down the hall.

"We'd like to help if we can," her mother said gently.

Her father came in, pawed pillows out of the upholstered arm chair onto the floor and dragged the chair over. Celia was amazed her mother didn't yell at him about the pillows, which meant her mother was really worried. Which made Celia feel even worse because there wasn't anything really wrong, she was just a screwup.

"I don't *know* what's wrong with me," she said, looking down. "I just can't seem to get it together anymore."

Her father reached over to hand her his handkerchief from his back pocket. "Try to explain what you're feeling," he said. "Describe it, lovey."

"I don't know, I'm just dead inside," she said, wiping her eyes. "I don't feel like doing anything anymore." She lowered the handkerchief. "I mean I can work, but that's about it. I don't want to go out anymore, I don't want to do anything. I get upset about shit— Sorry."

"When you say 'go out,'" her father said, "do you mean socializing? Or going out for a job or something?"

She looked at him, sniffing. "Both."

Her parents exchanged looks.

"Celia," her mother said, covering Celia's hand, "I don't want you to be angry with her, but not long ago Rachel called us."

Celia's head whipped in her direction.

"She's worried about you." She paused. "And so are we."

She looked to her father. He was nodding, trying to stop himself from cracking his knuckles, which is what he did when he was upset. "We think we might know what it is, too."

"What *what* is?"

"Why you're feeling like this."

"Ceil," her mother said, "Rachel said she found you crying the other day. In front of the TV."

Celia remembered. It had been humiliating.

"She said you were crying while watching a commercial about a man asking a woman to marry him."

Celia sighed. "I know. I don't know why."

Her parents were looking at each other again.

"Why do you guys keep looking at each other?"

Her father ran his hand back through his hair and sat forward again, still trying not to do the hand thing.

"We know you like to drink," her mother said. "Obviously we do, too. But how does it make you feel?"

"Better," she said without hesitation. And then she thought a minute. "And then worse sometimes." She felt her throat tightening. Why were they making such a big deal out of this? It didn't take a genius to see she was depressed because she was such a screwup in a family of superstars.

"Rachel said you would never get out of bed if she didn't wake you up."

Celia shrugged. "I work long hours. I get tired."

"And she says your room is impassable."

"It's not that bad," Celia said. "Rach is such a neat freak. I got that storage space and put half of my stuff in there. I don't know what she's complaining about, she's got this useless boyfriend lying around."

"She wasn't complaining, Celia," her mother said, putting

an arm around her. "And I'm very glad she called us. Because we think we might have an idea about what's going on."

"Something like this happened to your mother," her father said.

"When I stopped smoking," her mother added.

Celia's eyes flew wide open. "*You* smoked?"

She nodded, smiling apologetically. "I hid it from you children as best I could. I finally stopped when you were around, I don't know, eight?" The last was said to her father.

"But she chewed nicotine gum for a while after that, too. Four or five years. So it wasn't just smoking cigarettes, your mother was addicted to nicotine."

"But you're like a health nut," Celia said incredulously.

"I am now."

"The point is, Ceil," her father said, "your mother went into a downward spiral after she stopped chewing the nicotine gum. She got very depressed."

"I remember that gum," Celia said. "It was horrible, but we kept trying to chew it anyway."

"I gained weight," her mother said, "because I was eating sugar and carbohydrates night and day. And coffee, I drank a lot of coffee. Because I always felt like I was dragging, Celia, that's the only way I can explain it. It was like dragging a hundred pound sack of cement behind me. And I don't mean physically, but *mentally.* I couldn't cope."

"I remember when you locked yourself in the bathroom once," Celia said. "You wouldn't let us in." She looked at her father. "We were all fighting about something. You were away, Dad, and—" She looked at her mother in wonderment. "You said you couldn't take it anymore."

"I don't remember, lovey," her mother said. "But I do remember feeling like that a lot."

Celia felt like hiding most of the time, too.

"Your father made me get a physical and Dr. Stringer told me I was eating too much sugar and drinking too much caffeine. So I went on a diet and lost some weight and drank decaffeinated coffee. And I did feel a little better."

"But she was still crying at long distance commercials," her father added. "And anything with a child or an animal or an abused woman in it, which is to say just about everything on TV." He looked at Celia's mother. "We couldn't have people over, either. We used to entertain, but we stopped."

"I felt so overwhelmed," her mother said. "I just could not get organized."

"With three kids, Mom—"

"No, it was more than that, Celia," she said quickly. "I was emotionally exhausted all the time and there didn't seem to be any reason why." She bit her bottom lip for a moment. "Except when I had a few drinks. Then I felt better. Which made me wonder what was wrong."

"That's when Dr. Stringer sent her to a psychiatrist. He suspected your mother had some form of chemical depression."

"You can imagine how well that went over with me," her mother laughed. "Oh, I was *mortified,* Celia! A psychiatrist! But we went through the list. I had stopped sugar, I was exercising, I was getting at least seven hours of sleep, I was getting plenty of light and plenty of fresh air..." She dropped her hands in her lap. "And I still felt like I was on the outside looking in. While everybody else was having a great life, I felt like I was looking at everybody through a glass window, trying to drag my cement bag along with me, trying to find a way to get into that space so I could feel happy, too."

"That's exactly it," Celia said quietly. "You can see everybody, but you can't find a way in."

Her mother's mouth pressed into a line and her eyes began to tear. "I know, angel. That's why I'm upset that I didn't put it together before."

"Depression can run in families," her father said. "And you were such a go-getter kid we never worried about you."

"And then as soon as Rachel started telling us why she was worried," her mother said, "we knew. We just knew."

"But we're not doctors," her father added.

"Which is why you need to see one, Celia. And we want you to stay overnight because I've made arrangements for you to see my doctor at eight-thirty tomorrow morning. He's coming in especially to see you, because he knows how important it is to me."

"This guy's a shrink?"

She nodded. "He put me on an antidepressant, Prozac, nearly thirteen years ago. I'm on something else now, but the point is, Celia, it saved my life." She glanced at Celia's father. "And probably my marriage."

"What your mother is taking isn't addictive in any way. It's not a narcotic, or a tranquilizer—"

"In other words, it's no fun," Celia joked.

"I'll pretend I didn't hear that," her father said.

"If your brain chemistry doesn't need an antidepressant," her mother said, "then the drug doesn't do anything. It's only when there is a chemical deficiency that it works. But let's wait to see what the doctor says after you see him."

"Right. Wonder if nothing's wrong with me," Celia said, "except I'm a basket case?"

"That's *exactly* how I felt, Celia."

"And something else, Celia," her father said. "Your brother

wanted to come down tonight—not just because he wanted to see you, which he did, but because he was having similar problems."

"Three years ago," Celia's mother said. "He'd been having the same kind of feelings that we've been talking about. And it turned out, yes, he also has a problem with depression."

Celia was astonished. Her oldest brother was like Mr. Perfect. She never really saw him much anymore but no one had ever let on anything was wrong.

There was something to what her parents were saying, but Celia was almost scared to hope they were right.

30

The Autobiography of Georgiana Hamilton-Ayres

FIRST SHE COULD meet him and then she couldn't. Then she might be able to squeeze him in but then she called back to say she was sorry, she had to reschedule. Trying to meet with Georgiana Hamilton-Ayres while she was in New York was like chasing down a cat who wanted to be loved but not caught.

"Howard?" Gretchen said from the doorway of his office. "It's Georgiana Hamilton-Ayres again."

He picked up.

"I promise you, Howard, I am trying my best," the actress said in her British accent. "I have a fitting uptown at two and I should be able to see you at four. No, wait, then there's travel time."

"Wherever, whenever," he said. "Where is your fitting?"

"West Seventieth."

Howard named a few places where they could meet. "I know at this point you must believe me to be the most tiresome of all creatures," the actress said, "but is it possible we could meet somewhere a little less public?"

"My house," he said without hesitation. "And I'll shock you because my wife has trained me to serve a proper tea."

"Splendid! But a little less proper, please, Howard, because I'm only wearing slacks and a sweater."

He gave her their address, adding that she should take her time and he would expect her when he saw her. He hung up the phone and looked at his watch.

Of all the times he would finally get to see Georgiana Hamilton-Ayres it had to be the day Amanda was coming in. He had wanted to go over to Emma Goldblum's with her. If Mrs. Goldblum was half as bad as Rosanne had described it was going to be a terrible blow to Amanda. Mrs. Goldblum had been a surrogate mother to his wife for years and years, able to give Amanda the kind of practical advice she could never get from her own mother.

So it was going to be a very bad few days ahead. There was the situation with Mrs. Goldblum and then there was the situation with their finances he absolutely had to tell Amanda about. He had to tell her because at this point it appeared taking a mortgage out on the apartment was all that could save him.

She would be shocked. Of all the problems he could have brought home to their marriage, money was the one he had always assured her she need never fear. She was already upset with him and she didn't even know the story yet.

What if she told him no, she wouldn't take out a mortgage on the apartment? What then? He didn't have the slightest idea. The Hillingses were looking at the agency books now, but without Amanda's help in two weeks there would be no paychecks and the secret would be out—that Howard Stewart had run the once thriving Hillings & Hillings literary agency into the ground.

It was already getting dark outside. There was another storm forecast to move in tonight from the northeast—a direction that was never good. He wished Amanda was getting an earlier start but the snowfall in Woodbury last night had closed the schools this morning and Amanda said she needed to get things organized for her absence. She was an excellent driver, though, and the Navigator was as good a bodily protection as any other vehicle around.

"The super's coming up to see you, Howard," Gretchen told him, sticking her head into his office.

Damn. He'd forgotten about him. He'd been ducking him all through the holidays. The super was no doubt looking for his yearly extortion payment to keep the heat on in the winter, the air-conditioning on in the summer and to free up the freight elevator when needed, to say nothing of letting the electrician or painter or carpenter or computer guy in the building, and, of course, for not making the johns overflow into his office if Howard didn't pay up. A Rambo super was one of the unspoken business expenses every Manhattan businessperson had to deal with.

Howard needed three thousand in cash. He took his glasses off and cleaned them to give himself time to think. He didn't have three thousand dollars in cash. "Gretchen, tell him I need to run over to the bank and then will stop down in the basement to see him."

"Oh, good, then maybe he won't shut the elevator down again," Gretchen said. She swore he had purposely trapped three of them in one of the elevators their first day back after the holidays.

Howard took his wallet out of his back pocket and opened it. There was only one credit card left. It was the one in both his and Amanda's name, the one he swore he would never use.

Howard left the office and went to a large bank where he did not have an account. He walked up to the manager's desk and explained he needed three thousand dollars for an unexpected expense and could she please get it for him using this card. She looked at him, then at the card and then back at him in such a way as to make Howard wonder just how many stories like this she had heard from crooks.

"Do you have an account with us, sir?" she said.

"No. Here's my driver's license."

Reluctantly she took the card from him and excused herself. She needed to make a call. When she returned she was all smiles. "You have a fifty thousand dollar credit limit on this card, Mr. Stewart, are you sure three thousand will be enough?"

Howard could remember when, as a little boy, he had been taught that banks were in the business of investing. They used their depositors' money to build things, that was how they made their money. So when, exactly, had the business of banking become loan-sharking? He was both disgusted and relieved he could get the money, and he took an extra two thousand to put in their checking account.

He returned to the office building and took the elevator down to the basement. It was a pretty creepy place, where one could easily imagine a variety of crimes involving steamy heat and dark, dank concrete. Howard felt perspiration break out on him immediately. "Luis?" he called, walking to an area that reminded Howard of the bowels of an ancient warship.

Luis was busy in his dark and cramped workshop space. He was listening to his cell phone, with a dirty finger stuck in his ear to hear better. He kicked his head up in what Howard assumed was a greeting and Howard took a little walk around, wondering why he put up with the ridiculous rent in this "landmark" office building.

Sometimes he wished he'd just chuck it. Let someone else worry about the rent and the insurance and the payroll and the clients and the books and who could have vacation when and—

"Ehhh, Howard!" Luis said, coming out. "Sorrybuttahear-wifeyouknow," he confided, elbowing Howard in the side.

"I wanted to thank you for all your help and hard work over the year, Luis," Howard said, slapping the thick bank envelope of fifties into Luis's hand and shaking it.

"Soallrightsallright," Luis assured him under his breath.

"I hear our friend may be trying to sell the building," Howard said, rocking back on his heels, jingling the change in his pants pocket.

"Sallreadysold," Luis said. "Ileafnextweek."

"Excuse me?" Howard said.

"Fired." He drew a finger across his neck. "Cantell-youhowneedthis, mafamily," he said, holding up the envelope. "Savemylifethanks, youtheman."

Amanda called the apartment from the road at three-forty and Howard told her about his meeting with Georgiana. "I'll go straight over to Mrs. Goldblum's then," she said, sounding like a space alien on the car speakerphone. "I think it's probably better if I go alone anyway, until I know what condition she's in." He could imagine Amanda flicking her hair over her shoulder, trying to change tracks of her mind so she would not get upset while driving. "You *are* going to use the tea cart, aren't you?"

He turned around in their kitchen. "I'm looking at it this very moment."

Amanda had a sterling silver tea cart her grandmother's butler used to roll out. It was pretty handy, actually, and carried the teapot and cups and saucers and plates, food, napkins—everything.

"Don't put tea bags on the cart," she said, as if she could see the box on the cart from where she was. "Use loose Earl Grey in the ball, put it in the pot."

"Okay," he said, removing the box of tea bags from the cart.

"Bring the water to a boil and then turn it down to low. When she arrives turn it back up to high. Show her into the living room, then pour the hot water in and roll the cart out to her. She'll offer to pour and you might as well let her."

He smiled. How he loved Amanda.

He had to make this deal between Georgiana and Bennett, Fitzallen & Coe work. If he could get it done with that jumbo hunk of cash attached to the signing of the contract, then it wouldn't be nearly so bad telling Amanda about everything. A hundred-fifty-thousand-dollar commission would be a huge help.

"And what food do you have?" Amanda asked.

"I went to Zabar's and they made me those little—you know."

"Quiches?"

"Yeah, I got a couple of those, but I mean, you know, the little sandwiches, with the crusts cut off."

"What kind?"

"Water cress—"

"Excellent. She may not like them but it's always nice to show you made the effort."

"Cream cheese and some kind of peppers, or pepper—"

"Red or green?"

"Red."

"Pepper jelly, then, probably."

"That's the one. Um, and I got razor-thin Black Forest

ham. And then I think cucumber and something, the lady said to trust her, it was really good."

"What about sweets?"

"Those little things. Little éclair, cheesecake, napoleon, chocolate-covered strawberries—"

"That's a *lot* of food, Howard."

"I know but I thought maybe we could have a picnic or something. Tonight. Later. Build a fire." He swallowed. "If you felt like it. Just to talk and stuff."

After a long moment, Amanda said, "Sometimes you are the dearest man in all the world, Howard."

Dearest and the poorest if he didn't pull this deal off, he thought.

After the concierge announced the actress's arrival, Howard slipped on his suit jacket and straightened his tie in the front hall mirror. He'd already put a couple of Listerine strips in his mouth. He opened the door and stood next to the elevator to wait.

Nervous.

It was a lot of money.

The elevator arrived and Georgiana Hamilton-Ayres emerged, draped in fur. God she was gorgeous.

"Howard," she said, offering a dazzling smile while extending her hand. She kissed him on the cheek. He showed her into the apartment and took her fur coat and hat while she tugged off her gloves and shook out her blond hair.

"Gorgeous coat," he said, using a heavy wood hanger.

"It's not real," she said, handing him her gloves and turning to walk down the hall. "I think they must sew lead into it to make it feel like it." She was wearing jeans that had to be size four and a cashmere sweater that left very little to the imagination. Her boots with a spiked heel sounded surprisingly loud on the hall runner. "This is some apartment, Howard," she said admiringly.

The kettle started to shriek and he apologized, laughing a little, explaining he messed up the order of what his wife had instructed him to do. She went into the kitchen with him and helped him make the tea. "I love your wife's book," the actress said, sneaking a sandwich off the cart and taking a bite. "It's still under option, isn't it?"

He nodded.

"Then tell whoever has the option I want to play her. Catherine the Great."

He looked at her. "Really?"

She swallowed the rest of the sandwich quarter and plucked a napkin from the cart. "Really," she confirmed, touching it to her mouth.

Huh. Wait until he told Amanda. That would be something, wouldn't it? If a movie or miniseries finally did get made after all these years.

He showed her into the living room. "There are a lot of eighteenth-century costumes and sets and props and things lying idle all over Europe these days," she said. "The industry went through that streak of period films so now it wouldn't be nearly so expensive to do a film like this." She chose the early Victorian settee to sit on, which Howard always thought was uncomfortable but evidently Georgiana, like his wife, did not. The actress spread her arms along the back of the settee for a moment (*Now where does she expect me to look?* Howard thought) but then jumped up to pour the tea as Amanda said she probably would. "And there are tons of places in Eastern Europe to shoot," she added.

"Where they shot all the Jane Austen stuff?" he asked.

"Good grief, Howard," she scolded.

He looked at her.

"There is no *stuff* in Jane Austen."

They laughed. And then while they sipped tea and nibbled food she talked about friends of hers who had an incredible production facility she would love to use. Howard told her about what Amanda was working on now, about Catherine the Great's court. His mood was rapidly climbing toward euphoria. Since Hillings & Stewart represented Amanda, perhaps Georgiana Hamilton-Ayres could solve some of the agency's long-term problems, too!

"So we are in agreement?" Georgiana said. "You will ring my new agent?"

"Absolutely."

Soon the topic turned to the possibility of her autobiography. "It defies the imagination," she said, "that a casual comment to Spencer Hawes at a cocktail party in Los Angeles could translate into a three-and-a-half-million-dollar offer from a New York publisher scarcely a month later."

"That's what happens when it's a great idea."

"A great idea until paired with the prospect of working with Spencer," she said. "I shouldn't be unkind, I'm sorry, but it's very difficult for me to believe that anyone who willingly married Verity Rhodes is sane."

"No, no—you would work with Kate Weston." Then he explained Kate's history. Though recently named publisher, she was a great editor and planned to personally edit a few titles, one of which would be this one.

"I've met Kate. She was Jessica Wright's editor. Alexandra and I threw the publication party for Jessica's autobiography, as you may recall."

"Oh, that's right. Rockefeller Center."

"Which frankly is why I'm here, Howard, because Jessica told me I should hear what you have to say."

He smiled, pleased.

"I also met your wife at that party," Georgiana added, pointing to the painting of Amanda, Emily and baby Teddy, which hung over the fireplace, "which is what interested me in reading her book. She's lovely. I'd love to work with her. She believes *she's* Catherine the Great, too, as I recollect." They laughed and Georgiana sat forward to survey the desserts. "Go on, tell me more about Kate."

He listed many of the books and authors Kate had worked with over the years.

Georgiana muttered something about an extra half hour on the elliptical and finally selected a miniature chocolate layer cake, remembering as she did so, "I would beg Cook to make this for me when I was a child."

"Where was that? On your family's estate?" Howard asked.

"My father's home, yes," she nodded, carefully taking a bite. "The kitchen was always the warmest place at Greycliff Hall. I was always cold there." She smiled to herself. "In Beverly Hills Mummy had a Filipino kitchen boy who was always giving blow jobs behind the garage." She looked vaguely alarmed at what she had said. "I apologize. That isn't a very pleasant childhood memory to share." She ate the rest of the little cake. "Unless people might like to read about some of those men behind the garage with our kitchen boy, one or two of whom happened to be very famous actors and directors."

Howard only smiled slightly, trying not to appear like a ghoul.

"The situation is this, Howard," she continued, shaking out her napkin. "I have spent an inordinate amount of time and money trying to forget the times when I felt helpless to do anything about what was happening to me and my parents. I don't want to talk about my mother's illnesses or lovers or suicide attempts. I don't want to talk about what my father did to her, or what she did to him, or why I had to see all the things that I saw. I have no desire to talk about my ex-husband or anyone else in this world who has hurt me. Which means, Howard, unless people want to read about the role that dogs and cats and horses have played in my personal life, I have very little to offer in the way of an autobiography."

Howard felt his heart sinking. It wasn't going to happen. She wasn't going to do it.

"So you tell me, Howard, why on earth would I want to write my autobiography at this point in my life?"

"What exactly did you say to Spencer Hawes?" he asked her. "Because whatever it was made him think you'd do it. And sell him first serial rights to launch his new magazine."

"*What?* Muck about with *those* two? He must have been drunk."

"Do you remember what you said?"

"I remember quite clearly. Spencer asked me how I was doing. I told him I was fine. He asked me if I was still seeing Alexandra and I told him you never know, he might be reading all about it in a day or two." She leaned forward. "I meant in the *Inquiring Eye,* Howard, not writing my autobiography."

He nodded, feeling almost numb with disappointment. Well, that was that. Goodbye three-and-a-half-million-dollar book deal. Spencer Hawes must have been drunk.

All might not be lost, though. At least not for Amanda. "Georgiana, if Catherine the Great did get made..."

"Yes?"

"And you were to play her..."

"Yes?"

"Might you keep a journal and take pictures over the course of the making of the film? Soup to nuts? And then later, when you had time, work on transforming it into a book? A memoir of filmmaking?"

"That's not a three-and-a-half-million-dollar book, Howard."

"Who cares if it's a fifty-thousand dollar book if you enjoyed writing it and it was good?"

One exquisite eyebrow arched. "Like *The African Queen?* Only after thinking about it for thirty minutes instead of thirty years?"

"And with or without an Oscar." He smiled. "Well, let me start with the option status on Amanda's book and then—" He cocked his head and raised a hand to his ear. "I think that might be my wife coming in now."

Amanda Sees Her Old Friend

"SO YOU SEE, dear," Mrs. Goldblum said, holding Amanda's hand, "everything is quite all right."

Amanda's lower lip began to quiver and she bowed her head to hide it, looking at the hand-crocheted coverlet Mrs. Goldblum's mother had made that was spread over the hospital bed. The bed could be cranked up so that Mrs. Goldblum could look out over the park and the river, and it had sides so she could not fall out.

The Jamaican nurse's aide, Virginia, was pleasant enough. The room was lovely, with flowers and a lot of pictures. What Amanda still didn't understand was how all this could have transpired so quickly. She had seen Mrs. Goldblum a week before Christmas. Granted, she had seemed a little under the weather, and they had cut their tea short for Mrs. Goldblum to "have a rest," but now to see her friend in this bed, to hear her faltering speech, was heartbreaking.

"You—" Amanda's voice broke. She swallowed and raised her head, struggling to smile. "You know this is difficult news."

"Of course," the older woman said softly.

Mrs. Goldblum's hand felt so light in Amanda's, scarcely weighing a thing. Her nails were filed though, and carefully painted in a muted pink. That would be Rosanne. And Mrs. Goldblum's hair was done. It was not the way it used to be (her hairdresser had an unmistakable "do" for her), but it was still attractive. That was sure to cheer Mrs. Goldblum, Amanda knew, to be able to look at herself in the mirror and know however ill she might be she was still "tickety-boo."

"I'd like to the bring the children to see you, if that's all right," Amanda said.

She smiled, her head resting back against the pillow. "I would like to see the children."

Amanda wondered how much Emily and Teddy would understand. The woman they had played Chutes and Ladders with on Thanksgiving was now preparing to leave this world and wished the people she loved to see her on her way. That much she had understood from Rosanne. Hospice was a process to familiarize everyone with the rites of death and to make the passage a loving one for the patient and their family.

Daniel, Mrs. Goldblum's son, had been here this week, Rosanne had told Amanda. And he'd behaved well. (One would hope that at sixty years old he finally would!)

"I'm sure Howard will be dropping by very soon," Amanda said, taking a deep breath in an effort to maintain control. "I find it most fortunate that I was planning to spend much more time in Manhattan anyway."

This seemed to catch Mrs. Goldblum's interest. "Oh?"

Amanda nodded. "I need to be with Howard more. I want to spend more time with him."

Mrs. Goldblum made a sound expressing that she understood.

Amanda took another breath, looking out at the river, and gave Mrs. Goldblum's hand a squeeze. "I'm seriously thinking about moving the children back to Manhattan. Putting them in school here." She looked at the older woman, unsure of what she would think of this plan. After 9/11 Mrs. Goldblum had been all for the exodus of the Stewart children to the relative safety of the suburbs.

"A very wise decision, my dear," Mrs. Goldblum said.

Amanda blinked. She had not expected this answer. "You sound very sure."

There was a hint of a smile, but Mrs. Goldblum's eyes were growing weary. "I am sure."

A few minutes later she drifted off to sleep and after watching her awhile, Amanda went to the kitchen. "She's asleep," she reported to Rosanne.

"You okay?"

Amanda crossed her arms over her chest and nodded, but then felt herself starting to give way. Rosanne pulled out a kitchen chair and guided her down into it, and Amanda lowered her head to the table and wept. The pending loss of Mrs. Goldblum felt unbearable. Why had she wasted all that time in Connecticut?

She wasn't sure how long she cried, but after a while she sat up, reached for a paper napkin, and then wept a little into that. She started to get under control when she felt a hand on her shoulder and she looked up to see Cassy Cochran. "I'm so very glad you're here," Cassy said softly. "And that you know. I don't have to tell you how much you mean to Emma."

A Walk in the Park

CASSY AND AMANDA went for a walk in Riverside Park. "Look at the snow!" Cassy cried when they got outside. It was coming down thick and furious, blowing on the diagonal. It wasn't a cold wind, though, but eerily springlike. Cassy pulled up the hood up on her winter coat and Amanda put on a knit hat. They walked north at first, against the wind, not down into the park proper but along the perimeter brownstone wall. Way down, on the river level, they could see the West Side Highway was jammed with cars trying to make it out of the city before the roads got bad. Amanda said they were too late, the roads were already bad in the suburbs.

Amanda asked a great many questions about Emma's condition and Cassy answered them as best she could. She explained that there was a tumor near her lung, that it might possibly be surgically removed and followed by chemotherapy, but Mrs. Goldblum had chosen to forego that route.

"I don't blame her," Amanda said.

"In truth," Cassy said, slinging her arm through Amanda's, "nor do I."

"She looks so tiny in that bed," Amanda said. "She doesn't seem to be in pain, though."

"She's started on morphine," Cassy explained. "The nurse will increase the dose as the pain increases."

"What does the doctor say?"

"He's signed off the case."

Amanda looked at her, blinking rapidly. "Is that because—?"

"It's the hospice process. If she doesn't want to go back to the hospital, doesn't want to be treated any longer, the charge of care transfers away from her doctor. He came by, I think Rosanne said. Or he's going to. I'm afraid after a while I start to lose track. That's why Virginia keeps that log. So we can all see exactly what has happened every single day."

Amanda looked at her. "You've done a great deal, Cassy."

She shrugged. "I wish I could do more." She stopped. "This storm's getting worse, Amanda, maybe we should turn around."

They did, walking back down the Drive. Amanda suddenly stopped. "Five weeks, Cassy. Only five weeks ago she was sitting at our dining room table trying to decide between pumpkin pie or pecan pie and she ended up eating a little of both!"

Cassy didn't know what to say.

"Now she can barely—" Amanda held out her hand and then dropped it. "It's not fair," she said, starting to walk again. "Intellectually I understand she's eighty-nine years old, Cassy, but I don't care. Does that make any sense?"

"I know. Why does she have to go when there are so many—?"

"Vermin stalking the earth," Amanda finished for her. "Evil violent creatures from hell, yet Emma Goldblum has to die."

"We all have to die," Cassy said after a moment.

"I guess this is what it takes for us to remember that," Amanda said.

Sleet was mixing in with the snow now and it stung Cassy's face. The storm was turning into a nor'easter. They reached the Stewarts' building and Amanda asked Cassy up for a cup of tea. Cassy wanted to say no—she had work piled to the ceiling to do—but the sadness in Amanda's eyes prompted her to say yes, she would like that.

The doorman let them in and they shook themselves off in the lobby. They went up to the eleventh floor and Amanda unlocked the apartment door. Howard was having a client meeting here this afternoon—Amanda explained to Cassy, taking her coat and hanging it up—so if Cassy didn't mind they'd have tea in the kitchen. It was a large, bright, warm kitchen and Cassy helped herself to a seat at the round table in the bay window while Amanda put the kettle on. A moment later Howard came in through the swinging doors.

"Hi, Cassy," Howard said, seeing her first. He then went to Amanda and kissed her hello. Holding Amanda by the elbows he asked after Mrs. Goldblum.

Amanda nodded. "She's very ill."

"I'm so sorry," he said sympathetically.

"Cassy says it could be a matter of weeks." And then Amanda burst into tears on her husband's shoulder. Howard held her tight, stroking her hair and murmuring something. There was an exchange Cassy couldn't hear and then Howard looked at Cassy over Amanda's shoulder.

"Could you tell my client I need a minute?" he whispered.

"Howard, I'm fine—" Amanda started to protest.

Howard kept his hold on her and nodded to Cassy to please do as he asked.

Cassy touched at her hair for a moment before going through the swinging door into the dining room. She crossed the deep Persian rug and dark wood floors to reach the living room.

Once there she didn't know who was more surprised, she or Georgiana Hamilton-Ayres.

Cassy is Made to Feel Like the Lowest Form of Life

"CASSY! IT'S BEEN too long!" Georgiana said, jumping up from the settee to give her a kiss and a hug. She held Cassy's hands in her own for a minute, looking at her with genuine fondness. Then a hint of pain appeared in her eyes. Cassy knew she had to be thinking of all the dinner parties, cocktail parties, fund-raisers and birthday parties they had shared because of Alexandra.

"I'm so surprised to see you," Cassy said honestly.

"Howard and I are talking about some possible book projects," she said, releasing Cassy. She dropped her voice. "Bennett, Fitzallen & Coe wanted him to approach me about writing an autobiography. I told him a party or two might not be wild about me writing a kiss and tell—" She half grimaced. "And told him, no, I wouldn't do it."

Cassy nodded. What else could she do? Then she remembered why she had been sent out here. "Howard asked me to tell you he needed a minute with Amanda. A close mutual friend of ours is dying. Amanda just saw her."

"Oh, I'm so sorry. What does your friend have?"

"Cancer. But she's older—"

"That doesn't make it any easier when you love someone." She turned to look out the window. "That snow doesn't look too promising for my flight out tonight, does it?"

"I think the airports are probably closed," Cassy said. "It's only supposed to get worse."

Howard came in and Georgiana said she really needed to get going. When they moved to the front hall to retrieve Georgiana's coat, Amanda appeared, apologizing for barging in. Georgiana took one look at her and threw her arms around her in a hug, murmuring, "I know, I know, it's very difficult," while Howard and Cassy awkwardly looked on. Then Georgiana gave Amanda another brief hug, kissed Cassy goodbye, saying they should get together soon, and Howard saw her to the elevator while Amanda and Cassy returned to the kitchen.

Amanda made a pot of tea and Howard brought the tea cart in from the living room. Cassy drank a cup of tea but passed on the food, watching the clock. As soon as it was polite to do so she made her apologies to leave and promised Amanda they would keep in touch.

In the elevator, Cassy leaned back against the wall, holding the bridge of her nose a minute. She had the worst headache, either from the weather or the stress, she didn't know. She did know she was on overload.

As she crossed the lobby her heart sank when she saw the limousine waiting out front in the snowstorm. She knew who it was. She took a breath, pulled her shoulders back, and, as if she didn't know who it was waiting for her, stepped out under the awning and pulled up her hood. Almost immediately the mirrored rear window of the limo went down.

"You were right," Georgiana called, "the airports are closed."

"I thought they might be," Cassy said, pulling on her gloves as she walked over.

"Please get in," Georgiana said. Before Cassy could respond the door had swung open and Georgiana was sliding across the seat to make room for her.

She had no choice but to get in.

"Where are you going?" the actress asked her.

"Only home, at Eighty-eighth—"

Georgiana told the driver to go down Ninetieth and circle around to Eighty-eighth Street. Then she raised the barrier between them.

"I'd invite you up for a drink," Cassy said, pulling her sleeve back to look at her watch, "but I have a conference call shortly."

"This won't take long," the actress promised, unhooking her coat and crossing her legs in Cassy's direction. "I only wished to ask if you know what really happened, why Alexandra suddenly bolted."

Cassy was at a loss.

"At first I thought it was cold feet about the baby." She met Cassy's eyes. "But Alexandra's not the type to get cold feet about anything."

Georgiana was exquisitely beautiful and needed not a dab of makeup to achieve it. She had her mother's porcelain skin and some of Lillian Bartlett's features as well—certainly the eyes, hair and body—but it was the refined features of her father that most successfully contrasted her more sensuous gifts. They called her the sophisticated man's ideal.

"I've longed to call you, Cassy, but to be perfectly honest, I wasn't ready yet to hear what anybody else had to say." She paused, dropping her eyes. "I was too upset." Looking back up she said, "Please tell me what you know."

Cassy felt like the lowest form of life. "I can't speak for

Alexandra, but I think, given the circumstances of her life, she may have felt it wasn't fair to the child for her to become a parent."

"She used to say that. And I was the one pushing for a child," Georgiana said, dropping her eyes again. After a moment she looked up and touched Cassy's arm. "Thank you. I knew you would know."

She would probably burn in hell for this.

"I'm not convinced that was the reason, however," Georgiana added, withdrawing her hand. "From the beginning she always said that she loved me, but was afraid she might not love me the way she should."

Cassy's forehead wrinkled.

"She was being honest. You know Alexandra. She never pulls any punches." She looked out the window. "Except at the very end. One day we were going to have a child and the next—" She turned back to Cassy. "She said she was sorry. And that was the end of it. Gone. Like those four years had never happened."

"I'm sorry," Cassy said.

And she was.

Sitting here looking at Georgiana it was difficult to believe Alexandra had chosen her. Of course there was the child aspect; had that issue not come up Alexandra might very well still be with her.

It was pointless to try and second-guess what had happened and what could have happened.

"I'm sure there's somebody else," Georgiana said. "There was someone before, before me, who she would never talk about. So I knew." She started to cry. "I vowed I would not do this anymore." She leaned forward to snatch some tissues from the holder and looked out her window as she wiped her eyes. "I was so sure Alexandra was the one." She wiped her nose, sniffing. After a moment she turned to Cassy, trying to smile. "I'm sorry to do this to you."

"Please don't apologize," Cassy said. In this moment she thought if she had any decency left she would go home, call Alexandra and tell her she was never leaving Jackson and that Alexandra must reach out to Georgiana before it was too late. Georgiana would be so much better for Alexandra in so many ways.

Although, Cassy remembered, there had been clouds on the horizon of their relationship. Cassy got the distinct feeling from Alexandra that at one point Georgiana had some kind of fling with her male costar on location. (He was gorgeous, a kind of swashbuckling superstar.) Had that been the cause of their first separation? Cassy had never been sure.

"You would think with all the world has to offer, and all the world has blessed me with," Georgiana said, sitting back against the seat, "I could simply move on."

"Give yourself some time," Cassy said quietly. "I think it's clear you need to have some kind of resolution with Alexandra. When you're feeling up to it. To talk through it."

"The difficulty does not lie with me, Cassy. As you know, Alexandra is not terribly keen on messy emotional encounters."

And there you are wrong, Georgiana. Alexandra and I have done nothing but wade through messy emotions for years.

"She will opt, every time," Georgiana said, "to steal off in the night."

The limo had stopped on the side of Riverside Drive right across from the Soldiers' and Sailors' monument at 88th. There was almost no traffic now, though the M5 bus was braving Riverside Drive through the storm, the windshield wipers flailing madly, the glow of inside lights inviting.

"I only wish to know to whom she was going," Georgiana said to Cassy.

Her eyes were large, luminous. And moist. Georgiana was a wonderful actress, which Alexandra said had been part of the problem.

"If you knew who it was," Georgiana said, "would you tell me?"

Cassy shook her head. "I'm sorry, but it's not my place."

"So you do know who it is." Georgiana's voice had taken on a slightly accusatory tone. She looked out her window for a moment before turning back to Cassy. "You're right, of course, it's not your place. I must ask Alexandra directly."

"If it's that important to you, of course you must," Cassy said.

"Perhaps it's vain of me, Cassy, but I can't imagine what another woman could bring to the relationship that I didn't. We not only loved each other, but we got on so well! Surely you must have seen that."

Cassy nodded, looking down at her lap.

It was now or never.

Alexandra had never told Georgiana about her. She had been trying to protect her. And them. And others, including Jackson and DBS. If Georgiana ever decided to go public with the story, they would lose all control over the situation.

Cassy raised her head. "You don't have closure, do you?"

"No." She had reached for another tissue and was dabbing at her eyes.

After a moment she said, "I'll speak to Alexandra."

Georgiana lowered the tissue. "Would you? She'll listen to you. And then I won't have to get hysterical while trying to explain myself."

Cassy nodded. "Yes, I will," she promised.

The Mission of Sam Wyatt

SAM GOT ON the last flight out of LaGuardia. It was also the last to land in Binghamton before that airport shut down because of snow. When he emerged from the terminal it was practically a blizzard. Actually, it was a blizzard, but these Binghamton people seemed only energized by the storm and continued driving (and sliding) around on the roads muffled by snow. Sam climbed into a cab, gave the driver the address and off they went, tire chains spewing snow behind them. The address was on the south side of the city, the driver explained, and he thought it best to get on 81 for a while. Trucks and other high-riding four-wheel-drive vehicles kept a one-lane caravan moving on the New York State Thruway and there were only occasional passenger cars spun out and abandoned on the side of the road.

Sam had his seat belt buckled and looked out the window, willing the car to stay on the road until they reached the office complex. It appeared that snow never closed anything down around Binghamton except the airport.

"Mr. Washington?" an attractive secretary asked Sam when she appeared in the waiting room of Ericksson Laboratories & Pharmaceuticals. "Mr. Culmathson is ready to see you. If you'll just follow me."

"Mr. Washington," the man said jovially, striding to the door extending his hand. "Steve Culmathson."

Steve Culmathson was about Sam's height, six-two, and he was a big guy, just like Sam. Not overweight but later he'd have to watch it. He appeared to be in his late-thirties, maybe early-forties. He was definitely white. He had brown hair, a receding hairline and brown eyes. He was also a sharp dresser. His handshake was firm and dry and he touched Sam's arm with his other hand while they shook, implying he liked Sam already. Well, he should. Sam had told his office he was a purchasing agent for a group of New York hospitals who had heard so many great things about the service Culmathson's sales people provided.

Culmathson asked him if he'd had any trouble getting in from the airport and Sam told him, no, he'd taken a cab, but the airport was closed now. Culmathson said he'd get him a great hotel room nearby to stay over.

Sam tucked his folio under his arm and walked straight over to the windowsill to pick up an 8 1/2-by-11 framed picture. It was of an attractive but heavyset woman and two boys, around ten and six maybe. "Are you a family man, Mr. Culmathson?"

"Steve, call me Steve. And, yes, I am." He walked over. "That's my lovely wife, Karen, and our boys, Steve Jr. and Scooter. Well, Peter's his real name."

"Nice-looking family," Sam said, handing the picture off to him.

"Thanks. I think so." He put it back on the windowsill. "Help yourself to a seat."

"I will, thank you," Sam said, sitting down. "So how long have you been married?"

"Almost thirteen years."

"That's great," Sam said. "I find it's generally better to deal with family men in business."

"I couldn't agree more," Culmathson said, plunking down behind his desk and folding his hands on top of it.

He would agree with anything Sam said because he was a salesman. "Your children look very happy and very healthy."

He grinned. "They are. Karen says too healthy sometimes."

"And how do they do in school?"

There was the slightest flicker of a question in Culmathson's eyes. "Steve Jr.'s the scholar and Scooter's the athlete."

"Did you play sports?" Sam asked.

"Yeah. I wasn't great, but I got my three letters in high school. Football, basketball, baseball."

Sam was looking up at the degree on the wall.

"I went to Oswego State. I didn't play sports there. I was a business major."

Was his smile now just a trifle nervous? Whether it was or wasn't, Sam decided Culmathson's teeth were bonded. He hoped his grandchild wouldn't inherit bad teeth. They were excellent on Samantha's side of the family.

"So," Steve said, leaning forward, "I'm dying to know what hospitals you represent."

Sam opened his folio and took out a manilla folder. He saw Steve's smile expand in expectation. Sam leaned to hand it to him.

"Okay, let's see what we've got here," Steve said, opening the folder. Almost immediately he frowned, his eyes skipping around on the page. He turned to the next page and his look of dismay grew. He closed the folder. "Who the hell are you?"

"Name's Sam Wyatt." He let his words hang in the air a moment. "I'm a family man, too."

It could have been a full minute of silence that they glared at each other.

"What do you want?" Culmathson said, breaking eye contact. His face was set like granite.

"You have some papers there you need to sign." He kept his cool. "When you sign the top two you are giving up all rights to the child my daughter is about to give birth to." He pursed his lips for a moment. "Got a problem with that?"

The guy's stony expression didn't change. "No."

"Didn't think so," Sam said, looking at the picture of Culmathson's family.

"What are these other papers?" Culmathson asked. He had opened the folder again and was looking through it.

"Just fill in your social security number and then sign and date it. You've agreed to undergo a complete medical workup and to provide a complete medical—" his eyes narrowed slightly "—and dental history."

He had gone on to another page. "I can't just sign these without my lawyer looking at them."

"Sure you can. Or maybe you want your lovely wife, Karen, to look them over, too."

Culmathson was reading. "I don't know what Samantha's told you," he said quietly without looking up, "but she was not an innocent in this."

The rage caught Sam in the back of his throat and he told himself to hang on. "On the other hand, if you just out of the blue *died*," Sam mused aloud, "before you signed those papers, then your black child would get a nice chunk of your estate. And two half brothers. How much life insurance did you say you had?" He didn't wait for a response, but got up and went to the doorway. "Could I trouble you for a minute? We have some papers here that Mr. Culmathson is signing and we need a witness. Would you mind?"

The secretary came in and Sam and Culmathson locked eyes. "Unless you want her to proof them for you, Steve, it would be fine if you just signed and dated each document, and then had her sign and date them as well as you go through them."

The secretary smiled, raising her pen and waiting for where it was to be directed. After a moment Culmathson covered a document with his arm and then signed it. He waved her over. "Here?" she asked.

"Where it says *witness.*" She signed it. And then they worked their way through the folder. When Culmathson finally closed the folder his secretary left.

Sam reached over for the folder. "Thank you." He took care in putting it back in his folio.

"Samantha said she'd already taken care of this."

"I like filling in the blanks more than she does," Sam said, standing up. The two men gauged one another warily.

"I care about Samantha," Culmathson finally said. "Don't think I don't. Because I do."

"She's nineteen, shithead," Sam said. And then he left.

Howard and Amanda

AFTER CASSY COCHRAN left the Stewarts' apartment Amanda went into their bedroom to lie down. Howard cleaned up the tea cart and dishes, carefully wrapped the food and put it in the refrigerator. He walked back to their bedroom to check on Amanda and found her sleeping. He stood at the foot of the bed and leaned against the bedpost, watching her.

Amanda had always been perceived as the vulnerable one, and perhaps in the early years of their marriage that had been true. But at this point did Amanda even need him anymore? She could handle the children with or without Madame Moliere. She had her own money. She had this apartment. She had a career if she wanted it. He, on the other hand, was about to lose everything if Amanda didn't bail him out. He had been telling Amanda for years not to worry about money and now he had to tell her he was near bankruptcy.

It felt like a kind of death to have to tell Amanda how he'd failed her. She had never failed him. Ever.

He pushed off the bedpost and made his way through the apartment. While their room had not changed since they'd married, they had made two bedrooms out of the guest room for Emily and Teddy and then a second full bathroom and tiny guest room from the original third bedroom. When Grace arrived the tiny guest room became Madame Moliere's, with Grace shuffled between their room and Emily's.

Maybe they should just sell the apartment.

Howard went into the study he and Amanda shared and sat down at his desk. He opened the double drawer to remove the accordion file that held the papers outlining his disaster.

"You still haven't downsized the agency," the accountant had said. "You won't move to smaller offices, you won't tell the employees they have to contribute more to their health care plan, nobody seems to keep track of the expenses your clients are racking up, and you went ahead and gave your employees Christmas bonuses when you can't cover their salaries because you're paying all these damn interest charges on all these debts. And you're asking me why I can't make the books look any better?"

"I will not watch our marriage die with Mrs. Goldblum," Amanda's voice suddenly announced from behind Howard.

He turned around. Amanda was standing in the doorway, her arms crossed over her chest.

He brought his left arm up to rest on the back of the chair. "What do you mean?"

"I want to move back to New York, Howard."

He tried to think. "I thought you liked it out there. With the horses and everything."

Amanda walked over to her desk and slowly sat down sideways in her chair to face him. "I don't like anywhere if you're not with us."

He looked down at his lap. He had to tell her. All of it. He had to tell her now.

"Oh, Howard, don't you want me to live with you anymore?"

"Oh, my God, Amanda," he said, startled. "Yes, yes, yes I do. The question is—the question is whether you will want to after what I have to tell you."

Amanda took a sharp intake of breath and then slid her arms around to hold herself. She was preparing herself for a shock, he realized; good, she understood that what he had to tell her was bad. Her eyes moved up to the framed photograph of the five of them on the wall. It had been taken last summer by a neighbor, near the community garden in Riverside Park. Howard, Amanda, Teddy and Emily were standing arm in arm behind Grace's stroller. Ashette was sitting by the stroller, her tongue hanging out. It was a wonderful picture, filled with life and love and laughter. "I think I know already," she said quietly, still looking at the photograph.

"I don't know how you could. I was pretty careful to hide it from you."

She took another one of those short breaths and looked at him. "You've been avoiding me, Howard. Emotionally, mentally, physically. I know what that means."

"I'm not sure that you do," he said, starting to feel confused.

"I almost had an affair in Connecticut."

It took a moment before Howard realized he was standing up.

"I wasn't aware that I was moving in that direction," she continued. "I think, in the back of my mind, I didn't want to be completely bereft when you finally told me. Because then I'd have somebody who wanted me."

He felt sick. "My God, Amanda, I do want you. I've always wanted you." And then he felt the flush of anger. "Who is he?"

"It doesn't matter, Howard, because it didn't happen. Instead I'm sitting here."

He felt for the chair to sit down. An affair? Amanda? In Connecticut? Was she making this up?

Howard looked at his wife and knew that she wasn't. Of course she wasn't. With all the rich married guys out there, who wouldn't want to have an affair with Amanda? She was still a knockout, but it was her soaring spirit, that high passion and emotion that would have attracted him. A soccer game. That's just the venue where they would see it, Amanda with her arms shooting up in the air with a cheer, and then her suddenly cringing at a downward turn in the game, sighing with such sorrow it always made people laugh fondly. The looks of the men always lingered on his wife after she had drawn their attention. Three kids later and she still had that body. She dressed differently to disguise the fact it wasn't the same body, really, but the effect it had on men was still the same. They could imagine the bliss that lay there.

"Shit," he said out loud, taking his glasses off to hold his face in his hand a minute. He was sick at this point. And he just wanted to run. If things had gotten this bad—

"I know you're not in love with someone else," Amanda said. "I would know that."

He put his glasses back on. "You think I'm having an *affair?*"

"I think you have taken your needs somewhere."

"My needs," he said sarcastically. He looked up at the ceiling a minute. "My needs are close to a million needs." He brought his head down to look at her. "There is no one else, Amanda. I have not had sex with anyone else. I have not wanted to have an affair." A fleeting memory of kissing Celia Cavanaugh came and went. "The only secret I've been hiding from you is the fact I am in debt up to my ears. To the tune of close to a million dollars."

It took her a few seconds to absorb his words. "But we still have income from the trust fund, don't we?"

We, she'd said *we.* But his mind was elsewhere. "Who was it, Amanda? Someone I know?"

"I doubt it," she said.

She was lying. He knew whoever it was. It had to be one of the guys at the soccer games. If he had to guess, it was the investment banker. The guy had made millions and then retired at fifty with a second wife and a second set of kids. He'd break his friggin' face in.

"Who is it we owe?" Amanda asked.

"You don't owe anything, Amanda. It's me. I've wrung every penny out of the Woodbury property and have credit card bills up the gazoo." Her consternation made him angry. "I had to balance the books at the agency, pay some tax stuff I owed, and there simply wasn't enough cash coming in to pay for the heat, the light, the horses, the orthodontist, the piano lessons, Madame Moliere, the handyman, the pool man, the cleaning lady, the cars, the clothes, the vacations— You know, all the crap you kept asking me if we could afford!" He slammed his hand down on his desk for lack of knowing what else to do. "I've never been so ashamed in my life," he told her, his eyes down on his desk.

"I could petition the trust to see if—"

"No!" he shouted, slamming the desk again. "That's your money. Keep it safe and sound. The way we're going you're going to need it in your new life."

A moment later he felt Amanda's hand on his shoulder and he looked up. Her eyes were filled with tears but she was smiling. "I thought you didn't love me anymore, Howard."

He didn't know what to say and she sat down on the chair arm, took off his glasses and pulled his head to rest against her chest. After a moment he slid his arms around her waist.

"Money I can handle," she soothed, stroking his head. "Actually, I can handle anything as long as I have you and the children. I should hope you know that by now."

He was going to say, yeah, right, you were about to let another guy— He screwed his eyes shut, trying to get the image out of his head.

"Explain to me what happened," she said gently.

And so he did. He kept his head right where it was and told her how at first he had thought the problems started when Gertrude Bristol died but had since come to realize it went all the way back to when he bought Hillings & Hillings. How he had prided himself on not letting anyone go, of keeping those same offices in the landmark building, of being able to offer better benefits. No, it had started when he went big-time. "I wasn't thinking clearly when I bought the house," he said.

"None of us were thinking clearly after 9/11."

"But you and the kids were so excited when you saw it, what with the horse farm next door and the stable and everything." She murmured that she knew. "It was eight hundred thousand, I had two hundred sitting in the reserves at the agency and I used that as the down payment." He sighed. "Now I owe a million on it."

"But how were you to know Gertrude's niece would nix the estate deal?"

"Yeah," he agreed, "that was a part of it."

"And how were you supposed to know what's-her-name—"

He couldn't help but smile. Whenever Amanda didn't like how someone had behaved she refused to call them by name.

"—was going to steal your clients?" she finished.

"It wasn't quite like that." He sat up and pulled her down off the arm of the chair to sit in his lap. He brushed her hair back from her face. "Pride goeth before the fall. That's what the accountant said to me. He wanted me to slash the overhead a long time ago, but I kept thinking things would turn around."

"You only got into difficulty because you wanted to do what was best for everyone. Your family, your employees, your clients. You're a fabulous literary agent, Howard, everyone says so."

"So I used to think." He sighed.

"Surely this is a temporary state of affairs. It's not as though you don't make any money."

"The agency grossed almost seven million last year, bringing in nearly a million, and I made negative two hundred thirty-one thousand."

"Oh," Amanda said.

He looked at her. "Unless we take out a mortgage or home equity loan on this apartment, Amanda, we're going to lose the house."

"Then I say lose it."

He looked at her.

"I'm absolutely serious. Let's sell it and be done with it."

"I owe more than it's worth, though."

"The minute we don't own it anymore is the minute the other bills stop. Yes?"

He nodded. In all these months this idea had not occurred to him, to sell the house and get rid of that colossal ongoing expense. Of course he hadn't known Amanda was about to have an affair with another man. Damn right they were going to sell that house!

"And what about Henry's grandson?" Amanda said. "Didn't you say he might come in as a partner?"

"The agency still needs to be restructured."

"So you'll be the hatchet man."

He nodded.

"That's going to be difficult," Amanda sighed. "But we'd help people find jobs, wouldn't we?"

We.

"Yeah."

She ducked her head to see what expression was on his face. "What is it, Howard?"

He tried to think how best to phrase it without sounding ungrateful. If he had to make all the changes in the agency the accountant said had to be made, he wasn't going to feel the same about it. Because it wouldn't be the same. A more gracious professional atmosphere would break down into the usual sweatshop atmosphere that so much of book publishing had fallen into. And if he had to cut back on staff, it would meaning cutting down his time developing clients. Bestselling writers didn't just walk in the door. Most often, at least at his agency, they were writers he worked with (like the editor he had once been), whose books were sold to publishers only after they had been edited at least once. And that was the part that had made him want to be a literary agent, to work with writers.

"Don't freak out because I'm not going to do anything rash," he said, "but I'm beginning to wonder if this is how I want to spend the next twenty years."

"Being married or being an agent?" she said. She was smiling.

"Convincing you to marry me has been my only really great success in life."

"That and your love and support in producing three such wonderful, healthy children."

Howard shut his eyes, pressing his forehead into her shoulder.

"I know, darling," she murmured, rubbing his back. "But we're never living apart again." A tear rolled down her cheek and she kissed the side of his head. "Ever. Ever, ever, ever."

Cassy and Alexandra Have a Talk

ALEXANDRA WAS SITTING on the windowsill of the master bedroom in Cassy's old apartment, watching the storm. Jackson was stuck in Washington, and the only reason Alexandra had been able to get here after the newscast was because the man who plowed West End had given her a lift. She had showered; her hair was in a ponytail and she was naked beneath the terry-cloth robe. "I can't believe Georgiana has no idea it's you."

Cassy laughed softly into her pillow.

"Why are you laughing?"

Cassy drew herself up to sit, holding the sheet over her breasts. "Because, my darling, you are the only person on the face of the earth who would choose me over her."

"That's not true," Alexandra said, turning back to the window.

"I appreciate the sentiment, but it is true," Cassy said. "No doubt Georgiana thinks it's some lovely young woman who will keep the home fires burning for you."

"I bet Georgiana didn't say anything to you about how she would leave for a month at a time," Alexandra said, "and then reappear when she felt like it, expecting me to drop everything."

"I don't think Georgiana ever expected you to drop anything. It sounded to me as though she had been planning to stay home with the baby, at least for a while."

"Oh, come on, Cassy," Alexandra said, sliding off the windowsill, "give me some credit, will you? Don't you think I had a pretty good idea of what raising a child with Georgiana would have been like before I broke it off?" She walked over to stand at the foot of the bed. She had been eager to make love after her shower because of the storm, she said. There was something about storms that did it to her. But as soon as Cassy mentioned that she had seen Georgiana, Alexandra's desire had vanished and agitation had set in.

"Compared to Georgiana's upbringing," Alexandra said, "dragging a child and a nanny around the world with her would be, in Georgiana's eyes, idyllic. Punctuated by visits to the farm to ride in a pony cart with the child's other famous lesbian mother. Namely me." She sighed heavily and dropped down on the bed, her back to Cassy. "We had to have major battles before having a child. And I had to win those battles before I would agree to it."

Cassy felt a twist of something cold in her stomach. Alexandra had wanted a baby. She had wanted to have a baby with Georgiana, and only when they couldn't come to terms had she broken off the relationship.

Alexandra hadn't chosen her over Georgiana. She had broken it off with Georgiana over the child and then had come to Cassy.

She was Alexandra's second choice, not her first.

"I wanted the child's home base to be here, in the East," Alexandra said. "Not here a month, in California a month and then flitting around the world, Scotland this week, on location the next." She paused. "But Georgiana would have none of it, there was no way she was giving up California."

Alexandra headed into the bathroom. A short while later she came back out. She took one look at Cassy and hurried to sit next to her. "What's wrong? You look sick or something." She felt Cassy's forehead. "What is it?"

Cassy couldn't lie to her. It simply wasn't possible anymore. "I think I misunderstood why you broke up with Georgiana. I thought— Oh, it's stupid, it doesn't make any difference," she muttered, looking away.

Alexandra gently pulled her chin so Cassy had to look at her. "Tell me."

"I thought you left Georgiana because you couldn't live without me." She closed her eyes after tears sprang into them and offered a bitter laugh. "How could I be so stupid," she said, bringing a hand up to cover her face.

"What are you talking about?" Alexandra said, sounding irritated. When Cassy didn't answer, she pulled her hand away. "But I *did* leave Georgiana because I *don't* want to live without you. I never have."

"But that was only after you disagreed about—"

"What is the matter with you?" Alexandra interrupted. She gave Cassy's shoulders a little shake. "Look at me. I love you more than anything or anyone on the face of the earth. That is the truth. I tried to run away from it because I was so angry you wouldn't leave Jackson. And looking back, thank God you didn't leave him, because I think that would have been the end of DBS News."

Cassy's heart was beginning to slow down a little.

"I couldn't make you leave him, and it took me a while to realize that having part of a life with you was better than a wholehearted commitment from Georgiana, or at least what she considered was wholehearted." She had sadness in her eyes. "I spent twice as many nights with you, like this, than I ever did with Georgiana. And then to drag a child into it—" She held Cassy's face in her hands. "I wanted to be with you. Any way I could be." She kissed Cassy, but Cassy could tell her mind was elsewhere.

"I think I understand," Cassy said tentatively.

"I don't have a problem telling Georgiana about us," she said, brushing Cassy's hair back from her face. "But not yet." Alexandra lowered her hand, thinking. "Move over a little, will you?"

Alexandra always slept on the right side of the bed, but now she slipped under the sheets on the left and lay on her side to look at Cassy. "If you and I ever do get together, I mean *really* get together, you know there is going to be a lot to deal with."

Cassy had never truly been able to imagine *living* with Alexandra. And if she did some day, and word got around, it would take a long time before friends and family would come to believe it. Not because Alexandra was a woman, but because they wouldn't believe Cassy could ever fly in the face of her conventional upbringing.

"When and if we ever do make a life together," Alexandra continued, "I will tell Georgiana before anyone else."

"I felt like the lowest form of life today," Cassy said after a moment.

"I can imagine," Alexandra murmured.

"I almost told her."

"I'm not surprised." Cassy dropped her eyes and Alexandra reached for her hand.

"I'm scared," Cassy whispered.

Alexandra's grip tightened.

"I'm so much older than you are," Cassy said. "It's hard to believe—"

"Still beating that dead horse, are you?" Alexandra brought Cassy's hand up to her mouth to kiss. "May I make a suggestion?"

"Yes."

"Might you consider one day truly placing your trust in me? You did it with Michael. You did it with Jackson. Maybe you should try doing it with me."

Cassy closed her eyes, feeling the anxiety. "The thing is," she said, opening them, "I didn't trust them, Alexandra, not really. What I did was hand myself over to them and trusted that they would fix my life. Fix me."

Alexandra bit her lower lip.

"I pray to God I've learned to trust myself. To at least believe that I am the person who knows what's best for me." They looked at each for a minute and then Cassy smiled. "You are best for me."

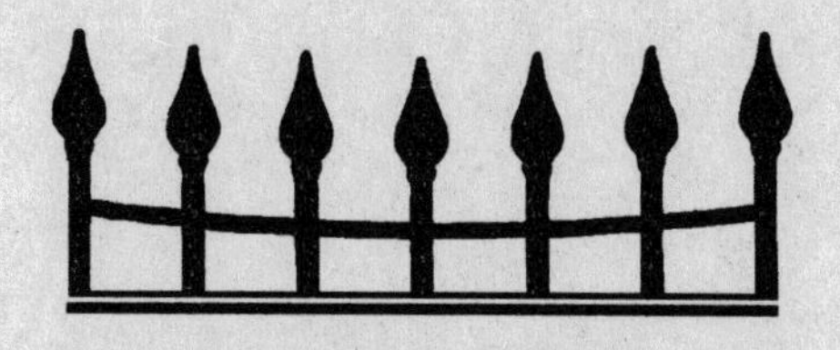

FEBRUARY

Celia and Her Auctions

"YOU *ARE* DIFFERENT," Rachel told Celia. Rachel and her boyfriend were sitting at the breakfast bar and the smell of fresh coffee had lured Celia from her bedroom. "We were just talking about it."

"It's not supposed to kick in for six weeks," Celia mumbled, getting a mug. "It hasn't even been a month." She was still feeling very self-conscious about the antidepressant her mother's doctor had persuaded her to try.

"Well, I'm telling you, Ceil, you're different."

"Okay," Celia said, pouring her coffee, "like how?" She went to the refrigerator to get some milk.

"Well, for one, you're up and it's nine o'clock in the morning," her roommate said, nodding in the direction of the kitchen clock.

"Two," Rachel's boyfriend piped up, "you haven't gotten blasted out of your mind."

"Three," Rachel continued, "you're putting your dirty clothes in the hamper that I've never seen you use before. And your room's not perfect, but it sure is a heck of a lot better than it was."

"And four," the boyfriend said, nudging Rachel, "she cooks now." He looked over at Celia. "I never knew you could cook. And be such a great cook. You've left us dinner like five times now."

Celia sipped her coffee, leaning back against the counter. She didn't feel different, really. Maybe a little more energetic. And she didn't seem to be so short-tempered. And impatient. And she felt, well, hopeful or something. Did antidepressants give somebody hope?

"And you haven't cried at a commercial for a while," Rachel added. Her boyfriend gave her a kiss and whispered something in her ear that made Rachel beam. "And we think maybe your junk habit is a career or something. It makes you really happy."

Celia smiled. She had been selling a few things on eBay. She did as much research as she could about the objects to get an idea of what they should at least sell for, but the world on eBay still held many surprises. One of the glass doorknobs she had listed she figured might go for ten bucks to someone looking to replace one in their old house. But the bidding went crazy in the last five hours of her seven-day listing and the bids rocketed up to $172. When she e-mailed the guy who had won it, asking why he had wanted it, he wrote back to say he believed it was a kind of crystal doorknob that could only have come from one of the old Russian palaces. Someone, perhaps a refugee, he said, must have brought it with them to New York.

But the most exciting thing that had happened was her mother had taken her to an auction house, Nest Egg Auctions, in Meriden, Connecticut. They called it a country-style auction, which appeared to Celia to be as different from a formal auction as a proper golfing outfit was to a tux. There was no catalog to follow, but each item—and there was tons of stuff—had been meticulously cataloged and put on preview so buyers could note their lot numbers. It was a family owned and operated enterprise, which cheered Celia up for some reason. Probably because all the family members seemed to be having so much fun with each other and with the bidders. There was the head auctioneer, Ryan Brechlin, his mother, Mary Ellen, Ryan's brother, Christopher and sister, Jen, and her husband, Adam.

Celia had not been prepared for how the atmosphere of Nest Egg would affect her. As soon as she came through the door of the vast auction hall she felt a buzz, the kind of buzz she felt around certain kinds of old things and places. It happened in museums and it was happening now. She looked in awe at the endless tables of boxed lots, at the pieces of furniture that circled the auction hall, and the paintings and prints and photographs hanging from, or leaning against, the walls. It was a stunning display.

"Isn't it marvelous?" Celia's mother whispered.

While her mother registered and got them a bidding number, Celia claimed two seats in the back and surveyed the room. There were only fifteen minutes before the auction started. Where should she begin? The buzz in her brain told her there was something very, very special in here. She just needed to find it.

She headed for a couple of paintings in lovely old gold-leaf frames. She guessed they were from the same owner because their theme—landscapes or waterscapes in oil—all resembled southern France. There were prints, some in good shape and others not. There were some framed magazine ads from the

1930s. Nothing spoke to her, though. The furniture lots were interesting. There were plenty of practical modern pieces, but a couple of the older pieces were intriguing. Celia waved to her mother after she looked under a pair of empire end tables. They were mahogany, with a single drawer, dull brass handle and claw-feet. Her mother nearly swooned. "How much do you think they will go for?"

"This far north? I have no idea." They were ninety miles from New York, twenty from the Fairfield County line and thirty from the Gold Coast. Celia looked around the auction room. There were people who looked well-heeled but for the most part the bidding crowd looked to be the kind of people she ran into at tag sales, flea markets and bazaars, which led her to believe they were here to buy things to resell, whereas people like her mother were looking to buy for themselves.

"Look at that," her mother had marveled, pointing to a hand-painted glass globe that belonged to a Victorian lamp. (Celia intuitively knew it was original. How did she know? She didn't, not for sure. Still, somehow she just *knew* it was.) "Your great-grandmother had something like this in her front hall. She lived in one of those painted ladies in Bronxville, a great Victorian mansion with all the gingerbread, porches and towers." (Celia's mother had told her about a hundred times.) "What is that, do you suppose?" She was pointing to a large brown metal box.

"I think they probably used it to measure electricity in the old days."

Her mother looked at her. "Celia, how on earth do you *know* these things?"

"I don't. Not for sure." She waved to one of the helpers on the floor. "Could you please tell us what this is?"

"It measured electrical currents so they could regulate the flow," the young man said.

"My littlest angel," her mother said after that, putting her arm around Celia, "I think you and I have some talking to do."

"About what?" She had been assessing a wood-and-string contraption she guessed was some kind of ancient cot. (It turned out to be an old officer's field bed.)

"I think we should come to these auctions and then you should sell things in New York."

"Old power meters?" Celia said absently, touching the stringing.

Her mother pulled her hair. "No, brat girl. Buy something and take it into that man you told us about in the Bronx. Put it in his auction. I'll stake you, Ceil. Two hundred fifty dollars. Buy something to sell in the city."

Celia looked around the auction room with new appreciation. What was in here that might sell well in New York? Definitely the end tables she had pointed out to her mother. Maybe the oil seascape, although she was certain it would go for far more than two hundred and fifty dollars. There was also a curved corner cabinet with panes of beveled glass that was very appealing.

Her mother gave Celia a little shove. "There might be a business in here, you never know."

Celia was almost afraid to speak. This would be too good to be true, too easy. To take her joyful pastime and try to make a little money at it? Wouldn't that wreck it? Jinx it? Take the fun out of it?

"The glass globe," she said to her mother. "If there's one thing I would like to try in New York it would be that. I can take it in on the train."

"How much would it go for, do you think?" her mother whispered, turning to look at it again.

"I haven't the slightest idea," Celia said.

"Oh, Celia, I can just feel it in my bones," her mother said, squeezing her arm. "We're onto something."

Celia smiled, uncertain. Still, she could try to sell a few things and see what it was like. No big deal.

In the few minutes left before the auction began Celia moved quickly through the goods going up for sale. There were boxes of old tools; toys and dolls and people's figurine collections, boxes of letters, postcard albums, photos from WWII, car manuals from the nineteen-sixties (those should fly, she thought, not as something she wanted but as the kind of thing people searched on eBay to find, a manual to the old car they were fixing up), odd lots of china for daily use, bone china teacups and saucers, candlesticks (brass, glass, silver plate), fireplace utensils, old cameras, a box of *Playboys*, a box of nineteen-thirties business records for a defunct department store. It went on and on, table after table. Celia felt almost shaky now, overwhelmed with the idea of exploring her mother's suggestion but also wondering what it was in this room that was setting her off? There was some *thing* here on her radar but she had yet to see it with her eyes.

Ryan Brechlin was up at the podium microphone warning the auction would be starting shortly. Something under one of the tables caught Celia's eye and she made her way over, excusing herself in the crush of people, and squatted. In a cut-down Arizona Iced Tea box there was a pile of magazines, the size of the old *Life,* the top one of which was blue with a black-and-white photograph of a mounted equestrian lady holding a trophy. *Saddle & Bridle* it was called. Celia looked for a date. *1932.* She took a sharp intake of breath through her nose and gently picked up the magazine to look under it. *August, 1932. September, 1932.* She straightened up, rising to her feet. This box was coming home with her.

A glossy equestrian magazine of high society after the great crash of 1929? How big could that audience have been? The magazines were heavily illustrated in black and white, on acid-free paper and had obviously been tucked away in someone's attic. She moved on. (And looked back at them over her shoulder, as if to signal to the magazines they were not to worry.)

People were sitting down now and the aisles were clearing so Celia moved fast. Then something lying across the table to the side caught her eye.

Shotguns. Four of them.

She edged closer, aware that Ryan was above her on the dais ready to start. But she couldn't help herself, she had to reach out to one of the guns and touch the fine wood of its gunstock. She knew nothing about guns but the wood was such a gorgeous nutty-brown and the signs of wear only seemed to enhance it. The barrels were sleek, smooth and cold to the touch. The shotgun was broken open and the precision cut of the shell chamber fittings was fine. The whole piece was exquisitely made and Celia's mouth had gone dry, which told her this was it. The shotgun was the star of the room.

"Do you like guns?" Ryan asked her, smiling down from the podium.

She shook her head. "But I know I love this one. It's one of the most beautifully made things I've ever seen in my life."

He smiled. "Then maybe you know more about guns than you thought."

Celia sat down next to her mother. "Mom, you've got to buy the shotgun that's up there and put it in your auction for the historical society."

"A shotgun?" she said, astonished.

"It's gorgeous."

"Does it work?"

"Who cares, it's the most gorgeous thing I've ever seen."

Her mother frowned a little. "I don't know, Celia."

The auction began with the sale of an oil painting for seven hundred dollars. The next item was a simple cherry chair from the nineteen-fifties that no one seemed to be the least bit interested in. "All right, who will start me with five dollars, five dollars for the nice cherry chair, five dollars, come on, people, five dollars, that's less than what delivery would be from a furniture store—for five dollars you can break it up and use it for firewood, I don't care—" Finally someone raised their hand. When the chair went for five dollars, the entire auction room cried, "Five dollars!" Celia and her mother looked at each other and burst out laughing.

No, this was not like any auction Celia had ever been to before.

It fascinated Celia what moved and what did not in this part of Connecticut. The mahogany end tables came up and her mother joined the bidding, which ended with her mother's winning bid of eighty dollars. "I can scarcely believe it," she gasped to Celia. "I feel as though I'm stealing."

It was amazing. The hoosier went for three hundred and twenty dollars but a modern dining room table and chairs for only two hundred(!). The electric meter went for five dollars ("Five dollars!" everybody, including the Cavanaughs, cried), but a box of postcards went for one hundred and ninety dollars! When the first of the shotguns came up Celia felt her stomach tighten. "Not that one," she whispered, which went for one hundred and ten dollars. "No," she whispered on the next three (one-fifty, eighty-five and two hundred and ten dollars in succession). When *her* shotgun came up Celia elbowed her mother. Ryan explained that it had been made in Connecticut around nineteen-ten. "Don't bid until the very last second," she told her mother.

"Celia, I don't really want it."

Celia took the bidding card from her.

"I have competing left bids on this," Ryan said, "and we also have two phone bidders." Two of the assistants, with cell phones to their ears, had moved toward the front. "With our competing left bids we can start this at two thousand six hundred dollars." A murmur rolled over the room as Celia handed the card back to her mother. "Do I see two thousand seven?" A bidding card went up and Ryan never even slowed until they hit the ten thousand mark. Finally, at "Eleven thousand two hundred fifty dollars… Sold!" the hammer came down.

"How did you know?" Celia's mother whispered.

"You could tell, it was gorgeous."

"Celia, I saw it and I thought it was a piece of junk."

"We also have competing left bids on this," Ryan announced when the glass globe for the Victorian lamp came up, "so we will open the bidding at eighty dollars. Do I see ninety?" He laughed as a number of bidding cards flew up. "I've got ninety dollars everywhere!" he exclaimed. People knew what this was, then, Celia thought. "One hundred in the back, one-ten, I've got one-ten. One-twenty? One-twenty. One-thirty? One-thirty. One-forty?" It was down to two men now and the second hesitated before nodding. "I've got one-forty, one hundred forty dollars for the circa eighteen-fifty Victorian hand-painted glass globe—" The other man nodded. Ryan pointed. "I've got one-fifty. One-sixty?" The second man shook his head, no. "You'll never find this at Target, people, this is the real thing. Do I see one-sixty?" He lifted the hammer, scanning the room. "It's going then for one hundred fifty—"

Celia shot her mother's card up. "Ah, one-sixty!" he said, pointing at Celia. "A new bidder, do I have one-seventy?" He was waiting for the first man, who nodded. "One-seventy, I have," he said, eyes coming back to Celia. "One-eighty?" Celia nodded. "We've got an auction going, people, great," Ryan said. "I don't mind working for it. I've got one-eighty. Do I have one-ninety?" The man hesitated and then shook his head. "One-eighty, we're at one-eighty," Ryan said, scanning the room. "Do I see one-ninety?"

Celia anxiously checked the room. The trick was going to be for her to match the globe with a lamp.

"I'm selling at one hundred and eighty dollars," Ryan said, hammer wavering in the air. And then it came down. "Sold! For one hundred eighty dollars to number—"

Celia held up her number.

"One-eighty-three."

"Oh, that's so exciting!" Celia's mother said.

She felt the same way and a ripple of pleasure ran through her when the assistant brought it to her and she actually held the globe in her hands. Then her mother took the globe to the back to ask for something to pack it in.

Celia was smiling. She was happy. Really happy. This was the coolest thing she had done in a very long time. When the box of equestrian magazines finally came up toward the end of the auction, a man who had bought the box of old *Playboys* made a halfhearted bid. Celia was shocked there weren't more hands in the air, but unless one knew something of the horsey set, she supposed people might not understand how rarified the content of these magazines had to be, given that they were published at the height of the Great Depression. She got the box of *Saddle & Bridle* magazines for forty dollars.

"So how are the horse magazines selling?" Rachel asked Celia now.

"The auction for the first one I listed," Celia said, "ends this morning. Around now," she added, feeling a surge of adrenaline.

"Cool, let's go see," Rachel said. "What was it at last night?" she asked while they all went trooping down to Celia's room to look at her computer. They were all getting into it, the eBay thing. For everything that Celia had sold it seemed like Rachel had asked her to buy at least two things for her.

"Nineteen dollars and fifty cents. Oh, my gosh," she said a few minutes later after she logged on to her account.

Rachel leaned closer to the screen. "Is that just for one magazine? Twenty-three dollars?"

"Yeah," Celia said, doing the math in her head. There had been seventeen magazines in the box, all in good shape. The one she had listed was the oldest. If each magazine brought at least fifteen dollars, that would be around two hundred fifty dollars. The buyer paid the postage and handling, but the listing fee, which Celia had heavily illustrated with photos of the content, plus a percentage to PayPal, her preferred method, meant that the expenses would be around a hundred dollars, which left one-twenty-five, less the forty-four that covered Nest Egg and the buyer's commission, which would be eighty-one.

Hmm. With time and effort taken into consideration it meant that although she had doubled her investment, she was paying herself eight dollars an hour to list these. That wasn't so hot. On the other hand, she was lowballing the magazines, so she would just have to see as she went. To say she was learning a lot in the meantime was putting it mildly.

Celia refreshed the page and Rachel screamed. "It went up to $25.50!"

"There's only seventeen minutes left," the boyfriend said.

How cool is this, how cool is this? Celia thought to herself.

They remained glued to the computer screen for the next seventeen minutes, Celia constantly refreshing the page. Not a thing happened until the very last minute when the number of bids jumped from five to nine.

"Look, look, look!" Rachel cried.

Thirty-two dollars it said.

Ten more seconds. But that was it. The time ran out, the magazine had sold for thirty-two dollars, plus two dollars for postage and one dollar for handling. Thirty-five dollars on the nose.

Rachel was screaming and running around in circles, she was so excited. She came back to do a drumroll on Celia's back, making them both laugh. "Your mom is like *so* right! You're in business, baby!"

An e-mail message appeared in Celia's eBay mailbox. The fellow who won the magazine, whose handle was AlfieRalphie, wanted to know if she had any more of them.

"What will you do, Celia," Rachel asked her, excited. "Sell them in one big deal or individually?"

"I don't know, I don't know," Celia laughed. It was hard to believe. This was just the coolest.

Rosanne Takes Samantha for a Walk

"NO, YOU *DON'T* KNOW, Rosanne!" Samantha Wyatt said, stamping her boot.

The women were standing in the last vestiges of sunshine on the terrace of the Soldiers' and Sailors' monument. Harriet had begged Rosanne to see if she could get Samantha outside for a little air, however chilly it was, and to make sure Samantha went to her four o'clock doctor's appointment. In terms of a walk they had not gotten very far. After two and a half blocks Samantha started throwing a fit, kicking chunks of ice and waving her arms around. Apparently Mrs. W had finally gotten the father's name out of Samantha and Mr. W had gone to upstate New York to pay him a visit.

"Seems to me your parents have left it up to you whether or not you want to see him again," Rosanne said.

"Oh, yeah, like he's going to want to see me when he knows I've got a lunatic for a father!"

"Sammy, listen, you said your father got him to sign the

papers needed to legally sever him from the baby. So all your father did was make sure the way's clear if you want to see your, um, friend, again." It took all of Rosanne's self-control not to shake Samantha by the shoulders and scream at her to wake up and grow up. She'd always known there was going to be trouble with this one. Samantha was too beautiful and too willful and too spoiled. It wouldn't surprise Rosanne in the least if Samantha had deliberately gotten pregnant in the belief her boyfriend would leave his family to be with her. She had always gotten what she wanted in the end, so why not the piece of crap she thought she was in love with?

Who did you blame for this situation? The W's, for allowing Samantha to get away with murder for all these years when, at the same time, they had always come down on Althea like a ton of bricks? Or do you blame Samantha for being so self-centered? Or blame the guy Rosanne would like to blame it all on, that fortysomething married piece of crap who had seduced a sheltered eighteen-year-old when she was a freshman.

"So what are you saying?" Samantha asked, drawing herself up to full height, which was considerably taller than Rosanne. Sammy was huge now, her condition obvious, even under the cascading winter cape her parents had bought her. Part of her size was hereditary but some of it, Mrs. W wailed, was inactivity and ordering junk food to be delivered while she and Mr. W were at work.

"I'm sayin' stick it out for a couple of weeks and then go back to school and do whatever you want to do. But understand, this guy's not leavin' his family. And if you want to be his mistress, then your parents are sayin' fine, go on, that's your affair."

"They're trying to buy me off, that's what they're doing!"

Samantha said, stamping her foot again. Some of the snow had melted in the sun but now a thin layer of ice was starting to form over the paving stones. "They're going to pay me to stay away so Althea can have my baby!"

"Are you saying maybe you want to keep the baby?"

"No!" she shouted. "But I don't see why Althea should have it. How am I supposed to come home now?"

Her hormones were all out of whack and who knew what Sammy's tears really meant at this point.

"You just come home," Rosanne said. "And be an aunt."

"I can't believe she's doing this to me!" Samantha wailed, looking up at the sky.

If Samantha did not get away from her soon Rosanne knew she was going to lose her temper. And that wasn't her place. Her place was to make sure the kid got to the doctor.

"She's not doing it to you, Samantha. Your sister is doing it to start her own family and she is bending over backward to let you be as involved as you want to be. Because she loves you and will always want to be a part of your life."

Samantha sniffed. She seemed to be listening.

"And your parents are going to be grandparents to this child. But they will always be your mother and father, they'll always be your parents first, and they will always be there for you—if you'll let them. Eventually you'll see that what they're doing is giving you back your freedom but also honoring Althea's desire to be a mother and honoring the baby as a new member of your family." She moved closer, touching Samantha's arm. "You're going to be an aunt, Samantha, and how much or how little you want to be in this kid's life is up to you."

"How am I going to look at it after it knows I gave it away?"

"I think it will be up to Althea to handle that when the time comes. But, Samantha, listen, who can you trust more to do the right thing than your sister?"

"Yeah, she's pretty good," Samantha admitted.

Rosanne looked at her watch. "We've got to get you a cab. It's getting near your appointment." They started walking toward Riverside Drive.

"All I know is if this baby doesn't come soon I'm going to go crazy," Samantha said, unconsciously placing her hands on her abdomen as she walked. "I can't sleep on my back."

"Oh, no," Rosanne said under breath.

"What?" Samantha said.

"The last person I want to see," Rosanne grumbled. It was the bartender, Celia, carrying a box and trying to hail a cab. She had seen Rosanne and was just standing there.

Samantha raised her arm to signal for a cab. The bartender chick called, "I'll get you one!" and moved out into the Drive to more aggressively hail one. An empty cab did a U-turn and pulled up on their side of the road. Rosanne walked Samantha over and opened the door for her.

"Thanks, Rosanne," Samantha said, kissing her on the cheek and then carefully climbing in. Rosanne shut the door and waved.

"Mrs. DiSantos?"

Reluctantly Rosanne turned around to face the bartender, wanting to claw her pretty eyes out.

"I've been trying to write you, but I keep ripping the letters up." She shrugged. "I guess it's stupid to think I can apologize."

"For what? For trying to screw up my son's whole life?" If Jason had not come back with a clean bill of health from the doctor Rosanne didn't know what she would have done.

The bartender chick lowered her eyes, toeing the large granules of salt on the sidewalk. "I thought maybe I should show you the letter Jason wrote me."

Rosanne got a chill. Is that what he was doing over at Mrs. C's place? Writing this slut?

"Because he sounds good. I mean, he says he's interested in a girl at school—"

There was a thud and crunch of colliding metal, followed by the tinkling sound of broken glass. For a moment all was quiet on the Drive, the traffic stopped, the birds and people hushed. The bartender chick had dropped her box and was already calling 911 while she and Rosanne hurried across the street toward the accident. It looked as though a cab coming up Riverside had clipped the back end of a cab turning onto 88th, sending it careening sideways into a parked car.

"Oh, my God," Celia said, "I think it's your friend."

Rosanne was already pushing through people. "I'm a nurse, I'm a nurse," she kept saying. The back door of the cab couldn't be opened and Rosanne could see Samantha lying on her side across the backseat. The cab driver was pinned between the wheel and the parked car. A man was shouting at him to unlock the doors but he was having trouble understanding or even hearing.

"I'm right here, Samantha!" Rosanne yelled through the shattered window. "Everything's going to be okay!"

Finally the driver managed to hit the button to unlock the doors and the man forced the front passenger door open. "Don't touch him until the ambulance gets here," Rosanne instructed.

"Smell the gas, lady."

"The engine's off, don't panic," Rosanne said, squeezing past him to climb into the front seat. "You're fine, Mister, don't sweat, you'll be out in a second," she said to the driver. She rose on her knees to peer back through the bulletproof glass into the backseat. "Sammy? Sammy? Can you hear me?

Samantha was lying on her side in Rosanne's direction and her eyes were open but she was clearly in shock. She was covered with safety glass but Rosanne couldn't see any blood. There was a police siren and Rosanne prayed an emergency unit was not far behind with tools to get Samantha out. Somebody was trying to drape an overcoat over Samantha through the twisted window frame but she did not move or respond. A police officer asked Rosanne to get out, which she did, aware that Celia was telling the cops about Samantha's pregnancy and the urgency of getting her out. A fire engine arrived with the ambulance and Rosanne refused to be pushed back into the crowd, continuing to talk to Samantha. They pulled the driver out through the passenger-side door and put him in an ambulance while the firemen started cutting the mangled rear door to get to Samantha.

Suddenly Samantha let out a bloodcurdling scream. "Sammy, I'm here, Sammy, I'm here!" Rosanne shouted as they gingerly tried to slide Samantha out the backseat, but she kept screaming that awful scream, her eyes wide with terror. They lowered her on a stretcher. She couldn't talk; she could only scream and scream.

Rosanne climbed into the ambulance with the medics. On the way to the hospital she helped them cut off Samantha's coat and clothes and kept telling Samantha everything was going to be okay. Samantha fainted, which gave them a minute to examine her. She had a broken arm and broken ribs and was in full labor, the child's head appearing. This was not going to be easy.

They reached St. Luke's at 113th Street and Amsterdam, by

which time Samantha had resumed screaming, but they couldn't give her anything for the pain because of the baby. By the time Samantha was in an E.R. cubicle the baby's shoulders were appearing and Rosanne kept thinking no one could keep up this kind of screaming for this long. *Please, God, don't let her die.* An obstetrician was there to meet them and in minutes the baby was out, the umbilical cord cut and they mercifully injected Samantha with a painkiller. Her screams subsided, and moments later she was out.

Had the baby cried? Rosanne couldn't remember. She turned to a nurse. "Is the baby—?"

"I'll check."

While they cleaned Samantha up Rosanne stepped outside the cubicle. A few minutes later a doctor appeared who told Rosanne the baby was fine, he had a little trouble getting started, but was breathing fine on his own. Samantha was wheeled past then to go into X-ray. She was still out.

"It's a boy?" Rosanne asked the doctor, her eyes filling with tears.

"Nine pounds ten ounces worth," he reported. "He's going to be a big boy."

Someone asked Rosanne if she would go up front to fill out the admittance forms. While she was struggling to come up with answers Mrs. W came barreling around the corner. Her eyes were as wide and terrified as her daughter's had been. She clutched Rosanne's arm.

"She's stable, Mrs. W," Rosanne said evenly. "She broke some ribs and her arm. She should be okay, though."

Harriet wept on her shoulder. "Thank you, God, thank you, God."

"And you're a grandmother," Rosanne told her. "You have

a grandson. Nine pounds ten ounces." It was only when Mrs. W stepped back to look at her that Rosanne realized she had blood on her clothes, because now it was on Mrs. W's, too.

Harriet trembled from head to toe while she answered the admission questions and Rosanne had to get the insurance card out of her wallet for her. Finally the forms seemed to be done, by which time the doctor had learned the patient's mother had arrived and came down to talk to Harriet. The break in Samantha's arm was clean. They could only tape the two ribs that had been fractured.

"What about her face?" Mrs. W asked.

"Not a mark on it," the doctor said kindly.

The E.R. doctor who had tended to Samantha came around and asked Mrs. W if she would like to see her grandson and Rosanne told her to go ahead, she wanted to wash up. She went into the bathroom off the E.R., took one look in the mirror and knew it was hopeless. There wasn't a thing she had on that wasn't stained with blood. She washed her hands and face, patted her hair, and wondered what crook in New York had her purse now. She had no memory of what had happened to it.

When she came out she saw Mr. W wandering the halls with a nurse chasing him, telling him he couldn't go where he was going. "Rosanne!" he cried, dodging a gurney with a groaning guy on it. Rosanne quickly brought him up to speed and a nurse's aide agreed to take him to find his wife. "Watch for Althea, will you, Ro?" he called. "She's on her way."

Rosanne wandered in the direction of the waiting room and slapped the button to open the double doors. She was in a kind of protective shock still, she knew, the kind where her body and training took over and left her emotions safely locked away.

She walked over to the soda machine and checked to see if she had any money in her pockets.

"Here's your purse, Mrs. DiSantos," Celia Cavanaugh said, handing it to her. "How is your friend?"

"She broke her arm and a couple of ribs. She should be okay." Rosanne had taken out her wallet and pulled out a one-dollar bill. She put it in the machine. "She had a little boy. Nine pounds ten ounces. He had a little trouble in the beginning but he's breathing fine now on his own." She pressed the button for a bottle of water. It came thunking down the chute.

"Did her mom get here?"

Rosanne nodded, unscrewing the water and taking a swig.

"Here's your friend's cell phone. I think her purse is at the desk. The cops brought it."

Rosanne nodded, taking Samantha's phone and flipping it open.

"I had to turn it off when I came in because the nurse said—"

"The equipment, I know," Rosanne told her.

"I saw *Mom* in her directory so I called the number," Celia said. "I figured I should let somebody know what was happening."

Rosanne brought the bottle down from her mouth. "You called Mrs. W? That's how she got here?"

"If that's your friend's mom, yeah. I guess."

Rosanne nodded, sliding the strap of her purse over her shoulder. "Yeah, well," she said after a moment, "you did good, kid. Thanks."

The girl's face instantly brightened. "You're welcome. Well," she said, starting to back away, "I guess I'll go now, then. Unless you need me to do anything."

Rosanne shook her head. The girl turned around and headed for the E.R. exit doors. "Celia!" Rosanne suddenly called. The girl turned around. "I'll let you know how she's doing."

Then Althea Wyatt came flying in through the doors and Rosanne had to move on to think about other things.

More Surprises for Celia

WHEN HOWARD STEWART'S wife greeted Celia by name in the lobby, Celia knew something other in the neighborhood must have changed besides the state of her own depression.

"Hello, Celia," Amanda Stewart said, leaving a large, thin cardboard box leaning against the concierge desk. She held her hand out to Celia.

Celia put down her bag of groceries. "Hi," Celia said, shaking her hand.

"I hear you were almost the first person to see Althea's little boy."

Celia hesitated. "Althea?"

"Oh." Amanda grimaced slightly. "Well, it's— Let me phrase it this way. Althea Wyatt is the little boy's mother. The—the young woman you assisted is her sister."

"I see," Celia said although she didn't. But it wasn't any of her business.

"Rosanne told us how wonderful you were, that you called 911, got Rosanne's purse, called Harriet, Samantha's mother—"

Celia shrugged. "Really, I didn't do much." Pause. "That's right, you're friends with Jason's mom and gran, right?"

"Yes. His gran is dying right now, it's a tough time."

"Yes, I know," Celia said. Jason had stopped by Captain Cook's the other day to say hi to everyone. He liked his new job and had a girlfriend, so life was much better, except that his grandmother was dying. Celia was unsure how to proceed with this conversation or if she was supposed to. "Um, I saw your husband. He told me you guys are moving back into the city."

"Yes, yes we are, as soon as the school year's over," Amanda said. "And I am *delighted*. I've missed Manhattan terribly."

"He's really happy. He's missed you guys a lot."

Amanda smiled. "That's nice to know."

Celia banished the thought of Howard kissing her in the elevator.

"So you cannot imagine the task that lies ahead of me, Celia," Amanda said, walking back to her big box. "Somehow I must reduce twenty rooms of furniture to eight."

Celia's ears pricked up. "You're getting rid of your house?"

Amanda nodded, sliding the box over to lean against her hip. "We might buy a smaller house in the country sometime later, but something low maintenance, that we can use for weekends and vacations." The cardboard box slipped and almost fell over but Celia moved quickly to catch it. "Thank you," Amanda said. "I'm supposed to be taking this over to storage."

They compared notes on storage units and Amanda said she should look into Celia's place, it sounded like a much better deal. "I'll drop the rate information for you at the desk," Celia promised, picking up her groceries. "They have some climate controlled areas that would be good for your paintings."

"I think my children are hoping this particular painting will rot somewhere so they don't have to inherit it," Amanda said, nudging the box. "It took us years to figure out that the vulture in it was giving Emily nightmares. It's been under our bed for I don't know how long."

Celia laughed. "Where did you get it?"

"My grandparents. I think my grandfather must have liked it because— Well, here, I'll show you."

Celia put her groceries on the concierge desk this time and helped Amanda take the painting out of the box. It wasn't wrapped in anything. Celia caught her breath when she saw the quality of the oil painting. But the subject was very strange, an Arab kneeling behind a camel in a desert, aiming a long rifle at a vulture circling in the sky.

"Rather ghastly, is it not?" Amanda said. "But in my family, when you inherit something you're supposed to keep it forever and ever, even if everyone hates it."

Celia laughed, carefully bringing the painting over to rest on the couch. "I've got some stuff upstairs to wrap this properly for storage," she told Amanda while she took a closer look. Celia kneeled, squinting.

"Don't tell me you like it," Amanda said.

"Not the subject, particularly, but as a well-executed painting, absolutely," Celia said, standing and tilting the painting to look at the back of the frame. "And if I were to guess, I would say someone would pay a bit of money to own this painting."

"Really?" Amanda said.

"Yeah." Celia came back to stand next to Amanda, eyes still on the painting. "It's well over a hundred years old. It's in the original frame, I think, which on its own is worth something." She looked at Amanda. "If you don't like it, and if your children are scared of it—" She shrugged, smiling. "If I were you, I would call Christie's or Sotheby's and have one of their appraisers look at it. You never know, you might get enough money to buy a painting that you like, instead of what your grandfather liked."

"That's an idea," Amanda said, crossing her arms and reconsidering the painting. "It is rather good, isn't it?"

"I think so. I mean, I don't really know for sure. I like old things and this is sort of jazzing me. It gives me a kind of a humming feeling, which makes me think it's valuable."

"A humming feeling?" Amanda repeated, fascinated. She looked at the painting again. "It does absolutely nothing for me." She looked back at Celia. "Tell me more about this humming."

Celia laughed, embarrassed. "It's the quality of it," she explained. "Everything feels real about it to me. There doesn't seem to be any restoration needed. I can check online for you about the artist, to at least give you an idea if he's listed."

"That would be wonderful," Amanda said, looking back at the painting. "And would you be willing to call one of the auction houses for me, as well? Get somebody to look at it?"

"Oh, it's very easy," Celia assured her. "I'll help you call, if you like."

"No," Amanda said, shaking her head, "I've got too much to do as it is. What I want is for you to take over now. I was only going to stick it into storage the way it is and probably ruin it. So please take it, Celia, find out if it's worth anything and if it is, sell it. You can be our agent. And take, I don't know, ten percent of gross? Is that fair?"

"But you don't have to pay me anything!" Celia sputtered. "It would be a great learning experience for me." She was also thinking how it might make up for the Victorian glass globe being destroyed. When Mrs. DiSantos' friends got hit in the cab, Celia had put the box down and somebody ran over it.

"My husband's a literary agent," Amanda said, "and I can assure you since he receives a percentage of the author's work he tries a great deal harder to sell things than he might otherwise. I'm not *that* generous. My guess is it will provide motivation."

Celia didn't know what to say. This was a real piece of art; this wasn't something she found in a Dumpster. "If they took it, there would also be the auction house commission—"

"Understand, my young friend," Amanda said, touching her arm, "this was practically going into the bin so whatever you can get is going to be a great deal more than nothing. So, it's all yours, take it away. Hallelujah, I don't have to go out after all!"

Celia tried one more time, although she did agree with Amanda; it would do nobody any good if the painting just got stuck away.

Emma

"NO, IT'S FINE, really," Cassy assured the nurse's aide in the kitchen. "I'll wait in the living room until the others leave. She has enough company right now."

"Yes, she does," the nurse's aide agreed. She smiled broadly. "It is a very cute little baby. Mrs. Goldblum's eyes lit up when she saw him."

"He's only a couple of weeks old."

The nurse's aide nodded and proceeded to set up some medications on a small tray.

Cassy lingered a moment, wanting to ask but not wanting to ask. She already sensed it, but wanted confirmation. "She's not very far away from it now, Virginia, is she?"

The aide waited a moment before looking at her. In a low voice she said, "But Rosanne does not see it. She won't allow herself to see it."

"She doesn't want to let her go."

"That makes it hard for Mrs. Goldblum," Virginia said solemnly. "Because she wants to go."

Cassy nodded. "Thank you for telling me."

Cassy went into the living room and sat down on the couch. She slid her glasses on and picked up the photo album Amanda and Rosanne had put together for Emma to look at. There were pictures of Emma as a girl, her parents, her dog. There was her wedding, Mr. Goldblum, Daniel as a baby, and the park. Those were the most amazing pictures, of Riverside Park over the decades, the glory years, the bad years, and then the glory of the past fifteen years or so when The Riverside Park Fund caught the hearts and imagination of the neighborhood residents. There were pictures from block parties that made Cassy laugh out loud. And then there was a photo of the day Rosanne and little Jason had moved into this apartment, standing with Mrs. Goldblum in this very living room, the DiSantoses looking almost like Ellis Island refugees.

What would Cassy's own scrapbook contain when she was old? She knew Henry would put in the picture of Cassy, at around age six, sitting in her father's lap with her arms around his neck. Cassy and her father had been very happy that day. It was before he couldn't hold a job. Henry would put at least one picture of Cassy's mother in it, but which one would he choose? Surely not the one where Cassy stood in her cap and gown at Northwestern and her mother, still stylishly attractive then, was giving such a poisonous look to the camera that anyone who saw the photograph burst out laughing. It so succinctly summarized her mother's feelings about the world! No, Cassy knew the picture Henry would put in. Of her mother holding Henry when he was a baby, because it was such a nice picture of her and it was clear that while she might hate the rest of the world, those feelings did not apply to her grandson.

Henry would put some pictures of Michael in, she supposed (how did you skip twenty years?), and he would make a big deal of her marriage to Jack. He would put in some pictures relating to DBS and her friends there, but what gave her such a hollow feeling was wondering where, outside of a picture of the gang from DBS, would Alexandra be in that book of pictures. And that thought, of everyone making it into her album as part of her personal life except the person she had come to realize she loved most, frightened her.

Cassy's head picked up at the sound of laughter coming down the hall; she closed the album and slipped off her glasses. A moment later a radiant Althea Wyatt appeared in the archway with the bundle of her baby son in her arms. Samantha had returned to school and so the rest of the Wyatts were free to joyfully tend to the new member of the family. He was beautiful. He had very light skin, lighter even than Samantha's. The nose must be the father's for Cassy did not recognize it, but the baby had the same high chiseled cheekbones Sam and Althea had. Cassy smiled to herself. This child could very well be Althea's because of the resemblance. In any case, he *was* her child.

"Hello there, Samuel," Cassy said gently to the child. "You are the most gorgeous creature on the face of the earth, yes you are. Except for my grandchildren. All right, I give in, you are just as gorgeous as they are."

"He is gorgeous, isn't he?" Amanda Stewart said, coming into the living room to stand with them. She peered down at the baby over Althea's shoulder. "You made Mrs. Goldblum smile and smile, didn't you, Samuel?"

Cassy glance up at Althea. "So how's the nanny hunt coming?"

"It's not," Althea said. "I mean, when the right one appears I figure I'll know it."

"Amanda's pushin' Madame DeFarge on her," Rosanne contributed, breezing by on her way to the kitchen.

"I am not, Rosanne," Amanda protested. To Cassy she explained, "We're not renewing Madame Moliere's contract."

"Really? Why not?"

"We frankly don't have the room for a live-in here. Not if we're living here full-time. I need her room for the baby."

"If we're going to Mrs. W's for tea," Rosanne announced, coming back in, "we need to get a move on. It's going to take a while to wrap Nanook of the North and then unwrap him again." Rosanne had already put on her coat and was holding the baby's outdoor garments. "Are you sure you don't want to go, Mrs. C? Because I'll stay."

"No, no, you go ahead," Cassy said. "I'd like to sit with Emma for a while. I brought the paper to read." Cassy used to read the paper to Emma but not anymore. She read it to herself while Emma dozed.

After the ladies bundled Samuel up to everyone's satisfaction, they left and Cassy walked back to Emma's bedroom. Virginia was smoothing the bed linens. The hospital bed was raised and Emma lay back against the pillow, her eyes closed. She looked very clean and tidy. Virginia dampened a washcloth and patted Emma's mouth with it, which made Emma open her eyes. They seemed to be very heavy for her. She made a sound, trying to say something Cassy couldn't understand.

"She knows it's you," Virginia told her, standing by the bed.

Cassy drew up a chair and sat down, reaching through the bed rail to take Emma's hand. The diamond in Emma's engagement ring caught the light coming through the window. The view was spectacular from here, of the park and the river and the setting sun.

Emma's hand seemed even lighter and more fragile than two

days ago. "I admire you above all others," Cassy heard herself say in a hushed voice. "Your faith, your loyalty, your strength, your love, Emma. You have always been there for everyone who loves you."

Mrs. Goldblum's eyes had closed and she whispered something. Cassy didn't dare ask her to repeat it because she was so obviously weak.

"She says you are like her," Virginia told her.

Cassy's eyes filled. "Oh, how I wish it were true." She sighed. She felt the tiniest little squeeze from Emma's hand. "But thank you, Emma, thank you for saying that." She stood up to kiss her on the forehead. "You give me the mark to which I aspire."

Emma's eyes opened. She looked past Cassy, searching for Virginia. Cassy sat down and the aide leaned close to Emma's mouth. "She wants to know if Rosanne's still here."

"No, Emma, she went out," Cassy said, still holding her hand. "With Althea and the baby and Amanda. They went over to Harriet's for tea."

Mrs. Goldblum's eyes trailed back up to Virginia and her lips moved again. Cassy thought she said, "Are they gone?"

Virginia nodded. "Yes, Mrs. Goldblum, everyone else has left."

Emma's eyes moved to Cassy and her lips moved, but there was no sound.

Cassy looked up at the aide.

"She's asking if she can go now."

Cassy tried not to cry. "Yes, Emma," she whispered, "yes, you can go now. It's all right."

"Did you hear that, Mrs. Goldblum?" Virginia murmured. "She said it was all right for you to go."

Emma did.

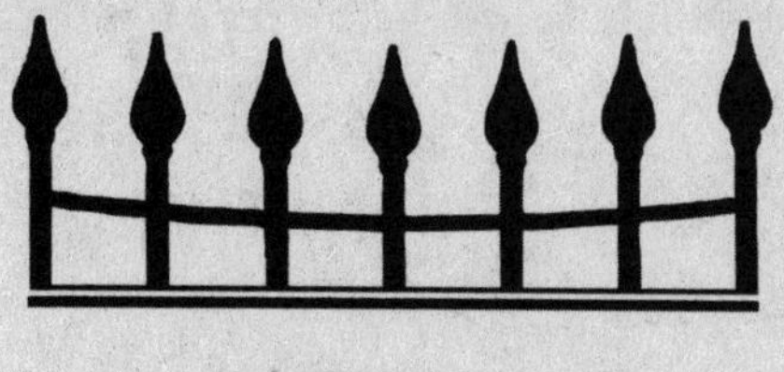

MARCH

41

The Memorial Service

THE DAY AFTER Emma Goldblum died she was laid to rest next to her husband in a Long Island cemetery. A few weeks later, as she requested, a small memorial service was held on the terrace of the Soldiers' and Sailors' Monument of Riverside Park. It was a bad day out, windy with rain threatening to turn to snow, but Jackson Darenbrook dispatched a crew from the West End Broadcasting Center with a corporate tent, which included attachable sides with plastic windows and space heaters. Between the whipping winds and rains and space heaters, however, everyone was either very cold or sweating while seated in their padded folding chair. Some were even simultaneously both, as young Emily Stewart claimed.

"Mother wrote everything out about how—*exactly*—she wanted this service to go," Daniel Goldblum said, holding up a sheaf of papers for everyone to see. "So if any of you have any complaints you'll have to take it up with her." Pause. "She even wrote that line for me to read—that you'll have to take it up with her." Everyone started laughing, which was a good beginning.

As his mother had directed, Daniel read from a history of Jewish immigration to New York, which focused on the arrival of Emma's own parents from Eastern Europe after World War I. Then Daniel read a brief outline of her life. Jason then got up to read a poem she loved, about God's green earth; Rosanne went up to read some remembrances of happy times Mrs. Goldblum had dictated, about Operation Sail on the nation's Bicentennial, when the great ships had sailed up the Hudson, about the block parties and about her friends and neighbors.

"'When you have lived in this neighborhood of New York for as long as I have,'" Rosanne read for Mrs. Goldblum, "'you come to appreciate its magnificence—and its significance.'"

Cassy noticed Amanda Stewart mouthing the words; she had helped Emma to write this.

"'Of how beautiful God made this place, and of how dramatic the city's history had to be in order for us to reach this special place. We are blessed in this community, as people who have come so far from so many places, to have this place and to have each other. Never in my life have I been prouder of this neighborhood, this city and this country, than I was after 9/11. God bless you all. I love you. And God bless America.'"

They were all crying their eyes out at this point, of course, and Jackson put his arm around Cassy. The baby Wyatt was crying and Althea carried him to the back of the tent. Howard and Amanda Stewart sat with their heads pressed together. Sam gave Harriet his handkerchief and put his arm around her. Daniel Goldblum's wife was patting his back, and Jason was holding his mother's hand.

Cassy had paid to place Emma's photograph and obituary in

the *New York Times.* It was not a remarkable life to read about but the obituary was meaningful to those who knew her. Perhaps most significant was how Emma had requested it to read:

> She is survived by her son, Daniel Goldblum, of Saddlebrook, New Jersey, and by her daughter, Rosanne DiSantos, and her grandson, Jason DiSantos, of New York City.

In lieu of flowers she wished donations to be made to The Riverside Park Fund.

Daniel and his second wife ("the floozy with a heart," Rosanne called her) elected to lunch with distant relatives while the neighbors went back to Mrs. Goldblum's for something to eat. It was a quiet affair, with people simply eating and drinking and talking about memories they shared of Mrs. Goldblum. Jason, in a sharp blue blazer, gray slacks and tie, acted every bit the polished young man he had become, playing host.

"Can you get over the changes in him?" Cassy asked Howard Stewart. "He's really a young man now."

"I look at those two—" he gestured to Emily and Teddy, playing a card game on the floor in the corner "—and I just can't believe it. Where does the time go?"

"I'm afraid it only gets worse, Howard. Time passes faster and faster."

He nodded. He was watching Amanda now, Cassy could see, and his expression made Cassy inwardly smile. Something had changed in the Stewart household recently. She assumed it had to do with Amanda and the children planning to move back to Manhattan this summer. Cassy was happy for the Stewarts because it was clear the bond between husband and wife had been renewed in an almost adoring way. At least that was the way Howard was looking at his wife in this moment.

Howard frowned suddenly. "Excuse me, Cassy," he said, touching her arm, "but my son is trying to sneak his twentieth brownie. Teddy!"

"So what do you think?" Jackson said, coming to stand next to Cassy. "Time to shove off?"

She sipped her iced tea. "Attorney Thatcher wants to read the will and then we can go."

Jackson looked at his watch. "So when will this happen, do you think?"

Cassy went over to confer with Rosanne and Thatcher, who both agreed now would be fine. Cassy made the rounds of the room, telling people what was happening next. "This is by Emma's request," she explained, encouraging people to fan out around the living room and take what seats were available.

"I don't care what she said," Rosanne said to Cassy, "I still think this is creepy."

"Just sit," Cassy instructed her, absently patting Rosanne's shoulder before moving on to steer more people into chairs.

"Very well," Attorney Thatcher said, drawing a piece of paper out of his breast pocket. "This is not a formal reading, but this is the last will and testament of Emma Goldblum—"

There was a short sob from Amanda Stewart, who had covered her face.

Attorney Thatcher was not unmoved. He cleared his throat and proceeded. "It meant a great deal to Mrs. Goldblum to have you all gathered here. She wanted you to hear this together, so there would be no question down the road as to what her last wishes were."

They all looked at each other.

"Separate from the will itself she left a detailed list regarding the distribution of her personal property. Anything not specified on this list shall go to her son, Daniel." Attorney Thatcher looked around the room. "You should know that Daniel has already agreed to fulfill the wishes of his late mother, although in regard to this list of personal property he has no legal obligation to do so."

They all looked at each other again, except for Rosanne, who kept her eyes on the window, looking neither right nor left. She was exhausted, Cassy knew, to the point of numbness.

"Mrs. Goldblum wanted her grandmother's walking stick, with the silver handle, to go to Amanda Miller Stewart," Attorney Thatcher said. Amanda's eyes filled again and her daughter went over to sit in her mother's lap. "She also wanted Amanda and Howard Stewart to have her signed, first edition of *The Painted Bird*."

"We're getting a bird?" Teddy whispered. A few people laughed.

"The watercolor of the Hudson River that hangs in the foyer—" there were murmurs because it was so beautiful and such a familiar sight to them all "—is to go to Cassy Cochran." Cassy was totally unprepared for this.

"She wanted Sam and Harriet Wyatt to have her husband's stamp collection."

The Wyatts looked thunderstruck. It was a valuable collection.

"Her engagement ring is to be held for Jason DiSantos until such a time as he marries."

There was a murmur of approval.

"And, finally, her tea service and set of bone china is to go to you, Rosanne."

Rosanne smiled slightly, eyes still on the window.

"Now, in terms of Mrs. Goldblum's estate," he said, consulting his paper again. "She has left two hundred thousand dollars to her son, Daniel, and she has also set up a trust for you, Rosanne, and you too, Jason, of ten thousand dollars a year for ten years. This is to commence in the new calendar year."

"What?" Rosanne said, turning to look up at the lawyer. "What are you talking about?"

"I also have an immediate gift for you, Rosanne and Jason, from Daniel Goldblum on behalf of his mother, of ten thousand dollars each."

"So it won't be subject to taxes," Sam murmured to Rosanne. "That's why the amount is ten thousand."

Jason went over to sit on the arm of the chair next to his mother. "But I don't get it," Rosanne said, clutching her son's hand. "What was she doing, robbin' banks? Where did this money come from?"

"I was about to ask the same thing," Sam said, confused.

"A large portion of this money is from a settlement Mrs. Goldblum reached with the owner of this building," Thatcher explained.

"Settlement for what?" Rosanne said.

"To move out of this apartment by July first of this year."

Rosanne looked to Cassy and Cassy looked, open-mouthed, at Attorney Thatcher. "Is that why Tarnucci was at your office that day?"

He nodded. "The open market value of this apartment has been estimated at three to four million dollars. Mr. Tarnucci had approached Mrs. Goldblum some time ago. And until recently she had not been interested in relocating."

There was a stunned silence and then Rosanne burst out laughing. "She knew she would be gone by July. That's why she made the deal."

Is that why Emma had refused treatment? Cassy wondered. *To obtain a significant inheritance for her son and Rosanne and Jason?*

"I hasten to add," Attorney Thatcher said, "that Mrs. Goldblum told me she was looking forward to moving."

"I bet she did," Rosanne said, making people half laugh and half cry.

"There was no fraud perpetrated!" Thatcher insisted.

"Of course not," Cassy said, "and no one is saying there was. I'm sure at the time Emma was planning to move into a senior's residence. Isn't that right, Sam?"

"Probably the one on West End at Ninety-sixth Street," Sam said, backing her up.

"I think I remember her saying something about that," Jackson said.

"Please continue, Attorney Thatcher," Cassy encouraged.

It took a moment for him to sort himself but then Attorney Thatcher said to Rosanne and Jason, "She set up this trust because she wanted very much to assist you in the next phase of your lives."

"This will really help out with school," Jason said.

"Yes," Rosanne said quietly.

"I don't know if everybody knows," Amanda said, "but Jason got accepted early decision at University of Pennsylvania."

"From Little League to Ivy League. Well done, Jason," Althea said.

Others extended their congratulations.

"She wanted to make a difference in your life," Attorney Thatcher said to Rosanne.

"Like she hadn't already," Rosanne said quietly.

"Gran was the best," her son agreed.

Cassy and Jackson started for home in the damp, cold wind. "Jack," Cassy said after a few paces, "I don't want to do this anymore. Go on like this."

Jackson stopped walking, pulling the collar of his coat up higher. "What are you talking about?"

She turned to face him. "I want a divorce."

They stood there for a long moment, eyes locked, strands of her hair whipping in the wind. "No divorce," he finally said, shaking his head. "Out of the question."

"I'm not doing this anymore," she said. "Not one more day."

He jammed his hands into his pockets before looking at her again. "Why are you doing this?"

"Because I want my life back."

He shut his eyes a moment, vigorously shaking his head, and reopened them. "You're just gonna blow up DBS? What are we supposed to tell my family?"

"The truth. That you and I have been living separate lives for years." It was starting to rain, but neither made any move to seek cover.

"Cass, shit, listen, this is crazy. We're not gettin' a divorce. You're just upset over Emma. When you calm down you'll remember that we're a team. With a *lot* of people depending on us. You just turned fifty-three for chrissakes, this is no time for you to pin your hopes on some forty-year-old dyke. You're gonna get killed."

"This isn't about Alexandra. It's about me, Jack. *Me.* I can't remember being me since I was about six. Dammit, Jack, I want my life back. And I'm *going* to have it back before it's too late."

42

The Stewarts

"COME, CHILDREN, we're crossing the street," Amanda suddenly said, veering off the sidewalk as the rain started.

"Amanda, what the heck—?" Howard said, holding the umbrella and hurrying to catch up with her.

"I don't think the Darenbrooks should be interrupted," Amanda said, glancing over to where the couple appeared to be in some sort of face-off. Jackson was shouting but Cassy was standing her ground, hands in the pockets of her raincoat, her hair getting soaked.

"Oh," Howard said, grabbing the back of Teddy's slicker as he charged by.

"Hey!" his son protested.

"Put your hood up," Howard told him.

"Oh, let them go, Howard," Amanda said. "I'll put them straight in the tub."

The children ran ahead, stomping happily through the puddles and looking up, holding their arms out to the rain.

"So you think the Wren School's the one," Howard said, taking his wife's arm.

"I think so. Don't you?"

"Yeah. I guess." He looked at her. "Are you sure you're still up for the great financial review today? It's been a long day as it is."

"Oh, yes," she assured him. "I'm anxious to see where we are." She made a face. "I'm afraid I've already busted the budget before we've even set it, Howard. I sent a check for five thousand to the Riverside Park Fund in Mrs. Goldblum's name."

"That's not the five thousand that will break us."

"I suppose not." The children had run over to see a golden retriever puppy that was being walked.

"I wish Madame Moliere didn't look so happy about the prospect of leaving us," Amanda said.

Howard laughed and she joined in. "You thought she'd be heartbroken and she can't wait to ditch us."

When they reached the apartment they hung up their wet coats and Amanda herded the children to their rooms to check in with Madame Moliere and start the baths running. Howard went back to change and supervise Teddy's bath while Amanda took on Emily's. Afterward they parked Madame Moliere, Grace, Emily, Teddy and Ashette in their bedroom with a fire in the fireplace and the movie *Swiss Family Robinson*. "The real one," as Howard called it, with John Mills.

"So, are you ready?" Howard asked Amanda, standing outside the study doors.

She nodded.

Howard pushed the door open and they both stood there a moment, taking in the piles and piles of papers that were stacked around the study.

"Oh, my," Amanda said.

43

Cassy

CASSY HEARD THE key in the door and got up from the couch where she had been dozing. She was in Alexandra's apartment at The Roehampton, on Central Park West, and it was nearly one-thirty in the morning. She had not been sure if Alexandra would make it back to New York tonight. She'd been in Alaska working on a story for *DBS Magazine* on the Arctic Reserve.

"You made it," Cassy said, walking into the foyer.

"I had to," Alexandra said, putting her bags down. "I wanted to find out why you were here." As she straightened up her eyes moved appreciatively over the silk negligee Cassy wore. She smiled. "Hi." They kissed. "So what's going on?" Alexandra said.

"We don't need to talk about it tonight," Cassy said, watching her hang up her coat.

Alexandra gave her a doubtful look and pushed the large suitcase with her foot next to the door. The housekeeper would go through it, wash or clean whatever clothes Alexandra had used, and then repack so it would be ready at a moment's notice for her next trip. "The mystery deepens," Alexandra mused, heading across the living room to enter the master bedroom.

"Are you hungry?"

"Not at all. On the layover in Chicago we had a steak." Alexandra opened a closet door and slipped her shoes off. "So what's going on?" she asked again, glancing over.

She didn't know where to begin. "Why don't you get ready for bed. You look tired."

Alexandra frowned slightly, unbuttoning her blouse and taking it off. She slipped off her skirt and pulled off her stockings, the last with impatience, and tossed all the garments into the hamper. She left the bedroom in her underwear and reappeared holding two large glasses of water. She gave one to Cassy, put the other on her bedside table and went into the bathroom. Keeping the door ajar she talked about her trip while Cassy turned the bed down. The she slipped off her negligee, put it on the foot of the bed, and slid under the sheets. When Alexandra emerged she was wearing a white silk nightie. "Bed never looked so good. I don't think I've slept more than three hours since I left." She climbed into bed and drank some of her water. Then she reached to turn off the bedside lamp.

One of the loveliest aspects of Alexandra's bedroom was how the gentle glow of city lights shone up through the window panes. Although the original steel casement windows had been replaced with energy efficient ones, the replicas still cast an alluring pattern across the ceiling.

"Come here," Alexandra said, pulling Cassy over to lie in her arms. She took the clip out of Cassy's hair and combed it out with her fingers. "So what is this all about? Why are you here?"

For some reason Cassy felt like her news would be anticlimactic. She settled in closer, feeling Alexandra's collarbone against her cheek. "I told Jackson I wanted a divorce. And I left him."

At first there was no reaction. And then Alexandra sat up, nearly throwing Cassy off. "You did what?"

"I've got my things in the East End apartment." Cassy could only see the outline of Alexandra's head because the window was behind it. After several moments she added, "You're making me nervous, Alexandra. You're not saying anything."

"Because I can't believe it. After all this time."

"I know."

"It's going to take awhile for this to sink in." Alexandra shifted slightly. "Are you scared?"

"No."

"I think I might be," Alexandra admitted.

Cassy sat up, propping herself with her arms. "Every day I stay in that marriage another little part of me dies. And that's the part I have finally come to realize is the best part of me."

"I don't know if that's true."

"I know," Cassy told her. "It's the part of me that loves and trusts. And it's the part of me I want to focus on you."

"My God," Alexandra said softly. "I just can't believe it." Then she climbed out of bed. "Hang on." Cassy saw her shadow glide across the bedroom and a few seconds later the hall light came on. Alexandra was gone for at least ten minutes. "I couldn't find the stupid combination," she said when she returned. "Shield your eyes because I need to turn on the light."

Cassy covered her eyes as the bedside lamp came on and Alexandra crawled back onto the bed. She pressed a small box into Cassy's hand. "I had it fitted for your right hand, for obvious reasons."

Cassy blinked, looking down at the box.

"It's been in my safe for months. To be honest I wasn't sure if I'd ever get up the nerve to give it to you."

Cassy opened the box. There was a large blue sapphire anchored between two diamonds, set in platinum. It was stunning. Not showy but eye-catching, not overstated and yet they were clearly excellent stones.

"The sapphire was my grandmother's," Alexandra explained. "The one who raised me on the farm. My grandfather gave it to her but she never wore it because she was terrified of losing it. So, she kept it in a safe-deposit box at the bank. She said I might need it someday for seed money if there was crop failure. She grew up in the Depression." Alexandra reached to take it out of the box. "I chose the diamonds." She slid it onto Cassy's right hand. Alexandra brought the hand up to her lips to kiss it once. "It's perfect."

"It is," Cassy managed to say, her eyes blurring with tears. She tried to blink them back.

"I know you've had just about every diamond ring a woman can possibly own—" Alexandra began.

"Shh," Cassy said, putting a finger against Alexandra's mouth. After a moment she lowered her hand. "I will never treasure anything more than I will always treasure this." She smiled. "Because you had faith in us, didn't you? And in me. That someday I would do it."

Alexandra nodded. "Yes, I did."

Cassy took Alexandra's face to hold in her hands. "I love you, Alexandra Waring. And I always will."

Doing the Books

THE STEWARTS' TREK through their trail of long and twisting finances took some time. Amanda took care to keep any unpleasant observations to herself because Howard was doing a fine job of beating himself up. When their accountant arrived, Amanda could see that her husband wanted to crawl into a hole, he felt so ashamed about their predicament. But as uncomfortable as the process was, the Stewarts laid it all out, the personal and the professional, every single outstanding bill, every single expense and every single asset.

Their situation turned out to be both better and worse than they had thought. The better part was that all taxes were current ("I'm a screwup, not a crook," Howard snarled at the accountant), all the insurance was paid up and the agency's retirement accounts were pristine. The worst part was coming to realize that instead of the "around twelve thousand" Howard thought they spent each month as a family, the actual amount turned out to be more like twenty.

"That can't be right," Howard said at the same time Amanda gasped, "That isn't possible!"

Oh, but it was.

"The numbers don't lie," their accountant said. "Add your expenses up yourself."

And so once they stumbled through their horror to see where the money was going, gradually a plan of action began to materialize. What expenses would stay, what would go. First, there was no question, the Woodbury house had to be sold. If they were lucky and found the right buyer, they might still get out of it relatively unscathed. The cars would be sold. The horses would be offered to Daffodil Hill to use for lessons in exchange for board until Amanda made up her mind what she wanted to do. Madame Moliere was leaving and Amanda would look for day care for Grace so she could finish her book.

The monthly check from Amanda's trust was established as the new baseline of the family's income. Everything in the household had to come out of that. And everything Howard made was going to go toward paying off whatever debts they had. If they absolutely had to, they would take out a line of credit against the apartment, but Amanda was very much against this. And, in the end, Howard came to agree.

"So here is the situation," Amanda told the children one night after dinner. "Daddy and I miss each other so much we want to live together all the time."

"We miss Daddy, too," Emily said.

"Well, that's what we wanted to talk to you about. Daddy and I want to live here, on Riverside Drive, all the time. Which would mean you will be attending a different school in the fall. A school here in New York."

The kids looked at each other, baffled. "What about soccer?"

"You'll play soccer here."

"But what are we going to do in the summer?" Teddy asked. "We don't have a pool here."

"You'll go to day camp, and then we'll go to the country, all of us, for a vacation."

"What country?" Teddy wanted to know.

"Maybe Maine or Nova Scotia, somewhere on the ocean."

"But what about our friends?" Emily asked, her lower lip starting to tremble. "What about Sweets and Maja?"

While Howard felt like hanging himself Amanda explained that the horses were going to stay with Jessica and they would visit them. Emily started to cry and buried her face in Amanda's lap.

"So we're going to be city slickers again?" Teddy asked his father.

"Yes, sir," Howard said.

"We'll all be together," Amanda said, stroking Emily's hair, "every day and every night. Ashette, too."

"Where are we going to keep the canoe, Dad?" Teddy asked.

"Oh, we'll find a place.

"I'm not sure I can take this," Howard said later, holding his wife in bed. "I can't believe what I've done."

"What *we've* done is save our marriage," she said. "If this hadn't happened who knows where you and I would be."

For a while Emily could not be consoled. She told her friends, her pony and her teachers in Woodbury that all was about to be lost forever and *ever.* ("Who does she remind you of, Amanda?" Amanda's mother had laughed.) But while Emily bemoaned her losses, Amanda was celebrating the soon to be lifted burdens of the gardener, the housekeeper, the pool man, the handyman, the oil man and all those other people who ratcheted up the costs of country living.

And while Amanda dreaded some of the hoops they were going to have to jump through to sort out their finances, she welcomed the new sense of partnership with Howard.

"Don't you feel, it, Howard?" she would ask. "How much closer we are now?"

Howard did feel it when he was at home with Amanda, but at the office he was still filled with guilt. He had to help find three assistants new jobs (or he'd have to pay their unemployment). Gretchen was floored. "What the hell?" she said to him. "I'm supposed to do the work of how many people now?"

"We're reassigning clients to the new agent," he told her, "so there will be less of a workload."

"Then maybe I need to reassign myself to another job somewhere else," Gretchen warned him.

"A girl's gotta do what she's gotta do," Howard told her, trying to sound casual but feeling miserable.

"Business is that bad?" another literary agent asked Howard, while calling for a reference for one of the assisstants.

"It's not bad," Howard explained, "the setup's just not cost-effective anymore."

"We always wondered how you were managing it," the agent said. "So now I guess we know that you weren't."

When Howard told Amanda that the agent was hiring the assistant she was elated. "Well, don't be too elated," he said glumly, "because I found another bunch of bills I forgot to put on the list."

Amanda made him sit down immediately and go over those bills and how they fit into their financial plan. "Don't you find it at all strange how much you seem to like this finance stuff?" he asked.

"No," Amanda said, "because unlike writing, finance has resolution. There's a finite beginning and end and specific values in between. As a writer you get tired of calling something finished only because you can't bear to look at it anymore."

"I'm not sure if our finances make me feel more sick or more despondent," Howard said.

"Come, come, darling," she said, sliding into his lap and putting her arms around his neck. "Admit it. It feels good for us to be a team on this. On everything." She smiled. "Doesn't it?" The last she asked more softly.

"I thank God every day for you, Amanda. I do." He kissed her and she kissed him back.

After so many months of feeling so self-consciously unsexual around each other, it was strange how normal it seemed to feel acute desire for one another again. Amanda was kissing Howard's neck and then whispering things in his ear that made him grin and flex his muscles. "Bills turn you on, huh?" he murmured, looking upward as he felt her mouth on his ear.

They kissed as he fumbled under her sweater to unhook her bra, allowing her breasts to fall into his hands. She made a sound he had almost forgotten as he touched her a certain way, and he found his lower body already straining upward, wanting to find her.

God it was great. They locked the door, pulled each other's clothes off and simply went down onto the oriental rug, knocking bills off the desk in the process, which only made them laugh. Then when Howard found his way inside of her, Amanda threw some of the bills on the floor up in the air like confetti, then groaned deeply, wrapping her legs around him. If anyone had told Howard even a month ago that he and Amanda would be gasping with passion with credit card bills sticking to their bodies he would not have believed it.

But he believed it now as he felt Amanda, finally sated, relax beneath him. Howard allowed himself that final shudder of pleasure and knew, in that moment, that he and Amanda could do anything.

Celia Has Some News

"MOM, MOM, WHERE are you?" Celia Cavanaugh shouted into her cell phone as she skipped up Fifth Avenue. All the tourists were staring at her while all the New Yorkers ignored her. "I have news!"

She stuck her phone back in her bag and smiled at herself in the reflection of a store window. Her cell phone rang. It was her mother. "Mom, guess what? Remember how I told you my neighbors the Stewarts asked me to research that weird painting for them?"

"Yes."

"Christie's is going to handle it!" She smiled at a German family of tourists. "Yes, Christie's, the famous auction house!" she told them.

They had not a clue what she was talking about but smiled politely nonetheless before moving on.

"You must be joking!" her mother cried.

"Nope," she declared, continuing uptown. "On first examination they think it might be worth between seven and ten thousand dollars!"

"You're joking!"

"They're putting it in a May auction."

To heck with walking home for exercise, Celia thought after hanging up with her mother, and she jumped into a cab. "Is Mrs. Stewart here, do you know?" Celia asked the concierge when she reached their building.

"I'm not sure."

"Could you call up, please?"

The concierge did as requested while Celia paced the lobby. It was the coolest thing. She had been shown into an appraisal room where the guy put the Stewarts' painting on a large counter and closely examined it with different magnifiers and under different lights. When the appraiser called in a colleague Celia sensed that she had been right, the painting really was worth something.

"She's here," the concierge reported, pressing the phone to the shoulder of his uniform.

"Ask her if I can come up."

"She says of course," the concierge reported a few seconds later. "Eleven-B."

"Celia," Amanda said, opening the door, "how are you?"

"Christie's says it's worth between seven and ten thousand dollars and they're putting it in one of their auctions in May!" she said breathlessly.

Amanda squinted slightly. "You cannot be speaking of—"

"The Arab, the camel and the vulture!" Celia cried. "Christie's! So who knows how much it will go for?"

Amanda beamed, shaking her head and opening the door wider. "Well, I must say, this is welcomed news. Come in, come in, I was just making a cup of tea."

"I gotta go to work soon," Celia said, her heart still racing as she followed Amanda into her kitchen. "But I wanted to tell you the good news. They're going to be—" Celia stopped when she saw Jason's mother sitting at the kitchen table.

There was an awkward moment when Amanda started to introduce them but Rosanne said they already knew each other, didn't Amanda remember how Celia had helped the day Samantha Wyatt had her accident. "So how are you doing?" Mrs. DiSantos asked Celia while Amanda was busy at the stove.

"I'm really sorry about Jason's grandmother."

"We got your card," she said. "Thank you."

Celia shrugged, wanting to bolt. At least she was dressed nicely in a skirt today because she had been to Christie's. She didn't look like a slut or anything.

"Jason got into Penn," Mrs. DiSantos said then.

"I heard. That's really great," Celia replied.

Amanda made Celia tell Jason's mother about the painting.

"I remember that thing," Mrs. DiSantos said with distaste. "The camel jockey shootin' buzzards." She kicked her head toward Amanda. "She used to have it up in the living room, if you can believe. Scared the heck out of the kids. Scared the heck out of *me,*" she laughed.

Celia tentatively smiled. When Amanda asked her some questions, Celia answered them, and then started over from the beginning to explain how the process worked. By the time she had described the kind of glossy, full-color catalog that would be produced, with Amanda's painting in it, she had forgotten to be uncomfortable.

Cassy and Henry Have Lunch

"YOU DIDN'T REALLY have to come out on business, did you, Mom?" Henry said.

They were eating lunch near Henry's office. Cassy had flown in yesterday, stopped in at the DBS San Francisco affiliate and then driven out with Henry to Palo Alto to stay overnight. "I wanted to talk to you about something," she admitted.

"Are you terribly sad about Mrs. Goldblum?"

"I'll miss her terribly, of course, but she was ready and she wanted to go. And she got to do it the way she wanted. At home." She took a sip from her water glass. "Henry, about our old apartment."

"What about it?"

"Well, it doesn't seem likely you and Maria will ever want to live in New York." Henry didn't say anything but his eyes told Cassy this was correct. "And that's the only reason why I hung on to it. In case you wanted it."

"I don't think so, Mom. I don't think I'll ever get Maria to leave California again. Not with her family here and everything." He looked at her. "Oh, no, if you sell it does that mean the next time we visit we'll have to stay with all the kooky Darenbrooks? I suppose we could stay in a hotel, though," he added to himself. "Maria would love the room service, though she'd probably want to stick the kids with you so we could enjoy room service in peace."

Cassy smiled. "I don't think that would be a hardship for me."

"And Jackson's good with kids."

"Yes, he is." Cassy's smile dissipated as she watched Henry bite into his sandwich. "Henry, I wanted to talk to you about some changes I want to make. In my life."

He swallowed. "What kind of changes?" He must have sensed it was serious because he put his sandwich down and wiped his mouth with his napkin. And waited for her to speak.

It had been Henry's habit ever since Cassy and Michael divorced not to ask probing questions, but to patiently wait for either one of them to volunteer information. That way he never appeared to be taking sides.

"I'm not sure where to begin," she confessed.

He offered an encouraging smile. "The beginning, maybe?"

The waiter came over and asked if they were finished eating. Henry said no but Cassy said yes, though she had scarcely touched her fish. "Mom, you want coffee?"

"Please. And also another glass of water, if you would be so kind."

"And bring me a coffee, too, please, with a piece of that Mississippi Mud Cake. I'll be done with my sandwich by the time you bring it."

Cassy found it amazing how grown-up Henry was now. It

wasn't so much that he was married and had children, or even that he supported them all (with a little help). The fact that her shy, sweet little boy had become this tall man who needed to shave sometimes twice a day still amazed her.

Her little boy wore a wedding band. She remembered Henry's wedding but she couldn't remember when he had grown up.

Their coffees arrived, their luncheon plates were taken away and Cassy had a taste of Henry's dessert. "Would you like me to guess what this is about, Mom?" Henry said after she put her dessert fork down.

"You don't have to guess," she said, sipping her coffee.

"You and Jackson are splitting up, aren't you?"

It took a moment for Cassy to completely swallow her coffee. He had caught her totally unawares. "I—" She watched him cut into his dessert. When she didn't continue, Henry looked up.

"I'm right, aren't I?"

She nodded. "Yes."

Henry lowered his eyes to his dessert, evidently thinking, and after a moment finished cutting the piece and put it into his mouth. Cassy knew he was trying very hard to carry on and appear unfazed by the news but she knew that was not the case. Henry had been in college when she remarried and Jack had spent a lot of time with Henry over the summers and on vacations. They got on very well and genuinely cared about each other.

"Charming Lydia—" Henry began. Henry had always called her that because Lydia's behavior had been so outrageous. "—has made a lot of claims about Jackson over the years." Henry met her eyes directly. "I always wondered if any of them had any validity."

"Such as?"

"Other women."

Cassy nodded, feeling her face starting to burn. "Yes. But the early years of our marriage were very good, Henry."

"You seemed really happy after you guys got married."

"I was." She looked down at the single flower that served as a centerpiece. "I was also very grateful to find someone who had so many of the traits I had loved in your father." She brought her eyes up. "But who didn't have a drinking problem. And Jack was a widower, he hadn't been divorced. And frankly, Henry, I was so deeply flattered that a man of Jackson's stature seemed to love me that I—" she offered a small shrug "—I wanted very much to marry him."

"But you loved him, too," Henry said, pushing his dessert plate away, most of the cake uneaten.

"Yes." She paused. "But never in the same way after— I haven't for a long time." Her eyes fell back to the flower. "I'll always be grateful to him. I felt so desperately humiliated about how my marriage to your father ended." She brought her eyes up. "Regardless of everything that happened between us, Henry, I hope you know how very much your father and I loved each other when we had you."

He smiled. "You always say that, Mom."

"But this is not what I wanted to talk about," she said, bowing her head.

"Then tell me what you want to talk about."

Cassy vowed not to cry but she felt choked by all the anger and shame and frustration over her failed marriages. Did she need to tell Henry about Sheila confessing her affair with Jackson? Or had she explained enough? She wanted him to understand how hard she had tried. "I was very happy with Jackson until a woman came to see me. She had been Jackson's mistress—and had been since before we were married."

She saw a flicker of anger in Henry's eyes. "He was seeing her the whole time?"

After a moment, she nodded.

"I know when it happened, when you found out," Henry said, "because you guys were never the same."

"You could tell?"

"In retrospect I can." He swallowed. "But you stayed, Mom."

She nodded. "I did. At first to see if things might change. I wanted him to get help, Henry. Because it wasn't just an occasional affair. It was constant."

Henry shifted in his chair. "It's like booze is to Dad, isn't it?"

"I'm afraid so."

"There're even rehabs for it now, you know, Mom. At Maria's old company they sent this corporate guy to one after a bunch of sexual harassment suits."

"I know. But Jack wouldn't go."

Henry hesitated. "And he won't even go to one now?"

"To be honest, it wouldn't matter to me if he did," Cassy said carefully. "Not in terms of our marriage. I'm only telling you this, Henry, because I want you to understand why, and how, it came to be that I went outside our marriage for a relationship."

Henry was kind enough not to gasp, but he was obviously shocked.

"It's taken me a very long time to come to terms with this relationship. I'm not getting a divorce because of this relationship, but getting a divorce is the first step I need to take in order to give this relationship my all. To see if it can work."

Henry fell back in his chair, blinking rapidly. "Wow," he finally said.

"I know," Cassy said.

The waiter came over to warm their coffees. Cassy hadn't even touched hers so he brought her an altogether new cup. Henry poured some cream into his. "I'm just glad you have someone, Mom. It would kill me to think of you being alone." He sipped his coffee and then set the cup down in the saucer. "The Darenbrooks are all going to go nuts, Mom. They're going to want to disown him to keep you. What are you going to tell them?"

Cassy shook her head. "I don't know."

"He'll probably tell them you met this other guy and blame it all on you."

She took a sip of her coffee, trying to think how next to proceed.

"He must be a great guy," Henry said loyally. "I look forward to meeting him."

She took a breath, returning her cup to its saucer. When Cassy looked up she found Henry was waiting for a response from her. She knew he was trying hard for her sake to keep up a cheerful facade but she also knew he was scared for her and scared for himself. Just how many failed relationships was his mother going to demand he and his family invest in?

"I don't know exactly how to tell you this, Henry, other than simply to say it. The relationship is with a woman."

He did a fairly good job of covering his surprise. He nodded, squinting slightly. "Wow," he finally said, trying to smile.

"Yes, wow is right," Cassy said, scanning the restaurant for lack of knowing what else to do.

"Maybe I shouldn't go out on a limb and say this, Mom," Henry said, waiting for her to look at him again, "but I sure as heck hope it's Alexandra."

Cassy nearly fell into her coffee cup.

Henry ducked his head a little to the right, looking to see her expression. "Is it?" he said hopefully.

Cassy still couldn't speak. Finally she sat back. "How did you know?"

"I didn't, not until you said it was a woman. And then everything started to make sense, Mom."

Cassy took a deep breath and sat forward in her chair. "What started to make sense, Henry?"

"I think she's been in love with you for a very long time, Mom. I mean, she's always been—" He shrugged. "I don't know, she's just always been— Well, you know."

"No, I don't know. Tell me."

"I don't know," he said, throwing his hands up. "I just know, okay? Even when she was with that actress, she used to look at you sometimes— Stop looking at me like that, Mom, I'm not making this up."

Cassy picked up her water glass. "Okay," she said before taking a sip.

"Just ask Rosanne, she saw it, too," Henry said, nearly making her spit out water.

47

Woodbury

THE FIRST DAY Amanda saw the For Sale sign hanging in front of the Woodbury house she felt a pang. But when she remembered how lonely it had been here without Howard it went away. They were a team again and it felt very, very good.

When she tried to remember why they had bought such a huge house and a property that required so much care, she realized Howard had been trying to compensate for the loss she had felt leaving Manhattan. She had not wanted to go. It was so hard to know, sometimes, what decision to make. At this point Amanda only knew she wanted them all to be together in the New York she so loved.

"I'm not worried about any old terrorist," Amanda overheard Teddy telling one of his friends. "My dad'll take care of them. And Ashette will bite 'em, won't you, girl?"

They had already started running fire drills with the children in New York on the weekends. "It's like soccer practice," Howard told them. "You practice enough so that if anything were ever to happen, you don't even have to think about it—you're gonna win no matter what."

"Luck is for people who are ready," Emily said, parroting her father.

The Stewarts were shocked and then elated when an offer was made on the house a week after it went on the market. But before long another sign was added below the first: Sold. That night Teddy came tearing down into the basement where Amanda was looking for Emily's blue pants. "Mom, Mickey-Luck's here!"

Miklov had kept a respectful distance since that awful day. Several times she had seen his red truck ride past the house during school hours but he never stopped. At soccer games he waved but never spoke to her, and phoned the house only to speak to one of the children about soccer.

Teddy went racing back up the stairs and Amanda heard him thunder across the kitchen overhead. Then she heard a slower, much heavier tread.

Teddy ran across the kitchen again to the stairs. "Mom! Mickey-Luck wants to talk to you!"

"Just a minute, I'll be right there!" she called. Surely he would not say or do anything in front of Madame Moliere and the children. She heard his footsteps overhead, and just as she was thinking, *He wouldn't dare,* a pair of work boots appeared on the stairs, clomping down, one by one. "Mrs. Stewart?" Miklov called.

"Hi," she said, taking the pile of clothes she had just folded and dumping them back into the dryer so she had something to do. "What's up, Miklov?" she asked without looking.

"The house," he said. "It is sold."

"Yes," she said. Here were Emily's blue pants. They had been in the pile the whole time.

"You are leaffing?"

"As soon as school is out," she said as she folded a shirt.

Silence.

"Why?" he asked.

She hazarded a look at him. He was very tan already from the outdoor spring practices.

"Because my husband and I want to be together every day." She took another piece of clothing out of the dryer and when she looked over at him she saw he was looking down at the floor.

"I am leaffing, too." He looked up. "I have been offert a job. A goot job. In Grenitch." They locked eyes. "So I am here to say gootbye. They give me a place to live. A nice place."

"I'm very pleased for you, Miklov."

He swallowed. "Now you do not haf to go. I leaf."

She dropped her eyes to the piece of clothing in her hands, then put it on the ironing board. "You are very kind, Miklov. And I thank you for your thoughtfulness. But we are moving back to New York because it is our home."

"Miklov!" Teddy called from the top of the stairs. "You wanna have ice cream with us?"

"I will be right there, Teddee." Miklov took a step in her direction and Amanda looked up in alarm. Miklov held up his hand to reassure her. "I only want to say," he said quietly, "you are so beautiful and Mr. Stewart is lucky man."

She smiled. "Thank you. But I'm the one who's lucky, Miklov." And then she turned her back to him, pretending to sort clothes, and waited until she heard his heavy tread leave the house.

The Wyatts

"BUT WHAT DO you really think?" Sam asked Harriet. They had valiantly tried the run-walking regimen one of Harriet's fitness authors was promoting, but they'd already pooped out, which had left them walking on the path between the West Side Highway and the Hudson River.

"I don't think the magnitude of all she's undertaken has dawned on Althea yet," Harriet said, finding her husband's hand.

He grunted in agreement.

"But she'll be a fine mother, Sam. I have no doubts on that score."

"I don't, either. It's amazing how much she reminds me of you, now. I never saw the resemblance before."

"I bet within three years Althea's married."

Sam stopped walking to look at her. "Who's she going to marry? Not that textile guy."

"She'll marry someone who will make a good father."

"She's got me to be a father figure for Samuel," he said when they resumed walking.

"It's the way things happen sometimes, Sam. A woman gets her priorities straight and suddenly she can see clearly. About who's right for her."

Sam ballooned his cheeks with air before letting it out. "That would be nice, if at least one of our girls was happy."

"Sam, look!" Harriet's hand shot out to point. "Some crazy person's already out sailing and it's not you!"

"What about Samantha?" he asked, sliding his arm around Harriet. "How long do you suppose she's going to hate us?" They had succeeded in getting Samantha to go into therapy in Utica and she had hinted she was blaming them for all of her bad decisions.

"I've been trying to imagine how she must feel right now," Harriet said. "How angry she is. I think she feels ostracized and that we chose Samuel over her."

"I wish I could stop wondering whether or not she's seeing Culmathson," Sam said. He pulled Harriet aside while a small woman with a pit bull passed by them. "Maybe we should take a ride up to Utica Saturday," he said. "Not tell her, just show up. Stay over Saturday night, *make* her do something with us."

"We can always take her shopping," Harriet said glumly. She was still hurting, Sam knew, big-time, feeling as though she had failed Samantha in some way.

"And if she won't hang out with us then we'll just hang out with each other," Sam said, pulling his wife closer. "We'll tell her that whether she likes it or not, we still love her, we're still her parents, and we're still her number one fans. Then she can either come with us or not. And if she doesn't we can go to an open meeting and then dinner or something."

He wasn't sure if it was a smile or a sense of resolve tightening Harriet's mouth. "We can try, I suppose." She stopped walking to look up at the top of the apartment buildings that could be seen over the trees of Riverside Park. He knew Harriet was looking at their building. "You'd think after all these years I'd know for sure what the right thing is for the girls."

"They're their own people now, honey," Sam said, looking up at their building, too.

Harriet leaned into him. "I love you, big guy."

"You know," Sam began, eyes still on their building, "after all these years, you'd think you could have promoted at least one fitness writer who isn't full of crap."

Harriet gave her husband a playful punch in the shoulder and then took him by the hand to continue walking on the path.

APRIL

The Ladies of the Neighborhood

"IT JUST DOESN'T look the same without Jason's knapsack on the floor," Rosanne joked to Cassy as they walked into the living room of the Cochran's old apartment. "I'm not sure how I'm going to get him used to living in a small apartment." She stood in front of the windows. "Remember the old windows, Mrs. C? Before you got these?"

"You mean do I miss how they rattled in the wind and let the cold air in?"

"To be honest," Rosanne said, "I was kinda thinkin' about when Mr. C threw the TV out of the window."

"Have a seat, Rosanne, the others should be here shortly. I need to do a few things in the kitchen."

"Oh, right," Rosanne said, following her out. "Like I'm gonna sit there like the Queen of Sheba. I only cleaned this place for eighteen years."

Cassy laughed. "I'll tell you this, Jason left this place better than he found it. He fixed the cabinet door in the bathroom while he was here." She started making a pot of coffee while Rosanne pulled a breakfast stool out to sit. "He fixed the silverware drawer in here. And the doorknob actually works now in the master bedroom."

"He's pretty good with his hands."

"When does he actually go to Penn?" Cassy asked, switching on the coffeemaker.

"Middle of August. He's going up in June, though, for some kind of freshman orientation."

"Hard to believe, isn't it?" Cassy said. She looked over to see that Rosanne was looking at some of the family pictures on the wall. "Rosanne, there's something I wanted to—"

The doorbell rang.

Cassy headed for the front door. Moments later there was a great deal of chattering and laughter in the front hall and then Althea came waltzing in with Samuel, followed by Harriet and Amanda, the latter lugging a snoozing Grace in a carrier. Cassy herded them into the living room, disappeared for a few minutes and then reappeared with the coffeepot, mugs and coffee cake.

"There's no sugar and very little canola oil in it," Cassy explained about the cake, prompting the ladies to all reach for it.

They chatted for a while: the Stewarts had sold their house in Connecticut and would be back in the city as soon as the children were out of school; Harriet said Samantha had signed up for the summer session at Cornell; Althea reported on Samuel's latest accomplishments in eating, sleeping and smiling, and Cassy shared some pictures of her granddaughter, Catherine.

"Rosanne," Harriet said, "I understand you've dropped your advanced nursing course."

Rosanne glanced at Althea, scowling slightly. "I never snitched on you."

"Yes, you did," Althea told her.

Rosanne rolled her eyes and turned back to Harriet. "Yes, Mrs. W, I dropped my class."

"Why?"

Rosanne looked at her. "Well, if it's any of your business…"

Harriet waited, clearly expecting an answer.

"I hated it, I don't know what else to tell you," Rosanne said flatly. "I hated it just about as much as I hate nursing. The illness part is fine, it's just the people that are hard to take. The crabby people, the rude people, the mean people and the doctors and RNs who pooh-pooh their noses at me because I'm only an LPN. So other than that, everything's great." She noticed some smiles being exchanged around the room. "What? What are you guys smiling about?"

"They're hopeful smiles," Cassy began. "Because we're hopeful you might consider a career detour for a year or so."

"And maybe longer," Althea added, "if you like it."

"And we really, really, *really* need you to seriously consider it," Amanda added, gently rocking Grace's carrier on the floor.

Althea's baby began to fret. "Oh, not now, Samuel," she whispered. But it was to be now and after he started crying she took him out of the room, baby bag slung over her shoulder. "You have to say my part, Mom!" she called from the hall.

"Right," Harriet said. "Rosanne."

"It is so great to see her like this," Rosanne whispered across the room, nodding in the direction of Althea's voice. "It's like night and day. She's so happy."

Harriet beamed. "I know."

"So, Rosanne," Cassy prompted.

"What, for Pete's sake?"

"Would you be Samuel and Grace's nanny?" Harriet said.

Rosanne's mouth fell open. "A *nanny?* You gotta be kidding."

"And live here, you and Jason," Cassy said, "with Althea and Samuel?"

"Althea's buying the apartment from Cassy," Harriet explained.

"And you'd have Henry's old room," Althea said, holding a bottle for Samuel, "Jason can have the guest room and we'll make the study into a nursery."

"It goes without saying how much better Sam and I would feel, Rosanne," Harriet said, "knowing that you were here with the baby." She smiled at Althea. "With both of my babies."

"This year," Althea said, standing as she fed Samuel, "Mom and Dad will be around almost all the time. You know, when I have to travel."

"And we'd take Samuel some nights," Harriet said.

"I'm going to be able to bunch my travel time," Althea continued. "So it will take place during the first and third week of each month."

"Althea and Sam have already found major medical insurance we can offer," Harriet said.

"And we'll do your taxes and stuff," Althea said. "Because, you know, you'll be paid a salary."

"And we will be paying you, as well," Amanda added. "If we can drop Grace off for a few hours each day."

"And it's important that you know, Rosanne," Cassy said, "that no one will expect you to continue after a year if you don't want to."

"We'd have a yearlong contract," Althea said, "so we would both know what to expect."

"And that would give you a year to figure out your housing situation," Cassy said.

"And give me a family to come home to," Althea said. She walked over to Rosanne and offered her the baby and the bottle, which Rosanne accepted. "And you can get Jason organized this summer for school."

"I need to take him to Philadelphia."

"And Sam and I will be here to take care of the baby while you're gone," Harriet said.

"It's not like I'm never going to be around," Althea told her mother.

Rosanne glanced up from the baby to Amanda. "So you're really givin' Madame DeFarge the heave-ho?"

Amanda nodded. "She leaves at the end of June."

Rosanne took the bottle out of Samuel's mouth and wordlessly accepted the towel from Althea to put over her shoulder before bringing Samuel up to burp him. "Okay," Rosanne said, gently patting Samuel's little back.

"What?" Harriet said.

"You mean you'll do it?" Althea said with wide eyes. Samuel burped and her face filled with love. "That was very good," she told her son.

"Are you finished, or do you need to do one more?" Rosanne asked the baby. She put him back on her shoulder and resumed patting. She looked up at Althea. "What?"

"Are you kidding? Rose, are you really going to do it?"

"Why not?" Rosanne asked her.

"I—I can't believe it," Althea said, a look of elation spreading over her face.

Howard Has Some News

THE CHANGES IN their relationship were not magical but were, as Amanda expressed it, indelibly wonderful. Their progress as a couple seemed to go two steps forward, one step back, two steps forward, one step back, but with a closeness and energy that felt new.

As for Howard, he felt as though he was falling in love all over again. "The better you feel about yourself," one of the pop psychologists he represented had written, "the more capable you are to love others."

Yeah, well, whatever.

Even worse than having to list the debts for Amanda had been fully recognizing the sacrifices he was asking Amanda and the children to make in order to clean up his mess. Putting the Woodbury house on the market had felt like death to him. But Amanda being so excited about moving back into Manhattan made the process that much easier. They had also found a summer soccer program the kids could get into, and since

Mickey-Luck had moved to Greenwich, anyway, Teddy and Emily didn't feel they were missing as much now by moving. (There would also be a week of science camp, music camp and art camp.)

"Howard," Gretchen announced from the doorway of his office, "Amanda's on two and I've got ten thousand people waiting for you to call them."

He snapped up the phone. "Hi, darling."

"I've got a surprise," Amanda said, sounding happy.

If Howard wasn't mistaken he could hear the theme song of *I Love Lucy* in the background. "Where are you?"

"We're on our way in." There were shrieks of laughter from the children. "Lucy and Ethel are in the chocolate factory."

He laughed. "So what's the surprise?"

"Celia Cavanaugh left us a Christie's catalog at the desk."

"Oh, right, the vulture and the camel."

"Howard, you'll never believe what she said the estimate is."

"I thought she said seven to ten thousand." Although they weren't counting on the money it sure would come in handy right now.

"Celia said they listed it for fifteen to seventeen!"

"You're kidding."

She was laughing. "Can you believe it? I just talked to her. They had a number of people look at it and that's the estimate now. I must go to that auction. Celia and her mother are going so I want to go with them. Anyway, Celia's coming out with us next week to see what we have in Woodbury we want to get rid of."

"They're your things, Amanda. I hope you're not selling them because—"

"We need to get rid of it, Howard. Remember, someday

the children are going to get all of my parents' stuff, too. How much stuff can one family possibly need?"

Gretchen was back in the doorway. "Kate Weston. She says it's very important she speak to you."

He held up one finger. "Don't you think we need someone other than a bartender handling your antiques?"

"I can't think of anyone else I would rather handle it. She's eager, grateful and she's working her derriere off."

"Whatever you say." Howard hung up with her and changed to the other line. "Kate," he said brightly, shifting his headset slightly in an attempt to veer his thoughts away from vultures, debts and pretty bartenders.

"You better go over to your fax machine, Howard," Kate said, "because I'm sending over a contract. So if you don't want anyone to see it—"

"That fast? A contract that fast?"

"And not to pressure you, but I need an answer before the end of Monday."

"Monday," he repeated.

By four-thirty Howard had sent everyone in the office home early for the weekend so that he was alone when the accountant came in. "Thank God you've dealt with everything," the accountant said as they went over the latest set of agency numbers. "It makes it all the less likely you will get into this position again."

Howard felt his dander rise but said nothing except what he needed to say, which was "I have to know by Monday if the deal can work."

Howard, Amanda, Emily and Teddy made homemade pizza and salad and played Pictionary on the floor in front of the fire in the living room. Howard was not sure if he had ever been happier in his life. It was going to work out. He really knew that for sure now. They heard the children's prayers, put them to bed and kissed them good-night. Only then did they pour a glass of wine and return to the living room to talk. "I've got news, Amanda," Howard said almost immediately.

"You sold something," she guessed.

"It's what I'm thinking of selling. I'm thinking about selling the agency back to the Hillingses, for their grandson."

She frowned.

"The whole thing."

It took a moment for Amanda to recover. "But you've worked so hard, Howard. It's called Hillings & Stewart for a reason."

"After this restructuring I don't think I want to do it anymore. It won't be the same."

Amanda took a sip of her wine. "So what would you do? Stay on as an agent and let their grandson run the business?"

"Well, that's just it." He smiled. "I've been offered a job, Amanda. To be an editor again. To take Kate Weston's place as editor in chief of Bennett, Fitzallen & Coe."

"Editor in chief!" Amanda cried. The light that appeared in her eyes told Howard what he needed to know. "Oh, darling!" She hastily put her glass down to throw her arms around him. She kissed him several times and then sat back a few inches to ask, "Are you going to accept this position?"

"The salary falls right down the middle of my best year and worst year," he said.

"Howard, you made negative I don't know how much last year," Amanda pointed out.

"My best year I made nearly four hundred."

She did the math. "A hundred-sixty?"

"They've offered two hundred. A regular paycheck, profit sharing and full major medical for all of us. And Kate's offering me a three-year contract. I brought it home for us to look over together."

She hugged and kissed him again. "So you'll be the editor in chief and Kate will be publisher?"

He nodded. "We're fairly like-minded, editorially, but she's going to be wrapped up with a lot more administrative tasks now. That's why she offered it to me."

"But it's been such a long time since you worked for anyone, Howard. Are you sure you're going to be happy?"

"I'm sure going to like Kate better than the boss I have now," he joked.

She put her hand on his arm. "I'm serious, darling. I don't want this episode in our life to push you into taking a job that will make you unhappy."

"Amanda, honest to God, I miss being an editor. And with the restructuring of the agency—"

"You'll have much less time working with the writers," she finished for him.

"At Bennett, Fitzallen & Coe I'll be overseeing the editors and overall list, but I still get my own list. And frankly I have a few writers I'd like to bring there. I know exactly what to do with them, how to break them out." He rattled on for a while, discussing his ideas about what he could do and what might happen down the road if Kate Weston ever left.

"I think it sounds as though you've already come to a decision, Howard."

He smiled, wrapping a strand of Amanda's hair around his finger. "I love you so much."

"And I, you." Her eyes were sparkling. She raised her glass. "May you always be happy in your work, Howard Stewart, and may your wife always be hopelessly in love with you."

"Hear, hear," he said.

Cassy and Rosanne Finally Talk

"I THINK THAT'S the last of it," Cassy said to Howard Stewart, pointing to the boxes by the door.

Howard wheeled the handcart over. "How's Rosanne doing?"

"Once this is finally out of here, I think she'll be fine," Cassy said. "She and Jason are sleeping over at the other apartment tonight."

Howard nodded. His job was to take Mrs. Goldblum's clothes and shoes to a charity in the morning. "You know that Amanda would have helped tonight, but seeing Mrs. Goldblum's things—"

"I know," Cassy said. "I wish Rosanne had just let me take care of it. It was very hard on her."

"Whispering about me again, Mrs. C?" Rosanne said, coming down the hall with her arms full of sheets and blankets.

"Cassy was just saying this is the last of the boxes," Howard said.

Rosanne continued into the kitchen and Howard said

good-night. Cassy headed into the kitchen to find Rosanne standing by the double-decker washer-dryer. She had dropped the bedclothes in a heap on the floor and was just standing there. "I wish you would leave that for now," Cassy said. "I think we could both do with a little rest."

"Almost twelve years," Rosanne said. "Do you know that's the longest I've ever lived in one place?"

Cassy finally persuaded her to leave everything and when they emerged outside it was to find it eerily warm. "You can't tell me we haven't messed with the weather," Rosanne said, craning her neck to look up at the night sky. "It feels weird, doesn't it?"

They saw streaks of lightning over New Jersey and then heard thunder. They walked down the Drive, each in her own thoughts. When they turned the corner of 88th Street they ran into Jason coming out of 162. With a girl. "Mom, this is my friend Allyson from school."

Rosanne extended her hand. "Hello, Allyson."

"This is my mom," Jason added. "And that's Mrs. C."

She was a sweet-looking girl with reddish hair pulled back in a French braid. "Hi."

"So where might you be going at this time of night?" Rosanne said, sounding remarkably like Mrs. Goldblum.

"I'm walking Allyson home. We had to do an Asian studies paper."

After the young people continued on their way Cassy remarked that Jason's friend seemed like a nice girl. "She did seem nice," Rosanne said. "I wonder if she's going to college."

They went upstairs to the old Cochran apartment. As tired as they were, they started walking around the apartment, taking inventory of things Cassy was willing to leave if Rosanne wanted them. "We have to think down the road, Rosanne,"

Cassy said, opening the cabinets in the kitchen. "Someday there will be a new place for you and at some point Jason's going to need things for an apartment." They went through flatware, pots and pans and dishes.

They eventually made their way to Henry's old room. "Are you sure he's not going to want this?" Rosanne asked, running her hand over the top of the faux-Stickley headboard.

"It doesn't seem to hold any particular significance for him," Cassy said. "And it would cost heaven and earth to ship across the country. You're welcome to the dresser, as well."

"This is great," Rosanne murmured, walking over to the dresser. "I knew there was a reason why I was careful to use scratch cover on it for all those years."

They laughed.

"I really oughta pay you something."

"Rosanne, honestly, I will only give it to someone else. Besides, it would give Henry enormous pleasure to know that you or Jason liked it."

"It's really great," she said, opening a drawer.

Cassy crossed her arms over her chest and leaned against the door frame. "Rosanne, there's something I've been wanting to talk to you about."

"Are you taking the rug?" Rosanne asked, surveying it.

"Please, it's yours. I got it cleaned not long ago."

Rosanne squatted to examine it more closely.

Cassy hesitated. "I guess you've heard that Jackson and I have separated."

"Only me and the rest of the civilized world," Rosanne said, reaching over to pull up the edge of the rug to look at the flip side. "I should definitely pay you something for this."

"I'm not living next door anymore, Rosanne," Cassy added.

"And you're getting divorced," Rosanne said, standing up. She glanced over. "I know that's not for public consumption yet, Mrs. C. I haven't said anything to anyone."

"How did you know?" Cassy asked as Rosanne crossed the room to the closet and opened the door.

"Henry told me." Rosanne closed the door and turned around, planting a hand on her hip. "I'm sorry Mr. D turned out to be such a dirty rat."

Cassy had to laugh. "He's not a dirty rat, Rosanne, though I do appreciate your loyalty."

"You know you can't leave the neighborhood or Mrs. G will come back from the grave to haunt you."

"We'll see."

Rosanne pointed at the picture hanging over the bed.

"Absolutely," Cassy said, "if you like it." She pushed off the door frame. "Let me show you the desk I was talking about."

"Waaait a minute," Rosanne said, turning fully around. "You just skipped, like, the whole thing."

"What whole thing?" Cassy said, coming back.

"Like how Henry knew it was Alexandra Waring."

Cassy felt herself blush. "Oh," she said, sagging against the doorway.

"Well, do ya want to know the story behind Henry knowing or not?"

Finally she nodded. "Yes, I would."

"Well, ya see, Mrs. C," Rosanne said, crossing her arms over her chest, "way back when, in ancient olden times, there was a boy who came to me who was scared his mother might run away with her friend."

Cassy was thunderstruck. *"What?"* she said, straightening up.

Rosanne nodded. "He knew without really knowing what it was that he knew. Does that make any sense?"

Cassy gripped the doorway with her left hand. She felt as though the world was turning upside down.

"He was scared that if you left Mr. C then something really bad was going to happen to his father because he was so sick and you were the only one who ever cared. And you were the only one who was ever there. Except for the boy."

Cassy could only look at Rosanne.

"He was also scared you might make him leave with you, which would mean leaving Mr. C by himself."

Cassy finally found her voice. "Where does Alexandra come into it?"

"He heard her asking you to move in with her."

Cassy dropped her face into her hand. Finally she said, "Good Lord, I had no idea."

"That's when he came to me. But it all worked out," Rosanne added brightly. Cassy raised her head. "Because I guessed right. I told him he had nothing to worry about because you'd never walk out. And that Alexandra just wanted to make sure you guys knew you always had somewhere to go if things got really bad." Rosanne shook her head. "He never put it together, Mrs. C. Not until you talked to him a couple weeks ago."

Cassy looked down at the floor for a long moment. "What must you think of me?"

"Don't tell me you'd really like to know because I just might tell ya."

"Then perhaps you should."

"I'll tell ya this much, it's about time you picked someone you know is right for you instead of someone you think you're supposed to think is right for you. If you know what I mean."

Cassy's head kicked back a little, a slight smile emerging on her face. "Yes. I do know what you mean."

"And you know what they always say, Mrs. C, don't you?" Rosanne continued.

"No. What is it that they always say, Rosanne?"

She grinned. "Third time's a charm."

Conclusion

THE PAINTING OF the Arab, the camel and the vulture that scared the Stewart children fetched sixteen thousand dollars at the Christie's auction. "I made a sixteen hundred dollar commission!" Celia Cavanaugh told her parents. ("Don't forget a Schedule C on your taxes next year!" Mr. Cavanaugh told his daughter.)

While Celia's life has not miraculously sorted itself out she is definitely a promising work-in-progress. With the encouragement of her parents, her roommate and Amanda Stewart, she has created the rudimentary outlines of what might one day become an antiques business. In the meantime she's sold things on eBay and some of Amanda's items through an auction house.

The really, really big news is that Celia took two classes at Columbia over the summer with plans to re-enroll full-time in the fall with a dual major in history and business. She was also pleasantly surprised to be offered the three most lucrative shifts at Captain Cook's while she attends school.

Shortly after Jason DiSantos really did turn eighteen he returned to Captain Cook's to wait tables over the summer. He was by this time in love with his classmate Allyson and Celia became his confidante and romance counselor. When Jason started making noises over the summer that maybe he didn't want to go to Penn after all, but to a school closer to where Allyson would be, in Massachusetts, it was Celia who got Jason back on track before his mother went completely off the deep end.

With the exception of Jason's ever-changing love life Rosanne's summer was an extremely busy but happy one. She resigned from her job at the hospital and took immediate charge of Samuel (although his grandmother was more than eager to take him). Since Rosanne had never been able to be a full-time mother to Jason she is somewhat fascinated by the experience. In the park she has bonded not with the nannies but with the other mothers who like to talk about what career paths they might pursue when the children are older. Rosanne has picked up some good ideas and is almost positive it will be a business of her own, having to do with the placement of LPNs, nurses' aides, housekeepers and companions in the homes of the elderly.

In the beginning of July little Grace Stewart began arriving at ten in the morning and that's when things became interesting. Still, on Saturday nights, Rosanne sees Randy and she's beginning to wonder if perhaps there might be a future there after all.

Althea Wyatt negotiated a limited partnership at her firm so that she has a relatively reliable schedule to care for her son. Her parents are still planning to take early retirement but it becomes increasingly doubtful how much time they'll actually spend away from Manhattan while their grandson is living there.

Never having had a son of his own, Sam is amassing a rather formidable collection of sporting equipment for the future, which he always claims is on sale.

The situation with Samantha Wyatt will take time to heal. She only came home once over the summer and did not go to see Samuel. She is living in an off-campus apartment and the Wyatts are upset because they think Steve Culmathson is still on the scene. But Sam and Harriet just keep calling and writing to Samantha, telling her their news and expressing their love for her. Althea sends a card to Samantha once in a while, but doesn't talk to her; Althea has no desire to talk to her sister, she says, until Samantha at least acknowledges that Althea is a mother.

Amanda Miller Stewart has seemingly been reborn since the day her family was permanently reunited under one roof. (Her happiness does much to smooth the family's readjustment to living in significantly less space.) She has put her book on the court of Catherine the Great aside to assist two writers in the adaptation of her biography into a script. She drops Grace off with Rosanne and Samuel at around ten in the morning and picks her up at four.

The naive excitement of striding through the halls of Bennett, Fitzallen & Coe as editor in chief wore off in about five minutes for Howard Stewart (after legal brought him up to speed on the plagiarism suit against the publishing house being notoriously played out in the headlines), but he still knew at once how much he had missed being on the publisher side of things. He also is enjoying the enormous difference of being an editor in chief instead of the powerless young editor he had been the last time around.

Amanda and Howard sometimes look at one another and try to remember how they could have ever felt anything except blessed in their marriage. After the house was sold to cover their debts they now spend a half hour each week going over their finances. Oddly enough there seems to be a correlation between them working as a team on their debts and money falling out of the sky. (Howard says he will never use anything else but bartenders to sell antiques from now on.)

Emily and Teddy are settling in well and are playing in a Manhattan soccer league. The big difference now, which sometimes makes Amanda want to weep for the sheer joy of it, is that their father is almost always there to watch them.

Hillings & Stewart has reverted to the agency's original name of Hillings & Hillings. The agency's most exciting deal at the moment is the development of Amanda Stewart's biography of Catherine the Great as a movie vehicle starring Georgiana Hamilton-Ayres.

Over the summer Georgiana surprised the world by announcing her engagement to Lord William Edward Mortimer Douglas, future Earl of Worthington. When Lord Douglas was asked how he felt about his glamorous fiancée's highly publicized bisexuality, he said, "Georgiana and I love each other above all others. Our pasts are exactly that—past." The couple intend to make their home base in Surrey, UK, and Bel Air, California.

The news of the divorce action between media mogul Jackson Darenbrook and DBS President Cassy Cochran came as a stunner to the industry. The corporation itself seemed to go into a kind of mourning. Once people saw, however, that Jackson and Cassy did not seem to bear animosity toward one another, the nervous anticipation of some sort of corporate cataclysm in the broadcasting division began to dissipate. The Board of Directors, however, are beside themselves that their brother is back on the "hoo-ha" babe pages of the tabloids.

Jackson is living in a hotel on Fifty-seventh Street and has put the penthouse on the market. Cassy has been staying with Alexandra Waring until she finishes renovating and remodeling a brownstone on Riverside Drive. It remains to be seen what the reaction will be when it becomes known that Alexandra Waring is the co-owner. In the meantime Cassy carries on with a greater degree of energy and happiness than people have ever seen. People also agree that Cassy is still very beautiful and will no doubt marry again.

They just don't know yet to whom.